Broken

Beautiful Monsters Volume III

Jex Lane

This is a work of fiction. Names, characters, businesses, places, events, and incidents are either the products of the author's imagination or used in a fictitious manner. Any resemblance to actual persons, living or dead, or actual events is purely coincidental—or used with permission.

JexLane.com

Edited by Michelle Rascon

Cover Design by Jay Aheer

Library of Congress Control Number: 2017903044

ISBN 978-0-9977533-2-5

For Michelle.
Who took a chance beta reading a book for a friend
and now journeys with me.

CHARACTER LIST

(As they are at the end of *Sire*)

Matthew — Demigod. Sired son of Lysandros, the vampire god of blood. Son of Ilertha, the incubus goddess of sex.

Incubi; ordered by social ranking:

High King Malarath — Monarch of the incubi people.
Queen Agleea — Social. Malarath's granddaughter.
Lady Rosaline — Social. Member of House Malarath.
High Lord General Tarrick — Warrior. Leader of the incubi armies.
General Tarquin — Warrior. Tarrick's eldest son. Leader of the Russian offensive.
Lord Ennius — Social. Queen Agleea's consort.
Lady Dennith — Warrior. Tarrick's "right-hand".
Lord Teleclus — Warrior. Retired. Lady Lillian's custodian.
Lord Vassu — Warrior. Largest of his people. Stationed on the vampire-infested West Coast.
Lady Talena "Lena" — Warrior. Tarrick's only living daughter. Rescued by Matthew.
Lord Tane — Warrior. Tarrick's youngest son.
Lady Lillian "Lily" — Matthew's daughter.

Hunters; ordered by hunter ranking:

Imperator Prescott — Leader of the Hunter Corps. Team leader of the Argonauts, High King Malarath's personal bodyguards.
Commander Hiroto — Assassin. Kitsune. Member of the Argonauts. Team leader of the Shadow Six.
Commander Cullip — Former leader of the Wardens.
Commander Silva — Team leader of the Wardens, Tarrick's personal bodyguards.

Vampires; in no particular order:

Samantha "Sam" — Oracle. Matthew's sired daughter.
Gwenyth — Vampire lord. Her estate was destroyed during the Solstice Masquerade.
Ascelina — Vampire lord. Gwenyth's sired daughter. Rescued by Matthew.
Emilia — Ascelina's sired daughter. Can manipulate minds to create illusions and nightmares.
Stolus — Ascelina's sired son. Emilia's protective younger brother. Dresses like a Spartan in battle.
Bryson — The vampire general. Ex-hunter. Ex-lover of Silva.
Vikentiy — Vampire lord. Member of the Russian Zhirov family. Betrayed Matthew at Delphi.

Humans:

Alyssa Callahan — Deceased. Matthew's wife. Mother of Lily.

The Divine:

Devak — Deceased. Pleasure Guardian. Matthew's lover. Killed by Prescott and Hiroto at Delphi.
Lysandros — The Blood God. Patron deity of vampires.
Ilertha — Goddess of sex. Patron deity of incubi.

Misc:

Jet — Gargoyle. Often accompanies Matthew but has an affinity with Samantha. Preferred form is a Rottweiler.
Asper — Gargoyle. Has an affinity with Tarrick.
Bloodreaver, Harbinger of Ruin — Matthew's axe.

Beautiful Monsters terms and definitions:

Blood Pouch — Internal organ that stores blood energy for vampires. Located in the lower torso. Most vampires have one or two, some lords have three. Matthew has four.

Soavik — Internal organ that stores sexual energy for incubi.

Vampire Lord — After three centuries or so, a vampire undergoes a physical change. Often, they grow wings and gain new abilities.

Sanguine Dominar — A vampire who can control blood at a distance. Extremely rare.

Transformation — Incubi undergo three transformations in their lifetime, each time growing in power. The first happens in late teens, granting them their incubus form and abilities. The second happens when they are around a century, and the third around three hundred. It is rumored that High King Malarath has undergone five. Matthew never finished his first transformation.

Prologue

MALARATH

Fifth Century BCE. Greece.

"He has arrived, Your Majesty." The gruff voice broke the King from his thoughts.

Malarath stared down from his golden throne. A warrior knelt at the foot of the steps and tucked his helmet under his arm, his hoplite armor shifting with him. Battle was upon them but he carried neither weapon nor shield.

Malarath had ordered him to leave days ago, but the human disobeyed and stayed behind despite the risk. Even the great black dragon, Zafirah, had fled, and now the fortress was empty save for the two of them.

With his pale blue eyes, the King studied the fearless warrior that had served him for many long years. His hair and beard were dark and his complexion tan from training in the sun during the days; although his nights were spent fighting, and he had the hardened body to prove it.

"You should have left, Prescott," Malarath said.

The warrior said nothing, only offering a slight nod of acknowledgement that he had heard the King.

Malarath stood. "You will be punished for disobeying me."

"If *he* doesn't kill us, then I accept the penalty."

A smile ghosted the edge of the King's lips, glad that there was one among his subjects with such courage, even if he was only a human.

Malarath unpinned the ruby pendant near his shoulder and let his blue cloak drift down onto the throne, exposing his tunic made of cloth so fine it was nearly transparent. The tunic draped loose around his body, ending mid-thigh.

Jewelry, as golden as his hair, adorned his limbs. He adjusted a bracelet, correcting the orientation of the gemstones. It would not be enough to look good—he needed to be irresistible. "Rise. You understand that I will be offering you to him?"

"Yes, Your Majesty," Prescott said as he stood, donning his helmet. It covered his face completely and made him look like an incubus— long horns curling out the top and curving towards the back.

The King drifted down the steps from his throne and waited for *him* to arrive.

Malarath considered moving to a different room, one more intimate. Around him, grand murals layered the walls, and marble statues rested at every corner. Expensive cloth and rich furs hung from the tall colonnades, all fashioned to draw the eye to the massive golden throne from which he ruled.

He had insisted that this fortress be as richly decorated as any palace or estate he attended.

No. This room would do. *He* would enjoy the feeling of power that manifested in this space.

Malarath forced his breath to stay, even as he heard heavy steps pounding down the great hall. The doors to the throne room burst open and standing there was the *Sanguine Dominar*—a vampire unlike any other, able to control blood with just a wave of his hand, bending it to his will. He wore the tight leather clothes that barbarians favored: dark trousers, a rough shirt, and an impressive fur cloak that dragged the floor behind him.

An Egyptian by birth, his skin was dark, but his eyes were a harsh golden amber. His thick long hair twisted in wild coils, draping about his neck. And, although Malarath was nearly half a foot taller, his presence was imposing.

Butcher. Slayer. Destroyer. Names the vampire's foes had given him.

But to the King, he was Apep: the boy he had found on the streets and shaped into the perfect companion.

On seeing him, Malarath clenched his jaw, reminding himself of what he needed to do, even as his heart beat faster in his chest.

The vampire glared at him; his irises burned red. "Is this fort all you have?"

Indeed. The King had no other keeps or strongholds left, just this single inconsequential fortress. It had been hidden, protected by magic. That is, until an hour ago when he lifted the veil, exposing the last bastion of what was once a mighty empire.

Apep held his hand forward and squeezed it into a fist. Prescott lifted off the ground as an invisible force began to crush him high in the air. "I expected a battle."

"Wait!" Malarath cried, and sunk down to his knees. "I surrender," he said, his voice almost shaking.

"...What?" Apep's hand dropped to his side, as if unsure of what he had heard. Released, Prescott fell with a sudden crash to the ground and he pushed himself to his knees.

Malarath bowed his head. "I surrender. You have won."

The vampire stood silent, his eyes raking over the two men. "An incubus deception."

"No. I can fight you no longer. All that I have is yours. I am yours. Is that not what you desire? What you have always desired?"

"What I desired—" Apep spat out, his fangs flashing, "—was for you to save me from *her*. I endured decades of torture by her hand, hoping my lover would come for me."

"You would have killed me if I had tried. As all vampires do to those they love after they are turned. It wasn't until you broke the bond that I could come for you."

"And even then, you still did not come. You used the war against me to rid those who stood over you. You chose to ascend to your throne, *High King*."

Malarath lowered his eyes and whispered, "And I regret that choice."

"Because I made you regret it. I've killed your warriors, taken your lands, and stripped you of your wealth."

"No," the King shook his head. "No. I regret it because you were not at my side. We should have done it together, and instead I was alone." Malarath looked up, his eyes turned from light blue to a bright gold as he met the gaze of his former lover. "And I have longed for you."

Apep came closer, crossing the distance of the room until he was standing directly in front of the kneeling king. "Does truth ever fall from your lips?"

Malarath stood, slow and deliberate. One by one he pulled off his golden rings, dropping them to the stone floor. Each heavy *clang* echoed in the massive room. When they were finally off, he removed the bracelets, and lastly a golden circlet from his head, which he dropped as well.

"I have no more magic that can prevent you from using your blood powers on me. You control me now. I am aware that you will torture me, and when you tire of that, kill me." Malarath dipped his head in a submissive gesture. "But I will not fight you anymore."

Apep reached out and placed his cold hand on Malarath's cheek. Claws dug into the incubus' face and he fell back to his knees once more.

"Your subjects? Your warrior?" Apep looked over to Prescott who had stayed on the ground, but his muscles were primed and ready to move into action if needed.

Trapped within his own body, Malarath struggled to answer and could only do so once Apep slacked his fingers. "They are yours. He is yours."

"Remove your armor," Apep ordered Prescott.

The warrior stood and removed his helmet, then unhooked the side of the cuirass that covered his torso and, when it was free, set it on the ground, revealing the saffron-tinted goat's hair that lined the inside. Lastly, he doffed the greaves that covered his shins.

The vampire appeared behind the warrior and wrapped his arms around the human, sinking his fangs deep into his neck. Prescott accepted his fate without struggle, and Apep released him with a disappointed grunt after taking only a few pulls of blood, tossing the human to the ground.

The warrior pressed his hand against his leaking wound and looked up.

"Pathetic," the vampire growled and raised his hand.

Prescott began to scream as his own blood became a weapon within him, squeezing and snapping his insides. Moments later he fell silent, his face pale and slack, his eyes dead.

"You have killed him?" Malarath asked, still unable to move. The loss of his warrior pained him, far more than he would ever allow anyone to see.

"I haven't decided yet."

Hope swept through Malarath. "And me? What is to be my fate?"

Apep walked around him, judging him from every angle. His eyes traced the incubus' body, lingering on his slender hips and backside. The vampire tried to mask his emotions but Malarath could feel desire welling within him.

The King waited, not daring to use any of his incubus abilities. The curse of the Sanguine Dominar made Apep too unpredictable. His mind had become warped with the thirst for blood and power.

The vampire stopped in front of him, his stature imposing. "I haven't decided that either."

One moment Malarath felt the binding blood grip ease and the next his back collided against a pillar. A hand wrapped around his pale neck, squeezing hard enough to labor his breathing.

Apep leaned in and whispered, his cold breath hitting Malarath's cheek with harsh bursts. "You were right, I will torture you…and I will use you."

Malarath wanted to reach out and touch him but it would be perilous. He balled his fists. "Let me pleasure you. It has been so long."

The Dominar's eyes flared. He released Malarath's neck, then ripped the front of the incubus' tunic open with his claws, exposing his aroused body.

The vampire pawed at him. Thin bloody marks flourished against Malarath's fair skin. The tangy smell of blood filled the air and the claws cut deeper. Fear rose in Malarath and the vampire's lips curled into a cruel smile, his fangs long with hunger.

He struck hard, sinking his teeth deep into the incubus' tender neck, sucking in greedy mouthfuls of blood. Malarath struggled against him, and out of instinct tried to wrap a hold on the Dominar to control him, but blood shifted and severe pain surged through him. He lost his ability to focus and cried out.

"Derin, *please*," he begged, using the incubus name of affection: *Beloved*. A name he had often called Apep in the moments he allowed passion to overtake him.

Apep broke away. "No, you have lost the privilege to call me that," he growled, bright red blood coating his fangs. "You will call me 'Your Majesty'."

Malarath lowered his gaze. "Yes, Your Majesty." The pain swelling within him subsided.

Apep pushed what was left of Malarath's tunic from his body, then grabbed his wrist and pulled him along as he ascended the stairs to the golden throne. They passed over Prescott, still unconscious, his chest rising and falling in a shallow rhythm.

Taking a seat on the throne, Apep pulled Malarath between his legs. Malarath sank to his knees, his naked body pressed against the vampire's leathers, and asked, "Will you let me satisfy you, Your Majesty?"

Apep nodded once.

Malarath placed his hands on the Dominar's powerful thighs. He took his time, tracing the lean, defined muscles through the leather. Gentle as a breeze, he pushed pleasure through the vampire's body and Apep let out a soft sound of approval in response. Malarath tugged at the bulging leather laces that barely contained Apep's hard erection.

The situation was delicate. At any moment Apep's mood could change. If Malarath was not perfect in every way, he would suffer agonizing pain. He resisted the urge to feed off the lustrous golden strands of energy pouring out from the vampire.

With the laces undone, Apep's thick cock popped free and Malarath ran his finger up the underside, stopping at the slit and applying pressure.

"It has been so long, Muri," Apep said, and let out a lustful moan.

Muri…the word for *lover*. Caught off-guard by the name, Malarath yanked his hand back, his golden eyes wide.

Sitting powerfully on the throne, Apep looked down at the naked incubus between his legs.

"You still love me, Derin?" Malarath asked, ignoring the command not to use the name and already knowing the answer.

Burning red eyes narrowed at him, then abruptly softened and returned to honey gold. His claws receded and he cupped Malarath's face, opening himself. For a moment, it was like it had been long ago; their emotions entwined, and they were one. Malarath couldn't tell where Apep ended and he began.

As suddenly as he opened himself, the vampire closed, leaving emptiness within them both. Apep reached down and grabbed Malarath's hips and yanked him into his lap, holding him tight. He ran his hand over the incubus' skin, tracing the cuts, devouring them. "Never has there been a moment where I've stopped loving you. I will love you for all time, and there is nothing that could change that."

The incubus sunk against the vampire's chest, taking comfort in the grip. "I am sorry," he whispered.

There was no response other than a tightening of the embrace. The cool night air seeped into the throne room and rays of moonlight streamed in from arches high above them.

"You're trembling," Apep said.

"I am sorry," Malarath whispered again, squeezing his eyes closed and allowing himself to take comfort in his lover.

Apep held him tighter, careful not to crush the more fragile incubus. "I've long waited for you to say that." They sat silent, their passion a low simmer. Finally, the vampire said, "You will be punished. And once I'm finished we can start anew."

Malarath pulled back to study Apep's face.

"No," Malarath said, forcing the word out. The war would be over in a few moments. His people—the few that were left—would be safe. But the price was steep: emptiness would plague him the rest of his days.

"No?" Confusion and anger boiled from the vampire.

"*Immol,*" Malarath said. An iron collar appeared around Apep's neck. In truth, the collar had been around his neck for a while. Malarath had slipped it on when he first came close and it was not until he uttered the word that it became tangible.

The collar had deep engravings of ancient runic symbols that drew their power from four evenly spaced black stones set into the metal. The stones were round, polished, and contained hundreds of tiny glowing pinpricks of light—each seemed to have a galaxy trapped within. Night Stones, witches called them. They were magic consolidated.

He had spent a small fortune to acquire the magic needed to contain the Dominar, but it would be worth it. For his people.

The vampire shot up, pushing Malarath off him and sending him tumbling down the steps. Malarath grunted and was still for a moment while his body healed. Apep reached out his hand to control him but nothing happened.

"My powers—*what have you done?*" Apep roared, and began to claw at the collar around his neck, trying to remove it.

Malarath stood. "You killed most of my people and destroyed my empire. You have no control over yourself, Dominar. You are driven to kill and you will purge this planet until there is no living being left upon it. You are tainted by cursed blood and I can no longer allow you to live."

"I'll kill you."

Malarath shook his head. "No. It is over now."

The vampire launched himself down the stairs, but he never made it to the bottom.

"*Olipsus,*" Malarath said, and the vampire's body went limp, crashing down.

The High King stepped over the unconscious body and went to his throne. He put on the blue cloak he had shed earlier, securing it once again with the ruby pendant.

Dragging the vampire over to his warrior, he cut Apep's wrist open with a single clawed finger, letting the blood flow into Prescott's mouth. Prescott began to gag and cough, choking down the blood as it healed him.

"You were successful, Your Majesty," he said, as he sat up and wiped the corner of his mouth.

"Yes. Don your armor and bring him to the place I prepared for him."

Prescott nodded and did as ordered.

Once outside, Apep was fastened to a worked boulder by heavy silver chains, his body stripped except for the collar, stretched out on the rock like an offering to the gods. Malarath gazed over his unconscious lover, memorizing every detail.

The silence was broken when Prescott held out his hand and, with a sizzle and green glow of light, a golden sword appeared in it, adorned with the markings of the incubus goddess.

"She's here, Your Majesty," he said and pointed to the sky. A swarm of screeching bats swirled against the fat moon. The bats came close and merged together, forming into a woman with dark skin and cruel eyes.

The Queen of Vampires.

"You should never have turned him, Nebethah," Malarath said.

The Queen's lips curled up, displaying her long fangs. "You should have chosen me, not him. He was unworthy of you."

"I never loved you."

"And you loved him?"

Malarath brushed his hand across Apep's face in a tender gesture. "He is the only one I have ever loved." Malarath's eyes narrowed and he set free his anger. *"And you took him from me."*

"You should have—"

Tired of hearing her speak, he raised his hand to cut her off. "I will wipe your species from this planet, and when you are the last vampire left—I will come for you. Perhaps then you will understand the depth of my loss. Perhaps then you will understand what you took from me."

She laughed at him, her white fangs catching the moonlight. "Most of your people are dead. You will never kill us all." Her body burst into a thousand bats and she flew off into the night.

"She's not wrong, Your Majesty. There aren't many incubi left," Prescott said, still holding the sword.

"There are enough. And with them, I will rebuild and raise a mighty empire to serve me."

Prescott nodded at Apep. "Are you going to wake him?"

Malarath held out his hand and Prescott gave him the sword. "Leave."

The warrior bowed and left.

"Suspilo," Malarath said, and the vampire woke. He tugged at the silver chains. Once he realized he was trapped, he said nothing as he scowled at the incubus king. "The sun is rising soon."

Apep squeezed his eyes shut and looked away.

Malarath touched his chin and turned his face back to him. "Look at me, Derin."

He did. His hard eyes hid none of his fury. "Don't let me burn in the sun. If I am to die, I would rather it be by your hand, Muri."

"I..." Malarath was not sure he had the strength to carry out the request.

"Kiss me," Apep said.

Malarath complied, leaning down over the rock, his full lips crashed against Apep's. Heat blazed inside of him. This was their last kiss. The last time he would feel his lover against him. When he broke away, he found it hard to catch his breath, as if a great statue pressed down on his chest.

He wanted to make love to him, to satisfy both their bodies. He ground his hips against the vampire, his sex straining for more.

"No," Apep rasped, his own desire clear. "It would be a mockery of what we had. End this. Please."

Malarath pulled back and stood before the rock, looking over him one last time.

"If there is a way to be with you again, I will find it," the incubus said and sliced his blade through Apep's neck, severing head from shoulders.

He watched as the vampire decayed into ash. The iron collar fell on the stone with a clank and tumbled to the ground.

Malarath picked it up and clutched it in his hand. He screamed as the sun rose behind him, burning away the last remnants of his lover's body.

One

MATTHEW

Roughly 2,500 Years Later. New York.

"*Devak*," Matthew said, his voice raw; strained. Delirious with hunger, he couldn't remember where he was or how he had come to be there.

He struggled against the unyielding restraints that kept him suspended in the air, but they didn't budge. His arms throbbed as if he'd been hanging for some time. The thick shackles around his ankles didn't feel much better. Heavy chains attached to the floor pulled at his legs, leaving only the tips of his toes touching the ground. A bright directional spotlight focused on him.

He was naked except for the shackles and heavy collar around his neck. His head lolled forward in his weakened condition. At least the metal wasn't silver. Small blessing.

He couldn't recall the last time blood crossed his lips.

His vampire aspect—claws, fangs, red irises—would not retreat no matter how hard he tried to return to human form. The creature inside of him was desperate to feed.

"*Devak*," Matthew said again, as if calling his name would summon him.

"Your blood guardian is long dead," a cruel voice whispered from the shadows.

That's right. The incubi had recaptured him. How long had it been? Weeks? Months?

Perhaps the worst part of Matthew's imprisonment wasn't the hunger but *him*.

Malarath.

The High King.

Every single time Matthew woke, *the creature* was there in the room. Watching and waiting in the shadows, just outside of the light.

With great effort, Matthew lifted his head and a glint of light caught on Malarath's pale blue eyes. The High King's presence turned the very air frigid and biting, and the faint scent of jasmine made Matthew dizzy.

Other than the first night of Matthew's capture, when Malarath had informed Matthew that he was to call him *Master*, this was the first time the King had said anything at all. And it was to remind him that Devak was gone. Dead.

Fucking asshole.

Matthew narrowed his eyes at him and growled. Or tried to anyways. It came out as more of a dry rumble.

Malarath stepped forward into the light, his greyish-blue robes drifted around him, settling into place when he stilled. The incubus ruler was nothing like what Matthew had envisioned when he first heard of him. He'd expected a hulking brute—someone who filled a throne with an immense masculine physique and overwhelming presence. A warrior. A general turned king.

But Malarath wasn't that. He was tall and lean, with an almost otherworldly appearance, and self-assured perfect posture.

Malarath ran a finger down Matthew's gaunt body, starting at the collar and ending at the base of his flaccid cock. The touch was much warmer than Matthew expected, and if he hadn't been starving for blood his dick would be rock fucking hard right now.

It was disgusting—although not surprising given that he was facing the oldest incubus on the planet—how Matthew's body responded to the King, as if he desired him. His stomach churned.

"Are you hungry, pet?" Malarath ask.

Matthew stared at the King's long neck, watching the vein pulse just below the skin. He dragged his eyes away and glowered at the High King. He wasn't going to answer such a stupid question. Or any questions for that matter.

Malarath, in turn, said nothing else. He stood motionless for what seemed like hours, as if unburdened by the passage of time, waiting for Matthew to respond.

Matthew drifted in and out of lucidness. Until, finally, the High King spoke again: "My general tells me that you were speaking to him in six days with minimal effort on his part. I could have you begging in six minutes. Do you wish to experience that?" Malarath asked, sounding indifferent; and maybe even bored. His face betrayed no emotions, which was a strange contrast to how alluring and attractive he was. But it was a hollow beauty, like that of a porcelain doll.

Incubi may have evolved to be arousing, to be perfect, so they could attract prey to feed upon, but they were as much monsters as vampires. At least vampires were honest about what they were.

Matthew closed his eyes, wondering just what the High King would do to him if he didn't answer. His only shred of happiness was that Samantha was away from here and safe. As far as he could tell, none of the incubi knew he had a vampire child.

His heart shattered as he thought of her.

Actually, *that* was the worst part about his imprisonment—the separation from her. Every now and then he could feel a thin thread tugging his chest, letting him know she was alive. Sometimes, through the bond, he could feel that she was terrified and it killed him that he was unable to help her.

Most of the time he couldn't feel her at all, and that was far worse because he had no idea what her fate was. It was strange he didn't fly into a blind rage each time the bond seem to fall away. But then again, he barely had the strength to keep his head up right now.

Matthew considered what the High King said…six minutes? Fuck, wave a blood bag in front of him and the words would tumble from his mouth. It wasn't that he didn't want to fight, but having already gone through one incubus bending him, the idea of going through it again made his soul heavy. Things would just be easier if he submitted to Malarath.

He opened his eyes and swallowed hard. "Yes, Master, I'm hungry." The words stuck in his throat. He hated them. Hated himself. And fucking hated his sire for doing this to him, for leaving him helpless on the ground for the incubi to recapture.

Malarath stood frozen in place for so long that Matthew had no idea if he was going to get blood or not. Maybe he had to ask for it like he did with Tarrick…

"May I have some blood, Master?"

Malarath's hand pressed so hard into Matthew's emaciated stomach that he cried out. An echoing sensation pulsed in his belly. He was being scanned. It was an ability that allowed an incubus to 'see' inside of him like an ultrasound. Not every incubus could do it, but it was hardly surprising the King could.

He already knew what the High King would find: four collapsed blood pouches and an empty soavik that was cramping with pain, although the lack of blood was far more agonizing.

Malarath stopped scanning him but left his hand on his abdomen. He said nothing, and eventually Matthew dropped his head forward. He wasn't going to get blood and the hunger was becoming too overwhelming and painful. He was surprised he'd been lucid for that long. Eventually his thoughts became disjointed and the world stopped making sense.

He closed his eyes and focused on trying to pull himself together. When he opened them, Malarath was no longer touching him…and he was wearing different robes, light green in color. His long golden hair was tied up. A night or more had passed and Matthew hadn't even realized it.

"You are doing well, pet," Malarath said. The praise was…unexpected.

"…What?" Matthew asked, grunting the word out of his raw throat.

Malarath stood unmoving, waiting on something.

It took a while but eventually Matthew remembered what it was that Malarath wanted and he tried again. "I'm not sure what you mean, Master," he said with some effort.

"I do not tolerate the loss of self-control. If you are hungry, you are to endure it until I decide to feed you. I have been training you to resist your hunger and to stop losing yourself to the blood rage."

Training? This felt like torture.

"I've been blood raging?" Matthew asked. Tarrick had told him once that vampires succumbed to a rage when starved. It was an instinctual response for a vampire to find blood. Once a vampire got to that point, they went wild until they gorged on humans.

Malarath took a step closer. The air around him dropped a few degrees. "How much time do you think has passed since my warrior brought you in?"

Matthew would have shrugged if he could move. "A few weeks, maybe a month."

"Nine months."

Matthew blinked.

Nine months? Nine fucking months since Devak had died? Since he had last seen Samantha? Nine months strung up in this...cell? At least he assumed it was a cell, his senses were too dull, his eyes too weak to see anything outside of the circle of light.

Memories came flooding back. For months he had been alone. Starved, he begged for blood. He begged for company—just one person to talk to. He begged for Devak...for Tarrick...for anyone to come and save him.

Then he fell to the blood rage and the memories went blank.

Turmoil plagued him. He feared the High King...but there was a part of him that didn't want him to leave, if only so he wouldn't be alone anymore.

It was sick.

Matthew wanted to scream, or maybe cry, but he had no energy for either.

Instead, he slipped back into darkness. When he came to, Malarath was wearing a dark blue robe with golden embroidery, his hair down, his pale eyes examining Matthew. "You are close, pet. When you are able to go a whole night without succumbing to your hunger, we will move on."

An entire night? He wasn't sure he could do it but he had to try if he had any hope of getting out of these chains.

Hours later, he couldn't fight the pangs any longer and he slipped into darkness.

He woke again, and again Malarath was in new clothes. Standing there, unmoving.

Watching Malarath at the edge of the light, Matthew noticed that he rarely blinked, maybe once every few minutes. As a distraction, he began to count each blink and try to guess how much time was passing. He had to make it an entire night.

He didn't.

Not that night. Nor the next. Or the one after. But each night he was awake longer and longer. Each night Malarath said nothing, not even when Matthew begged for blood again or tried to wrap a hold around the High King. It didn't even so much as tickle him, not that Matthew expected to actually sway such an old creature. He could barely sway humans with it.

One night he tried to compel Malarath, who wore no preventive contacts or glasses, with a 'release me'. That earned him a small half smile from the High King.

Malarath came forward and grabbed Matthew's side, running his hand down his bony ribcage. Matthew wanted to squirm away from the touch...and lean into it. He craved it and wanted more. It was humiliating.

"For nine months you were not able to pull yourself out of the rage for even a few moments and now you can almost last the night. Another month and you will be strong enough to resist," Malarath said.

A month? No. Tonight.

He narrowed his eyes at Malarath, determined to prove the High King wrong, and focused on his anger, using it to distract himself from the pain.

Time crawled by and the urge to surrender to the darkness crept around him, but he beat it back.

In the long hours of silence, his thoughts turned to Devak and he fell to grief. He'd never again feel Devak's warm touch, or soft lips. He'd never see his amber eyes or hear his serene voice wrap around him.

They only had a few months together, yet it had seemed like so much more.

And now Matthew was alone again. No family around him; no lovers—just a cold, uncaring incubus monarch lingering in the shadows. '*Master*' Matthew would be forced to call him. Again, he considered resisting, but he knew where this road led and he wasn't sure he had it in him to fight.

Matthew's eyelids felt like they had boulders chained to them. Keeping them open was a near insurmountable feat, but he refused to succumb to the exhaustion tonight. He had something to prove.

Survive. Don't let him break you. That was the last thing Samantha had said to him. Matthew had assumed that she was talking about his sire, the Blood God, but he'd been wrong. She'd been talking about the High King. Oracles were funny that way; they spoke in mystery and misdirection.

Matthew wasn't so sure he'd come out of this whole—but he'd try, for her sake.

Time ticked by and, although he couldn't see it, he could feel the sun approaching the horizon. He shot Malarath a triumphant look.

Malarath's mouth curled up into a smile. "Well done, pet."

Matthew cringed, horrified by how much pleasure he took in the praise.

Two

In what Matthew could only describe as a divine experience, life flooded his mouth. Delicious, heavenly, essence-restoring blood seeped over his tongue and trickled down his throat. He was too weak to open his eyes, but he did suck harder on some sort of tube that penetrated his lips.

The blood stopped flowing, followed by a loud slurping sound. The tube was yanked away from him and he whimpered. He needed more.

Within him, he focused on healing his body. His muscles were weak, his senses dull, blood pouches collapsed, and he even had some fractures, especially where his wrists were shackled.

"How much so far?" a male asked, standing close by. Probably the person feeding him.

A different male answered. "Two gallons, sir. Want me to get more?"

"Yeah. He's burning it quick. Bring another two and start a line."

Two gallons already? The blood burned away inside of him as he healed himself. Or at least that's what it felt like. He wasn't really sure how his body got rid of the physical blood. He sure as hell didn't piss it out. He'd have to ask someone someday how it all worked.

He smiled to himself. He was an undead incubus that fed on sex and blood and here he was looking for some sort of scientific explanation. Next he'd be wanting to know just how guardians flew with wings made of blood or how shifters gained mass when they changed form...

God, he was being absurd right now, but it just felt so damn wonderful to have blood again. He was buzzing with delight and began to purr.

"Someone's happy," the male standing close by said.

Matthew snapped his eyes open and forced them to focus.

The cell—no, scratch that—*the cage* was now illuminated by lights on the high ceiling. He was shackled to the middle of what looked like an enormous round birdcage. Silver bars rose from the concrete ground and curved together into a point above him.

Surrounding the cage was empty space, then a round concrete wall with glowing runes painted on it. A vamp trap.

There were no windows and only one heavy silvered door that looked like it belonged in a military bunker. Several cameras hung from the ceiling, along with a single shower head positioned above the cage.

Matthew noticed there was a section of bars that looked freshly welded on. There was also dried blood everywhere. And there were claw marks on the walls outside of the cage, in the concrete itself. Something big and strong had broken the bars and tried to break out of the room. Matthew was 99.9 percent sure it had been him, although he couldn't recall doing so.

Imperator Prescott stood before him.

Leader of the Hunter Corps.

The High King's personal bodyguard. Rumor had it that he was over a few thousand years old, but he looked younger than Matthew; somewhere in his mid-twenties.

He wore his usual hunter armor: Greek design with a sculpted breastplate, thick arm and leg guards, and a skirt made of wide leather straps that would look lame on nearly anyone else, but he managed to pull it off.

When Matthew had seen him in the past, he always had his helmet on, hiding his features. It was missing now, exposing his short hair, maintained beard, and straight nose.

The fucker had murdered Devak.

Anger surged through Matthew and he jerked and hissed at the Imperator, chains rattling.

Prescott patted Matthew's chest, as if to mock him. "Settle down. It took us a few tries but these chains will hold even you." Prescott looked around at the damage in the room. "You were a little stronger than I expected."

"I'm going to kill you," Matthew snarled.

Prescott shook his head. "No. But it'll be fun watching you try."

Matthew curled his lips, displaying his fangs.

"You should be nicer to me, I'm the one with the blood," Prescott said, holding up a full blood bag and waving it.

Matthew fantasized about draining him near death, healing him, then doing it again. Over and over until his need for revenge was satisfied. But it was a foolish fantasy since hunters poisoned their blood. He wondered how long it would take to purge it from Prescott's system.

Prescott shoved a tube connected to a blood pack into Matthew's mouth. Matthew scowled at him. *Murderer.*

"Suck," Prescott ordered, squeezing the bag. Blood dribbled from Matthew's mouth as he narrowed his eyes. Prescott shrugged and started to pull the tube out. "If you don't want blood…"

Matthew clamped down on the tube with his teeth and grudgingly began to suck on it like a straw. Cold blood, reminding him of coffee that sat out too long, but to him it was ecstasy. And as pissed as he was, Matthew was thrilled he was getting more. He had a feeling it would be too much to hope for clothes next.

Over the next seven nights, a hunter entered the cage every two hours to swap out the blood bag on an IV line they attached, but otherwise Matthew was alone. His soavik cramped and he was tempted to try to get a hunter to blow him so he could feed sexually and stop the pain.

Not that he was strong enough to wrap a hold on a hunter, especially not these hunters—the one's that worked for Prescott and Malarath directly were among the best. Or so he had overheard when he'd trained with hunter cadets down at Ashwood Vampire Hunter Academy. Compelling was off the table since all hunters wore contacts to prevent it from happening.

He was miserable alone in the cage, but at least he had blood.

Before the sunset on the eighth night, the crack of a whip against his bare back woke him. He was unable to move since it was still day but he could scream and, with tremendous effort, keep his eyes open.

The High King was standing before him wearing maroon robes with silver embroidery and a high collar that gave him a sinister look. He wore gemmed rings on each of his fingers—he always had them on—and a golden circlet weaved into his hair.

Another lash of the whip broke against his back and Matthew managed to suppress his cry with a grunt.

"Oh. You are awake," Malarath said, the edges of his lips pulled into a disturbingly playful smile. Bastard.

Matthew could smell Prescott standing behind him, wielding the bullwhip no doubt. He also smelled foxglove, a poison for vampires that slowed healing. It stung like a bitch too.

As Malarath stepped forward, the temperature dropped a few degrees. He ran his hand along the top of Matthew's right arm then back down again, tracing the tendril pattern of the tattoo that covered it.

Some of Matthew's muscles had regrown over the past week—perk of being a vampire—but he'd still have to work for the rest of them. He wished Malarath would stop touching him though. The soft contact repulsed him…and yet he wanted more of it.

He was thankful his dick wasn't rock-solid right now, but as soon as the sun set his traitorous cock would probably rise. Maybe by then they'd get to the torture part and he wouldn't have to worry about what his cock was up to. Maybe he'd even get clothes at some point. Heh.

"Have him moved to my room. I will enjoy him there," Malarath said, lowering his hand.

Matthew growled and another lash fell upon his back. Still unable to move, Matthew could do nothing but accept the pain.

"You growl at him again and I'll cut out your tongue," Prescott said from behind.

Matthew resisted the temptation to growl just to spite him.

Malarath ran his knuckles down the side of Matthew's cheek, the gemmed rings cold against his flesh.

"You like him, huh?" Prescott asked.

The High King grabbed Matthew's chin, moving his head around to inspect him. "He will make an adequate pet."

"Fuck you," Matthew said before he could stop himself.

Fingers tightened on Matthew's chin as the whip cracked against his back again. He cried out.

Prescott stepped closer. "Don't speak unless spoken to and each time you do speak, you *will* address the High King properly. You'll call him 'Master' and I am to be addressed as 'Imperator'. Am I clear?"

"Fuck you too, *Imperator*."

Another four blows striped his skin and Matthew ground his teeth, grunting with the pain. He nearly passed out. Staying awake during the daytime was always exhausting and this was pushing him to his limit.

"Try that answer again," Prescott said.

Matthew was feeling rebellious but he'd made his point the best he could. Anything more would earn him more lashes. "You're clear, Imperator."

The sun set and Matthew could move around again, kind of. He could jerk around a bit but the chains kept his body taut and didn't allow for any motion beyond that. Out of instinct, he yanked his head away from Malarath's tight grip. To his surprise, Malarath released him.

"You sure he'll behave in your room?" Prescott asked.

"Yes. He will behave," Malarath said and left the cage.

Three

Prescott stood alone at the open door of the cage, a bullwhip coiled in his hand. *"Rayak,"* he said and the chains holding Matthew up disconnected from the shackle. Matthew, who hadn't been standing on his own in months, crumpled to the floor in a heap.

But now he was free and the man who killed Devak was in the cage with him.

His fucking mistake.

Matthew shrugged off the pain and surged at Prescott. His fangs came down and he called forward his axe, *Bloodreaver, Harbinger of Ruin*. According to Samantha, the axe had named itself. It was an egocentric little bitch.

The normally black tattoos on his right arm turned crimson as they split open. Blood poured out but the axe didn't form.

Instead, the blood simply dropped to the ground, failing to take shape in his hand. Before he could figure out what the fuck was going on, Prescott uttered the word, *"Raylo."*

The shackles on Matthew's arms snapped together behind his back as if magnetized. The shackles on his legs also came together and he tripped and tumbled along the ground, leaving a trail of blood behind him as he slammed full-force into the bars of the cage. The silver burned his naked flesh.

He tried not to scream but wasn't able to stop panicked grunts from escaping his lungs.

Prescott looked down at him, unimpressed. "You done?"

Matthew flashed his fangs at him as he tried to writhe away from the silver bars only to have a heavy armored boot land on his shoulder, keeping him pressed against the cage. The smell and sizzle of flesh burning filled the air.

Prescott smiled. "We're in no hurry."

Matthew snarled, and Prescott took a few steps back, a shit-eating grin plastered his face. Matthew rolled to his stomach and struggled to get onto his knees—not an easy task with all his limbs on lockdown.

"What's your plan here?" Prescott asked. "Assuming you can stand, going to hop over to me bunny style and try to bite me a few times? Maybe headbutt me? I took a punch from your daddy and it didn't do shit to me. You need to stop and think before you try again."

Yes. Yes, that had been his plan. But now that Prescott said it out loud, it sounded dumb. The words sedated his blind rage as he realized there was nothing he could do right now. He felt fucking helpless as he forced the stripes of silver burns to heal. He also closed his bleeding tattoos, wondering why the fuck he couldn't summon his axe.

Matthew tilted his head forward, and narrowed his eyes at Prescott.

"All done?" Prescott asked.

Matthew wasn't even close to being done, but he'd wait for a better opportunity before trying to attack again. He nodded once.

"*Rayal*," Prescott said as he hooked the bullwhip to his belt. The shackles around Matthew's feet disconnected and he pushed himself up. Whatever force that kept his arm shackles glued behind his back together didn't budge.

Fucking magic.

He hated magic and these stupid fucking words: *Rayak, Raylo*, and now *Rayal*; each doing some new bullshit thing to him.

Prescott motioned his hand towards the bloody mark on the floor and Matthew's blood-covered body. "We had these shackles made special just for you. Trying to summon your blessed weapon will do nothing except make a big mess."

Fuuuuuuck magic.

At least now he knew why his weapon didn't form.

"Try and escape again and you'll learn just what the collar is capable of. I wouldn't recommend it, personally. It was made for someone far stronger than you." Prescott grabbed Matthew's elbow and ushered him from the cage.

They waited at the thick door leading out of the room before it unlocked and swung open. Bright light flooded him from the other side and he forced his eyes to adjust as he was pushed through the doorway.

They walked down a long concrete hall lined with more reinforced doors. Matthew could sense other powerful creatures locked up down here but had no idea what they were. A team of six hunters stood guard. All looked gruff, with a don't-fuck-with-me attitude. Each saluted Prescott.

Matthew hated that he was naked. As an incubus, it shouldn't bother him as much as it did, but he wished he had clothes. At least Tarrick had always given him clothes.

"Need an escort, sir?" one of the hunters asked Prescott.

"Nah, he's not going to give me any trouble."

Matthew frowned. He sure as hell would give him trouble if he could...

Prescott tapped his boot against Matthew's calf to get him moving. Matthew scowled and walked forward. At the end of the hall was another thick door. They waited and it opened into a round room with three elevator doors. The middle elevator slid open and they stepped in.

The inside was massive, able to hold two hunter teams—twelve people—easily. There were no buttons, but glowing green runes blanketed the reflective metal walls. Prescott placed his hand where the button panel would normally be and runes became visible. There were nearly a hundred.

He touched the rune second from the top then grinned at Matthew. "If you are plotting your escape, you'll need someone who can activate magic for this elevator. If you do make it this far, you'd be the first."

Matthew pretended to ignore him, but he *was* planning his escape. He needed to learn the layout of this place. As the elevator began its ascent, he stared at his reflection in the metal. He looked miserable: covered in blood, his brown hair matted, his body thin and boney, and his silver eyes dull.

His hair was far longer than it used to be. He wasn't sure why or when it grew out, usually he had to force it to grow. Never having to get a haircut was a strangely nice perk of being a vampire. He wasn't too thrilled to see his pubic hair had grown too, looking like a messy nest. He liked to keep the hedges trimmed.

The heavy iron collar around his neck drew his eye. It had runes that glowed a soft green every so often. Four black stones, set evenly around the collar, were the most attention grabbing. Each stone had fine pinpoints of light, like twinkling stars.

Matthew recognized them. It was the same type of stone they had used as an offering to break Devak's curse—a Night Stone Samantha had called it. Matthew had never asked her specifically why she'd needed one, but now he could guess because they could fuel powerful magic. Like an empowered collar to keep a demigod in line.

He twisted his body to look at the shackles. They also had engraved runes, but these were different from the cuff-bracers General Tarrick had put on him. Those had been thinner, covered most of his forearm, and designed for use in battle...designed for a warrior. These shackles were meant for a slave, tight and heavy around his wrist.

The ones on his ankles were the same.

He noticed Prescott was watching him, but the hunter said nothing. Moments later, the elevator doors opened to another concrete room. This was some serious security. As far as Matthew could tell, there was no way to get through the doors unless someone watching through the cameras unlocked them from some remote location.

Any hope of escape was shrinking fast. This place was a fortress and, though Matthew loathed to admit it, his jailer was skilled.

Another two doors later, Prescott ushered Matthew into a hallway that looked nothing like the concrete rooms they'd just left. Richly colored rugs covered the marble floors and contemporary art hung on the walls. There were other entries, but it was the ornately carved door at the end of the hall where, unsurprisingly, he was being led.

The High King's room.

Prescott went inside, expecting Matthew to follow. Matthew walked forward and froze at the doorway.

Inside wasn't just a 'room', as Malarath had called it. Inside was a fucking apartment that took up most of the level. It was massive with high ceilings. A spiral staircase led up to a second level balcony that wrapped around the room. The walls were lined with books.

Everything was modern, decorated white and slate grey with hints of maroon brick and artwork adding splashes of color.

There was a sitting area with white leather furniture that seemed more for looks than comfort. To his left, not far from the door, a platform rose two steps. On it, a minimalist bed with a wooden headboard and, naturally, silk sheets.

Perhaps the most eye-catching feature was the floor to ceiling windows overlooking the Manhattan nightscape.

The view was fucking impressive.

Central park sprawled out before him and downtown twinkled in the distance. Matthew knew the High King lived somewhere in New York City but he hadn't expected this. How did the incubi and so many hunters go unnoticed by humans? Surely someone would've seen them from time to time.

This place was nothing like Tarrick's estate. Tarrick's room was too clean and orderly for Matthew's tastes, but it was still warm and inviting…well, except the wall shackles. Malarath's space was something out of the pages of a design magazine—sterile and untouchable.

After taking in everything, he noticed the High King sitting on a large, almost throne-like chair, looking out the window.

The King stood and studied Matthew. Under the cold gaze, Matthew fought the urge to take a step backwards. For the tenth time in the last hour, he wished he had pants on. Hell, he'd even take underwear…or a Speedo, or jockstrap. Anything besides having his dick flopping around for everyone to see.

"He misbehaved," Malarath stated, his voice cold, his eyes lingering on the blood.

"He tried to summon his weapon, but I think he knows better now," Prescott said.

"Come in, pet."

Matthew pushed back a growl that sat deep in his chest and took a few steps into the room. The door swung closed behind him automatically.

From the corner of his eye, he noticed that the wall to his left was metal covered with runes inscribed across it. The tiled floor had a drain in the center. And there were chains. It seems Tarrick wasn't the only incubus with the proclivity to keep vampires chained up in their room. He wondered if it was a common fetish among them.

"*Olyar*," Prescott said, and the shackles detached from each other, leaving Matthew's hands free. They grew into long claws and he flexed them. Prescott raised an eyebrow and motioned to the runed wall. "Go stand over there."

Matthew didn't move.

Prescott sighed and walked over to Matthew. He didn't seem the least bit threatened and he had good reason for it: his armor made him invincible. But Matthew had a plan that didn't involve killing him, he just needed to shut him up for a few moments so that he couldn't say any of the words that bound his shackles together.

Then Matthew was going to kill the High King.

When Prescott was close enough, Matthew drove his fist into the hunter's neck. Prescott went flying, but Matthew didn't wait to see where he landed. He dumped power into his speed and, in a blur of movement, was on Malarath.

He grabbed the High King by his neck and pushed him down onto a white leather chaise lounge, pinning him.

All Matthew had to do was squeeze just a little tighter to crush Malarath's trachea and he'd be dead.

But he didn't squeeze.

He slipped his hand behind Malarath's neck, and pulled the incubus up with the desperate need to taste him. He licked the King's lips, careful not to cut him with his fangs. The last thing he wanted to do was damage Malarath's supple skin or soft, pink tongue.

Between his legs, Matthew's length was as hard as iron and already leaking precum. The pearl fluid dampened the King's robe. He ground his hips into the High King. Never in his life had so much pleasure pulsed through him. He was on the verge of an orgasm and his dick was untouched.

He moaned into Malarath's mouth, then pulled back and looked down at him. He was so magnificent, so beautiful, that it moved Matthew nearly to tears. He needed more of the incubus—*now*.

Matthew ripped open the top half of the robes that separated them and leaned in to worship his chest, his light nipples, the hollow of his collarbone, his neck, everywhere. He licked, sucked, and kissed his way across Malarath's delicate skin, thinking of nothing but bringing the King pleasure, and he cursed himself for being inexperienced, for being so close to coming already.

And then it stopped.

Malarath loosened the hold and Matthew's mind cleared. He panted. His lungs burned within him as if he was still alive and needed more air. Propped up on his arms he looked down at the High King, their faces inches apart.

The incubus' hold was unlike anything Matthew had ever experienced. Normally it was a pushing and pulling of emotions, but this was something different: a complete domination of his thoughts.

Panic set in and Matthew tried to get away but he was stuck in place; it was as if his body was no longer his.

Malarath gripped Matthew's hips, pulling their bodies closer together, and Matthew's sex ground into the King's robes, sending a jolt of stimulation through him. His body began to tremble out of strain and fear and pleasure.

"Are you going to rape me?" Matthew asked. Raw fear clung at the edge of the words.

Malarath said nothing as his hand snaked up Matthew's back.

"Ask him again, but this time address him correctly," Prescott said, his voice hoarse. He was standing just a few feet away, rubbing his throat.

Matthew struggled to move again but it was in vain. He closed his eyes for a moment to collect himself. "Are you going to rape me, Master?"

"You fear that?" the King asked. "Being taken against your will? The loss of control?" Matthew swallowed hard. Yes. He feared it. He lost control too often and it pained him. He said nothing though. Malarath ran a finger down Matthew's cheek. "You are easy to read, pet."

The hold fell away and he could move again. With his vampire speed, he pushed himself off the incubus and rushed to the door, trying frantically to open it. But it was no use. The door was locked, and when Matthew tried to smash it apart nothing happened. It didn't make sense, the door was made from wood, it should be shattering under his strength.

"Matthew," Prescott said, but Matthew ignored him and continued to try to escape, scratching at it with his claws, leaving deep grooves behind. But they didn't stay...the door *healed* the claw marks. He had to get away from this fucking madhouse. He didn't want to be tortured or raped, or forced to kill, or be alone. He didn't want any of this. He didn't want to be some sort of *pet*. He wanted Samantha back. He wanted Devak.

"*Matthew*," Prescott repeated.

Matthew stilled. Getting away was hopeless. He looked back. Malarath was standing, his robe had slipped off his shoulders and clung to his hips, exposing his slender chest, now dirtied by dried blood.

Prescott had his hand on the whip but hadn't bothered to uncoil it. "No prisoner has ever escaped here and we have creatures far more powerful than you. You won't get through a single door unless we allow it."

Matthew looked at the windows.

"You won't have any luck with them either. They're not made of glass. I promise you, you aren't going anywhere, vampire."

Matthew flexed his claws. The High King's pale blue eyes bore into him, making his skin feel itchy and tight. His stomach churned with dread and it took every ounce of restraint not to succumb to a panicked rage.

What hope did he have escaping this place?

Survive. Don't let him break you. Samantha's words echoed through him.

Matthew closed his eyes and pushed his vampire side away. If he was going to survive, provoking his captors was not the way to do it.

"Go to the wall," Prescott said, repeating the order he'd given earlier.

With no small amount of reluctance, Matthew followed the command this time. He stood with his back to the metal wall, the tile floor cold against the soles of his feet.

"*Kayar*," Prescott said. The hanging chains came to life like snakes, twisting in the air, then connecting to Matthew's shackles. Once attached they reeled into the wall, yanking Matthew back and spreading his limbs apart.

He looked like an X, his backside pressed against the metal, his feet off the ground. The High King eyed him as if he was a piece of artwork. He nodded his approval then, moving like a breeze, left the room through a side door.

A few moments later, a male and female incubus entered the room. They were somewhat androgynous, slight in stature, and wore short, nearly transparent robes. If one didn't have small breasts, it'd be hard to tell she was a female. Both had the same thick brown hair, big hazel eyes, and small noses. They looked young, somewhere in their early or mid-teens, and Matthew guessed they were siblings, twins maybe.

They bowed to Prescott and shot Matthew a nervous glance as they scurried into the room that Malarath had disappeared into.

Prescott crossed his arms over his chest. "The punch to my throat was a good idea but it only takes me about a second to shake it off. I knew you had a brain in there somewhere. It's nice to see that you actually use it." He sounded sincere with the odd compliment, but Matthew had nothing nice to say in response. "Attacking the King isn't all that smart, though." The hunter leaned against a pillar, making himself more comfortable. "Your life will be easier and less painful if you obey. Each time you act out you'll be punished."

Matthew wondered just how terrible the punishments would be. Worse than being alone in a cage for months on end? As an incubus, it was a terrible fate.

Prescott studied Matthew. "Over the next few weeks I'll teach you all the rules but for now you should know that I hate begging. And no amount of it will get me to stop whatever I'm ordered to do to you. Understand?"

Matthew didn't answer.

The Imperator rubbed his beard. "I also hate repeating myself. If you don't want to answer questions that's up to you, but there'll be consequences."

Malarath re-entered the room and the temperature dropped a few degrees. He had cleaned off the blood and was wearing a new robe, this one dark green with white embroidery. The top of his golden hair was pinned back while the rest flowed down his back. Trailing behind him were the two smaller incubi. Malarath waved them out and they bowed deeply before leaving the room.

Malarath sat on his bed, smoothing out his robes as he settled down. "Remove his fangs."

Four

R*emove his fangs?* What the literal fuck? Matthew fought against the chains that kept him suspended.

Prescott touched the wall and a single rune began to glow bright green. The section that Matthew was pinned to, began to move. He felt himself going forward, then swinging upwards until he was lying horizontal, facing the ceiling. It took him a moment to realize that the wall itself had detached. He felt as if he was chained to an autopsy table.

"I told you, attacking the King was foolish," Prescott said. "Now, open your mouth."

Yeah. Right. Matthew pressed his lips closed.

Prescott waited and after a while, he held out his hand. With a green flash, a vial filled with a silver liquid appeared. He popped the lid off with his thumb and poured it onto Matthew's abdomen, starting at his naval and moving down. Matthew's skin began to burn and bubble and he bucked under the pain.

Before Prescott could pour the shit onto Matthew's dick, Matthew opened his mouth with a scream.

"Good. Keep it open," Prescott said, corking the vial and slipping it into a loop on his belt. In his hand, he summoned in a long metal device and he shoved it into Matthew's mouth, squeezing a handle that hung out the side. It took Matthew a moment to realize it was a mouth spreader. The metal expanded, forcing his jaw open wide until he was unable to bite down. It hurt, but not as much as the silver still burning into his stomach.

"Fangs," Prescott said.

Matthew grunted, the pain increasing as his skin burned away. When he didn't bring his fangs down, Prescott picked up the vial of silver fluid and held it over Matthew's flaccid cock.

"Wait!" Matthew said—or tried to. He couldn't really talk with the damn thing in his mouth and it came out more like, "Wauh!"

Prescott raised an eyebrow and Matthew struggled against the chains again. Helpless to escape, he stilled and brought all four fangs out.

"This is going to hurt. Leave them out. If you retract them, I finish pouring."

Jesus Christ. Fucking sick son of a bitch.

Dental pliers appeared in his hand and in one smooth motion he clamped onto one of Matthew's top fangs and yanked it out. Matthew screamed. It took everything he had to not retract the other three but he really didn't want silver burning his dick away.

The sharp tooth hit the metal table with a clank and with a cold efficiency Prescott pulled the second. The pain of the root being ripped out shot through Matthew and he struggled again.

Prescott placed the pliers on the bottom fang and plucked it out, dropped it on the table, and did the same with the last one. Matthew's jaw ached. He was tempted to use blood energy to push away the pain but he only had one half-healed pouch right now and it was nearly empty. He wasn't sure what other tortures awaited him but he had a feeling it'd be worse than this shit, so he wanted to conserve what he could.

With a green flash, a small box appeared in the Imperator's hand. He flipped it open and pulled out what looked like a metal tooth with a long pin for the root. Prescott pushed one into Matthew's gums.

"Muher ucker," Matthew said as the pin burned into him. The ends of the pin seemed to have a small amount of silver on them—enough that it prevented his fangs from growing back, but not so much that it burned away the skin and slipped out.

Prescott repeated the process, filling in the gaps with metal teeth. When he was done, he released the mouth spreader. Matthew ran his tongue over the metal teeth. They were blunt. His body kept trying to retract his missing fangs but nothing happened.

How was he going to feed now?

Prescott activated a rune and the metal table went back to being a metal wall. "These aren't permanent," the Imperator said, "your fangs will regrow if you pull them out, but doing so without permission means losing them forever. I'll make it so they won't regrow again. Behave and maybe the King will let you have them back one day."

Matthew glared at Malarath, who still sat on his raised bed. His expression was blank; uncaring. Matthew curled his lips up to growl at him only to cry out when a lash of the whip hit his chest.

"How many, Your Majesty?" Prescott asked.

"Two hundred," Malarath answered.

Prescott nodded, then got started. Two hundred lashes would kill a human and with such low blood, it wouldn't be easy for Matthew either.

The first ten weren't too bad. Matthew had, after all, gotten used to the lash while he was with Tarrick. But then the whip landed across his hips and brushed his cock.

"Jesus Christ," Matthew hissed.

"Hit him there again," Malarath said.

"Oh god, please don't. Not there…"

Prescott cracked the whip against his cock. Matthew's chains rattled as he struggled against them.

The King looked at his nails; bored. "Ten more on his penis and perhaps he will remember the proper way to address me."

Ten more lashes licked Matthew's hips and dick. He leaned his head back and tears pricked his eyes. He grunted with each strike and, eventually, accepted what was happening, because what else could he do?

Prescott moved back to whipping his chest and Matthew had never felt so relieved to be whipped elsewhere. He kept his head up, too scared to look down.

Every twenty lashes or so, Prescott would immerse the whip into a bucket at his feet to coat it with foxglove. Each lash burned like the sun, splitting open Matthew's skin. He tried to heal but the foxglove prevented him from keeping up, and he was rapidly running out of blood.

Somewhere in the hundreds Matthew's head dropped forward. His entire chest, abdomen, and hips looked like shredded beef. Skin was peeled back, exposing muscle, and blood oozed from the wounds. It was nauseating. Matthew tried to heal again to stop the blood loss but he felt drained.

He looked to Prescott, who was dipping the whip back in the bucket.

"Imperator, please, I need blood," he pleaded desperately.

"Well, at least he is addressing you correctly," Malarath said from the bed.

Prescott chuckled. "Forty-three more, Matthew. Don't blood rage or I'll start from the beginning."

Matthew held off pushing healing. Vampires still healed fast enough without forcing it. He'd have to suffer the pain and let that kick in. After the foxglove wore off, that is.

Strike after strike, the sound of the cracking whip thundered in the air. His body and mind went numb, suffering the rhythmic pain with indignant cries until—finally—it ended.

His body slumped against the chains holding him up and his head hung forward. He needed blood. A sob escaped when he remembered that his fangs were gone.

Malarath stood before him, his hand came to rest on Matthew's shoulder. The touch was tender, taking away some of the pain that throbbed across his front side.

Matthew didn't even have the energy to be disgusted and instead surrendered to the small mercy, even if he didn't understand the reasoning.

"We are done. Do not attack me again," Malarath said.

Prescott coiled up the whip behind the King. "I knew you'd like him."

"Mm." Malarath gave a slight nod and a dismissive wave. Prescott bowed and left the room, bucket and whip in hand.

Malarath kept his hand on Matthew's shoulder. He stayed there watching him. Unmoving. It was unsettling at first, but a few hours later it became downright unnerving. And yet, Matthew didn't want it to stop. He enjoyed being touched after spending so much time alone. He closed his eyes and surrendered to the feeling.

"Wake up," Prescott said, his voice gruff as always.

Matthew blinked hard, his body aching. He hadn't even realized the sun had come and gone. Malarath wasn't in the room, only the Imperator.

He looked down at himself, his body was littered with bruises and cuts but the major bleeding had stopped. His dick looked better, thank god. Well, not god. It was a god that had put him in this situation. *Thanks, Dad.*

And where the fuck was his mom, anyways? If his sire could show up and kick his ass, why hadn't she shown up to save him?

It seemed as if the incubi had no idea who Matthew's mother was… or Devak. Malarath had, after all, called him a *blood guardian*, not a *pleasure guardian*. Whatever the case, Matthew sure as fuck wouldn't offer the information freely. He wouldn't put it past the High King to simply end him for being the child of the sex goddess. Or to use the information in some other grotesque play of power.

"May I have some blood, Imperator?" If he didn't get some soon, there was no way he'd make it through another night of torture.

"Tarrick made you ask like that, didn't he?"

Matthew nodded.

"That's not how it's going to be here. If you are going to get blood, the King or I will be giving it to you when we feel you should have some. You are not to accept any from anyone else, and gods help you if you try to feed without permission. Is that clear?"

It took everything Matthew had not to give a smartass remark. "Yes, Imperator, it's clear."

Prescott clasped his hands behind his back and waited.

"Is there something I should be doing right now, Imperator?" Matthew asked, feeling squeezed under Prescott's gaze.

"Nope. I'll tell you when you need to do something. Don't talk unless you are addressed, but I'll give you a pass on that one."

"Kind of you, Imperator."

Prescott chuckled. "You like to push boundaries, don't you?"

"I suppose so." Matthew wondered if he could push a little farther. "May I ask something, Imperator?"

Prescott sighed. "Sure, Matthew."

"Is my daughter safe? Is she going to be punished for my fuck ups?" Other than in photos, he hadn't seen Lily since he was turned into a vampire. He abandoned her and his wife to protect them. Maybe the only gift his sire had given him was that he wasn't compelled to kill them like other vampires when they were newly turned. Nothing had surprised him more than learning that she was a succubus.

Prescott looked genuinely caught off-guard. "…Daughter?"

"You are dismissed, warrior," a cold voice said. Malarath was standing by the side door, his two young attendants trailing behind him.

Prescott covered his confusion quickly but Matthew could see that he hadn't been informed about Lily. He assumed the leader of the Hunter Corps would have known. Both Commanders Silva and Cullip had known.

Malarath waved away the siblings, who, along with Prescott, left with a bow. The King came to stand before Matthew. "Lily is a handsome creature, untouched by the vampirism that taints you. I have not yet used her against you and if you behave, I will not need to. Understand?"

Matthew wanted to scream at him. Cuss him out. Fucking beat him within an inch of his life for even implying that he might one day hurt her. But instead he just said, "Yes, Master."

Malarath touched a rune on the wall and the metal plate behind Matthew moved and extended out, becoming horizontal once again. The High King stared down at him.

Wait.

An incubus activated a rune? Incubi couldn't use magic. Matthew glanced up at Malarath, then to the wall, then back to him. As if knowing what he was thinking, the smallest crack of a smile formed along Malarath's lips, but he offered no explanation.

"Do not mention your daughter to anyone again, even my warrior. If her lineage is made known, it will make her life difficult."

"I won't, Master."

"I know, pet. You are young and predictable," Malarath said, sounding almost disappointed. He left the room and Matthew didn't see him again until the next night.

Five

The sun had just set and the sky was glowing a dramatic pink and orange, but Matthew didn't notice. He was focused on Prescott and Malarath, who were looking down at him like a pair of evil scientists about to start an experiment.

"Where would you like it, Your Majesty?" Prescott asked, holding something in his hand. Matthew couldn't see what.

Malarath ran his fingers across Matthew's flesh, tracing down his abs until stopping just above his pelvis. The King moved his fingers to the left side of his body and tapped the area above Matthew's left hip. "Here."

Prescott held something that looked like a metal block the size of a brick. One side of it had some sort of raised design, like a stamp. Prescott set it down on the area that Malarath had pointed.

The design itself was silver…it was a brand. They were going to fucking brand him. Prescott produced some leather straps and used them to secure the brand in place. Then he brought out a vial of brown liquid—it smelled like foxglove—with an eyedropper. He dropped the liquid into the holes in the back of the brand.

Matthew wasn't sure what could actually cause a vampire to scar, but it seemed he'd be finding out first hand. He didn't bother struggling. If it came off, he'd probably be beaten before they simply started over again. As far as pain went, it wasn't so bad—so long as he ignored the smell of burning flesh that filled the air.

The next few nights passed in silence with Prescott returning every few hours to drop more liquid into the holes. Matthew was hoping he might get some blood but he wasn't so lucky. Maybe low blood helped the branding take to the skin.

Malarath spent the nights sitting in a chair, looking out over the city. It was odd behavior. He rarely left the room and Matthew never saw him feed, maybe he did during the daytime. And, being an older incubus, he wouldn't need much sleep.

Matthew found the silence chilling but it was better than the crack of the whip or screaming. He thought about trying to talk to Prescott but every time he opened his mouth, the Imperator shot him a warning glance. So instead, Matthew used the down time to memorize the small details of the room.

Many of the books were in foreign languages and almost all of them were ancient looking: handwritten and bound by old materials. The books that were in English were mostly classics: Brontë, Fitzgerald, Dickens, Austen…

Matthew nearly laughed when he spotted *Dracula* on the shelf.

It was the statue of Ilertha, his mother, that held his attention the longest. He *hated* it. The statue reminded him of Devak, who served her loyally. Who died trying to protect Matthew from this fate.

He pictured Devak's kind, honey colored eyes and how he had felt tremendous serenity whenever he looked into them. And now he'd never see them again.

"Contemplating gods?" Prescott asked, taking him out of his thoughts.

Matthew looked away from the statue. "Something like that, Imperator."

Prescott—*Devak's murderer*—removed the silver branding stamp from Matthew's body, the skin tearing away from it. The brand was the image of a shield with a jeweled design in the center and a crown above it. A thick line, ending in an arrow, twisted around the shield—an incubus tail. It was the symbol of House Malarath.

The King came over to inspect the brand, touching Matthew's lower abdomen. His fingers traced the fresh scar. He nodded to Prescott who shoved a tube into Matthew's mouth. Matthew drank his blood without a sound.

"Try to heal it, Matthew," Prescott ordered when the blood pack was empty.

Matthew pushed energy into healing the brand. The open wound healed but the scar was left behind; the lines crisp and clear. He wondered if there was any way to get rid of it or if he was stuck with the brand for the rest of his life.

"That's the best I can do, Imperator."

Prescott activated a rune and Matthew's table returned to being part of the wall. He wished they'd have left it flat, because the upright position put stress on his arms and shoulders. And it was too much to hope they'd let him out of the chains for a little while, even though all his joints ached. And the brand ached. As did his empty soavik, his blood pouches, his healing cuts and whip marks, his missing fangs, the silver burns...his heart...Matthew ached everywhere.

"Open your mouth," Prescott ordered. In his hand was a vial of silver liquid.

"Wait. You're going to make me drink that?" Matthew asked.

"Yes. I was only going to do half, but since you didn't address me correctly it'll be the whole bottle."

Matthew grimaced. "Please...no, Imperator. I've been following your rules. I'm doing what you tell me to." He looked to Malarath who stood expressionless.

"What did I tell you about begging?" Prescott asked, his armored hand grabbed the bottom of Matthew's jaw. He wasn't rough but it was clear he'd pry it open if he needed to.

Matthew fought the urge to yank away from Prescott. "You told me that begging wouldn't end the torture early, Imperator."

"Nor will it change my mind once it's made. Open up." Prescott raised the glass bottle to Matthew's lips and paused. "Swallow it quick. You spit it out, it'll be two vials."

He poured the silvery contents into Matthew's mouth and the moment it hit his tongue it began to burn. Matthew forced it down. His throat blazed as the silver ate away his mouth, neck, vocal cords...it kept burning as the liquid slid down inside of him. He let out a gargled scream.

His insides started to dissolve from the inside out. He screamed again but no sound came this time. All the pain and suffering he'd felt before was nothing like this.

Malarath grabbed Matthew's ear and painfully forced his head up. "You have killed many of my people—did you think such acts would go unpunished?"

Matthew tried to answer but the pain overtook him and he passed out.

When he came to, none of the pain had lessened. He looked down to see small beads of silver clinging to each of his pores; his body seemed to be sweating the silver out. His skin was red and blistered.

"Welcome back," Prescott said. He was standing close by, scrutinizing Matthew.

Malarath was on the far side of his room, standing before a three-paneled mirror, his back to Matthew. He was being attended to by the sibling incubus. They carefully removed his outer robe, revealing more cloth underneath. The female began to undo the intricate ties and laces that held the outfit together while the other started pressing kisses on the revealed skin.

It was strange behavior and Malarath seemed to ignore the attention, holding his arms out so they could remove what was covering his chest. When they were finished unknotting him, they slipped the layers off.

Malarath stood naked. He was tall. Taller than Matthew, but not by much. His skin was pale and flawless. His muscles were subtle; fine. The lines and curves of his body were statuesque.

Matthew didn't believe for a moment that the King was as delicate as he looked. He wondered what Malarath looked like in his incubus form. Was he huge like a warrior incubus or svelte as a social one? It was easy to assume he would be sizable since he'd been a general before he took the throne, or so Devak had told him. He didn't look like a general.

The succubus joined her brother in lightly kissing Malarath's chest and arms, which was about as high up as she could reach. Malarath brushed his two attendants away as if they were pests. Disappointment crossed their faces as they began redressing him in new burgundy velvet robes.

"How is my pet doing?" Malarath asked, using the mirror to glance at Matthew.

Matthew mouthed a 'fuck you' that was followed by a fit of coughing and gagging, which only aggravated his pain. Worth it.

Prescott smiled. "He's feisty tonight. Maybe it wasn't enough silver…"

A sad, low whine escaped Matthew. Okay, maybe the attitude hadn't been worth it. He needed blood to stop the burning and Prescott controlled the blood.

With fluid strides, Malarath walked over to Matthew and looked him up and down. The siblings trailed behind, trying to finish tying up the rest of the robe, but stopped when Malarath came too close to Matthew. They feared him, which was ridiculous considering his current chained up state.

Matthew wanted to glare at Malarath but the moment their eyes met, a terrifying chill made its way down his spine and he thought better than to challenge the person torturing him. Resigned, he lowered his eyes to the ground. He could practically hear the evil smiles crossing Malarath and Prescott's faces.

Malarath ran his fingers over the brand, his nails scraping the skin. The beads of silver sweat that collected there smeared, igniting the area with fresh pain. Matthew threw his head back in a silent scream.

"Look at me, pet."

Matthew rolled his head forward and looked at Malarath, whose hand was still touching the brand on his skin.

"You are mine," Malarath said, his voice dark; threatening. His pale blue eyes shifted to a vibrant gold. Matthew was stunned, both because he had never heard of an incubus who had golden eyes in their true form and because Malarath—who never showed much emotion beyond boredom—looked pissed off. "You exist for my pleasure. Every time you forget that, you will bear agony considerably worse than what you are suffering now. For you, we started with simple silver and whippings, but those are nothing compared to the true torments I can unleash upon you. Learn to hold your tongue and do not disrespect me again."

Malarath removed his hand, holding it out to the side for one of his attendants to come forward and clean the silver and blood from it. When they were done, he waved them away and they hurried from the room. "Get the Death's Bite."

Prescott paused. "Are you sure? That seems—"

He shut up when Malarath shot him a severe glance.

Prescott bowed and teleported away with a green flash and reappeared a few moments later holding a syringe filled with a dark liquid. He didn't look happy as he turned it over to Malarath.

Matthew's body shook as the silver continued to poison him. Or maybe it was the fear; or both.

Mercy. He mouthed.

"No, pet. You have not yet earned the right to my mercy." And with that, Malarath stabbed the syringe into Matthew's chest.

Before he could inject the liquid, a sharp gasp came from the doorway.

All three heads turned.

A succubus was standing there; horrified.

Malarath removed the syringe from Matthew. "Lady Rosaline."

Six

Seeing Lady Rosaline standing in shock caused a torrential crash of emotions in Matthew. Humiliation and remorse flooded him.

She had always been so kind to him. She was the succubus that had helped him through his partial transformation and taught him how to be an incubus. And after, she had used her considerable influence to try to get others to accept him. Even though things hadn't worked out in the end, he owed her more than he could ever repay. The last thing he wanted was to see her frightened, or to see him in such a sorry state...especially when she was a vision of perfection.

Her hair was like a fire: red and vibrant. Its tight curls cascaded down her back. Her matching lipstick contrasted with her milky skin. The short champagne colored dress she wore showed off each salacious curve.

She was beautiful and removed from of all the shit he'd gone through. Deep down he knew his picture of her was skewed. She was a succubus after all, skilled in the art of manipulation, but she'd always been honest with Matthew. At least as far as he could tell.

Her intense green eyes darted between all three men before finally settling on Malarath. She forced her body to dip into a curtsy. "Your Majesty."

"You have returned early," he said, his voice tempered and face impassive.

She rose and her eyes fell back to Matthew. "What are you doing to him?" Her voice sounded strained, trying to conceal anger and failing at it. Matthew wished he wasn't chained to a metal wall. He wished he could go to her and tell her that it would be okay.

Prescott crossed the room, removed his gauntlet, and rested his bare hand on her shoulder. "I think it's pretty clear what we're doing, my lady." He leaned in and lowered his voice, "And you should watch yourself tonight. He's in a mood."

Matthew looked back to Malarath, who didn't react to what Prescott said, although he clearly had heard it...and Matthew found it strange that Rosaline wasn't being kicked out of the room either.

Rosaline yanked her shoulder away from Prescott's hand. She marched forward, her heels clicking on the wooden floor, and stopped before Malarath. Her face flushed with fury that she was no longer trying to conceal as she stared at him.

Malarath slipped the still-full syringe into his robe then held up his arm, tugging the loose sleeve back to expose his wrist to her. She shook her head and took a step away from him.

His face cracked, lips pulling down into a frown. Matthew wasn't sure what had just passed between them, but it was clear something had.

Malarath lowered his arm and turned his attention back to Matthew. Rosaline's anger perfumed the air and Malarath's own anger joined it. Juuuust great. Matthew totally wanted the guy torturing him to be even more pissed off.

"I underestimated how much you cared for him," Malarath said, his eyes locked on Matthew like a panther about to pounce on its prey.

Rosaline nodded slowly. "I care for every incubus I help through their transformation, Didi." Matthew wondered what 'Didi' meant— it sounded like a term of endearment. "You've had him for over ten months. Why are you still doing this to him?"

Malarath didn't answer but Prescott stepped forward and did. "Did you see the footage from the Solstice Masquerade? What he did? What he became?"

The solstice attack...that was the night of the masquerade, and the night Matthew had lost complete control because he had thought Samantha was dead. He had become some sort of unstoppable force, killing hundreds of hunters and incubi warriors. He hadn't realized there was footage from the attack and found himself morbidly curious about it.

Rosaline shook her head. "Tarrick wouldn't let me watch it. But... I've heard the stories from the hunters and warriors."

"We were training him not to rage—"

Good, at least they thought he had lost control that night because of blood rage and not because of Samantha. Vikentiy, the fucking traitorous Russian vampire, had taken Samantha away right before the hunters had shown up to kill Devak and capture Matthew. At least he hadn't handed Samantha over to them. If they knew she existed, it would put her in incredible danger.

"—imagine if he lost control like that during a ball—"

"Are you going to take him to a ball?" she asked, looking to Malarath, cutting Prescott off. Her eyes widened, excited at the prospect. "You haven't attended one in so long. So many of our people don't even know what you look like…"

Malarath said nothing.

Rosaline looked at Matthew once more and her face fell. He lowered his head, unable to bear her distress. Only then did he realize how terrible his appearance was. His skin was red and blistered from the silver his body was trying to expel and the whip marks were healing much slower than they should have been. He was filthy too—unable to remember the last time he had showered… He desperately wished that Rosaline would leave.

His wish came true when he heard her heels clicking away. He looked up in time to see her exit through the side door Malarath often used. Matthew was unsure where it led, a bathroom or dressing room was his best guess.

He looked back to Malarath, whose oppressive gaze was still upon him. Matthew wanted to shrink away and become nothing. He was so helpless right now.

Rosaline emerged from the room holding a porcelain washbasin full of water. A big sponge floated on the top.

Prescott intercepted her, blocking her path to Matthew. "Please, my lady. If you clean it off, I'll just have to have him drink more later."

Matthew couldn't drink more silver. He began to panic. Aspirated gasps escaped him and he struggled against the chains holding him to the wall.

Rosaline's eyes reddened as tears collected along the bottom but didn't drop. She looked to Malarath. "Please, Didi. Please."

Malarath repeated his earlier behavior, holding out his arm and exposing his wrist to her. Rosaline pushed the basin of water into Prescott's arms then went to Malarath. She leaned over to the wrist and pressed a delicate kiss to it. When she broke away, he brushed his fingers along her jawline. "I do not wish you to suffer."

She leaned into his touch. "Are you going to do to him what you've done to the others?"

Malarath nodded and a single sob escaped Rosaline. Matthew wasn't sure who the 'others' were but Prescott had mentioned other prisoners, and there had been other creatures down by his cage. Maybe it was them. He wondered just what the King had done to them.

"He's an incubus," she whispered.

"Tainted."

"Beautiful." Rosaline stepped in and carefully kissed the bottom of Malarath's jaw. Matthew wasn't quite sure what to make of the behavior. It looked submissive in nature and out of place for her. She was delicate, sure, but strong too, and he had never seen her submit to anyone. Not Tarrick, not warriors double her size, not even queens.

"He would destroy us all if he could," Prescott said.

Rosaline shook her head. "Not me. He'd never hurt me."

That made Matthew smile. It was true, he'd never hurt her. Prescott was wrong, he wouldn't destroy all incubi, just the ones that wanted to cage him. His smiled dropped when he noticed Malarath was watching him.

"I will retire to my room," she said, her voice unsteady as she backed away.

Malarath grabbed her arm. "You may wash him."

She dipped her head with gratitude and went to stand before Matthew. Prescott stood by her, holding the basin of water. She grabbed the wet sponge and brought it to Matthew's chest. The silver mixed with the water and dripped down his body, stinging his skin. He hissed, curling his lips and clenching his teeth.

Rosaline looked at his mouth and gasped again. She snapped her head to Prescott. "You removed his fangs?"

"Yes."

She shoved the sponge back into the water and it splashed over the edge, dripping against Prescott's armor. He glowered at her but said nothing.

Again she brought the sponge to Matthew, but this time worked slower and took greater care to collect the silver rather than let it run down his skin. But it didn't matter how careful she was, each stroke of the sponge brought intense pain. He braced against it, grinding the back of his teeth so hard he nearly broke them, determined to not let her see how much he was suffering because of her actions. Other than a slight involuntary spasm of his muscles, he kept his torment hidden from her.

The water in the basin clouded with dried blood and flakes of silver. When she was done with his upper body she told Prescott to get fresh water. He obeyed without a word of protest.

Rosaline frowned as she eyed Matthew's crotch, his sex red and torn. Without thinking, he opened his mouth to try to tell her not to worry, that it would heal, but no words came out. Frustrated, he snapped his mouth shut and hung his head.

It was probably for the better since he wasn't quite sure when he'd be allowed to heal, or that he would even come out of this unscarred.

She ran her fingers over the brand near his hips then continued up his body, exploring his chest. Long months of continued starvation had taken a toll on Matthew. She touched the twisting tattoos over his right arm. They were new to her.

He looked into her eyes and a small, sad smile appeared on her lips before dropping away.

"He can't speak," she said when Prescott returned.

He held the water basin up. "Not right now. And even if he could, he's not allowed to unless addressed."

"That's a cruel thing to do to an incubus."

"A vampire," Prescott said.

Her green eyes clouded and she looked down to hide how upset she was, her face twisting. She swallowed hard a few times. "Didi…" she whispered.

Malarath came behind her and rested his hand on her shoulder. He was far taller than she was and she craned her neck to look up at him.

"Please don't do to him what you've done to the others. I beg of you."

Malarath slid his gaze to Matthew. Matthew bowed his head. He didn't know what was going on here but hated seeing Rosaline beg on his behalf. He hoped the High King would send her away.

"I will think on it," he said, his fingers squeezing her shoulder. "Ezra and Ophelia will finish washing him tonight. Go. Be with others."

Rosaline nodded, pressed a kiss on the top of his hand, and left the room, pausing at the doorway to look Matthew up and down one more time.

When the door shut behind her, Matthew slumped against his shackles, his chains rattling. No longer having to mask the pain, his body began to shake. His teeth ached. Fangs he no longer possessed wanted to come down, yearning to sink into soft flesh and pull blood into him. Both the High King's and Imperator's heartbeats called to him and he closed his eyes to listen to their rhythmic patterns.

The air around Matthew turned frigid and when he opened his eyes again, the High King was inches away.

From behind Malarath, Prescott dropped the basin on the ground with a thud, water splashing over and onto the tiles. "Over seven billion people on this planet and none can manipulate you like that one does. She bats her pretty eyes and you practically bend over."

Malarath raised an eyebrow. "Do you think I do not know what she is doing?"

"No. I know you know exactly what she is doing and you let her do it anyway. It's ridiculous." Matthew was stunned that Prescott spoke so candidly to the King. He guessed that thousands of years of service had earned him that right.

Awkward moments followed as Malarath stood watching Matthew, who kept his head bowed, hoping not to incur the King's wrath.

"He hid his pain from her," Malarath finally said.

Prescott, who had taken up a spot leaning against the wall, arms crossed, nodded. "Yeah. I noticed that too. Are you considering stopping?"

"Perhaps."

"That's dangerous. A few more weeks of this and he'll do anything you command."

Weeks? *No.* Matthew struggled against the chains. He couldn't take *weeks* of this. He couldn't.

Malarath smiled and looked over at Prescott. "Do you think I will be unable to tame him without the torture?"

Prescott gave an exaggerated sigh. "I wasn't issuing a challenge, Your Majesty. I know full well what you are capable of. It's that we don't know what *he* is capable of that worries me. There are just too many unknowns. The last time we dealt with such a powerful vampire he nearly wiped out your race."

"This one is not a Sanguine Dominar."

"But he was sired by the Blood God and we don't know all of his abilities. Break him and be done with it."

Don't let him break you. Samantha's words bounced around inside Matthew's head. If they kept going, he would be broken. This was too much.

Matthew looked up at Malarath and mouthed: *Master...I submit...*

Malarath laughed. The sound was soft and wicked. "No. I do not think you know what true submission is...but you will." He turned and walked out of the room, Prescott trailing behind him, leaving Matthew alone and hanging from the wall for the rest of the night.

Seven

The sun sank below the horizon and Matthew's silver eyes opened. He was lying down on the metal table but everything was different. His body still ached but it was manageable; healing. His arms were by his side and not stretched or pinned...he wasn't chained.

Matthew shot up and pushed himself off the table, stumbling and nearly falling on the floor before recovering. He looked around the High King's room. He was alone in the dark. Through the windows, Manhattan sprawled out before him.

He was clean and—with the exception of the brand—his wounds had faded to light pink scars. They must have knocked him out for days to let him heal. Matthew patted himself to make sure he was whole and was surprised to find he was wearing jeans. Glorious jeans.

He scrambled to undo the button and held them open so that he could check out his penis. It had healed. Thank all that was holy.

Matthew sighed in relief, then began laughing. He continued for a while, unable to stop until the laugh turned to desperate sobs. He wasn't chained right now but he knew this room was just another cage—one he had no idea how to escape.

He pressed his hand to his eyes and finally got a hold of himself, feeling a little better from the emotional release.

Able to see just fine in the dark, he looked around again. For the first time, he saw just how the table/wall thing worked. In the table form right now, it had pistons and gears on the underside that pushed it out. He ran his hand over the runes on the wall behind him, wondering what it felt like to be able to use magic.

Below him was the area of tiles, maybe ten feet wide and going eight feet into the room. Then the floors turned to wood with huge stylish rugs.

Time ticked by and Matthew wasn't sure what he should be doing. He considered going to the bookshelf and grabbing a book but stopped at the edge of the tiled floor. He couldn't cross it. There wasn't anything holding him back, it was just...he didn't want to do anything that would risk him being punished more.

Having memorized the entire room, he hopped back up onto the table and waited. He watched the city as the night passed, the dazzling lights flickering like stars, calling to him. He was content to sit here, even if he was lonely, because it was better than being in a cage.

He thought of Samantha, missing her terribly. Closing his eyes, he felt the thin strands of the bond that tied them together. Lately he had tried to shut himself away from the bond, hoping that Samantha couldn't feel what he was going through. He felt a gentle tug, letting him know that she was alive and he smiled.

The footfalls of four people walking down the hallway outside grabbed Matthew's attention. The lights flickered on in the room. He was already standing when the door flew open and Malarath glided inside. Trailing after was Prescott and the two young attendants, who Matthew assumed were Ezra and Ophelia.

"You need to approve the attack," Prescott said. His face strained and voice harsh.

Matthew took a step back as Malarath walked past him to one of the side rooms. The attendants, with their much shorter legs, were nearly running after him to keep up. "No. I do not."

"On your knees, Matthew," Prescott barked, not even giving him a glance. Matthew sank to both knees without hesitation, bowing his head. Prescott marched past him, following in Malarath's wake. "Do you want the vampires to hold Russia forever? Tarrick's plan is sound—approve it."

"No," Malarath said one more time and disappeared into the side room, the attendants and Prescott behind him. The door slammed and Matthew could no longer hear their argument. He had already suspected some of the room was magically warded to prevent people from listening in, but this confirmed it.

Still on his knees, Matthew watched as they came parading out of the side room minutes later in much the same state they entered it.

"I have hunters dying out there and if this is your way of punishing him—"

Malarath turned sharply and held up his hand, cutting Prescott off. "I will be punishing my general for his recent failures and when I do, you and everyone else will know it. I am rejecting his plan for other reasons. We are done with this discussion."

Prescott's mouth opened as if to argue another point but instead he snapped it shut and bowed. "Yes, Your Majesty."

Malarath went to the lounge area of the room and took a seat in the throne-chair, which faced the window. Ezra and Ophelia stood out of the way, near the corner of the room. They were always sure to keep Malarath or Prescott between themselves and Matthew. He could smell their fear too. The vampire inside of him wanted to chase them around a little.

"Have you found a replacement member for your team?" Malarath asked after he settled.

Prescott, who didn't sit, shook his head. His face still hard from the argument but his voice was measured. "Not yet. I'm still holding out hope Cullip will rejoin. I'm giving it another few weeks, then I'm thinking of offering the spot to Fendrel."

"He works alone."

"Given his past, we let him, but he really should be on a team. Besides, there hasn't been a dragon in centuries and he's been running with the Argonauts the past few months anyways. He and Lock are, as they put it, 'tight'. It'll be a good fit."

The High King tilted his head to the side. "Tight?"

"It means close. They're good friends," Prescott said.

"Ah. Come here, pet."

It took Matthew a moment to process that the King was addressing him. He rose, far slower than he should have, and paused before stepping onto the wooden floor. He swallowed hard then walked over to where Prescott was standing, keeping an arm's distance between them.

He kept his head down and shoulders slumped so that he wouldn't seem large or threatening. It was hard to do when he was far taller than Prescott. As they watched him, he wondered if he should return to kneeling but decided not to; they'd let him know if they wanted him down.

Malarath leaned forward slightly. "Do you plan on trying to escape?"

Matthew blinked at the question. Yes. Of course he was going to try and escape if he could. Not right now or anything, but once he knew this place, and if an opportunity presented itself...he didn't want to admit it to his captors but there was no way that Prescott and Malarath didn't know that already. This was a freakin' trap in question form.

"Not at this moment, Master," he answered honestly, hoping the punishment he'd get for telling the truth would be less than that for lying.

Malarath stood and began to circle Matthew. "And in the future?"

"If I see a way out, then yes, Master."

From behind him, Malarath asked, "And would you kill me if you could?"

"Yes, Master."

"And Prescott, would you kill him too?"

Matthew's eyes narrowed. "If I had to choose between you and the Imperator, I'd choose him. Master."

"Oh?"

Prescott smirked. "He doesn't like that I killed his blood guardian."

The casual way Prescott spoke about killing Devak made Matthew's claws come out and his irises turned from silver to red. It took great restraint to not swipe at him.

A soft whimper coming from the corner of the room helped rein his anger back a bit. Ezra and Ophelia were clinging to each other, their pubescent bodies trembling at the sight of Matthew. He wondered if they had ever even seen a vampire before.

"I took your fangs, Matthew, don't make me take the claws too. Put them away," Prescott said.

Matthew flexed them once, then they melted back into fingers. But his eyes stayed red. Malarath continued his walk around, when he was at Matthew's side he asked: "Would you kill Rosaline?"

Matthew snapped his head up and glared at the King. "I would *never* harm her, Master. Never."

Malarath tilted his head at Ezra and Ophelia, who were still in the corner. "What about them?"

What the fuck was up with this twenty questions bullshit? "I don't have a desire to kill them, Master. But if I was hungry enough, I suppose I'd eat them." Matthew hated himself for saying the last part, but he was enjoying smelling their fear and didn't want it to stop. Fuck, he was a terrible creature.

Malarath looked amused and it made Matthew feel even shittier.

"And Tarrick?" the words oozed out of the King like a seducer whose efforts were about to come to fruition. Was that what this was all about? Tarrick?

Matthew didn't know how to answer right away. His feelings about Tarrick were…muddied.

Tarrick was the enemy. He had manipulated Matthew into loving him so that he'd be easier for him to control.

'It's just an obsession. Lust. You don't love me.' Tarrick's words. Matthew had refused to believe them at the time, but maybe he was right. Maybe he was just a fucking fool—but…

A metal fist crashing into his jaw sent him tumbling to the ground. Prescott was standing above him. "When the High King asks you a question, you answer it right away."

Matthew's eyes flared and he sprung back up. Squaring his shoulders, he growled at the Imperator, his claws coming out for a second time.

Prescott smiled as he spread his feet into a defensive stance and waited. Matthew wanted to smack that bitchy smile right off his bearded face.

"No, Master," Matthew hissed, ignoring Prescott the best he could. "I don't want to kill Tarrick."

"'Lord General' is how you'll address Tarrick from now on," Prescott said, still waiting on the attack. "And those claws better be away in three seconds or I'm going to cut them off and replace them with silver caps."

Matthew grunted and pushed his vampire aspect back inside of him.

Prescott straightened up from his stance. "I already told you that I hate repeating myself. Don't bring them out again, there won't be another warning."

Malarath came around to stand before Matthew. "Remove your pants, pet."

Damn it. He just got them too. With no small amount of resentment, Matthew took his pants off. He left them on the floor near his feet. Maybe clutter would bother the High King as much as it bothered

Tarrick. But if it did, Malarath didn't show it as he inspected Matthew.

"I want his body bare and hair short." He grabbed Matthew's arm, pinching the skin. "I want him training. Bring his muscles back."

Prescott cocked his head. "You are actually going to rejoin your people, aren't you?"

"I told you as much."

"You told me that last century too and changed your mind." Then a realization dawned on Prescott: "You've rejected Tarrick's plan because you're going to take down Russia yourself—with your unruly demigod under your heel."

A corner of Malarath's mouth pulled up.

Prescott shook his head. "It'll take centuries to battle your way across Russia. Even for you. The vampires there have old strongholds."

"And?"

"Your people are war weary."

"My people are strong and can withstand a few more centuries of strife."

Prescott looked as if he wanted to argue but dropped the issue. "More silver for him?"

Matthew whimpered. He hadn't meant to, it just escaped.

"No."

A frustrated grunt came from Prescott. "Because of Rosaline? She has you wrapped around her finger."

"No. I had already made the decision to cut the punishment short." Malarath gripped Matthew's jaw hard. "I find myself savoring the battle between his desire and hatred for me. If I break him too quickly, he will be as boring as the others."

Matthew curled up his lips and bared his teeth. A low growl vibrated across his chest.

He jumped when Malarath abruptly grabbed his cock. For a moment, he thought this was going to turn painful, or sexual, but that didn't happen. Instead, Malarath studied his flaccid dick. "Apadravya," he said and released his member.

Matthew had no idea what that meant, but Prescott smiled so it couldn't be good.

"He will sleep up here. Go get bedding."

Ezra and Ophelia bowed and dashed from the room. Matthew

leaned towards them, his vampire scratching at the surface, begging to give chase.

"What would you do with them if you caught them?" Malarath asked.

Matthew forced his tense body to relax. "I don't know, Master. Normally I'd feed...but...I guess I'd just let them go."

"And not try to seduce them?"

"Jesus Christ, no. They look like they're thirteen," Matthew quickly tacked on a, "Master."

"Do you not wish to feed your incubus side?"

Matthew laughed. The normal pain he got from an empty soavik seemed so minuscule compared to what he had just gone through that he could completely ignore it. "No. I suppose I don't, Master."

"Dress and return to your area, pet."

Matthew snatched his jeans from the floor and pulled them on. He didn't need any explanation as to which area was his. He walked back to the wall.

Prescott trailed behind him. "You need permission to leave this area. And Matthew?"

"Yes, Imperator?"

"We never got to the truly bad tortures."

"I'll keep that in mind, Imperator."

"Well, there's one you need to experience firsthand. *Asonda*."

Around Matthew's neck the collar heated and he felt strands of magic weaving through his body, penetrating every inch of him, inside and out. An instant later, pain wracked through every ounce of him, twisting and tormenting his body. He might have been screaming but he couldn't hear anything as he slumped to the ground and passed out.

Eight

Matthew appeared in a dark room filled with burning incense. In the center was a single light focused on a young, mostly naked, Japanese man who sat cross-legged with his arms clasped in front of him. Wearing only strips of cloth tied around his waist and crotch, he'd pass as human except his ears were fluffy fox ears surrounded by neck-length white hair, and the shadow he cast had many tails.

Hunter Commander Hiroto.

Assassin.

Card carrying member of Prescott's team of badasses—the Argonauts.

Matthew stopped breathing and sank into the shadows. He didn't want his presence known. This was Hiroto's mind and Matthew was an intruder here.

Hiroto sniffed the air and his eyes slowly opened; brown orbs with long slits down the center. "Who's there?"

Matthew scowled. Hiroto had poisoned Devak so that he was weak enough for Prescott to kill him. He was just as culpable in his death, and the longer he watched the kitsune, the angrier he became. He stalked forward into the light.

Hiroto bounced up and daggers appeared in his hands.

"Matthew…" he gasped. "How—" he stopped, then changed the question, "What are you doing here?"

Matthew answered by baring his teeth.

Hiroto took a step away from him. "You should leave. Now."

"You poisoned him," Matthew said and launched himself at Hiroto.

Hiroto tumbled away, narrowly avoiding the attack. "Matthew! Stop, please. This will only end badly for you."

Matthew spun around and tried to push power into his speed but it didn't work. This wasn't the real world; none of the rules were the same. Again, Hiroto dodged out of the way, his dagger slicing the top of Matthew's forearm, just above the shackle.

Matthew roared and swiped at Hiroto with his claws. The assassin evaded each attack, rolling around him effortlessly.

Hiroto bounded away and held his daggers out. Dark writhing shadows moved behind him. They twisted and turned, forming into tentacles that headed towards Matthew. He swiped at the closest one. It felt real for a moment, then dissolved into smoke. A second shadowy tentacle grabbed his wrist, yanking him down.

Matthew attacked that one as well but it was followed by another, and another. Hiroto had his eyes closed, controlling the illusionary constructs.

If Hiroto could control this shit, maybe he could too.

A tentacle twisted around his torso and began to squeeze. Matthew focused on it, *willing* it to release him. Another wrapped around his neck and a third around his legs. He closed his eyes and concentrated. It was a subtle thing, each of the constructs were part of Hiroto, his mind, his will. Fighting against it felt the same as when he compelled a creature.

The tentacle around his torso released him. Hiroto's eyes snapped open. *"No."*

Matthew smiled, then took control of the other tentacles. They turned on Hiroto, lashing at him.

The kitsune tried to get away—to return into the waking world—but Matthew wouldn't let him go. A high-pitched shriek escaped Hiroto's mouth as the twisting limbs surrounded him. He tried furiously to slice them, but each time he got one down two more shadows replaced it.

Matthew rushed to him, grabbed his wrists, and *willed* the daggers away. They disappeared with a pop.

"How—" Hiroto was cut off as the tentacles squeezed him. Another whimper.

"You killed him!" Matthew yelled.

Hiroto stopped struggling and sucked in a labored breath. "Please. I had no choice."

"You took him from me!"

Matthew's focus dissolved and the tentacles melted away as he punched Hiroto in the face. Then he came around with another swing. Hiroto didn't fight back. "Matthew," he forced out between gasps.

Matthew didn't stop his assault, landing blow after blow against Hiroto's small body, his face bloodied and already bruised.

Hiroto shifted into a white fox with red lines running over his face and down the side. Seven bushy tails fanned out behind him. He whined and went to his back, exposing his belly to Matthew.

Matthew held up his fist and stopped. He'd won this. "Shift back."

Hiroto became human again.

"I should kill you," Matthew hissed.

Hiroto, still on his back, wiped the wet from his eyes. "Please no, Matthew. I'm not like everyone else. My god has rejected me and when I die my soul will be destroyed. I'll cease to be. Please don't kill me."

"And Devak, if his god didn't reject him…"

"No…the sword…he's gone. I'm sorry."

Matthew struck the ground beside Hiroto and screamed to the empty blackness above him. The idea that Devak was just gone was devastating. There'd be no meeting him in the afterlife, no hope he might be reborn, nothing. *Nothing.*

He had lost everyone. His wife and Devak, dead. Tarrick, Samantha, Lily, even Jet…all taken from him.

He was alone.

He collapsed to his knees and screamed again, the sound raw and desperate. His heart shattered with him.

When he could scream no more, he sat still for a while, empty and numb.

"I loved him," Matthew finally said.

Hiroto sat up and put his hand on Matthew's shoulder. "I know."

Time passed between them as Matthew collected himself. Despite his anger, he found Hiroto's touch comforting. "When you take a life, do you feel anything?"

Hiroto took his hand back and placed it in his lap. "Is it important?"

"I have to know if you felt anything when you took him from me."

Hiroto paused and adjusted his weight on his knees, the question clearly making him uncomfortable. "I used to," he finally said. "I used to love all life. It was my purpose to bring joy to those I met. Now it's my purpose to kill whomever Malarath orders me to."

"Why would you work for such an evil creature?"

"I have no choice," he whispered.

Matthew shifted on the ground, crossing his legs. "You told me he saved your life, that you owe him a debt…"

"I lied." Hiroto's bowed his head forward. When it seemed like he wasn't going to elaborate any further, Matthew sighed and started to stand but Hiroto began to speak, stopping him. "I-I lied because I'm ashamed of the truth…I'm the only kitsune that's ever been cast out. The High King found me at the time I was most vulnerable. He…he treated me like a toy…played with me. For decades I tried to escape him but it's impossible.

"He hides how truly powerful he is because he wants everyone to underestimate him but I promise you, whatever powers he's shown you are nothing compared to what he is capable of. If he wants you, you become his. There's no way out of it. The best you can hope for is for something else to catch his attention."

Hiroto wiped some blood from his cheek with the back of his hand. "I stopped fighting him a long time ago, and my life isn't terrible. I enjoy being a hunter. I'm good at it."

Matthew absentmindedly rubbed his chest. "You think I should do the same? Just give in to him?"

"You don't have a choice. In the end you will. Unless your sire steps in…but he left you to the incubi. I doubt he'll intervene anytime soon."

Matthew was calmer now. The urge to kill Hiroto lessened. Old, unanswered questions bubbled up and since the fox had served a god, he might have some answers. But there was something else he wanted to do first. Matthew sprang to his feet. In reaction, Hiroto leaped to his, backing up and getting into a defensive stance.

Matthew smiled and closed his eyes. He willed the mindscape around him to reshape itself and when he opened them again, he and Hiroto were standing in a small, fully stocked kitchen. It was bright here, the sun streaming through the big windows from outside. There were stools by the island with place settings already out.

Blue kitchen towels hung from the oven door and a young child's crude drawings were magnetized to the fridge. The kitchen was warm and cozy.

"Where are we?" Hiroto asked, rubbing his hand along the top of the wooden island.

"The first apartment I rented with my wife."

Hiroto walked over to the fridge and looked at the drawings. "I didn't know you had a child. I'm sorry."

Matthew didn't correct Hiroto's assumption that he had killed Lily after he was turned. The less people that knew about her, the better.

He put his hand on Hiroto's shoulder and pushed him gently to the side so he could get into the fridge.

"What are you doing?" Hiroto asked as he watched Matthew pull out eggs, bacon, cheese, an onion, and milk.

"Dude, I haven't had real food in ten years. You think I'm going to pass this up?"

Hiroto smiled and Matthew cracked eggs into a bowl.

"And I'll have you know," Matthew said, pouring in a dash of milk, "I was an excellent cook. So long as it was an omelet."

Hiroto jumped onto the island and crouched down, watching Matthew prepare an omelet in silence. Matthew enjoyed the mindless task of chopping while the warmness of the sun hit him.

"What's a champion?" he asked as he fired up the gas stove and put the bacon on once the pan was hot.

"Uh—" Hiroto, caught off-guard, stuttered then smiled slightly. "You are endlessly curious."

Matthew returned the smile. "I'm an incubus."

"Champions are the right hand of a god. They are gifted a domain they can call upon for power, essentially making them a mini god in their own right, but they can freely walk this realm. The rules that restrict a god here don't restrict a champion. Those chosen are insanely powerful." Hiroto studied Matthew for a moment, who was pulling the bacon out of the pan and readying it for the eggs. "No…"

"Yeah."

"Lysandros wants you to be his champion?"

"Yeah."

Hiroto hopped down and walked around Matthew in the small space. He was getting sick of people walking around him, judging him, but he didn't protest. "Matthew, you're powerful but not at the level a champion is. Having Lysandros sire you has made you a strong vampire—and you're still considered a demigod—but being turned into one isn't quite the same as being born to a god."

"And what if I was born as one?"

Hiroto hopped back onto the island, sitting on the edge of it, his legs swinging over. "Born to a god? I think everyone would know if that happened. And besides, the Judge would have come for you by now."

Matthew cut up the bacon and added it to the bowl with the eggs. He salted and peppered it. "The Judge?"

"Eons ago the gods had children freely but the children were so powerful that they began to kill their parents and take over as gods themselves. It was a time of chaos from what I've been told. The Judge was created to kill any demigod born. Blessed by the entire pantheon, she's the most powerful creature in the universe, save for Oa itself."

"And she's supposed to come kill me? Awesome. Can't wait."

Hiroto smiled. "Well, she's always killed the others at birth but maybe because you were turned instead of born she can't sense you. Maybe Lysandros found a loophole. I don't know."

Hiroto was wrong about that, of course, but Matthew only asked, "What's an Oa?" as he poured the egg mixture into the pan.

"The god of gods. The god of this realm. They say it made the universe and all the realms but none of the other gods have seen it in… well, I'm not sure any of them have met it actually."

"It?"

"Him? Her? Who knows."

Matthew smirked. So there was a God. "I thought realms were like heavens."

"Sort of. It's just a place where a certain god rules. Oa is this realm's god. Each god has their own. And technically the Pit is a realm, one that broke away from the fabric of the others. It's like a whole universe they control, except all souls come from this realm, which is what makes this one so important. When I was a messenger, I was able to traverse them all freely…I can't anymore."

Matthew fell silent. He had spent so much time looking forward to talking about all this with Devak, waiting for the curse to be gone. Now his loss seemed even greater.

Although, he was glad that Hiroto had some answers for him.

It was nice to be talking to someone.

He hated that he wasn't allowed to speak unless addressed. It made him appreciate how much Tarrick let him get away with, and how willing he'd been to answer all of Matthew's foolish questions.

Matthew pulled the omelet off the heat and fucked it up with cheese before sliding it onto a plate, making sure it folded correctly. He grabbed two forks from a drawer and handed one to Hiroto.

"Split it with me," he said, walking around to the barstools. Hiroto came and sat on the second stool, the plate of food between them. "Oh wait," Matthew said and got up. He grabbed some sour cream from the fridge and added a dollop on top. Fork in hand, he sliced off a piece and held it before him.

"It smells delicious," Hiroto said and took a bite. "Mmm." The small sound of approval came from him.

Matthew smiled and ate his bite. Then immediately spat it out. "Gross, that's nasty! And really? I can stand in a fake sun but fake food is off-limits? How is that fair?"

Hiroto laughed and grabbed his bruised ribs with his free hand. "It really is good too," he said as he shoveled more into his mouth.

"At least one of us can enjoy it." Matthew moped over to the fridge and pulled out a pitcher of blood. He grabbed a cup and poured himself a glass. "And if you're eating, so am I."

He drank his glass of blood while standing. It was warm (because he willed it so) and divine. He couldn't remember the last time he had drunk fresh blood. Eggs and bacon couldn't compare to the joy of drinking the rich life essence. He only wished this was real and that he'd have the blood in him when he returned to the waking world.

"Hiroto?" he said as he put down his empty glass.

"Yes?"

"My mother is Ilertha." Matthew wasn't quite sure why he said it. It wasn't that he trusted Hiroto—he couldn't. But he had to tell someone and maybe if the High King knew, he wouldn't be so severely punished. Telling Hiroto first seemed a good way to test the idea out, and the fox would no doubt report it. It'd save him the awkwardness of telling the High King himself.

Hiroto blinked once. Set down his fork. Stood up. Then sat back down, blinked one more time, and swallowed the food that was in his mouth. "Say that again."

"My mother is the incubus goddess. I was born a demigod."

"No. You can't be the son of Ilertha."

"Why not?"

"Because your incubus powers would rival that of Malarath's. And—no offense—but you can barely sway a human."

"You mean my incubus powers would rival that of Malarath's if I hadn't been turned by Lysandros, stopping my transformation before it was complete. A transformation that didn't even trigger until my thirties, meaning I would have been extremely powerful."

Hiroto fell silent once again. Then finally said, "Ilertha has been missing for a long time. Most of those that serve her think she's dead. There's a struggle for power, a civil war going on in her realm right now. Who told you that you are her child?"

"My guardian did."

Hiroto shook his head. "The blood guardian? He's lying to you. He couldn't possibly know—"

"Devak was Ilertha's guardian. Lysandros called him Cel'ii."

Hiroto hopped back up to his feet again, the stool nearly falling over. His fluffy ears twitched. *The traitor?* The only guardian to betray his god and be taken in by another? Holy shit."

He smiled at Hiroto's reaction.

Hiroto rubbed his face. "Are you really Ilertha's son?"

"I guess I can't know for sure since I never finished my transformation, but her statues used to sing to me. Not anymore though."

Hiroto got back onto the island and kneeled down before Matthew, their height nearly the same. He grabbed Matthew's shoulders. "You haven't told the High King yet, have you?"

"No."

"Don't. Don't tell him any of this."

"Why not? Doesn't he worship Ilertha?"

"Publicly, yes. He's the King, he has to. I can't know for sure but...I think he means to try and ascend and become her champion, or maybe even replace her and become a god. He's never said as much but through centuries I've seen signs...if you're her child, you're a threat to that goal. Matthew, not telling him was the smartest thing you've ever done. Keep this hidden."

"You won't tell him?"

"No."

"Why not?"

Hiroto's big eyes darted back and forth, searching for an answer. "I…" he began but looked lost.

Matthew patted the fox's hand. "Maybe you never did stop fighting him."

Looking down, Hiroto bit his bottom lip. He nodded slowly and asked, "Why did you say no to Lysandros' offer to be his champion?"

"He wanted me to kill Devak to prove myself to him and I refused. In the end it didn't really matter, Devak died all the same."

Hiroto flinched. "I wonder if it was Ilertha's blade or my poison that killed him."

"Why would that matter?" Matthew couldn't hide the pain in his voice, or the anger.

"I—I guess it doesn't. Never mind. If Lysandros offers to make you his champion again, you should take him up on it."

"No." Matthew shook his head. "I don't want to be anyone's pawn. Not to the High King or any of the gods. Fuck 'em all."

"And in the meantime, you'll be bowing down to Malarath. Wouldn't it be better to bow down to your sire?"

Matthew rubbed his face, scraping his hand along his stubble. Lysandros would probably make him kill Samantha to prove himself. That was not something he'd ever even consider doing, not even to get out from under Malarath's thumb.

"Sun's about to set in New York." He could feel the call of night.

"I have to report that you were here. Prescott will figure it out the moment he sees me," Hiroto waved his hand over the bruises and cuts that Matthew had given him. "We're set for a mission later tonight. I can't hide it."

"What happens in here shows up in the real world, Matrix style?"

Hiroto laughed. "Yeah. Not food though. I'm going to be hungry when I wake up."

"Me too. So what do we do?"

"I have an idea."

∗∗∗∗

Matthew's eye snapped open. He was lying on a pallet, soft blankets under him. He even had a pillow. Whatever that collar had done to him last night, the effects of it lingered and everything was sore.

"Vampire, I can choose to make it so the collar will keep you conscious."

Matthew looked up at Prescott towering above him, adjusting a strap on his armor. "And you'll no doubt use it on me in a few moments, Imperator."

Prescott smiled. "Why? Have you done something to deserve it?"

"Yes, Imperator." Matthew rubbed his forearm where Hiroto had cut him during the fight. The wound had mostly healed except for a thin pink line.

"You've been in the same place all day, I couldn't imagine you—"

He was cut off by a white light lingering in the air. Hiroto teleported in beside Prescott. Unlike in his mind, he was wearing his full assassin hunter attire: a cloak cascading over his leather outfit with a red mask over his mouth and nose.

Prescott's smile dropped and his voice turned grim. "What did he do?"

Hiroto pushed his hood back and pulled off his mask. His face was covered in bruises. "Mind breach. I was meditating. He attacked. It didn't go well for me."

"You couldn't eject him from your own mind?"

"No. And he locked me out from leaving."

"He did not kill you?" a voice asked from across the room. "Interesting," Malarath rose from a chair that faced the city.

"Master." Hiroto kneeled on both knees. "I think he knew how dire the consequences would be if he killed me. I think he lost momentary restraint, like any young vampire facing his lover's killer."

Malarath studied Hiroto. Matthew wished the King wasn't so hard to read; Matthew had no idea if he was buying it. Finally, the King addressed Prescott. "Have Ester set up the collar to trigger each time he mind breaches."

"And his punishment?" Prescott asked.

"Two hundred lashes. His back this time."

Nine

Taking the whip to the back was far better than taking it on the front. Matthew's dick wasn't exposed for one, and his butt had some small amount of cushion for two. But beyond that, the punishment was excruciating. He had some blood in him, but around the halfway mark he no longer had enough to push the pain away. It was hell.

After the punishment, they left him hanging, face and chest pressed against the wall, and gave him no blood for days.

He woke one morning unchained and slumped down on the floor. He sat up to see Prescott looming over him. "I don't get offended if you take a few shots at me, you'll be punished for it but I'll get over it, but if you beat up one of my teammates again, it will be my mission to make you as miserable as possible for the rest of your life. And if you think what I've done so far is bad, just wait until you push me. Do I make myself clear?"

"Yes, Imperator," Matthew answered quickly to avoid pissing off Prescott any further.

Prescott stared down at Matthew, then finally nodded, satisfied with the answer. "Stand up."

Matthew pushed himself up. Looking around the room, he noticed that the High King wasn't there, and he had no pants. Seems he managed to lose that privilege after a single day. He laughed.

"Something funny?" Prescott asked.

"Just wondering whose dick I have to suck to get some pants, Imperator."

Prescott smirked. "Of all the comforts we took from you, pants are at the top of your list?"

"I wouldn't mind some blood, a shower, and, Imperator, if you are feeling generous, some sex. But since you haven't offered any of that, I'll settle for pants."

Prescott gave an amused snort and raised his wrist to his mouth, "Gavyn, I'm ready for you." He lowered his arm. "And for the record,

Matthew, I prefer women and hate undead. It's not my dick you'll be on. Ever."

An outline of green light appeared in the air, replaced by a hunter teleporting in a fraction of a second later. The hunter, Gavyn, looked like a rock star. He wore a ribbed tank top with black pants. There were tattoos covering nearly every inch of his skin, save his face, where he had lip and ear piercings. His visible tattoos weren't the silver hunter ones, but rather colorful designs, each a piece of art. His dark hair was shaved short on the sides and long and messy on the top. It was one of those styles that someone spent a long time making it look like they didn't spend a long time on it.

On his belt was a single stake and two silver daggers. For a hunter, he didn't carry much on him in the way of weaponry. He set down a Styrofoam cooler and smaller metal case. Matthew could smell blood in the cooler and took a step towards it.

"Easy, Matthew. If you behave you'll get the blood soon," Prescott said.

Wanna-be-rocker Gavyn dropped the box and case on a nearby table. "King say what gauge he wanted?"

...gauge?

"Nope, use your best judgment," Prescott said.

Matthew watched as Gavyn opened the case and pulled out disinfectant wipes and set them to the side. He looked Matthew up and down while he snapped on some blue exam gloves. "I guess we don't have to worry about him getting an infection, even if he does look like he has ten diseases."

Matthew curled back his lips, showing off his metal teeth, and growled at the hunter. The hunter was right, Matthew's back looked like raw meat from the lashings and he hadn't washed since Rosaline had begged the King. Dried blood stained his back, butt, and legs. His skin had turned a corpse-like grey and his hair was still too long everywhere, despite the High King's orders to have him shaved—but still, even if he did look terrible, the hunter was being rude.

"You see those shiners Hiroto was rocking a few nights ago?" Prescott asked.

"Damn. The commander let him get close enough to touch him?"

"Mind breach. And Matthew's fast. Don't underestimate him."

Gavyn nodded. "Yeah, I've seen the footage...hard to believe I guess."

Matthew's ego inflated just a little bit...and quickly deflated when Gavyn came forward—pen in hand—and grabbed his dick.

Matthew jerked back and his claws came out. "What the—"

Gavyn took some steps back. "I thought you said he wouldn't attack."

Prescott wore a devious grin. "He won't. Not if he wants blood."

The tattooed hunter looked unsure. "Alright...You have to stay still, big guy, I just need to put some marks on."

"Marks? What the hell for?" Matthew asked.

Prescott chuckled, trying to hold it back until he snorted with amusement.

"Aw, shit, Imperator. You didn't tell him?" Gavyn said, looking just as displeased as Matthew did.

"He heard the High King say he was getting an apadravya piercing," Prescott said between the laughter.

Matthew shook his head and took another step back, bumping against the metal wall. "Wait. No. Imperator, the word 'piercing' was never used and 'apadravya' sounds like a spell from Harry Potter. What the fuck is it?"

"It's a vertical piercing through your glands. It won't hurt that bad. I'll be quick," Gavyn said. At least the hunter had the decency to feign some concern. Most hunters would be laughing right along Prescott with an 'Oh look, the poor little vampire is in pain—let's mock him! Ha, ha!' attitude.

"You're going to pierce my dick? No. I don't want you anywhere near my dick." Matthew cupped himself and was ready to run away if he had to. He'd happily take more whippings instead.

Prescott's laughter died down. "And to think just a few minutes ago you wanted sex...*Kayar*."

The shackles on Matthew's arms and legs flew backwards, meeting the chains midair. The chains reeled in tight and once again he was hanging, unable to move.

Gavyn came forward and grabbed his cock, inspecting it on each side. He placed a mark on the top of the head and one under, then grabbed forceps, lined them up with the marks, and clamped them on. In his hand was a needle.

"God, please, don't do this. I really don't—"

"Quiet, Matthew," Prescott said.

Matthew snapped his mouth closed. He knew he was being a little bitch right now and that begging wasn't going to change anything but still, he really didn't want this.

"Alright, just breathe in and out, or uh, pretend to," Gavyn said with a nervous smile. Matthew narrowed his eyes and when he exhaled the hunter pressed the needle in. Fuck, it hurt. Matthew pulled against the chains and ground his teeth. For a moment he felt as if his dick was going to fall off, but as suddenly as it started, the pain subsided.

"We're almost done." Gavyn looked to Prescott, "Silver or normal?"

"Normal for now. But, Matthew, if you take it out, we'll redo it with silver and I'll make the hole permanent."

At least he could remove it at some point down the road and it would heal. Gavyn finished by pressing a bar through, pushing the needle out, and screwing on the ball at the end.

"See?" Prescott said. "That wasn't so bad. *Rayak*." The chains released and Matthew landed on his feet. He grabbed his cock and looked at the piercing. Now that it wasn't hurting as bad, he wondered what benefit there was to it. Would it make sex better for his partners? For him?

"You're dismissed, Gavyn. Send up Ezra and Ophelia," Prescott said. Gavyn saluted by pressing his right fist to his left shoulder, then he grabbed his box of tools and teleported away. Prescott grabbed the cooler and tossed it to Matthew. "Drink up."

It was filled with blood packs. Matthew nabbed one, bit off the top and consumed the blood. The first thing he poured healing energy into was his dick, then he shotgunned the rest of the packs as fast as he could.

"Alright, let's go over a few rules," Prescott started. "The High Lord General taught you about kneeling, so you should be familiar with it. It was good you went to both knees—" both knees for slaves, Tarrick had told him, left for warriors, right for everyone else. It was a strange practice but that's how it was done and it removed all doubts that he was a slave, "—but what's different to know is that you'll only be kneeling to the High King unless I order you down. You'll bow to Lords and Ladies, Kings and Queens, hunter commanders, and me. I want you showing respect to my hunters but you don't have to bow to them."

Prescott went over hand gestures for kneeling, when to rise, halting, etc. It made Matthew feel like a dog. The Imperator had him repeat all the other rules: no blood unless it was given to him, no leaving his area without permission, follow any commands that Prescott or the High King gave him, don't remove the dick piercing or metal teeth, no blood raging, use correct titles, and no speaking unless addressed.

"If we put you on the battlefield you'll follow the High Lord General's orders. No compelling any incubi or hunters," Prescott said, adding to the list. "Oh, and just like blood, no coming without permission. That means no self-gratification either."

Awesome.

The door to the room crept open and Ezra and Ophelia silently drifted in. They bowed to Prescott and looked around for Malarath.

"Take him down and clean him up. Shave him. Cut his hair too," Prescott ordered. Their eyes went wide as they looked from Prescott to Matthew. "Is anything I'm saying confusing?" he asked when they didn't move.

"Are you—" the male, Ezra, started to ask.

"—coming with us?" Ophelia finished the question. It was a little eerie.

"No. I have more important things to do tonight. You can handle it." Prescott teleported away before they could protest.

Ezra and Ophelia stood there, frozen in place. Matthew could hear their little hearts beating fast and smell their fear. Now that he was fed, he didn't quite feel the uncontrollable need to chase them, but he still thought it'd be fun to stalk them for a while.

After three minutes passed, Matthew sighed and came to the edge of his area. "I'm not supposed to talk to you unless you talk to me first but I'm going to risk it because I'm getting a little sick of standing here. Are you going to take me to a shower? Because I could really use one."

They didn't move.

"I'm not going to hurt you." They weren't the type of victims Matthew favored anyways. He didn't prefer the young or the innocent if he could avoid it. Still, he'd play with them if he were ever allowed. God, he couldn't believe he was fantasizing about playing what was essentially vampire tag with them.

"Follow—"

"—us," they finally said and slowly backed out of the room, their eyes never leaving Matthew.

Matthew did as instructed. He paused for just a moment before stepping onto the wood flooring, then paused again before leaving the room. Not having Prescott escort him around or the High King lording over him made it feel like he was breaking some sort of rule. He really wanted to try to minimize getting in trouble until he could learn more about this tower and its weaknesses.

Talking to Hiroto had given him a small amount of hope that he thought lost. Sure, Hiroto hadn't found a way out and realistically Matthew knew he wouldn't either—it had, after all, taken the High King all of a fraction of a second to make Matthew his bitch—but that didn't mean he was going to give up.

It might take years to find a way out, but it was all he had right now and he was going to hold onto it.

Ezra and Ophelia led him down the hall, through the metal doors, onto the elevator (where Matthew got to see just how awful he looked), out onto a new floor, through some more metal doors, and out into a wide hallway.

The two small incubi kept as much distance between them and him as possible, and Matthew, for his part, tried to follow along as non-threateningly as possible. They went through a set of double doors and led him into a windowless bathhouse.

Greek-looking marble pillars flanked an enormous blue tiled soaking pool. There was also a spa off to the side, along with showers, marble chairs, statues, fountains, and lush green plants. The air was warm and perfumed.

Ezra and Ophelia pulled on the ribbon that tied their nearly transparent robes to their lissome bodies and shed them. Naked, it was easier to tell them apart only because of Ezra's small package and Ophelia's nearly flat breasts. Both were smooth and hairless, which gave them an even younger appearance. Matthew guessed they shaved or waxed since they were past the age hair would have begun growing.

Even still, they were beautiful, graceful creatures. They tied up each other's long hair with ribbons, then motioned to a showerhead on the wall. Matthew diligently stood under it.

When the water hit Matthew, he could have orgasmed from it. It was already warm, the water massaging every inch of his skin. Matthew closed his eyes and enjoyed the feeling. A washcloth ran down his back. Ezra was scrubbing him.

From a small pitcher, Ophelia poured a blue liquid onto a washcloth and began to clean him as well. Matthew loathed admitting it, but having their hands on him felt pleasant. He was still an incubus, even if he wasn't treated like one, and he desired the contact. He wanted to be touched, to be cared for, and to care for others.

Ophelia's hand dropped low on his abdomen, scrubbing the area there and going lower still. Matthew grabbed her wrist and she froze. Ezra froze as well. Their fear spiked as adrenaline hit them.

"I can wash there myself," Matthew said as he took the cloth and let her go. He went about finishing washing his privates. The gel tingled.

Ezra tapped his shoulder and gave him the sign to get on his knees. He didn't think he'd be kneeling to them but he wasn't going to argue, not while he had access to a shower. He lowered himself before the incubus, who grabbed a white bottle, poured the contents on Matthew's head, and massaged it into his scalp. Ah, Matthew was too tall for Ezra to reach his hair otherwise.

They rinsed him off and when the water shut off, Matthew began to stand, but Ophelia pressed on his shoulder so that he would stay put. Ezra left and returned with wireless electric clippers and shears. Matthew stilled as they clipped the hair on his head short.

When he finished, Ophelia used a brush to mix shaving cream in a dish then spread it on Matthew's face. She tilted his head back and brought up a straight razor, her hand trembling.

"Wait," Matthew said. She stopped. "Not that I don't appreciate being shaved, but you're going to slice me up if you don't stop trembling. Why don't you let me do it?"

She paused. Then brought the razor up, her hand a little steadier, and began to shave him. Matthew didn't move a muscle, worried she might cut him. Wait. He was being ridiculous. After what he just went through, a cut would feel like nothing. Fuck, even when Samantha had stabbed him in the blood pouch to open a portal to hell all he did was scowl a little. This was just a mental thing, a holdover from when he was human. He forced himself to relax a little.

Ophelia proved to be efficient with the blade, shaving him close and smooth. Matthew was hoping that maybe he could grow back a little stubble, it made him feel a little more masculine. The succubus slathered shaving cream onto his chest and shaved there, then his arms (except where the shackles were), back, legs, anyplace with hair.

She left the crotch for last but Matthew knew it was coming. With a sharp blade so close to his junk, he did everything in his power to keep his movements as minimal as possible.

When she grabbed his dick to move it out of the way, Matthew sucked in a sharp breath, and Matthew Jr. responded to the touch in kind.

Ophelia looked up at him and her small pink tongue darted out to wet her lips. Matthew pushed away some shamefully inappropriate thoughts. "You sure you don't want me to finish?" he asked, hoping she'd either finish quick or hand him the razor.

She went back to her task. The water turned back on when she was done and Matthew rinsed off, trying to ignore his half-hard dick.

Picking up a white towel, he dried off and waited, expecting to be led back to the King's room. But Ezra and Ophelia motioned for him to get into the soaking pool. The siblings walked in from the steps and began to float around.

Obeying, Matthew felt smooth as a seal as he sank into the silky water. He ran his hands through his hair, thrown off by how short it was now. It was a little longer than a buzz, but not by much.

After floating around for a bit, he settled down on an underwater ledge and leaned against the wall, spreading his arm out along it. He relaxed as Ezra and Ophelia playfully splashed each other. For the first time in a long while he was…comfortable. He was in no pain, he actually had blood in him, and he was around other incubi. He reached out and felt Samantha through the bond. She was alive and wasn't in any distress.

He sank a little lower into the water and wondered what the rest of his life was going to be like. Eventually he'd have to kill vampires. What would happen when he faced someone he actually cared about?

Rubbing his shackles, he wondered what terrible things the High King would have him do. His future seemed so entirely out of his hands. The only plan he had was 'wait' and that was a shitty plan.

A soft moaning pulled him from his contemplation. He looked up and saw Ezra and Ophelia making out in the water. Matthew frowned. Incest wasn't his thing—it really wasn't—yet, he couldn't look away from the depraved scene unfolding in front of him. He watched as their hands began to explore each other.

"Jesus," he muttered.

Their heads turned to him seductively and their eyes began to glow. Ezra's left eye was bright blue and his right green, while Ophelia's were opposite, blue right, green left. It was startling. Fascinating.

The twins—he had no more doubts they were twins with eyes like those—descended on him. Matthew pushed himself up as they came close. He felt lethargic as they reached out and ran their hands over his chest.

"What are you doing?" he asked.

On his right, Ophelia leaned in and pressed a warm kiss to his neck, above his collar. Matthew leaned his head back and moaned. God, it had been so long since he had fed sexually.

On his left, Ezra ground his hips into Matthew's side. The incubus' small cock was hardening with each thrust against Matthew's skin. Matthew brought his arms down around each of their shoulders, pulling them in closer. They licked and sucked at his neck, their hands exploring his chest and abs.

Matthew's eyes drifted closed as he enjoyed the feeling of their delicate fingers caressing him. His chest rumbled with a low purr as they moved lower.

His eyes shot open when they gripped his iron hard cock. Jesus, they were too young. He couldn't do this. Not with them. No matter how much his hunger pained him.

"Stop," he said, his voice strained.

They didn't.

Their hands moved in tandem, sliding up and down his cock. Ophelia moved her thumb around his new piercing and it vibrated inside his shaft, drawing another moan from his lips and highlighting just how long it had been since he'd last had sex.

Matthew tried to stand only to find his body heavy in the water. They had holds on him. They were strong, far stronger than he would have thought given their age but the holds weren't impossible to break. He fought against their holds, snapping away from them, and attempted to stand again but his body was still sluggish.

He pushed blood energy into his muscles and forced himself up. Ezra and Ophelia pursued him and he stumbled backwards out of the water, scrambling to his feet and backing away as fast as he could.

Until he ran into someone.

Surprised, his vampire side came forward as he whipped around with a swipe.

Malarath grabbed his wrist with astonishing strength and held him in place.

"Master," Matthew gasped and dropped to his knees.

Ten

The High King shook the water from his hand and brushed off his now damp robe.

How long had the King been in here? Matthew hadn't sensed him. The warm room had no noticeable temperature drop, he couldn't smell any jasmine, or even hear his heartbeat. He couldn't hear Ezra's or Ophelia's hearts either. All his senses were dull.

…The body wash…there had to be something in it that numbed him.

He shot a glare over his shoulder at the twins, still in the water, looking pretty proud of themselves.

Matthew was half-tempted to run over there and slam their heads against the tiles. They wouldn't be so arrogant then.

"Did he break any rules?" Malarath asked.

At first, Matthew thought he was asking the twins, but Prescott appeared out of thin air, arms crossed, leaning against a pillar.

Fucking hunters and their bullshit ability to make themselves invisible to vampires. Prescott had probably been in here the entire fucking time.

"Except for some talking when he wasn't addressed, he behaved. I thought for sure he was going to come without permission but—" Prescott waved his hand up, pointing to the wet spot on Malarath's robe.

"Look at me, pet." Matthew raised his head and Malarath grabbed his jaw. "Speaking without being addressed is a privilege you have not yet earned. You will not do it again."

Matthew said nothing, unsure if Malarath expected a response or not. He did find himself a little optimistic that maybe one day he'd be able to speak to others. Then he realized that he was looking forward to being given permission to speak, and that was depressing as shit.

"Give him venom bites. Perhaps those will help him remember the rules if he is tempted to talk out of turn."

Matthew had no clue what a venom bite was but it was probably horrific and would have him begging.

"You want it tonight? Gavyn had the rest of the evening off and I think he went out drinking. I might have to go pull him from a bar," Prescott said.

Ah, so another piercing. Matthew really hoped it was something for his tongue and not his balls, or lips, or anywhere else actually—especially not his dick again.

Malarath released Matthew's jaw. "Yes."

"I'll be back," Prescott said and teleported away.

Malarath gave a hand signal for Matthew to rise. He did, but kept his eyes down and shoulders hunched. He really hoped there'd be no punishment for the swipe. He feared the High King. From what little he had seen it was clear his powers were off the chart, but Matthew still had no idea what he was really capable of and, coupled with Hiroto's warnings, that scared him.

Behind him Matthew heard Ezra and Ophelia leave the pool.

"You may take of them, pet," Malarath said, nodding to the twins.

Matthew turned and looked at them. Their eyes flared with desire. "Uh, that's...nice of you...but I really don't want them, Master."

Malarath pressed his hand into Matthew's abdomen, scanning him. "You are hungry—" Then he let his hand drift downwards, brushing against Matthew's dick. Oh god, the touch was electric, rocketing him from half-hard to full attention. "—in more ways than one."

"They're so young. I can't. Master, please." Matthew said the words but his resolve was rapidly declining as Ezra and Ophelia began to touch him again. He backed away from them but they stayed with him until he ran into a pillar. The twins pressed in close, the heat of their bodies warming his skin.

They kissed his chest and nibbled at his nipples, swirling their tongues around the hard peaks. When they went down to their knees all willpower to fight drained from Matthew. His brain turned off and his body took over as his incubus side surged. It had been neglected for so long...

He focused on the golden strands of sexual energy that curled and danced around them.

Ophelia began to lick Matthew's heavy balls. Each lap of her delicate tongue shot pleasure up to Matthew's cock, which wasn't forgotten either. Ezra's lips parted as he took Matthew's head into his mouth. His small lips had to stretch wide to accommodate the girth and he looked up with his shining mismatched eyes. Matthew wondered just how much of him Ezra could take.

Pleasure rippled through him as Ophelia sucked a testicle into her mouth and Ezra pushed the piercing around with his tongue. Matthew rested one hand on the back of Ezra's head and the other on Ophelia's cheek. He didn't push them to do anything but he didn't want them to stop until he was finished feeding.

Fuck, he was hungry. He wasn't sure how much he could take from them, he didn't want to hurt them, but once he started consuming their energy it was hard for him to stop.

Ezra pressed down, taking in more of Matthew while Ophelia's hands slid up the back of Matthew's legs and to the area just behind his balls and applied pressure. Matthew rocked his hips forward, holding Ezra in place. The incubus choked but Matthew didn't let him go. After a moment, he relaxed his throat and pushed deeper. Ophelia's fingers circled Matthew's hole and she moved her mouth to the other testicle.

Matthew's muscles tensed as he neared the end. Ezra moved up and down the shaft while Ophelia fingered his hole. Matthew lost control, emptying himself down the boy's throat. His orgasm was almost painful the way it ripped through him. His muscles cramped and his body became insanely sensitive. The twins hummed quiet whimpers of delight and didn't stop their movements. When it became unbearable, Matthew shoved them away and slid down the pillar onto his ass.

The haze of hunger and lust faded away.

What the fuck had he just done? They were barely teens. Teens who stood there smiling at him. Triumphant.

He couldn't stand to look at them. He closed his eyes and buried his forehead in his hands.

"Pet," Malarath's evil voice pierced him. Matthew looked up at the High King standing over him. "Dry off and return to your area." Ezra and Ophelia began to undress Malarath, their skin still flush with arousal.

Matthew pushed himself up and went over to the towels. Without glancing back, he dried off and left the room, leaving the towel behind since he wasn't sure he was allowed to take it with him.

There were no hunters outside. Or escort of any sort. It didn't matter—he could hear hidden cameras buzzing everywhere. Hunters could teleport to him if they needed to.

The doors opened and the elevator automatically took him up to the floor with the High King's room. When he entered, it was empty and the lights were off.

With no clothes set out for him, he laid down naked on his pallet and wished the release of the sun was far closer than it was. Then he wouldn't have to think about the horrific act he had just committed. His heart ached and he wasn't sure he could do this anymore, he didn't want to be this monster, and yet he couldn't escape it.

He wondered how hard it would be to kill himself. A sudden breaking of the bond would hurt Samantha but she was strong and it would be safer for her in the long run. And it would be safer for all the vampires if he wasn't used against them.

He looked across the room at the statue of his mother. The statue was beautiful with soft features and kind eyes, but Matthew wondered if she actually looked like that or if it was just an artist's rendition of her. Whatever her appearance, the only thing she'd ever done for him was send him a lover who had died. Fuck her.

Matthew curled up and pulled a blanket over his head, as if it would help him forget how truly terrible he was. It didn't work. His whole being felt numb…except for one small area of skin on his lower right hip—opposite the brand. Under the sheets, he looked down and a quarter-sized patch of skin there was red with black around the edges. Where the fuck had it come from?

Matthew ran his finger over it. Some of the skin peeled away.

Gross.

He forced the area to heal and it disappeared.

Then he tucked his knees into his chest and tried to block out the world.

"Matthew—"

He pushed the sheet off him and sat up. The lights were on and Prescott was there with Gavyn, wearing a button-down shirt and dark jeans, and most notably he had no visible weapons on him. His eyes were glossy but focused, like someone trying to sober up quick.

"—back against the wall," Prescott ordered.

Matthew did as he was told. Like a good fucking pet.

Gavyn snapped on disposable gloves. "He's too tall, I need him lower."

Matthew went to his knees without being asked. Prescott raised an eyebrow but Matthew said nothing.

"Stick out your tongue," Gavyn said and put two marks on it with some sort of strange looking pen. Ah, okay, venom bites were two tongue piercings. That wasn't so bad he guessed. Gavyn ran his finger down Matthew's metal cuspids. "His teeth match his eyes."

"You sure you're sober enough to do this, hunter?" Prescott asked. "'Cus I'll go get you some vamp blood..."

Gavyn shook his head. "Naw, Imperator. I could do this shit in my sleep. Vamp blood will mess up my plans for tonight."

"Plans with Johnnie Walker?"

"Yeah, and he's wearing blue."

Prescott sighed. "Just make sure they're straight."

"Always, I have a rep to maintain." Gavyn went about prepping. The piercings themselves didn't take long. Matthew didn't even move when the needle went through. Some blood covered his tongue but he healed it right away—same with some swelling. He wasn't sure how humans could stand the long healing process.

The piercings sat strange in his mouth.

Gavyn stood back, admiring his work. "See? They're perfect."

"Yeah. If you're into that sort of thing, I guess."

"Hey, don't knock them. I bet that lady of yours would love it if you had a tongue piercing. When you're going down on her—"

Prescott held up his hand. "You're dismissed, hunter."

Matthew wasn't sure if Gavyn was so brazen because he was buzzed or if the elite hunters had that sort of camaraderie, but it made him long to be part of something like that again.

Gavyn teleported away. Matthew slumped against the wall and zoned out.

Survive. Don't let him break you. Well, he was broken now and he didn't feel much like surviving. What he wouldn't give to hear Samantha's voice again.

"They're two hundred and eighty-three years old, Matthew."

Matthew looked up at Prescott, who actually looked concerned. "Imperator?"

"Ezra and Ophelia. Sometimes an incubus doesn't fully develop their human form as a way to feed off sexual predators. They love it. And they're not children."

Two hundred and eighty-three…

"And you're an incubus, a hungry one. Don't beat yourself up for giving into them."

"Thank you, Imperator," Matthew whispered, but knowing they weren't actually young didn't make him feel any better. He should have been able to stop himself. He should have been able to resist his hunger.

When Matthew looked up next, Prescott was already gone. On his pallet was a pair of jeans. Matthew slipped them on, laid down, and went back to his self-loathing.

Eleven

The following few nights were strange. Each time Matthew woke, he kneeled because the High King was in the room. But Malarath never addressed or acknowledged him and no one else entered the room.

Malarath sat in a chair that faced out the window, overlooking the city.

Motionless.

All night long.

It was creepy as shit.

After the fourth night, Matthew stopped kneeling. His knees were aching and he hadn't been fed. With his blood pouches still repairing, he needed more blood than usual. That small reddish, black area of peeling skin by his hip would reappear but Matthew healed it away without paying it any mind.

From the eight-by-ten-foot tiled area that was now his home, he watched the High King, wondering what the hell was going on. Out of morbid curiosity, Matthew focused on him and, holy shit, it was like someone flashed their high beams right into his eyes. He was nearly blinded by the bright golden sexual energy that surrounded the King.

Matthew looked away but not before he saw strands floating in from the city to the High King. Was he feeding? Matthew couldn't pull energy from someone unless he was a few inches away. Was it possible the King could feed off sex that was happening anywhere in New York City?

He knew that older incubi could pull energy at range, that they didn't have to actually participate in the sex act, but to get it from miles away? No wonder the King had picked this city to live in. There'd always be plenty of sex.

When Matthew had first heard of the High King he had assumed that everything around him would be about coitus: non-stop orgies, dungeons, naked bodies everywhere. But no. At least not that Matthew had seen.

The door to the room swung open and a familiar scent of rain and apple blossoms enveloped him. Matthew was at the edge of his area and bowed as Rosaline entered the room, wearing a short lavender dress with a high neckline.

She smiled at him. "Hello, Matthew."

Matthew dipped his head a little deeper. "Lady Rosaline," he said, sounding a little muffled because he wasn't used to talking with two tongue piercings.

She went over to where the High King was sitting. From his angle, Matthew had a hard time seeing what she was doing. It looked like she had placed her hand on his face.

"How long has he been like this?" she asked.

"Uh, four nights now, my lady."

Rosaline sighed and walked over to Matthew. When she reached out to put her hand on his arm he took a step away from her. He hadn't meant to, it was just he really didn't want an incubus touching him—not even her.

She frowned, and guilt washed over him.

"You don't have to fear me, Matthew," she said, "I'd never hurt you." He knew that but still, he didn't want anyone touching him any- more. He looked down and said nothing to her. She could do what- ever she wanted to his body, stopping her would mean more punish- ments he didn't want to suffer. Mercifully, she didn't reach for him again. "When was the last time you were fed?"

"Four nights ago, my lady."

"Prescott hasn't been in here?"

Matthew shook his head.

She frowned and crossed the room. From the drawer of a sleek looking side table, she pulled out a comm that looked like one the hunters wore around their wrists: a black bracelet with buttons on it. Rosaline turned it on.

The sounds of explosions and gunshots came through the speaker.

"Your Majesty?" Prescott said between labored breaths. It sounded like he was running.

"It's me."

"Lady Rosaline, right now isn't really a good—" another explosion cut him off followed by sounds of hunters yelling.

The mic picked up a new voice in the background—General Tarrick's. "Ashwood Blue and Crimson Ash cover the South building, and where are my gargoyle busters?"

"Are you safe?" Prescott asked Rosaline.

Rosaline held the comm to her lips, "Yes, but—"

"Then it's going to have to wait." There was more shouting behind him and abruptly the comm cut off.

Rosaline schooled her pouty expression, and put the comm away.

She crossed the floor back to the High King and placed her hand on his face. "Come back to us, Didi, please." When nothing happened, she let out a frustrated sigh. Her green eyes quivered and she began to shake him. "Didi, *Didi*. Don't leave us again. *Please.*"

"Calm yourself, young one," Malarath said, his voice cold and even.

Relief seemed to wash over Rosaline as she fell to her knees. "I didn't think you were coming back."

Malarath's arm moved from the chair rest, and he patted the top of her head. She crooked her head up and began to kiss his wrist.

"I told you that I was returning," he said.

Rosaline broke away from his wrist, "You told me that decades ago."

An unsettling chuckle came from the High King. "When you begin to count your age in millennia, you will find that decades are little more than a single breath."

Rosaline looked up at the High King with warm admiration. "Queen Agleea is holding her Christmas ball next month. Didi, please come to it. Our people need you. They need to see you, be close to you. Please."

"I allow some of my people to see me."

"Only a small handful. It's not enough. All of us feel your absence. As long as I've been alive, you haven't been to one. I'd love to see—"

Malarath stood abruptly, pulling Rosaline with him. He went over and sat on his bed, grabbing Rosaline by her hips and set her on his lap.

Now that the King was awake, Matthew went to his knees and watched as Malarath ran his fingers through her red curls. She leaned into the touch and a soft moan escaped her. Malarath ran his hand down her arm and side, then caressed her legs.

Rosaline's breath grew heavy and her nipples became small hard pebbles under her dress. The sounds that came from her were deep and truthful, and her eyes rolled back into her head.

A flood of pheromones hit Matthew and his eyes turned red as he watched Rosaline orgasm. Small red horns came out from the top of her forehead, her ears became pointed, fingers clawed, and her red tail came out from under her dress. She wasn't in her full form, no wings or hooves, but she was close. The High King pulled her into his chest as her body quaked in his arms. Sharp sighs escaped her.

Watching her climax was beautiful.

And surprising. The High King had brought her to orgasm quickly, and with just a few touches. Matthew envied that power and thought of all the terrible things he would do to a partner if he possessed it. How many times could he make someone come in an hour? Or in the entire night?

A long golden tail that ended in a thick arrow, twisted around her body then intertwined with her own tail. It was the first time Matthew had seen any part of Malarath's incubus form besides his eyes.

"I will attend the ball."

Rosaline's now glowing green eyes widened, her body vibrated with excitement, and she wore the widest smile Matthew had ever seen.

"But," Malarath said, "do not tell anyone. I wish to make an entrance."

"I won't tell a soul, but I'll make sure there is a large attendance."

"That is acceptable. Be sure all the generals attend, including the High Lord."

"He'll be there if I have to tie him up and drag him." Rosaline untwisted her tail from Malarath's and she pushed herself off his lap. She began pacing the room. Malarath seemed content to just sit there and watch her. "I need to have you fitted for a tux."

Malarath frowned. "I do not like modern attire."

"You *don't* like modern attire. If you are going to rejoin the world, you should use contractions, Didi."

Malarath waved his hand, dismissing the notion. "I do not like them, they sound crass."

"It's how people speak, otherwise you sound too formal. You'd stand out to humans."

"I care little about humans."

"Well, the rest of us still have to hunt for our meals. And, unlike you, I'm under orders from my High King to keep our race concealed and blend in."

"You know my reasons for that order."

"I wasn't criticizing the order, Didi. And you're going to wear a tux," Rosaline crossed her arms, looking resolute.

"Are you giving me a command?"

She frowned. "No, I would never presu—"

Malarath held up his hand. "I am only playing with you."

Rosaline blushed, and a small smile crept up Malarath's lips.

Matthew was amazed how different he was around her. She was like the sun melting away his frosty veneer. From what Rosaline had told him, an incubus had saved her when she was undergoing her transformation during the 1920s. She had no idea that she was a succubus and was killing humans during sex, unable to feed correctly. He later learned that the incubus who rescued her was Malarath himself.

Matthew was completely perplexed by their relationship. Malarath doted on her like she was a daughter, but what he just witnessed made her seem more like a lover of sorts. She was the only one that carried the title 'of House Malarath', which made her extremely popular and high ranked among the incubi, despite her relatively young age.

She was also strong in her own right, able to wrap holds so subtle that not even other incubi could feel she was doing it—an impressive feat for one who had only been through a single transformation. Matthew suspected that Malarath had taught her how to master her abilities.

Rosaline sat down next to Malarath again. "If you wear robes, then all incubi will start wearing robes and it'll make us stand out. Please, let me dress you."

"I already let you decorate my room, must you decorate me as well?"

"Yes. And if I didn't decorate this," she motioned her hand around the room, "You'd still be sleeping on a bed made with ropes and a bag stuffed with wool as a mattress."

"I will concede that this mattress is more comfortable, but I still do not like the art. It did not 'grow on me' as you insisted it would."

Matthew had to agree with the High King on this one. Splashes of paint on a canvas was a style he was never into.

Rosaline chuckled. "I'll buy you new art if you wear a tuxedo to the ball...and maybe let me pick out a few other outfits for you."

"I will consider the tuxedo."

Rosaline looked positively thrilled.

"And my pet, he needs one too."

Matthew shifted on his knees under the dual gazes of Malarath and Rosaline. He had been ignored until now and that was just fine with him.

"You're bringing Matthew? Why?" Rosaline asked.

"You tell me, young one. What purpose would he serve?" Malarath asked, his voice kind but stern, like an instructor teaching a student.

Rosaline thought for a moment. "To embarrass him? A punishment maybe."

"No. I possess more painful means of punishment."

Rosaline sat silent for a moment then said, "He's the son of the Blood God...you're bringing him to show you've conquered him. To show you've done to him what Tarrick was unable to."

"Well done." The High King rubbed his hand down her back and looped his tail around her waist. "Get him a full wardrobe. I do not want him in jeans anymore."

Matthew stifled a frown and wondered what he'd be wearing if not jeans. He'd miss jeans.

"He's thin," she said.

"He will not be for long."

A green glow outlined the air and Prescott appeared in the room. He looked awful, covered in dirt, black soot, and blood. In one hand was a silver sword, in the other his horned helmet.

He looked around then checked over Rosaline. "Is everything okay, my lady?"

"It is now, yes. I'm sorry, I didn't know you were in a battle."

Prescott waved his hand as if it was no big deal.

"How did it go?" Malarath asked.

Prescott unsummoned his weapon. "Not good. We lost a lot tonight. The vampire general has changed his tactics again. This time they used high yield bombs by running them in right before they exploded, and they don't give a shit about hiding from humans anymore. We barely got veils up in time. It doesn't help that they seem to know where we'll be long before we get there."

"They are desperate."

"Maybe. But if they keep this up, we'll be the desperate ones. They're fighting guerrilla style and it's working. No big battles, just picking us off."

Abruptly, a searing pain ripped through Matthew's shoulder. He grabbed it and cried out.

The High King rose, his tail unraveling from Rosaline.

"What the blazes is wrong with you, Matthew?" Prescott asked.

Matthew's vampire side ripped forward. It was Samantha. She was in danger. And she was near.

Twelve

Only a single thought raced through Matthew: Save Samantha. She was in pain and she was scared.

Matthew stood. He had to get to her. Except he was in a room with Prescott and Malarath who could shut him off with a single word. He had no idea what the range of the collar was but he didn't much care, he had to try something—anything—to save his daughter.

He looked around the room. There was no way through the door and even if he could break it down, there were huge metal doors at the end of the hall that he wasn't going to be getting through anytime soon.

Prescott told him the windows were impenetrable and Matthew had no reason not to believe him. They were probably magic bullshit. But the walls…he wondered if he could get through those. He wasn't sure he was strong enough to just power through them though, not without all four blood pouches full.

He had an idea. It was a long shot.

"Back to your knees," Prescott said.

Matthew sunk to his knees, removing his hand from his shoulder. There was no mark there.

"My apologies, Imperator." He nodded to Prescott then to Malarath. "Master."

"Are you okay?" Rosaline asked.

Prescott talked over her. "What the hell were you doing?"

"I'm not entirely sure, Imperator. I sensed gargoyles, lots of them coming this way. When I was with the vampires they called me a gargoyle commander. I can feel when they are around. I guess I can feel when they're hurt too." Matthew really hoped he had gotten better at lying since this was probably the most important one he had ever told.

Prescott raised his comm to his mouth. "Dispatch, are there any reports of gargoyles nearby?"

There was a brief pause then, "Affirmative, Imperator. One report-ed sighting just north of the tower, the Misfits were sent to handle it but they ran into a fledgling, they're dealing with the vampire first."

"Let them know that I'll handle the gargoyle," Prescott said and summoned in a short, electrified mace. It buzzed and lightning ran across it. It was a gargoyle buster—strong enough to smash holes through the nearly indestructible stony skin of a gargoyle.

Matthew was up and running faster than he ever had in his life. He plucked the weapon from Prescott's hand and raced at a small part of the wall between the windows.

Behind him, Malarath, Prescott, and Rosaline looked as if they were frozen in time. He wouldn't be able to keep this speed up for more than a few moments but it was all he needed.

Swinging the weapon forward, he crashed into the wall. It broke under the force of his speed and the power of the mace. He could see the actual sound waves from the mace start to form in the air and ripple outwards at a snail's pace.

The first syllable of the word that would trigger Matthew's collar was forming on Prescott's lips. Matthew needed to get distance between them—*now*. He burst through the wall and was airborne for a moment before he started plummeting to the ground, which was—Jesus Christ—nearly a thousand feet down. The High King's tower was fucking massive. It took up a whole city block and was over a hundred stories tall.

He raked his claws down the side of the tower, trying to slow his fall. It didn't do much, but it was better than hitting the ground at terminal velocity.

He preemptively poured energy into his bones and muscles to bolster them since they were all about to break when he hit the ground.

The concrete came up on him fast and he slammed into it. Every part of him shattered. He didn't care about the pain. All he cared about was healing as fast as possible and getting to Samantha.

It took him a moment before he could push himself up. A green light hung in the air. Matthew finished healing his legs and bolted away before Prescott appeared.

Feeling the tug of the bond, he raced after it. Dodging cars and humans that were out late at night, Matthew crossed the city in a blink of an eye.

And then he slowed. The pain coupled with rapidly declining blood reserves caught up to him. He heard hunters nearby. There were green flashes behind him. Bolts soared through the air and a few hit him in the back and arm. He didn't pause.

He hardly registered Prescott's voice coming through their comms, issuing orders. More bolts hit him and still he didn't stop.

Turning a corner, he ended up on a dimly lit side street that would normally be busy but there were magic veils up, displaying the visage of a roadblock. Matthew pressed through the veil, and on the other side saw a team of hunters—wanna-be-rocker Gavyn included—surrounding Samantha. A hunter towered over her, stake in hand, about to take her down.

She held her hands up in fear, her large brown eyes wide and teary. She was lying on the asphalt, a single bolt embedded in her shoulder. It looked as if she had tried to grab it out at one point; the palm of her hand had burns on it. The silver from the bolt crippled her.

Faster than the hunter could see, Matthew ran into him, launching him into the air, sending him down the street. Time returned to normal and there was a bunch of commotion from the hunter team as they were figuring out what the fuck was going on. Matthew ignored them as he scooped Samantha up, pulling her into his chest.

More silver bolts hit his back. He ignored them. He ignored everything except his daughter.

He yanked the bolt from her shoulder and she looked up at him, smiling.

"What are you doing here?" was all Matthew could think to say. She should have been far away from this place and safe under Ascelina's or Bryson's care. Any happiness he should have felt by seeing her was crushed under his fear that she was going to be killed soon. Matthew couldn't get away from the hunters nor could he outrun Prescott's teleporting. There was no escape.

"I had to come," she said, tears falling down her face. "You were going to leave me if I didn't."

Matthew felt confused. Then he remembered earlier this week he had wanted to kill himself. Had she felt his distress the same way he could feel hers? Had she felt all the tortures he had gone through? He hoped not.

He noticed that behind him the hunters had stopped firing. And he smelled Prescott.

"That trick was impressive, Matthew, but it won't happen again. Why did you blow it for some nothing fledgling vampire?"

Matthew growled. Samantha was not 'some nothing fledgling'. He set her down on her feet and turned around to face Prescott—and the hunter team called Misfits—and another dozen hunters teleporting in, no doubt summoned because he was on the loose.

He pushed Samantha behind him so that he was between her and the hunters, and took a step backwards to the brick wall of a building. Samantha stayed a step away from him because of all the silver bolts sticking out of his body but he kept his hand on her arm, refusing to let her go.

Prescott looked from Samantha, to Matthew, then to Samantha again. "That's the oracle...no, Matthew, you didn't...you turned her?"

Matthew dropped to his knees. "Please, Imperator, don't kill her. I'll do anything you ask but, please, don't hurt my child."

"It's not my call, Matthew. But if either of you move I'll put you both down." He pulled off his helmet and rubbed the bottom of his beard. The other hunters in the area looked ready, eager even, to attack on his order. "Are you really a gargoyle commander? Or was that just part of your lie so you could get a buster off me? That was clever by the way. Now we have to reinforce all the walls. I'm not really looking forward to organizing that."

"People keep telling me I am, Imperator."

"Call that gargoyle that's flying around."

It was Jet, no doubt, here with Samantha but Matthew had never called him from a distance before. "Jet, come."

A deep growl came from an alleyway behind the hunters. They turned and Jet, in his dark terrifying gargoyle form, sat crouched, ready to attack.

"Jet, sit," Matthew said. If Jet attacked, the situation would get far worse.

The gargoyle obeyed, falling silent and sitting down, still as a statue.

"If it moves again, kill it," Prescott ordered his hunters.

Behind him, Samantha had ripped off part of her shirt, wrapped her palm, and begun removing the bolts from his back and arms one at a time. Truth be told, Matthew was thankful for it. He was starting to come down hard, exhaustion was overtaking him as his energy was nearly gone.

A caravan of five black SUVs with blindingly bright headlights came down the street and more hunters filled the area. The extra numbers weren't necessary but, like everything with the incubi, this was a show. The cars parked and a hunter opened the door to the middle SUV. Malarath exited in one graceful motion, his blue robe had not a single wrinkle on it.

Matthew's hand tightened on Samantha, and he could feel the hunters on edge. They were the elite who worked in his tower but he got the sense they didn't see the King often, and certainly not outside.

Freshly snapped flares lit up the area.

It took every ounce of control for Matthew not to pick Samantha up and run as Malarath approached. The King's oppressive presence felt like someone was stacking weights on his shoulders. He managed to stay on his knees with Samantha standing behind him.

Tall and regal, the King stood before them. The street was quiet, everyone waiting for him to speak. The only sounds were muted traffic from a few blocks away and a couple of humans laughing from outside of the veil, blissfully unaware that there were supernatural creatures just a few hundred feet from them.

Matthew bowed his head and said nothing as Malarath scrutinized them.

"Samantha Elizabeth Bree," the High King began, "I was most disappointed when my general failed to deliver you last year. I had hoped when you escaped you would be found and captured at a later time. I hardly expected you to show up in my city. You held worth as an oracle, but as a vampire you are useless." Malarath turned and started to walk back to the SUV. He waved his hand to Prescott, "Kill her. Destroy the gargoyle. Cage my pet."

Prescott put his helmet back on and the hunters began to move in for a kill. Matthew had no idea how to get out of this but he sure as shit wasn't going to let Samantha die without a fight. Before he could stand, Samantha squeezed his shoulder.

"You're wrong," she said, her voice small and shaky.

Malarath held his hand up and the hunters gave pause. He looked back. "Am I?"

"I'm a crappy vampire, I was a mistake. My father didn't mean to turn me and I was made weak but because of that, Fate allowed me to retain my oracle powers."

Matthew frowned, she was an accident but he'd never call her a mistake. Never.

Malarath turned. He was hard to read but Matthew thought he looked almost thrilled. He knew that Malarath had wanted an oracle, they were used to cast powerful spells. It required their death though. Malarath looked at Matthew, then back to Samantha. "You retained your oracle abilities?"

"Unfortunately for you."

Prescott laughed and Malarath smiled as if they were sharing a joke between them.

"You took my father from me." Samantha's eyes turned red and her small claws dug into Matthew's shoulder. She was trembling now but not from fear. "I felt it when you left him hungry, confused, and raging. I felt it as you tortured him. And that pissed me off."

"Did it?" Malarath asked.

"Yes. And to punish you, I woke all the dragons."

Prescott's face dropped. "You did what?"

"And you," she sneered at Prescott, "*you killed Devak.* So, I woke the vampire queen as well." She turned back to Malarath. "And all of them are so fucking pissed at you."

Matthew couldn't help but feel a twinge of pride in his chest. Everyone always assumed she was just a diffident, weak vampire but he knew better: she could see the future. And she was smarter than him (although he'd never admit it to her).

Malarath's eyes began to glow a bright gold and Matthew sensed a ridiculous amount of power flowing out of him. For a moment, Matthew thought the King was going to order their deaths again, but instead Malarath's lips twitched, then the power subsided as he calmed himself. "I will use you to put them back to sleep."

Matthew wanted to rip his throat out for implying that he'd kill Samantha but she gave his shoulder another squeeze. "You won't."

"You have an annoying habit of contradicting me."

"Because I see the future. And I put them under an obscuring spell.

You put them to sleep once, you won't be able to again. At least not until you find another oracle besides me and—spoiler alert—I'm the only one Fate is going to spit out for a few centuries."

Prescott stepped forward but before he could say anything Malarath held up two fingers to stop him, then he crooked a finger at Samantha. "Come here."

Matthew clung to her tight for a moment and only released her when she kissed the top of his head and pulled away. Carefully, she approached Malarath and he ran his hand down her face and through her brown hair. He grabbed a handful of it and pulled, forcing her to look up at him. "Devious little creature." Malarath kept a tight hold on her as he looked to Matthew, his golden eyes meeting Matthew's silver ones. "Your existence explains much of my pet's past behavior."

He leaned down and whispered something into Samantha's ear. Matthew couldn't hear it and he should have been able to, but it sounded muffled to him.

Samantha looked up at Malarath, her face frozen between anger and fear.

Malarath released her hair. "She will ride with me."

"And the gargoyle?" Prescott asked.

Samantha grabbed the front of the High King's robes. "Please don't kill him."

Malarath frowned at her touch. Sensing the danger, she released him and took a step back.

"Kneel," he commanded.

Samantha paused for a moment then looked back at Matthew. He could do nothing but nod, not out of approval but more of a 'we don't have a lot of choices here'. She went down to both of her knees, copying his posture.

"You will address me as 'Master'."

Samantha swallowed. "Please don't kill him, Master."

"Is he your familiar?" Malarath asked.

"Um," Samantha looked over her shoulder to Matthew for the answer. Matthew didn't know much about familiars but Jet had chosen Samantha.

"He's hers, Master. Jet traveled with me for a while but she's the one he protects. He was originally on the Lord General's estate. He showed up a month after I escaped. After I turned Sam, he took to her."

Malarath looked down at Samantha. "Keeping him is a privilege. One I will revoke if you displease me. Do you understand what I expect from you?"

Matthew didn't understand what the High King wanted but Samantha nodded her head. "Thank you."

"*Master*," Prescott said, correcting her. He wasn't nearly as harsh about it as he was with Matthew.

"Oh right. Thank you, Master."

Malarath looked over to Jet, who hadn't moved. "You will stay on the roof until you are summoned. Go."

Jet leaped into the air and flew away, his stony wings flapping against the night sky.

Without any forewarning Malarath walked back to his car. A hunter opened the door for him. Matthew watched as Gavyn grabbed Samantha by the arm and escorted her into the car. His heart sank as the door shut. Samantha alone with Malarath was a nightmare. That said, she was the one that saved her own life here. Matthew had done little.

"Come on, Matthew."

Prescott was standing by the open door of the last SUV. Matthew went to it, with a whole mess of hunters following close by. Once he was in, Prescott took the seat beside him.

A hunter took shotgun and the driver took off. Matthew watched the cars ahead, trying to listen in on Samantha.

"His car is warded," Prescott said.

Matthew sighed and rubbed his face. "Do you think he's going to kill her, Imperator?

Prescott said nothing as the car turned out into a busy street. After a while he answered. "Do you know how oracles can be used in the casting of some spells?"

Matthew nodded.

"If her predictions about the future are useful to him, he'll most likely leave her be. If he needs her for a spell, he'll use her. But those types of spells aren't often cast and, if she's telling the truth and made the dragons immune, it could be many centuries before he needs her."

"That's what he expects from her, Imperator? Her predictions?"

Prescott nodded.

"She's not like me, Imperator. She's only a year old and she wasn't lying about being a weak vampire. That single silver bolt I pulled out of her caused her more pain than a thousand bolts would cause me—"

"Matthew, I'm nearly three thousand years old and have been fighting monsters since I was a teenager. I know more about vampires than you do."

"She has bad days—"

"She's not my first oracle either. I know how the visions work."

Matthew looked through the windshield at the cars ahead of him. "I would do anything to protect her, Imperator."

"I know. You just spent the last ten months hiding your vampire child from us. I know what the bond is like and how hard that must have been for you to be away from her. I don't yet know how the King will want her treated but I have a feeling much of her comfort or discomfort will come from your actions. Getting her to do what we want will be easy. You're the one who acts out."

Matthew leaned back into his seat and sunk down a little. "Not anymore, Imperator."

Thirteen

The cars began to slow and Matthew opened his eyes again. This was the first time he had ever seen the tower from the outside. It was an impressive building: slightly rounded; a marble exterior with lots of windows. The building stuck out from the surrounding short, red brick residential buildings, but permanent veils were hiding the tower from humans.

The SUVs stopped in front of it and Prescott pulled Matthew from the car. Led by the High King, with Samantha trailing behind him, hunters held the doors open and the group entered a massive lobby.

Waiting on the other side were even more hunters and a few incubi, including the twins, who watched Samantha with curious eyes. Matthew wanted to growl at them and tell them that they wouldn't be getting their hands on her, but it'd be an empty threat as he had no way to stop them.

The elevator doors dinged and Rosaline exited, escorted by two hunters.

Samantha squealed—actually squealed—and Matthew was at her side grabbing her shoulders before anyone stopped him. "Are you okay?" he asked, looking her up and down for any injury.

She leaned into him and whispered, "She's wearing Marcel Vernier shoes."

Matthew let out a relieved breath. He had no idea who or what Marcel Vernier was but it was probably expensive. A few nearby incubi chuckled.

Rosaline came closer but still kept a healthy distance away from Samantha. "Who is this?"

The King motioned his hand to Samantha. "This is my pet's sired child, Samantha. An oracle."

Matthew moved out of the way so that Rosaline could see her, but he kept a protective hand on her shoulder. Rosaline looked her over for a few moments, then looked to Matthew. "I've never heard of a vampire as young as Matthew siring another."

"It was an accident," Samantha said, "I got shot and he tried to save me and he didn't know that vampires could prevent a turning with their venom. You're insanely gorgeous. Are you Rosaline?"

"I am. You know me?"

Samantha motioned to Matthew. "My father told me about his time in captivity. Well the first time he was captured, anyways. You look just like he described. You can call me Sam. Our lives are closely tied together."

A warm smile lit up Rosaline's face. "Are they?"

"Yes, but I don't know how yet. I know you don't like vampires but I think we're going to be friends."

Rosaline chuckled nervously.

"Come, oracle," Malarath said and made his way to the elevator.

When Matthew started to follow, Prescott stopped him. "No. You're with me."

Matthew's heart sank as he watched Samantha, Rosaline, Malarath, and the hunter team, Misfits, step into the large elevator. He was grateful Rosaline was there, hoping that maybe she would watch over Samantha.

Once they were gone, Prescott took Matthew down to the jail.

Prescott said nothing as he placed Matthew into the silver birdcage. This time there was a cot in it and he wasn't chained up, which was nice. Matthew wanted to ask how long he'd be in here for but he doubted Prescott would tell him.

Alone, he lay down on the bed and let out a long sigh. Only now did he begin to register how much pain he was in. He still had some broken bones and he was bleeding from bolt wounds.

He tried to ignore the feeling of dread that filled his chest. The memories of the months he'd spent starved and raging came back to him in flashes. He really didn't want to be in here.

Reaching out through the bond, he could feel that Samantha wasn't in any pain, and as the rising of the sun pulled at his being he felt content that she was nearby, even if he did end up alone and back in the cage.

****

When he woke the next night, there were folded clothes and boots just inside the cage, as well as a gallon of blood in a sealed bag. Matthew looked at the clothes. This had to be Rosaline's doing. The pants were soft leather and the shirt was a white button-down.

He ignored the items and waited for the shower…and sure enough, an hour later it turned on. In the hot water, he washed off the dried blood covering his body and spent a little too long running his fingers through his shorter hair. Once the water shut off, he dressed. Everything fit perfectly.

Then he waited.

A few hours later, Prescott came in. Matthew bowed to him.

"Didn't want your blood?" he asked.

"Uh, yes. I do, Imperator. But you said only you or the King would be giving it to me. I wasn't sure if I was allowed to drink it."

"Ah. If it shows up in here, you can have it. Not that shit though—even I can smell it's gone bad." Prescott raised his comm and ordered for more blood to be brought down. A hunter teleported in moments later with a new gallon of blood, slid it inside the cage at Prescott's command, and teleported away. The Imperator motioned to the blood.

Matthew ripped into the bag and downed it in record time.

"How are your blood pouches healing?" Prescott asked.

Matthew tossed the bag to the ground and touched his stomach. Jumping off a building hadn't helped things. "Slow, Imperator, but getting there. If I get this much blood every day they'll be healed in a week."

"Tomorrow night you start training. This is your home for a while. I don't know when you'll see your child next, so don't ask." And with that, Prescott teleported away.

Matthew passed the rest of the night alone and bored, often tugging at the bond to make sure Samantha was still okay.

The next night, workout clothes and blood were set out for him. Prescott was there an hour after sunset to take Matthew up a few floors to a training center. He passed weight and sparring rooms. Hunters everywhere did double takes when he walked by, but returned to their workouts when they saw Prescott.

One even teleported next to Matthew with a stake out, a rune on his shoulder glowing bright green—a tracker hunter that could sense vampires nearby. Prescott waved him away.

Unlike the trainees at Ashwood, there were no rude comments or gawking. These hunters had shit to do and they did it. At least for now. Matthew knew that hunters were terrible gossips when they were alone. Hell, they could be worse than incubi sometimes.

They ended up in a sparring room. Prescott evaluated Matthew's skill; they went through stances, attacks, weapons. Prescott didn't seem all that impressed, making small adjustments to each of his moves and making him repeat them until he'd mastered them. He was a demanding perfectionist, who made no small talk while working. He reminded Matthew of Cullip, except Cullip looked like an old man.

Shortly before dawn, Matthew was taken back to his cage where he showered and plopped onto the cot.

The next few weeks were the same: cold blood, dress, train, shower, bed. No Samantha. But he could feel her emotions all the time now that they were closer. Sometimes she felt happy, elated even, others she seemed fearful. In the minutes before the sun rose, she always seemed so sad. That broke his heart.

During training, even though he rarely spoke with the other hunters, he began to memorize their names, faces, and teams.

The different teams fascinated him. Some were full of big, stocky hunters that wore thick armor and had oversized weapons, while other teams seemed specialized: assassins, or long ranged specialists, or trackers.

Matthew, for his part, obeyed every order to the letter and did everything he could to keep out of trouble. He wasn't willing to risk Samantha's well-being for his failure.

Even when they brought him back to his cage, he didn't protest, despite the feeling of dread that filled his chest. But he'd remind himself that it was only for the day and he'd be let out to train the next night.

Sometimes the strange patch of red and black decaying skin on his hip reappeared. It was still palm-sized but blacker and bluer than before. If he poked at it, the skin would rub off. Nasty. He finally decided to ask Prescott about it but never got the chance.

He woke to Prescott standing outside his cell. The Imperator had scorch marks across his armor and face. There was no blood waiting for Matthew. He didn't really need it nightly anymore. His blood pouches had healed and now he was just working on packing on muscle.

The Imperator glared at him, and Matthew knew whatever came next was going to hurt.

Fourteen

"**W**orkout clothes. Now," Prescott said, his command short and grim.

Matthew dressed into the clothes that had been laid out for him and followed Prescott up to a floor he had never been. It was an open area, the center surrounded by a wall and bleachers, like a miniature arena with rubber flooring.

There were a few hunters sparring in the middle but when they saw Prescott marching over, followed by Matthew, they saluted him and teleported out of the way to the bleachers.

There was a vamp trap around the wall. Matthew stepped into the center, knowing he wasn't going anywhere until they let him out.

Without any warning, Prescott turned and punched Matthew square in the chest, sending him flying high into the air and slamming into the invisible wall of the vamp trap. Matthew fell to the ground with an 'oof'.

"Defend yourself," Prescott growled and held out his hand. With a green flash a silver sword appeared.

Matthew got to his feet and let his vampire rip forward.

"*Saa'nile*," Prescott said and Matthew's right shackle fell off. The moment it was gone, a dark voice called to him.

Blood. Feed me. It said.

The black swirling tattoos that ran up Matthew's right arm and over his shoulder turned red and broke open. Blood began to pour down his skin. From the blood, a double-headed battleaxe formed in his hand. It had a continuously bleeding vampire skull in the center, complete with twisting horns and terrifyingly long fangs.

Prescott lunged at Matthew, who parried the attack with his weapon. In the first exchange of blows, neither landed a hit. It was Prescott who broke through Matthew's defenses first.

Matthew sped out of the way of an aggressive thrust only to find Prescott had teleported behind him. He failed to dodge in time and Prescott's weapon pierced his side, barely missing a blood pouch.

Matthew grabbed the hilt and pulled it with him, disarming Prescott before pulling the blade out and tossing it away.

Prescott summoned in another weapon—a silver tipped longspear. He took a defensive stance.

Blood. Matthew's axe called.

"I know, I'm working on it," Matthew said.

"I do hope you weren't addressing me, vampire." Prescott was in a sour fucking mood.

"No, Imperator," Matthew growled. "Bloodreaver, Harbinger of Ruin won't shut the fuck up."

"That's a hell of a name."

Matthew gripped his axe tight in one hand and flexed the claws of the other. "Not one I came up with, Imperator."

Prescott came at Matthew again. Matthew dodged the attacks but only by inches. Nearly a year of being tortured had taken a heavy toll on his body. It didn't help that the axe was trying to take control of Matthew and he had to fight it off while Prescott hounded him.

If Matthew had any doubt of the Imperators skills, they were erased during the fight. Prescott seemed to know where Matthew would be before he did. Every time it felt like Matthew might have an opportunity to connect a blow, the opening would close and Prescott would slice, punch, or kick Matthew as a counter.

He backed away to try to come up with a new plan since he'd lost every exchange they had so far. Green flashes distracted him for a moment. The bleachers were filling up with hunters. If they wanted a show, Matthew was more than happy to give it to them. But before he could make a move, Prescott used the distraction to sink the head of the spear into his ribs then back out.

God damn that hurt. He couldn't let that happen again.

He tossed his axe at Prescott, it turned to blood midair and sprayed across the hunter, blinding him. Matthew followed it up by clawing Prescott across the face and yanking off Prescott's left gauntlet with such force the leather straps that secured it snapped. Removing Prescott's armor was the only way to beat him and Matthew would have to do it even if it was piece by piece.

Prescott dropped his spear and punched Matthew in the jaw, sending him airborne again. The Imperator's runes gave him incredible strength, more than any other hunter he had ever faced.

Matthew landed and rolled to his feet, the axe reforming in his hand. Prescott wiped his face and smiled. This time he summoned a golden longsword with the marks of Ilertha on it—it was the weapon that had killed Devak.

Matthew raged. His eyes burned, turning completely red as he surged forward. The two clashed in the center of the ring. Matthew used his speed to try to break Prescott's defenses while Prescott teleported around. He summoned in a silver bomb and hit Matthew square in the chest with it, sending silver powder flying everywhere. Matthew stopped breathing just in time to avoid it going down his throat, but it boiled at his skin.

Blood. His axe demanded again. The tattoos began to snake across his skin, moving up his neck and down his chest. He was losing control here and he needed a moment to regain it.

He didn't get that moment. Prescott sliced him across the abdomen with the golden sword. It felt strange...like power touching him, filling him. And for a moment he felt...safe.

The next thing he felt was a spear skewering him through the chest. Matthew raised his axe but he was too slow. The Imperator brought the sword down and chopped off Matthew's arm at the elbow. The pain was excruciating and Matthew howled while stumbling backwards, falling as blood sprayed the air.

Prescott came at him.

"That is enough, warrior," Malarath said. "You have bested him."

Matthew poured energy into sealing the wound so that he'd stop bleeding and his tattoos faded back to black. He felt like he was going to pass out. A blood bag was tossed onto his chest.

"Drink," Prescott ordered. Still on the ground, Matthew grabbed the bag and pierced it with his claws. The cold blood tasted amazing. He couldn't help letting out a soft moan as it filled him. When he was done, he gripped his arm and worked his way to his feet.

The place was packed. At some point during the fighting hunters, and even some incubi, had filled the stands. Matthew didn't think their fight had gone on that long...fucking axe. It must have taken over at some point.

It fell eerily silent.

The High King, seated in an intricate chair with Samantha sitting on a large pillow beside him, had his hand held up. Rosaline and the twins were nearby in the stands.

Matthew went to his knees and bowed his head. His detached arm was decaying on the ground. Prescott—putting his gauntlet back on, his wounds already healed—still seemed angry despite his victory. He hadn't let go of whatever bullshit had put him in this mood.

"Am I to assume that it did not go well tonight?" Malarath asked his warrior.

Prescott's jaw clenched. "No. The dragon got away and I lost two teams tonight. All thanks to that oracle."

He had fought a *dragon* earlier? Shit.

Malarath pet the top of Samantha's head. "You do not like her?"

"I'd kill her if you'd let me."

A deep, threatening snarl came from Matthew.

"Shut up, vampire," Prescott said.

Samantha leaned forward and locked her eyes on him. "I could beat you."

Malarath looked down at her. "Do you think so, young one?"

She nodded. "Let me fight him, Master."

New rage bubbled up in Matthew's belly. The word 'Master' from her lips was all wrong. He should have found a way to protect her from this. And what the hell did she think she was doing by asking to fight?

Prescott smiled. "I'd happily take her on. Give me five minutes with her, I'll keep her alive."

"Didi," Rosaline stood up, "she can't take him. It would be cruel."

Malarath waved her aside and nodded to Prescott. "If the oracle thinks she can handle you, who am I to argue?" Rosaline opened her mouth to protest again but Malarath silenced her. "One minute, that is all."

Holy shit. Matthew started to get to his feet. He couldn't let Prescott at her for a minute—he'd beat the crap out of her. Before he could finish standing, Prescott was behind him, kicking the back of his knees. Matthew fell and a heavy boot pressed down on the back of his neck. "Did anyone tell you to rise?" Matthew growled and the boot came down harder. "I asked you a question, vampire."

"No. Imperator."

"You may stand, pet," Malarath said after a few humiliating moments passed.

"Put him in the circle," Prescott said to some hunters. "And, vampire, if a single word comes out of your mouth I'm going to remove your tongue for a month."

They pushed Matthew into a ringside holding area and activated a vamp trap around it with a touch. He had a perfect view of what was about to unfold.

Samantha, who wore black slacks and a blouse with loose, long sleeves stood up and walked into the arena.

Prescott eyed her up and down. "You wanna change or fight me like this?"

Samantha straightened out her sleeves. "This is fine, Imperator. Oh wait! I forgot. If I win, I get to spend a week with my father."

The hunter laughed, which was joined by other hunters in the stands. Matthew pressed his one hand up to the invisible barrier of the vamp trap. He hoped beyond hope that Prescott wouldn't hurt her too much. He could do a lot of damage to her in a minute.

Samantha looked back at Malarath. "Well, Master?"

Malarath smiled. "That is acceptable."

Still standing, Rosaline's face twisted with worry.

Malarath nodded to a hunter with a stopwatch. "One minute. You may begin, now."

Prescott summoned back his golden sword and swiped it at Samantha's neck. She held up her hands defensively but didn't move out of the way. He came to a stop, pressing the blade against her flesh. "You should at least try to dodge the attack, vampire."

"Oh, I didn't need to. I knew you wouldn't chop my head off."

"Fine, I won't stop my next swing. You and your father will have matching limbs," Prescott said, taking back the sword and swinging it at Samantha's arm.

Then he screamed and the sword tumbled out of his hand to the ground. He held up his arm and pulled out a syringe that was stuck between his armor plating. "What the—" He didn't finish the question as he fell to the ground, his body seizing.

Samantha turned to the High King. "Can I spend time with my

father now?"

Malarath rose to his feet. "What did you inject him with?"

"Death's Bite."

"From where did you acquire it?"

"I took it from your side table." Prescott screamed on the ground, his face bright red, foam leaking from his mouth. His eyes were turning black. "I hope his armor can keep up with the damage. If not, he'll be the first person I've ever killed," she said with a frown. "The time had started, I didn't break any rules. Did I need to do anything else, Master?"

"No, the fight is done. You have won."

She looked to Matthew and smiled. Matthew stood stunned. She'd beaten him in like twelve seconds and he couldn't even land a blow with his axe.

"Take him to the infirmary and the vampires down to the cage," Malarath said to a big, mean looking hunter who was probably Prescott's number two. None of the hunters in the room looked happy, but Matthew couldn't care less.

Samantha and Matthew were roughly escorted down to the cage and shoved in. Once inside, Matthew ripped off his silver dust covered shirt as Samantha rushed into his chest and clamped onto him. "I've missed you more than you could know, Father."

Matthew put his one arm around her and smiled so wide it hurt. "I think I might have some idea."

Fifteen

For over an hour Matthew held onto Samantha, refusing to let her go. They moved over to the bed but otherwise stayed in an embrace while she sat on his lap. Samantha cried and truth be told, Matthew wanted to as well, but he also wanted to be strong for her so he didn't let tears fall.

Finally, she pulled away from the hug but stayed sitting on his lap. Matthew let his arm drop around her hips.

"You look different," she said, rubbing her hands over his short hair.

"Well. I have only one arm now," Matthew said, waving his limb around. Thank god for vampire healing.

She laughed then pulled his mouth open. She ran her fingers over his metal teeth then pulled his tongue out to look at the piercings. "They took your fangs?"

He nodded.

"How do you feed?"

Matthew shrugged. "Blood bags. I haven't had fresh blood since being here."

Her face twisted, as if she might start crying again. He ran his fingers through her hair. "Darling, don't worry about me. Tell me what you've been up to. I want to hear you talk."

Samantha swallowed back her sadness and offered a small smile. "Let's see, there's so much…"

"Start with the night—" Matthew almost said 'Devak died', "—I was captured. Vikentiy, he betrayed us, what happened with him?"

Samantha shook her head. "Vikentiy took me from there—he got me to the witches and we teleported out. It wasn't really him that betrayed us, it was his sire, Klavd Zhirov. His family controls all the Russian vampires and Vikentiy has to report to them. When the war is over, they want to rule everywhere and they saw you as a threat. The Zhirov family saw an opportunity to get you out of the way and get Vikentiy's sister back, so they took it.

"Vikentiy didn't know about it until after. Bryson nearly killed him.

Well, it was Gwenyth that nearly killed him on Bryson's order…he's kind of a weak vampire even if he is the general."

Matthew tried to rub his eyes only to remember he was missing his arm. Politics gave him a headache.

"Good," Matthew said.

"Vikentiy wouldn't have hurt me, he protected me while I was in Russia—"

"You were in Russia?"

"Yeah, that's where the Queen was. I went to wake her. And to wake the dragons. The Russian vampires are way more brutal than the one's here. And crazy, too."

"If any of them laid a hand on you—"

She shifted on his lap and laughed. "No. They thought I was crazier than them. They helped me wake the Queen."

"If they want to rule, why would they help you with the Queen?"

"She doesn't really rule. She just kinda *is*. I mean, if she tells you to do something, you do it or she'll kill you, and she expects tribute and stuff but she doesn't lay out law or anything. She seems content just being worshiped and pampered. To be honest, I found her frivolous. But she's super strong and she really, really hates Malarath. It was obsessive…I think she might have loved him once or something."

"You weren't scared of her?" he asked.

"A little, but I wasn't around her long and she hardly took notice of me." The showers in the cage spurted on and Samantha scooted off him. "You stink, go shower."

She was right. The fight with Prescott had left him bloody and silver flecks covered his face—he didn't want to risk them getting onto her. Samantha folded her legs as he stood.

She covered her eyes as he dropped his pants. Matthew chuckled as he got in the hot water, his back to her.

"You're all smooth," she said.

Matthew looked over his shoulder. She was peeking and wore a flustered smile. "Yeah. I have a dick piercing too, want to see it?" He started to turn and she squeezed her eyes closed, laughing.

"Oh, sweet Fate, no," she said, but peeked again anyways once he had turned. She laughed harder when she saw it. "Did it hurt?"

"Yeah. I don't recommend getting one."

"What does it feel like during sex?"

"I don't know. I haven't…not in a while." He wasn't going to mention that it had felt good during the blowjob. He didn't want to think about that. "What about you? Did you find anyone? Or has anyone here touched you?" He wanted to say 'I'll destroy anyone that lays a hand on you against your will' but he knew he didn't have the ability to do that. He closed his eyes and hung his head, ashamed. He should be able to protect his child…

He wasn't sure how long he stood silent under the water but Samantha's hand touched his face. He opened his eyes to see her also naked in the shower. She didn't have a mark or wound on her. "No." Her hand dropped to the High King's brand on his abdomen. "I'm still a virgin and no one has touched me. And I know you want to protect me but I've learned how to protect myself."

Matthew forced a smile. "I'm proud of you."

She looked up at him, water running down her face. He pulled her into him and refused to release her. Being close to his child again filled him in a way he hadn't even realized he needed to be filled. He missed her so much. It was more than just a supernatural bond that tied them together. He genuinely cared for her.

She settled against his chest and they stayed that way until the water shut off.

Matthew broke away first and tossed her the only towel.

"I watched some porn. Cum seems kind of gross," she said while rubbing a towel over her body.

Matthew choked on laughter.

When he settled down, she tossed the towel to him and redressed. "You don't talk as much."

He wasn't sure what to say to that. He wasn't allowed to talk unless spoken to and months before that he had no one to talk to anyway.

"You don't have to explain it to me. I have a lot to tell you anyways."

Matthew felt thankful for that; thankful for her. He dried and slipped on clean clothes: leather pants, grey shirt, tall boots. Samantha studied him. "You look good. Rosaline pick the clothes?"

Matthew feigned offense. "What? You think I can't pick out something stylish for myself?"

She laughed. "Nope."

"Okay, fine. She did. Do you see her often?"

"She comes down to my room all the time."

"You have a room?"

"Yep! And they let me walk around too. Well, I always have a hunter escorting me. I've found a swimming pool, and a library, and there's a maze...I think the High King has a minotaur in his zoo, and—"

"Zoo?"

"Oh, uh." She averted her eyes.

Matthew grit his teeth and pointed to the cage surrounding them. "This is the zoo, isn't it?"

"I haven't seen it but I think the walls here all lift up and you can see all the cages...that's why this cage is in the center of the room like this."

He wasn't really surprised.

Samantha was eyeing the claw marks on the walls outside the cage. "Did you do those?"

"Yeah. But I really don't want to talk about my time in here. Tell me about dragons, what are they like?"

"I only met a few. They helped me with the spells to wake the rest of them. They look human until they shift. And then they're massive." She spread her arms as wide as they would go and outlined an enormous creature, "Oh! They can mask themselves when they fly around. One could fly past here and you'd never know unless it wanted you to. They come in all shapes and colors..."

Matthew listened to Samantha talk about dragons for a long time and by the end he knew a handful of their names, dimensions, what type of element they could breathe—most breathed fire but some could shoot long lines of lightning or even exhale gas clouds—and that Samantha had, in exchange for some fortune telling, managed to convince one to fly her around. It sounded fun.

That morning they settled down together on the bed and he clung to her as the sun put them to sleep. His last thought was how happy it made him to have her near again.

✷✷✷✷

The following night, Matthew rose before Samantha. In the cage, he found a gallon of blood for him and a quart in a bag for her. He drank both and took off his shirt. His arm was regrowing at a rapid pace, the bones and muscles already reforming. It looked nasty but didn't hurt and he figured he'd have his arm back by the end of the week.

He nudged Samantha awake, and her eyes cracked open, blinking away sleep. "Father?"

Matthew tilted his head to the side, exposing his neck. Her fangs came down and in a flash she was on him, her arms wrapped around his shoulders to hold him in place. Soft moans escaped her as she fed from him.

"Best. Blood. Ever," she said as she broke away. "I've missed that so much."

He had too.

Samantha passed the rest of the night giving him a detailed account of her two weeks in the tower. Rosaline, it seemed, was keeping an eye on her. She even helped Samantha acquire a new wardrobe, which, according to Samantha, was extremely expensive and all designer. Matthew didn't share in her enthusiasm but feigned interest to keep her talking.

The rest of their week together passed much the same way—Samantha talking and Matthew listening with a few comments. She spoke of books she'd read, places she'd visited, and languages she'd learned. And even though the incubi almost certainly had the cage bugged, she told him that Bryson had leveraged her abilities against the incubi, and how eventually she decided she needed to return to Matthew. She had to sneak out with Jet because if Bryson or Gwenyth—whom she had been staying with—knew of her plan to leave, they would have stopped her.

Matthew spent the week worried that Prescott would return and punish him for something else but the High King kept his end of the bargain. The two of them had the entire week together. Other than the fresh clothes and blood waiting for them each morning, there were no interruptions. Matthew was in heaven.

When their week together was over, he woke to find Prescott standing outside of his cage. Matthew bowed to him but pulled Samantha behind him instinctually.

Prescott looked like shit. He was in his armor, as always, but he had deep bags under his eyes, his hair was a mess, and his lips thin and pressed together. He looked as if he had just gone through hell.

The cage door unlocked and swung open. "Come with me, oracle."

Matthew didn't want to let her go. "Please don't hur—"

Prescott raised his hand and pointed at him. "One week and you've forgotten the rules?"

Matthew fell silent and let Samantha go. She kissed him on the cheek then followed Prescott out, the cage relocking automatically once they were gone.

And Matthew was alone again.

Hopeless in a cage.

For days, two things plagued him. The first was that pesky patch of skin Matthew now realized was rotting. It hadn't shown up when Samantha was around but after a few nights of loneliness, it reappeared. This time it had a putrid green sheen around the red and black. He got enough blood each night to heal it away, but he was starting to become concerned about it.

The second was his blood axe. As soon as Matthew's arm had finished regrowing, Bloodreaver began to whisper to him again. It was hungry and wanted to feed. It wanted blood. It wanted death. And Matthew couldn't turn off its voice.

Death. Blood. Kill. The same words over and over.

Thankfully, he didn't have to put up with it for too long. A hunter came in and put the shackle back on him, silencing the voice. But it didn't silence his desire to kill and he found it a little worrisome, even if there was nothing he could do about it.

Five isolated nights later, Prescott showed up to take him for training. The Imperator looked better, although he still had bags under his eyes. He said nothing as he led Matthew up to the training rooms. This one had blue mats on the floor and padded walls. There were some chairs in the corner and a few sparring weapons on a rack.

Prescott summoned in a battleaxe and tossed it to Matthew. "It's time you actually learn how to fight with an axe."

He kicked Matthew's feet apart and had just finished positioning his body into stance when the sound of heels came clicking down the hallway.

Prescott groaned as Rosaline came through the door.

Matthew bowed to her.

"Can I help you, my lady?" Prescott asked, his tone stiff.

Rosaline smiled. "I just wanted to observe for a bit."

Prescott balled his hand into a fist. "Why?"

She shrugged. "I suppose I could tell you that I'm curious about hunters and how they train or that I wanted to watch two incredibly hunky men sweating together as they practiced," her eyes grew dark, "but you know I'm here because of that bullshit you pulled with Matthew and I don't trust you to be alone with him."

Prescott's jaw clenched. "I more than paid the price for that."

She pulled a chair over. Her green flowing dress spilled to the sides as she sat, showing off her long legs and metallic pumps. "All the same, I think I'll stay."

"Surely you can find better uses for your time. Clothes to try on, nails to paint—"

She stood abruptly and narrowed her eyes. Matthew didn't blame her, that comment was pretty fucking demeaning. He could only guess that something had crawled up the Imperator's ass and died up there with the dreadful mood he had been in lately.

"Come with me, Matthew," Rosaline said.

Before Matthew could even think about moving, Prescott came between him and Rosaline. "Stay, vampire."

Matthew looked from one to the other. This was a pissing match he couldn't afford to be in the middle of. He had no idea who actually ranked higher nor any template on how to behave here.

"Imperator?" a voice came over Prescott's comm, interrupting the tense standoff.

"What?" he barked into his comm, still scowling at Rosaline.

"Your girl is on her way up."

"She is?" Rosaline said, alarmed.

"And, Imperator," the voice continued, "she's irate about something. I tried to stop her but she kicked me in the shin then wrapped a hold—"

"It's alright, Stephens."

"Matthew, leave now," Rosaline said, pointing to the second door that led to an adjoining training room.

Prescott sneered. "No. Stay. I have to handle this."

Matthew stood frozen. A distant scent of summer and peaches hit him. It seemed familiar, but he couldn't place it.

Rosaline's eyes widened. "You don't understand—"

"Jason—" an angry voice said as the doors were shoved open. "—you can't just ignore me. I deserve better than—" A young succubus walked through the doors. Her hair was a dusty blonde, her eyes a light bluish-grey. She was tall, fit…the type of girl who would get her nails in pink then jump on the back of a motorcycle. She was in jeans and a t-shirt.

When she saw Matthew, a gasp escaped her.

Prescott sighed and moved his body into an almost defeated stance. "Darling, I work with dangerous creatures, next time call up and I'll come down to you. It's not safe for you to just—"

The succubus' eyes darted up and down Matthew.

"Dad?"

Sixteen

L ily looked so much like her mother.

What little color Matthew had drained from him and the axe he was holding slipped from his hand, bouncing on the ground. "Lily…" The last time he had seen her in person she was eleven years old. The night he had been turned into a vampire and ran away from his family to protect them.

He had seen pictures of her since, but seeing her here before him was paralyzing. He had no idea what to say to her. 'I'm sorry I abandoned you.' 'I'm sorry I wasn't there when your mother died.' 'I'm sorry I'm a pathetic creature who doesn't have the freedom to be part of your life.' It all felt so hollow.

Lily's eyes darted back and forth across Matthew's face. "…How? …What? …You're dead."

"I—"

"They told me you were dead."

"Lily…" Rosaline said, walking to her.

Lily took a step away. "You knew?" Her face twisted up as an array of emotions rocketed through her.

"I'm sorry, darling, I was under orders—"

"*You knew.* My best friend and my boyfriend? Both of you kept this from me? I-I can't…I need to…They told me you were dead…" she repeated, trying to process what was happening. Then she backed out of the room and was gone.

Matthew trembled all over and he didn't even realize he was crying.

Prescott stood bewildered, his jaw open like he was about to say something and couldn't find the words.

"I'm going to go try to fix this mess," Rosaline said and went after Lily, leaving Prescott alone with Matthew.

Matthew stared at the door, his hand clutching at his chest.

"Lily's your daughter?" Prescott finally asked, his voice measured. "The one you asked me about weeks ago?"

"Yes, Imperator."

"You didn't kill her when you were turned?"

"No, Imperator." Matthew wasn't really in the mood to elaborate. Prescott could put together that being turned by a god wasn't quite the same as being turned by other vampires.

Prescott teleported away, leaving Matthew alone without any instructions.

Matthew fell into a torpor-like state, so pale and unmoving he could easily be mistaken for a statue. After a while the lights in the room shut off automatically and he lost track of time as he stood there. He had seen Lily for the first time in ten years and she had run away from him.

No. Not him…she had run from the situation. She had been overwhelmed is all, or so he told himself. But fear crept into his heart. What if he had messed everything up? What if he never got to see her again? It was probably better that way, there'd be less of a chance of hurting her.

He clutched at his right hip, the rotting skin there aching.

There were hunters down the hall, running sweeps of every room. Tattoo-emblazoned Gavyn entered and the lights came on. He nearly jumped out of his skin when he saw Matthew, grabbing the stake from his belt out of reflex.

"Christ in a hand basket," he cussed. "What are you doing in here?"

"The Imperator left me here. I wasn't sure where to go."

"Jeez, the Imperator hasn't answered his comm in two hours. Have you been standing here all this time?"

Matthew nodded.

"Do you know where he went?" Gavyn asked.

"After Lily, I think."

Gavyn put his stake back on his belt. "Aw shit, those two are fighting again? Well, uh, come with me. I'll put you back in your cage."

Matthew followed Gavyn to the elevator. Once inside, he noticed that the hunter seemed a little nervous. He kept glancing up then looking away.

"What's it like being bonded to your daughter?" Gavyn asked after a few moments of awkward silence.

"I am not bonded to her," Matthew said without thinking.

Gavyn stared at him.

"Oh, you mean Sam." Matthew felt like an idiot. "It…it's the worst and best feeling in the world. I share her pain and happiness. The need I feel to protect her is unlike anything I can describe."

"So…if someone harmed her…"

"I broke out of this place because she was shot and I felt her pain. The only thing that stopped me from killing your entire team was knowing I couldn't escape with her afterwards…knowing that killing you would anger the King and put her at risk." Matthew rubbed his hand over his short hair. "You're a hunter, don't you know about the bonds?"

Gavyn nodded. "I know what I've seen. Sires go crazy when we kill their children, and vice versa. And I know what we've been taught, but I've never had a chance to actually ask a vampire what it's really like. Or ask a vampire anything really. I'm usually too busy stabbing them." Gavyn made a stabbing motion with his hand.

His attention was pulled away by chatter coming through his ear-piece. Matthew overheard hunters reporting that Prescott had been located and that he was currently with the King.

"Gavyn, new orders," a dispatcher said, "bring Matthew to the throne room."

"Copy that." Gavyn halted the elevator and pressed the top rune. It resumed going the other direction. "You weren't with Sam very long before you were recaptured, were you?"

Matthew raised an eyebrow. "'Sam'? She only lets friends call her Sam."

Gavyn shifted away from Matthew, his hand dropping to the weapons on his hip. "Uh, I'm on her escort detail. She told me to call her Sam, she didn't really give me an option."

A half smile crossed Matthew's lips. "Sounds like her. And no, we weren't together long. But make no mistake, I love her and would do anything to protect her. Anything."

"Gotcha," Gavyn said. He seemed preoccupied by something on his mind and asked, "I've heard that some sires don't let their children do anything without their permission, that they control all aspects of their lives."

"I'm sure some are like that but I would never do that to Sam. She's a young vampire but she's an adult, one who was on her own long before I came along. She's allowed to make her own decisions. Besides, if I tried to pull any shit on her, she'd manipulate me until she got her way. I swear, she seems more like an incubus than I do."

Gavyn smiled.

"Still, it's hard for me to not want to rip the throat out of anyone who touches her."

Gavyn's smile dropped and the elevator doors slid open. Matthew exited into what he could only describe as a lavish receiving area. Pillows and plush couches adorned the room and expensive artwork covered the walls. There was even a fountain in the center. Matthew would have been impressed with the luxury of it all if his mind wasn't preoccupied.

The hunter led him through heavy double doors into a wide hallway. Polished marble floors, heavy drapes, and statues were all there to create the impression of power and wealth.

Matthew looked ahead at the second set of doors. He froze in place. He couldn't hear or smell anything from the other room because of the wards, but he could smell who had passed through this hallway recently: Rosaline, Prescott, and another male incubus whose scent he didn't recognize. The slight temperature drop meant the King was in there too. But the scent that was most important was Lily's. She was in there.

Gavyn, who was leading, halted when he noticed that Matthew had stopped following him. "Come on."

Matthew didn't move.

Gavyn walked back to him. "I'm not strong enough to push you, let's go."

Matthew didn't budge. Gavyn raised his comm to his mouth, "Imperator?"

"*What?*"

"The big guy is at the end of the hallway, refusing to move."

A grumbled acknowledgement came through the comm and Prescott teleported in front of them. "You're dismissed, hunter," he said, waving Gavyn away.

Gavyn saluted and disappeared.

"Let's go," Prescott ordered and began to march down the hall. Matthew stayed where he was. He'd be punished but he couldn't bring himself to move. After a few steps, Prescott turned around. "I have ways of making you move."

Matthew closed his eyes and hung his head. "Imperator—" he started, but wasn't sure what to follow it up with.

"Don't you want to see your daughter?" Prescott asked.

"More than anything, but I don't want her to see me like this." The collar around Matthew's neck had never felt so heavy. He rubbed the shackles around his wrists and that weird rotting spot at his hip ached. "Who would want to see their father as a slave?"

Prescott's face softened. "I just spent the last couple of hours talking with her and I can tell you that she doesn't care. She wants to see you."

Matthew looked down at his clothes and wished he was in something nicer than his workout outfit. Nothing about him felt good enough for her. "She deserves so much better than me."

"Why don't you let her decide that?"

Matthew nodded and took a step forward but found himself faltering and he stopped again. "How long have you two been together, Imperator?"

Prescott looked as if he might not answer the question for a moment then said, "Not long but long enough to know that you aren't the only person in this hall that would do anything to protect her."

"Is she happy, Imperator? I mean, her life, is it a happy one?"

"You should ask her yourself." Prescott motioned his head to the double doors. "Come on. Keeping her waiting just pisses her off, and she has a hell of a temper. Now I know where she gets it from."

Matthew scoffed, then smiled at the idea that she might be a little bit like him.

Prescott didn't wait on his answer. He took the lead, and when he arrived at the double doors he pushed them both open.

Matthew, following, took a deep breath and stepped into the throne room to face his daughter.

Seventeen

The High King's throne room was breathtaking, a full panoply of riches and affluence. Large windows offered a spectacular view of the winter cityscape. Carved white columns inlaid with gold flanked the sides. The floor was polished marble. There were armchairs surrounding the center of the room as well as standing areas, but the most prominent feature was the dais with a gold throne, where Malarath, wearing silver robes with intricate red embroidery, sat. A thin golden crown circled his head.

Below him, standing at the foot of the stairs was Rosaline, wearing an encouraging smile, and next to her stood Lily, looking apprehensive. Behind her stood a man, his hand on her shoulder. Matthew had never seen him before but could guess who he was: Lord Teleclus; a personal friend of Tarrick's and the incubus that had taken Lily in right before her transformation into a succubus.

Lord Teleclus had been an actual Spartan way back when and his obvious muscles under the suit he wore proved it. He had a sculpted chin, a straight nose, and his long dark hair was tied back. His eyes glowed an intense bright green.

Tarrick had told Matthew that Teleclus had retired, only battling when the situation was dire. He protected Lily…and had likely been the one to train her how to be a succubus. He pushed that thought away. The last thing he needed right now was to start growling at someone she clearly trusted.

The massive room looked empty with so few occupants.

Matthew absentmindedly clutched at his hip and followed Prescott to stand before the High King. At the foot of the stairs to the dais, he sank to his knees and bowed his head.

"Rise," Malarath said.

Standing, Matthew couldn't stop looking at Lily. When he had last seen her, her eyes had been hazel and her hair brown, but both had considerably lightened while her features had sharpened. She had turned from a child to a statuesque young succubus.

She stepped forward and swallowed. Teleclus let her go, but he looked ready to defend her at a moment's notice.

"I-I've never seen a vampire before," she said.

Matthew gave a nervous smile. He wasn't sure what to say to that. Or to her.

She came to stand before him. He couldn't help but notice that in heels she would tower over Prescott, but right now she wore flat boots. For an incubus, she didn't look all that concerned about fashion. Matthew envied her jeans and t-shirt.

Lily reached out and ran her hand down his arm, tracing his tattoos. "Your skin is cold."

"I'm sorry," Matthew whispered, not at all talking about his skin.

She looked up at him, her bluish-green eyes darting back and forth as she studied his face. "They explained to me what happened. That you left because you were turned. So that you wouldn't hurt me or mom..."

"The bloodlust of a new vampire is...it's bad. And I had no idea how to control my strength back then. Leaving you and your mother was the hardest thing I've ever done in my life but I didn't know how else to keep you safe...I had to leave...I play through that moment over and over again. I wish there had been another way...I'm sorry." Matthew was rambling. He had so much he wanted to say but wasn't sure how to say it.

"Can you control your strength now?"

"Yes. No one here would let me near you if I cou—"

Before he could finish Lily leaned forward and wrapped her arms around his chest, pressing her whole body into him. "I've missed you, Daddy."

Matthew's eyes filled with tears and he folded his arm around his daughter, leaning his head against her shoulder. "I've missed you too, Lil. More than you could know."

They held their embrace until Rosaline politely coughed.

"Your eyes have changed color," Lily said as she pulled away.

"Yours too. And your hair...what color is your incubus form?" Matthew asked, dying to know. Since he had no incubus form himself, he wondered if he would've had the same coloring as her.

Lily looked back to Teleclus, who nodded approval. She took her shirt off. Under was a black bra. She wasn't the least bit shy or had any of the hang-ups Matthew had about undressing in front of others. Black wings emerged from her back, each of the ridges along the bones were lined with silver. Long horns, the same color as the wings, came from the top of her head, coming forward towards her face before curling upwards and back. Her ears became slight points and her irises turned a glowing bluish-silver. They weren't quite as pure whitish-silver as Matthew's, but the similarity was undeniable.

From the waist of her jeans, a tail emerged, black at the base and silver at the tip. It wrapped around her body. She didn't bring out her hooves but she had grown about three inches in height.

"Incredible," Matthew said.

She smiled. "They told me you never finished your first transformation."

"No. The eyes and the soavik were all I got. Oh, and the gel."

"I wonder if you would have become a social incubus or a warrior," she mused.

"Social," Rosaline said and at the same moment Prescott said, "Warrior."

Rosaline glared at Prescott.

"What?" He shrugged. "It's obvious he'd be a warrior."

"I disagree," Rosaline said. "The way he interacts with other incubi and the extreme way he desires company are social incubi traits."

Lily laughed and Matthew joined her with a smile.

"Did you ever find out who my grandparents are?" Lily asked, "What house we came from? I'm too strong for my age to have come from anything but a noble house."

Matthew shook his head. He hated to lie to her but he couldn't say 'oh yeah, you are the granddaughter of a goddess' in this company. "I searched but I never found them."

Lily looked up to the King. "Do you know, Your Majesty?"

"Lily—" Teleclus said, his voice a warning.

"It is all right, warrior," Malarath said, holding up his heavily jeweled fingers as reassurance. "I can forgive a young incubus the faux pas, and I will even answer the question. No, Lady Lillian, I do not know your lineage. It is a mystery I will solve eventually."

"Well, at least it's not some sort of Skywalker situation up in here," she said.

Matthew laughed.

"Skywalker?" Malarath asked, his head cocked slightly.

Prescott sighed. "Characters from a film, Your Majesty. She means that might have turned out you were Matthew's father."

"Ah." He looked almost amused by the idea. "No."

Matthew reached out and touched Lily's wings. They fluttered as she turned back to him. "Can you fly?" he asked.

"A little. I'm still learning. Can vampires really move as fast as they say?"

Matthew pushed power in his speed and was standing behind her before she even realized he had left. "Some can," he said. She whipped around at the sound of his voice. "But most can't move this fast unless they're old."

"But you can because you were turned by a god?"

Matthew wasn't sure how much she was allowed to know and looked to Prescott.

Prescott gave a nod of approval. "You can tell her."

"Yes. The Blood God, Lysandros, is my sire." Matthew rubbed his tattoo.

"You never really believed in God before."

"Yeah, then you meet one and that changes."

"I'm not sure I believe in them, but Jason tells me I'm wrong and last year everyone was talking about how he stabbed the Blood God."

Matthew wasn't fond of that night but he did like the part where Lysandros had smacked Prescott across the theater.

When Matthew said nothing, she smiled deviously at him. "Is it true you've slept with the High Lord General?"

Matthew nearly choked on his saliva.

She laughed while her incubus form retreated into her body. "You don't have to answer that, everyone already knows."

Rosaline was also laughing.

Matthew shot her a glare and she stopped, but the wide smile on her face didn't go away. "Well, I'm certainly thrilled my daughter knows all about my sex life."

Lily smiled, then her face dropped and she looked serious. She placed her hand on his chest. "I forgive you."

Matthew stilled. Those were three words that he needed to hear more than anything. He fought to keep his emotions in check but they seemed to want to pour out. He rested his hand on her face and kissed the top of her head. "Thank you."

They stayed close for a bit until Teleclus said, "Lily, it's late and we've taken far more of the King's time than we should have."

Lily stepped away from Matthew.

Teleclus bowed to Malarath. "Thank you, Your Majesty. You've been quite generous with us tonight."

With a flick of a few fingers, Malarath gave them permission to leave.

Lily threw her shirt back on and bowed to the King, then looked over to Prescott.

"I have something I need to do here," he said to her. "I'll come to you when I can."

She nodded, then followed Teleclus out.

Matthew watched her as long as he could, not taking his eyes off her until the doors closed. He scratched at the area above his heart, wondering if or when he'd see her again.

"Matthew," Prescott said.

Matthew turned to face him, Rosaline, and the High King. "Yes, Imperator?"

"Did any of the hunters hurt you tonight?"

"No, Imperator, the only hunter I was around was Gavyn. And he didn't do anything to me."

Prescott motioned his head to Matthew's hip. "Then why are you bleeding?"

Matthew looked down, a dark red spot had appeared on his shirt. "Oh, that. It just keeps coming back, Imperator. I can heal it away."

"No, lift your shirt."

Matthew did as ordered, exposing the area of rotting skin on his hip. The red, black, and pus-green patch had grown a little bigger while he had been caged alone. The top layer of skin there had peeled in a web formation and it was oozing. It didn't smell all that great either.

"Fuck," Prescott said. Matthew couldn't recall ever hearing Prescott cuss.

Rosaline gasped and turned to Malarath. "You promised me. You gave me your word," she said, clearly hurt by whatever was happening.

Malarath frowned. "When did it first appear, pet?"

"Um," Matthew was starting to get really nervous, "after the twins, Master."

"You let *them* at him?" Rosaline said to Malarath.

The King waved off her comment. "He was hungry."

"He wasn't born into our world, he'd see them as children. You shouldn't have—"

"My lady," Prescott said, and put a hand on her shoulder to stop her from going too far.

She looked down, jaw clenched, as she took a moment to get control of herself. "I apologize, Your Majesty."

The High King held out his hand to her. She climbed the steps and took a seat on his lap. He began to stroke her hair, calming her. When she spoke again, she kept her voice tempered and controlled. "I know you see him as tainted but he's still an incubus, Didi. He's been lonely for so long. Each time you cage him, it damages him. Please don't let him turn."

Turn? What the shit was going on here?

Malarath ran his hand down her back. "I did give you my word, and I will not break it. I sometimes forget the needs of youth. Both yours and his." He kissed her neck and a breathy sound of pleasure escaped her. "I will fix this. Go."

"Thank you, Didi," she said and slid off his lap.

Malarath dismissed Prescott from the room as well. He left with a bow, following Rosaline out.

Alone in the enormous room, standing below the High King on his throne, Matthew suddenly felt extremely small. He wasn't sure what to do as Malarath stared at him, so he lowered his eyes to the ground.

"You may speak, pet."

"Thank you for letting me see my daughter, Master."

Malarath gave a single nod then curled his hand and rested his chin on it, contemplating something.

"What is happening to me, Master?"

"It will be explained to you later. For now, come sit by me." Malarath motioned to a pillow on the ground beside the throne.

Matthew ascended the stairs and kneeled on it. Before he could figure out what he should be doing next, Malarath ran his hand over Matthew's hair and stroked the back of his neck, just above his collar. Matthew fought the urge to jerk away.

"You resist your incubus side. Why?"

"It's just...I don't want to be touched, Master."

Malarath hummed, his rings tingled against Matthew's skin as he stroked him. "I am not talking about right now. You have always been wary of the part of you that is incubus, feeding but never truly giving in."

The High King wasn't wrong. Being with Tarrick and Rosaline had been the closest he'd come to giving himself over to his incubus side, but he was a vampire too. He couldn't ignore that.

"I'm an incomplete incubus and despite what Lady Rosaline believes, I'm tainted. You're right about that. My vampire side has only brought me pain and loss. Well, it brought me Samantha, whom I love, but other than her..." Matthew trailed off for a moment. He yielded to Malarath's soft touch, leaning into it without even realizing he was doing so. "I don't fit anywhere, Master."

"Belonging is important to you? Having a place?"

"Yes, Master, I guess it is. I thought I had a place with the incubi once, with the Lord General, and after I escaped I thought I had one with Sam...with Devak...but it never seems to work out. Now I only exist to protect my daughters. I'll do whatever you ask if it means keeping them safe."

And that's when Matthew realized the High King had a hold on him. Not because he could feel it—he couldn't—but because he was pouring his heart out to someone he hated. The only reason he'd do that is if Malarath pushed him to.

Matthew tried to struggle against it but he couldn't feel anything to fight; not like with Tarrick or other incubi.

"Do you ever tire of resisting everything?" Malarath asked after watching him struggle for a few moments.

God, he was so sick of it. Nothing he ever did seemed to work out in the end and it was tearing at him. "Yes, Master, I'm tired."

"Then stop fighting."

"I think, Master, it's my nature to fight." A joyless laugh escaped

Matthew. "Isn't that what you want from me? To be your weapon? Destroy vampires for you?"

"Close your eyes," Malarath instructed. Matthew did so. The High King continued to pet the back of his head with slow steady strokes. It started to feel good, comforting, and Matthew leaned his head forward to allow more contact.

His mind began to wander, and at the edges of his consciousness he felt something…he focused harder and he could feel the presence of other incubi from all around the world. Silk strands of their lives weaved past his awareness, all heading to a central location—the High King.

Could Malarath sense all incubi this way? Tarrick had once told Matthew that the High King's decisions could be swayed by the influence of his court. Was it because they were all connected in some sort of spiritual way? None of the other incubi had ever mentioned it around him.

Within him, Matthew sensed his own thread. It was broken and buried deep, shriveled like a wounded animal.

"What is this?" Matthew whispered, keeping his eyes closed. He didn't want to risk losing whatever this was.

Malarath's hand gripped the back of Matthew's neck. "It is the power of my people. They are all part of me and I of them."

"Why have none of them ever mentioned this before, Master?"

"They are not aware of it. Only divine creatures—such as the sired son of Lysandros—can see the fabric of the realm and the threads that tie us together."

Matthew opened his eyes and looked up, his movements felt slow and drugged and the hand at his neck was heavy. "That means you're a divine creature, too?"

Malarath said nothing. He reached down with his other hand and dragged his fingers over Matthew's eyelids to force them shut. Then he placed his hand on Matthew's chest. The High King started to coax his thread out from him.

As Matthew tried to pull away, sharp nails dug into the back of his neck and Malarath leaned in closer. "I am your King and Master. Submit."

Matthew yielded. The thread came out and joined with the others and he felt…a longing desire to please his King.

A hum of triumph came from Malarath. His hand resumed stroking Matthew. This time, a tingling sensation began to build, spreading across his chest and down to his cock, which pressed hard against the material of his workout shorts.

Matthew's eyes rolled closed and he leaned against the side of the throne. Malarath sat back, pulling his hands away. Matthew whimpered. He wanted to be touched, *needed* it.

Matthew wasn't sure what to say. He wanted to beg for more but worried about displeasing the King. His incubus side scratched below his skin, longing for a deeper connection.

He was experiencing a union between the King and his people that he hadn't even known existed. This had to be why incubi didn't have many titles or ranks, they just *knew* who was more powerful than them even if they didn't know the reason they felt it.

Without thinking, he grabbed Malarath's wrist and began to kiss it. Slow at first, worried it might anger him, then rougher when the King made no move to stop him.

He traveled up the arm, stopping only when the sleeve of the robe would allow him to go no further. His senses returned to him and he pulled away from the King. "Master, I'm sorry, I'm not sure why—"

Malarath rested his jeweled hand on Matthew's shoulder. "Hush, pet. That is what was supposed to happen."

"The other incubi, that's how they feel around you, Master? That's why they're always kissing you…"

"Yes."

Matthew licked his lips. Never before had he seen the High King look so magnificent. "What can I do to please you, Master?"

Malarath grabbed Matthew's collar and pulled him up higher on his knees. The King leaned over and pressed his lips to Matthew's. Barely a brush, yet electric. Erotic pleasure ripped through Matthew's body, and he came with a sudden, shattering orgasm. Malarath grabbed the back of his neck tighter to keep him from jerking around too much and pushed sexual energy into him, filling his empty soavik.

When it was over, Matthew slumped down, stunned. A spot of wetness seeped through the front of his pants. He burned with embarrassment as the High King's now golden eyes raked over him.

"I didn't mean to—"

Malarath placed a finger over his lips. "Shhh. Rest."

Matthew sank down on the pillow and leaned his head against the arm of the throne. Malarath stroked his head well into the night, leaving Matthew to wonder what the fuck was happening to him.

Eighteen

Matthew didn't remember the coming of dawn, nor falling asleep, but he must have because when he woke the next night he was lying in a bed; Samantha sleeping in his arms, and something heavy on his feet.

When he sat up, a black furry form moved up the bed and began to lick his face.

"Jet. It's been a while, boy," Matthew said, half hugging, half petting the happy wiggling Rottweiler.

"Five more minutes," Samantha said and pulled the blue cotton sheet over her face.

Matthew looked around. This had to be Samantha's room. Windowless and decorated in shades of blues and pinks, it wasn't very big but it had enough space for a queen-sized bed, a nightstand littered with small trinkets, a bookshelf that was absolutely packed with books, and a recliner that had clothes for him folded on it. There was a door to a messy walk-in closet and another leading to the bathroom.

Matthew scooted out of the bed carefully to find he was wearing fresh boxers. He grabbed his clothes and headed to the shower. When he went to close the bathroom door, he found Jet in his way.

"I'm fine."

Jet's nose nudged at the rotting skin patch on Matthew's hip. "Deeeaaatth," Jet said, the gargoyle's voice sounding like rocks crushing together. And seeing him speak in his dog form was always a trip.

Matthew touched the skin then healed it away so that Samantha wouldn't see it. "I'll be fine, boy. Now let me shower," he said as he pushed Jet out of the way and shut the door.

In the shower, his thoughts turned to what the King had done to him. He hated Malarath, but the connection he'd felt was overwhelming. It had been comforting in a strange way, like he was part of something bigger and more important than a single man. Now that his thread had shriveled back inside of him, he found himself envying other incubi who shared the connection at all times.

After he spent way too long letting the hot water run over him, he dried and tossed on his clothes—leather pants, heavy boots, and a soft, black fitted t-shirt. It gave him a look somewhere between badass biker and let's-head-to-Folsom that would have been better if he didn't have shackles and a collar—or maybe that just added to it—but whatever, he rocked this.

When he exited the bathroom, Samantha, wearing a white tank top and pj shorts, tried to tackle him with a running jump. He snatched her from the air and deposited her back on the bed, her body bouncing on the mattress. She jumped up, her eyes red and her little fangs out. Hissing at him playfully she came at him again. Matthew didn't let her catch him as he dashed around the room.

After a few minutes, she jumped up on top of the bookshelf and was about to leap off when the door opened.

"Hey, Sunshine, I've got your blood—"

Matthew growled at Gavyn and his dumb tattoos. The hunter was holding up a bag of blood.

Samantha leaped onto Matthew's back and sank her fangs into his neck. Matthew didn't take his eyes off Gavyn, who raised his comm to his mouth. "Dispatch, can I get confirmation that Matthew is supposed to be in Samantha's room?"

Dispatch came back with an 'affirmative' and Gavyn set down the blood on the side table. "I'll just, uh, leave this here," he said and backed out of the room.

When Samantha finished feeding, she slid off his back.

"'Sunshine'?" Matthew asked, his eyebrow raised.

She shrugged. "The hunters like me. Well, some of them anyways."

Matthew grabbed her shoulder. "Be careful around them. It's their job to kill vampires and these hunters are good at it."

"I know, I'm careful." She broke away from him and went to pick out her clothes for the day, returning with them under her arm.

"Since when did you become so fashionable?" Matthew asked her, recalling the terrible dress she was wearing the first time he'd seen her.

"Since always. When I was human I watched a lot of fashion shows on TV and dreamed about having money. Who knew all I'd have to do is become a slave to get the clothes I've always wanted."

Matthew frowned. "I would have gotten you better clothes. You know, if things had worked out differently."

She smiled and disappeared into the bathroom, leaving the door open. "I know."

"Did you ever try to compel a human?"

The shower water turned on. "Nah. I never had the chance," she shouted out. "But I can sink into the dirt like a pro now."

Matthew wished he could watch her do it, but he doubted he'd ever be allowed outside with her.

While she showered, he rough housed with Jet on the bed. Jet accidentally ripped the sheets with his paws and Matthew tried to cover the tear with the comforter.

"If you're going to stay in my room can you please not ruin it?" Samantha said, drying her hair with a towel. She had on a flattering cotton dress with blue flowers on it.

Busted, both Jet and Matthew cowered back.

"Father," she said, her face long and voice serious.

"Is everything okay, sweetheart?"

"The Judge is coming."

"Now?" Matthew's claws came forward as he prepared to fight a demigod-slayer.

She shook her head. "No. But the Judge knows of you and is trying to find you."

Matthew relaxed a little, his claws returning to soft flesh.

"Devak masked you somehow. Now that he's gone…" She trailed off. Losing Devak had been just as hard for her. They hadn't gotten along at first but in the end, even she loved him.

"Do you know a way to fight or kill the Judge?"

Samantha's face twisted as she tried to mask pain from him. "No," she whispered. "I can see so much but not that. Please don't leave me again. I need you."

"I'll do whatever I can to stay with you. I'll figure something out." Matthew scooped her up in an embrace. After a while, she grew restless and started to fidget in his arms.

"Lily is a lot like you," she said when he released her.

"Ah, yeah. They let me see her."

"I know. She doesn't know about me yet."

"Oh. I didn't think about that. I wasn't trying to keep you hidden from her but there wasn't really a lot of time to talk. Maybe you could ask Rosaline to tell her, or maybe ask to meet her—"

"Nah, we share the same father but we aren't sisters."

Matthew frowned. That was true—there was no blood relation between them. Still, he hoped that maybe if they ever did meet, they'd get along.

Matthew and Samantha spent the next few hours talking about nothing really. Then Samantha needed some quiet time so Matthew thumbed through some of her books—most of them romances.

Later into the night, Rosaline showed up. Matthew bowed when she entered.

"How are you three doing?" she asked. "And what happened to the bed?"

"Jet got excited, my lady," Matthew said, pointing to the dog-gargoyle. Jet clamped down on Matthew's hand, breaking the skin. "Alright, fine. I might have been part of it, too. Stop biting me."

Rosaline laughed as Matthew licked his hand to heal the wound.

"Come with me," she ordered.

Outside was a team of hunters, they looked like Rosaline's escort. She opened the door to the room next to Samantha's and disappeared inside. "In here."

Matthew, trailed by Samantha and Jet, entered the room. It was about the same size as Samantha's but the furniture was dark heavy wood and the bed plush red velvet. The bookshelves were full of hunter training manuals and books on supernatural creatures. In the corner was an empty armor stand.

The look reminded him of Tarrick's room—old, warm, and comfortable.

"I wasn't sure about your tastes so I just guessed," Rosaline said as he looked around.

Matthew ran his hand over the velvet bedspread, and counted three 'hidden' cameras. "This is my room, my lady?"

"Yes."

Matthew couldn't believe it. He'd been in the cage for so long, that he never even dreamed of getting his own room. Nor did he think the High King would show him any charity, no matter how small. Matthew dipped his head to her. "Thank you, my lady.

"You're welcome, Matthew." She pointed at the wall. "I'll have a door put between the two rooms if you'd like."

"I'd like that," Samantha said, "but if he's going to be having sex in here can you *please* ward the wall?"

Rosaline's bright red lips pulled up into a wide smile. "I'll see what I can do."

Matthew doubted he'd be having sex in here. He hadn't actually had sex in…eleven months now? More? Jeez. And he was trying his hardest not to think about what happened last night with the High King…or the twins.

"Oh," Rosaline said to Matthew. "You're allowed in Samantha's room but nowhere else unless given permission. And," Rosaline pulled a cloth measuring tape from a pocket in her dress, "I need to measure you for adjustments. You've gotten wider. Even your shirt is too tight."

Matthew pawed at his t-shirt. "I like it this way, my lady."

She chuckled. "Only because it makes your muscles look huge."

Matthew flexed a little. "It makes my muscles look huge, my lady?"

Samantha rolled her eyes. "Seriously?"

When Rosaline put her hand on Matthew's arm, he froze in place. She noticed and took her hand away. "I'm sorry, my lady, it's not you. It's just—" Matthew looked her up and down, trying to come up with a reason her touch bothered him. He couldn't think of any. "I'm sorry," he repeated.

"It's alright."

Matthew was relieved when she looked concerned instead of offended or hurt. She handed the measuring tape to Samantha and told her where to hold it. As she finished writing down the sizes, Prescott teleported in.

Matthew instinctively pulled Samantha behind him.

Prescott scoffed. "She should be pulling you behind her, not the other way around."

Matthew said nothing while he bowed but that was a fair point.

"Starting tomorrow, training is two hours after sunset." The Imperator pointed to the bookshelf. "I expect you to finish that top row of books by the end of the week. You can accept blood from any hunter who delivers it. And don't break the cameras or you'll lose the privilege of this room."

"I won't, Imperator." Matthew wanted to ask about the rotten skin but he'd wait until Samantha wasn't around.

The moment Prescott and Rosaline left, Samantha was bouncing on his bed. "It's so cliché in here. Very *I vant to suck your blud.*"

"Yeah, a little, but I like it."

"I know," she said as she hopped down and explored his closet. "You're going to be pissed. No jeans," she called out from inside.

"I'll live." Matthew pulled a book from the top shelf and began to read on the bed. Jet curled at his feet. The book had the rousing title of 'Hunter Code of Conduct and Regulations'. Ug.

Samantha grabbed a book of her own and joined them on the bed. They passed the rest of the night that way, falling asleep together in Matthew's new room.

****

Two hours after sunset the next night, Matthew exited his room. The hunter standing guard outside gave him a weary look.

"Um. The Imperator said I had training but I'm not sure if I should wait here or—"

The hunter pointed her hand towards the elevator room at the end of the hall. "Just go."

Matthew was buzzed through the door and he walked onto the already waiting elevator. The doors closed but the elevator didn't move.

Prescott teleported in beside him. Matthew bowed and hoped he wasn't in some sort of trouble. Prescott grabbed Matthew's shirt and pushed it up, looking at his right hip. The skin there was smooth.

"You healed it away?"

"I didn't want Sam seeing it, Imperator. Are you going to tell me what's happening to me?"

Prescott released the shirt and pressed one of the bottom runes on the elevator without answering Matthew's question.

When the doors opened, Matthew knew he was back down in the zoo. He hung his head and swallowed hard. He really didn't want to be back in the cage again and began to rack his brain trying to figure out how he had managed to lose the privilege of his room in one night. Maybe Samantha wasn't supposed to sleep with him, or maybe he had spoken incorrectly to that hunter.

Prescott marched off the elevator. When Matthew didn't move, Prescott shot a glare that made Matthew's skin crawl and he reluctantly followed.

Dread filled him as they headed towards the door at the end of the hallway—his prison. The team of hunters standing guard in the room all saluted to the Imperator as he passed.

Abruptly, Prescott stopped midway down the hall. A heavy door buzzed open and he went in. Relief washed over Matthew but was quickly replaced by confusion. There was another hallway down here and more doors. This place was like a labyrinth.

"You might want to stop breathing," Prescott warned before he led them into a prisoner's room.

As Matthew stepped inside his stomach twisted. The smell that hit him was rancid, like that of a decaying corpse. And when he saw what the smell was coming from, he nearly vomited.

In the center of the room was a silver cage, just like his but this one was smeared with blood. The floor was littered with bones and torn cloth, but none of that was as disgusting as the cell's occupant. Crouched down was an emaciated creature. It had no hair, no clothes, and chunks of its skin were hanging off its body, exposing bone and muscle.

What skin it had left was greenish with black and red surrounding several wounds. The creature was decomposing but still animated. It hissed at them, showing long yellow fangs.

Matthew looked to Prescott for some sort of explanation.

"This is a ghoul. It's a mindless creature that lives off the flesh and blood of the living." Prescott paused and scratched his beard. "Ghouls are fast, strong, and have insatiable hunger…and you are turning into one, Matthew."

"What—?"

"Ghouls are vampires. Or, more accurately, *were* vampires before they turned to ghouls." Prescott paused, giving Matthew a moment to absorb what he had just said.

Matthew rubbed at his hip. "He was a vampire?" he asked, talking to himself.

"His name was Atieno, he was a vampire lord. About a hundred years into his captivity, Atieno *ghouled*. He used to have wings before he ripped them off."

Matthew was unable to look away from the miserable creature. Its huge lidless eyes darted around wildly before grabbing a bone from the floor and chewing on it.

"How long do I have before I turn into that, Imperator?"

"It depends. For him the process only took a few days. You've already surpassed that so it's clear you're fighting it. Could take a year or it could reverse and you won't turn into one at all."

"Is it a disease, Imperator?"

"No. Ghouling happens when a vampire—for lack of a better explanation—falls to despair. It's not uncommon with vampires who've been in captivity for a long time, but we're pretty good about managing it. I've never seen it trigger as quickly as it did with you. Normally it takes decades, so I wasn't watching for it."

"Imperator—" Matthew ripped his eyes away from the pathetic creature, unable to look at it anymore, "—I don't want to turn into that thing."

"Good. Now let's go train," Prescott said and marched out of the room, Matthew trailing behind, glad to be away from the creature.

Nineteen

The High King wanted Matthew back in fighting shape and the hunters pulled no punches with getting him there. Training wasn't easy. He was pushed to his absolute limits each session.

Prescott wasn't around much and the burden of Matthew's training fell on other hunters or a warrior incubus. Whenever the Imperator did show up, he was always in a foul mood. There was no further discussion about becoming a ghoul. Matthew healed away the rotting skin each time it showed back up so that he wouldn't upset Samantha.

In fact, Matthew did everything he could to make sure she couldn't see how depressed he was. He was stuck in a terrible situation, training to kill vampires, body rotting around him, no hope of escape… and the worst was knowing he couldn't keep his daughter from all this. He felt so…powerless. Although, it was nice to have her around again. Almost every night they slept together, trading off whose room they'd use.

He loved having her close, even if he couldn't keep her safe.

After he stepped out of the shower one night, she was waiting in the bathroom and she ran her hand over the currently smooth skin at his hip. She frowned, then left the room without a word. She never mentioned anything. Sometimes living around an oracle was infuriating.

As Matthew was heading down to train one night, a mean-looking hunter waylaid him in the hallway with, "The High King wants to see you." Matthew followed the hunter, stepping into the elevator. A few moments into the ride he noticed that he couldn't hear the usual buzz of electricity that powered the cameras.

He looked at the hunter standing beside him, really studying him for the first time. He was an average looking guy, wearing his hunter leathers and a cloak, the hood pulled up over his head. He had his full weapons load out, including silver stakes, a crossbow on his back, silver bombs, and a silver sword and dagger, along with plenty of vials on his belt.

Matthew leaned forward a little to get a better look at his face. The man had sharp features and seemed intensely focused on the closed door.

Whispers floated past Matthew's ears, so quiet that he almost didn't hear them. The words were demonic. Matthew took a deep breath in, smelling the man.

Death.

"Fucking demon," Matthew said.

The man turned. He blinked and his eyes turned black. A wide smile crossed his face and his teeth sharpened to terrifying points.

Matthew's claws burst forward and he swiped at the demon masquerading as a hunter. It dodged him, drew its silver dagger, and lunged.

Pushing power into his speed, Matthew kicked the demon in its stomach before the swing could land, sending it hard into the runed metal wall of the elevator. It pushed off the wall and rolled across the floor, slicing Matthew's legs with the dagger.

Matthew countered by stomping on its hand, shattering the bones and forcing the creature to relinquish the weapon. The demon swept its leg up and a heavy leather boot drove into Matthew's blood pouches. He struggled to keep the blood down as he reeled back.

The demon's fingers turned to claws and it slashed across Matthew's chest. Matthew responded in kind by slicing the demon's neck with his own sharp claws. Blood sprayed across the elevator but it didn't slow.

Matthew's tattoos split open and his right arm began to bleed, his weapon begging to come out. But the shackle prevented it from forming in his hand.

The demon licked Matthew's blood off its fingers. *"You live,"* it hissed, then jumped up to the ceiling and stuck to it like a fucking lizard.

"Get down here you son of a bitch," Matthew yelled as he jumped and grabbed the demon.

The doors to the elevator slid open and seven hunters were waiting in the concrete security room.

The hunters watched as the two of them fell to the floor, wrestling and getting blood everywhere.

"*Kayar*," Prescott said. Matthew went flying to the floor and his arm and leg shackles stuck to the runes in the back wall of the elevator. Like a note pinned to a corkboard, he wasn't going anywhere.

The demon stood and brushed himself off. It had returned to his human form before the other hunters had seen the teeth or black eyes.

"Report," Prescott said.

It downed a bottle of vampire blood to heal its neck and shattered hand. "I was escorting Matthew down to training when he punched out the damn cameras and attacked me," it said, coughing.

"That's not what happened, Imperator," Matthew growled, struggling against his shackles.

"Not another word, Matthew," Prescott said. "We saw the cameras go out. Why did the elevator end up on this floor?"

The demon shrugged. "I think I hit it by mistake when he first came at me."

"*He's a fucking demon*," Matthew yelled.

Prescott raised his finger to Matthew. "I told you to shut the hell up. Harlan, go get cleaned up. I want the written in thirty."

"Yes, sir." The demon grabbed his chest and hit the button to call a different elevator.

Matthew rolled his eyes. "Isn't it weird how he's not just teleporting away?"

Prescott gave pause.

The demon-wearing-a-Harlan-body dropped his hand to his swords.

In frustration, Matthew thumped his head on the wall behind him. "Maybe it can't use hunter runes because, oh I don't know, *it's a fucking demon*. Food for thought, Imperator."

Prescott summoned the golden blade of Ilertha—Matthew made a mental note to find out the sword's actual name sometime in the future—and launched himself at the demon. Before Prescott could reach it, it jumped up the wall and crawled along it. Its eyes were black again and teeth sharp.

The other hunters opened fire, bolts riddling the body. It opened its mouth and black smoke poured out of it. A high-pitched hissing, like that of a kettle, filled the air as the demon left the body.

The smoke left the room through cracks in the door and the body of the hunter fell to the ground with a thud.

"Get Harlan to the infirmary," Prescott ordered. A hunter grabbed the body and carried it into the elevator that had been called up by the demon. Prescott raised his comm to his mouth. "Alarm, code red. We have a possession demon in the tower. All Argonauts to the High King. Warkeepers get to Rosaline. Close all doors and seal the vents— no one in or out. Keep an eye on your teammates, it can't use runes. It has two minutes to find a host or it dies."

Alarms sounded and the hunters teleported away, leaving Matthew alone.

"No. That's cool. I'll just hang out here. Helpless in this elevator with a creepy ass demon on the loose."

An hour later the alarms stopped, and Prescott appeared before him. It took everything he had to hold back a 'I told you so'.

A moment of awkward staring later, the heavy door that led to the King's hallway swung open and Malarath entered. Matthew's attitude died a quick death.

"How did you know it was a demon?" Prescott asked.

"I heard demonic whispering, kind of like what I hear before an incursion happens but it was quiet. And he smelled like death, Imperator. Did you find it?"

Prescott shook his head. "No. Demon body jumpers haven't been an issue for over two thousand years, my hunters aren't trained to handle them. *Rayak.*"

The shackles disconnected from the wall. Matthew stretched his back and rubbed at his arm, now covered in dried blood. The tattoos had turned back to black a while ago but the desire to kill still welled inside of him. He stepped out of the blood-covered elevator and kneeled before the King.

Prescott eyed his bloody arm. "Why did you bother with the axe? You know you can't bring it out."

"I didn't, Imperator, it did that all on its own. It started talking to me even through the shackle's magic. It wants to feed. My desire to kill is stronger than normal."

That last part was something he hadn't wanted to admit. The High King had to be influencing him to be a little more forthcoming. God damn, he hated that.

Malarath finally spoke. "Use him to sweep the tower. Then get him some humans to kill. Let his weapon feed."

****

Getting to see the lobbies of each tower floor was fascinating.

The upper ten or so levels were mainly for the King. Rosaline's room was a level down from Malarath's and it was nearly as big from what Matthew could tell, although he didn't actually get to go into each room.

There was the spa and some levels designed for hosting, including a ballroom. Below that were rooms for visiting incubi and succubi that lived in the tower. It surprised the shit out of Matthew that there were actually a lot of incubi living in the tower.

He learned most of them lived there for the pleasure and service of visiting incubi while some served the High King in other ways. There were business leaders, financial advisers, investment managers, purchasing agents, stylists, feeders, etc.

About twenty floors were allocated to hunters and included their personal rooms, the training centers, the arena, a theater, and so on.

The last level he checked was the zoo but he wasn't permitted in any of the rooms. Instead he had to stand by each door and check from there. In the end, he never did find the demon but did overhear reports of a missing hunter.

When they were finished sweeping the tower, Prescott took Matthew to his cage. Matthew was hesitant to enter the room but did anyways.

Inside of the cage were three terrified humans.

Matthew's tattoos split open and began to bleed—not by choice. His vampire side scratched at him, begging to get out, his gums itching for fangs he no longer possessed.

"Please let us out of here," one of the humans begged.

"We don't deserve this," another joined in. The third cowered against the back of the cage.

Matthew hadn't had a human in so long and their scent was driving him crazy.

Prescott opened the cage door and when Matthew didn't move he motioned to the humans. "Well?"

"I can't, Imperator," Matthew said taking a step away.

"Your arm is bleeding all over the floor. Your axe needs to feed."

"But they're innocent people, Imperator."

"You're a damn vampire. You've killed innocent people before."

He had. Many. "When I couldn't control myself, yes, but not anymore, Imperator."

Prescott didn't look amused. "Blessed weapons carry a price. Yours needs blood, which is unsurprising given that the Blood God gave it to you. If you don't feed it, it will take over until it's sated and when that happens it won't care who it kills to get its blood. It won't care that you're slicing up your daughter or destroying a whole tower of my people. But once it's done feeding you're the one that'll have to deal with the fallout."

Matthew clutched his arm, the tattoos red and seeping. He wondered how long he could resist it but he didn't want to put Samantha or Lily at risk. Devak had warned him that the weapon was a curse not a blessing. He wished he'd listened, but at the time he had thought it was the only way to save everyone.

"Does your sword need to feed also, Imperator?"

"Aurous? Yeah, but not on blood and I don't have to pay the cost, it's not my blade."

"But—"

"Belongs to the High King, I only use it when I need to kill a demon or divine creature."

Matthew didn't really need the reminder that Prescott had killed Devak. Not when part of him was begging to kill something.

Prescott held the door open a little more. The humans cowered at the back of the cage.

Matthew looked at them. Both his vampire and his bloody axe wanted to kill them. But there was a small sliver of himself that didn't think they deserved this, that thought this whole situation was fucked up.

Prescott sighed. "If it'll ease your conscience these three fools used to work for Lord Aapo. They sold him out to vampires who ambushed him and his hunter team and killed them all. Their sentence is death. If we didn't bring them here they'd be executed anyway. Now go kill them, that's an order. One you don't want to disobey."

"No wait—" one of the humans cried.

"He was a terrible incubus, he treated us like slaves," another said.

Another wave of fear flooded them, and Matthew couldn't hold back any longer.

He needed this.

His eyes went red and claws came out. The humans panicked and tried to run but there was nowhere for them to go.

Matthew rushed inside, and Prescott uttered the word, *"Sa'nile."* The shackle on Matthew's right arm fell to the ground and Bloodreaver formed in his hand.

Feed me, its dark voice said within him.

Matthew focused on the first human, a male in his thirties. The human balled his fists as if he meant to fight but he never got the chance. Matthew swung and cleaved the man in half, starting at his neck and slicing down through his chest to his hip. The man's blood sprayed so far it hit the wall outside the cage.

Screams from the other two humans filled Matthew's ears.

Beautiful music.

Matthew grabbed one by her neck and ripped her open with his claws while cutting off her arm. As she bled out, he sank his axe into the head of the third, killing him right away.

Unable to stop himself, Matthew gripped the still-living woman and frantically licked the blood flowing out of the wound along her neck. It tasted like ambrosia, a gift from the gods themselves. He growled in frustration as his saliva closed her wounds and her heart stopped pumping.

He grabbed one of the dead males and licked the blood off him, then the other, stopping short of getting on his knees and licking the floor.

More.

Reason returned and Matthew looked around at the carnage. The gruesome mess sent waves of shame through him.

"No. We're done," Matthew said to it. Bloodreaver tried to fight him but he wasn't going to let it have its way. The axe returned to blood, retreating into Matthew's body, and the tattoos closed up.

"If you want out of the cage, put the cuff back on," Prescott said.

Matthew turned to look at the Imperator who seemed unfazed by what he had just witnessed, leaning against the wall, his arms crossed. "I've never seen a vampire so hung up about killing." He chuckled to himself. "Or an incubus so hung up about sex."

Matthew picked up the shackle and slapped it back onto his arm. He didn't really feel like engaging with Prescott right now. Or anyone. The sun would be up soon and he wanted to sleep this terrible event away.

Twenty

When Matthew got to his room, he was glad Samantha wasn't there. He showered for as long as he could and made it to his bed seconds before the sun rose, collapsing naked and wet on top of it.

The next night he woke to Rosaline sitting on his bed frowning at him.

Matthew sat up with the intention to stand and bow or toss on some pants, but she held up her hand to stop him.

"Stay," she said. He stilled as she ran her fingers over his brand then across his belly to the patch of rotting skin. "It's gotten bigger."

He looked at it and it had grown by a few inches. Spreading far closer to his crotch than he wanted. His cock lay soft against his thigh. There was a time her touch would have stirred him but now the only times it roused was when the High King was influencing him.

She smoothed her blue skirt out and folded her hands on her lap. "I hate vampires."

Okay, ouch. Matthew lowered his eyes away from her.

"No, look at me," she said. He did. Her face was hard, as if she was masking pain. "I was captured by them for almost ten years. I was kept in a cramped cage and only brought out so they could use my body and blood for their pleasures. At first, I had hope I would be rescued. I know Tarrick tried, some nights I would hear battles going on outside, but they couldn't break through and as the years ticked by, I gave up. After I was finally rescued, it took me a long time to come back from that and I still haven't entirely recovered.

"When you told me that you wiped out the lords of New Orleans because you were angry that they touched me, I had never felt so safe in my life. I hate vampires because for ten years, they took away every part of me. I hate vampires, but not you, Matthew. I don't want to see you turn into a ghoul."

Matthew felt...numb inside. He was also put in cages and used in ways that were beyond his control. He'd lost his freedom, his lover, his ability to protect those he cared for...what kind of man was he?

Pathetic. Piece by piece, the High King had chiseled chunks of him away, and Matthew wondered how much longer it would be until he was nothing but a shell. "The incubi are no better, my lady."

"How could you say that?"

Matthew reached up and touched his heavy collar, then let his hand fall back down beside him.

Rosaline sat silent for a while. She adjusted her position slightly on the bed, pulling her knees up as if ashamed. "They won't tell me what they do to you. I only know what I walked in on."

Good. He didn't want her to know.

"When you were with Tarrick, almost everything was the same and you were satisfied. What is so different now?"

When he was with Tarrick, he'd had a role and belief that his people would accept him. Or at least Tarrick had been kind enough to trick him into thinking those things. He had none of that now.

"Talk to me, Matthew. Please, you need to talk to someone."

"I...I don't know what you want from me, my lady."

"When we're alone, you don't have to say 'my lady'. I'd rather you use my name."

Matthew felt weary. There were cameras in the room, and he didn't know who was watching. He didn't want to be punished or, even worse, get Samantha punished.

"What I want," she said, "is for you to see that we live long lives and nothing stays the same. It's bad for you right now but your future might be completely different. You used to be so optimistic and now you've given up."

Matthew offered her a sad smile. "I'm not that person anymore." The smile dropped and he closed his eyes in an effort to control his emotions. "Rosaline, I don't have a whole army trying to rescue me like you did. I'm not getting out of here. Not ever. I'm an incubus with no place, no reason to exist, except to be used at the High King's pleasure...as a weapon."

"Your daughters—"

"Would be safer if I were dead. Lily's a strong incubus who has a home and people who care for her, and Samantha has proven she can take care of herself. She's valuable as an oracle and she can use that to keep herself alive. If I lose control it might be them that the High King punishes and I can't bear the thought. Why do you think I've stopped resisting?"

She reached out to touch him again but stopped when he flinched away.

"It doesn't matter anyway," he said, "the Judge is coming to kill me. I'm not going to survive that."

"The Judge? Who's that?"

Matthew was surprised she didn't know. "I don't know much. Some sort of creature that kills demigods. It's supposed to be unbeatable."

"How could you know it's coming for you?"

"My future-seeing daughter told me. My guardian kept me hidden. With him dead, it's only a matter of time."

"You loved him, your guardian, didn't you?"

Matthew nodded.

"Have you ever taken the time to mourn him?"

Guilt flooded Matthew. He had been avoiding thinking of Devak. Devak was dead. Nothing was going to change that. Intense pain shot across his body. All of this was too much. His hip burned. He grabbed at it and screamed, arching his ass and back off the bed.

Rosaline shot to her feet and covered her mouth with her hand.

The patch of red and black skin had spread even more, creeping up his stomach and down his upper thigh.

When the pain subsided, Matthew remained still, not wanting to move and not wanting to speak anymore. Wordless, Rosaline left the room.

Matthew tried to shut everything out. Devak's face kept crossing his mind. His handsome features, his bronze skin, his gentle eyes. Matthew could even smell sweet wine and fragrant oil in the air. What he wouldn't give for just one more night with him.

Prescott teleported into the room.

Matthew pushed himself off the bed and bowed, then braced himself for his punishment for being late to training.

Prescott eyed the rotting skin. "Go get dressed. Normal clothes," he said. His voice gave no hint as to what he had planned.

Matthew did as ordered, tossing on leather pants and a t-shirt. He followed Prescott onto the elevator, praying he wouldn't be put back in the cage. He wasn't. But his heart still sank when Prescott pressed the button to the King's floor.

He wondered if he'd be whipped or if silver would be poured on him. His body trembled and he clutched at his hip, the pain intense.

Getting to the High King's room seemed to take forever. The elevator was slow, the doors took their sweet time to unlock, and the hallway stretched on and on. When he finally made it inside, it was empty.

He walked over to his area without instruction and waited. Prescott took a seat but said nothing. Time crawled by.

From the side door, Ezra and Ophelia entered the room. Their eyes began to glow blue and green when they fell on Matthew, who looked away.

"Out you two," Prescott barked. They sneered and left.

Malarath entered and Matthew went to his knees.

"Stand and lift your shirt," the King said. Matthew did as commanded. Malarath ran his finger down the rotting skin. "You are scared, pet."

Matthew wasn't sure what to say. He was terrified...of turning into a ghoul, of punishment, of being killed by the Judge for simply existing.

The temperature dropped a few degrees and Malarath's gaze fell to Prescott. "I am displeased, warrior."

"I know, Your Majesty."

"He is getting worse."

"He was doing better when he was with Samantha but killing the humans last night triggered this episode...I don't always agree with Lady Rosaline but in this case I think her recommendation is sound. Short of letting him and his daughter go, I'm not sure what else we can do to stop it. Unless you want to put him under your hold for the rest of his life."

Matthew cringed at that. Could the High King just place a hold on him forever? He imagined it'd be like spending the rest of his life drugged out.

"Leave," Malarath said. Prescott bowed and teleported away, leaving Matthew alone with the High King. Malarath went to the window and stood before it, his hands clasped behind his back. After a long while he finally spoke again. "Come here, pet."

Matthew came to him, facing the window as well. Feathery snow flurries floated outside and the city lights twinkled like stars. He wanted to be out there, walking and hunting among the humans…feeling life buzz around him.

He was brought out of his thoughts when Malarath slipped his hand under Matthew's shirt and scanned his abdomen.

"Your soavik is almost empty again, would you like me to fill it?"

Matthew couldn't believe he was being given a choice. "I—no, Master."

Malarath cocked his head. "You enjoyed it when I fed you last time."

"Because you forced me to enjoy it, Master. I don't need it filled—the pain doesn't bother me."

Malarath removed his hand. "You are an unusual creature. Most of my people would quite literally kill for the opportunity to be fed by me."

The feeding had felt phenomenal and he could understand why the incubi would go to extremes to be around their King. But it had been forced upon him.

Malarath sat down in a chair facing the window but didn't give Matthew any new orders. "You worry about the Judge coming."

Matthew turned to face him. "Yes, Master."

"The oracle was only partly correct. The protection your guardian placed on you faded long ago, but you are safe from the Judge. The collar you wear hides you. If you ever remove it, the Judge will come."

Matthew ran his fingers across the collar. The magic from the four Night Stones buzzed under his touch. He had no way of knowing if the King was telling him the truth, but it seemed likely since the Judge had yet to show up to kill him.

Malarath's eyes turned from their pale blue to a vivid gold and his hands became clawed. They were as golden as his eyes and as long as any vampire's claws. He tapped them against the arm of his chair and a low growl came from the King. "I have much invested in you. That I might lose you to something as trivial as you turning into a ghoul angers me."

"I don't mean to anger you, Master." It wasn't as if he wanted to turn into a rotting, mindless, flesh-eating creature.

The King waved Matthew back to his area.

"*Olipsus*," Malarath said. The collar around Matthew's neck surged with power and his body went limp, falling to the ground with a heavy thud. The world turned black around him.

Twenty-One

When the world returned to Matthew, a vision of beauty stood over him, her red lips in a wide smile.

"You have to hurry," Rosaline said. Her red hair was pinned behind a diamond and emerald tiara. She wore a floor-length, green ball gown. The bottom spilled out wide and diamonds—beaded throughout the garment—glittered. Matthew didn't know much about jewelry but the rings and bracelets she wore looked real...and insanely expensive. She was a vision of beauty.

Matthew sat up. He was still in the High King's room. Outside the window, the sky had a faint pink glow as the last moments of day slipped to night.

"I wish I could go," a sleepy voice beside him said. Samantha was on the pallet with him.

Rosaline reached down and brushed Samantha's messy hair back. "I'll see if I can get you along to one in the future. But you have to understand how much my people fear vampires. We have to be delicate about it."

Samantha huffed. "I know." She pushed Matthew up. "Go. Get ready."

"I'm sorry, my lady. But what's going on?" Matthew asked as he stood. He was still wearing the leather pants and t-shirt.

"Oh. You were out for a few days. Queen Agleea's winter ball is tonight," Rosaline said.

After a few nights of sleep, Matthew still felt down but he had better control of his emotions. "You look breathtaking, my lady."

Samantha groaned while Rosaline feigned a blush.

"Are you flirting with me?" she asked, her voice cheery.

Before Matthew could answer, Prescott teleported into the King's room. Matthew did a double take. Prescott was wearing a tux. No armor. An actual fucking tux. And his beard was shaved, revealing a strong jawline. He looked younger—so much so, he might have issues ordering a beer—and not at all like the leader of the Hunter Corps.

Matthew almost forgot to bow he was so stunned.

Rosaline chuckled. "I see Lily won the battle."

Prescott ran his hand over his chin, looking unhappy his beard was missing. "Yeah, yeah. Laugh it up. And why are you not dressed, Matthew?"

Rosaline pointed to a suit bag hanging from the corner of the three-paneled mirror. "Use that vampire speed and dress fast."

He ran over and opened the bag. Inside, a tuxedo. He undressed and redressed faster than any of them could see. He slowed as he knotted his bow tie.

Samantha gasped and ran over to him, running her fingers down the front of Matthew's tuxedo. She turned her head back to Rosaline, her eyes wide. "Is this a D'Leva?"

"It is. I thought you'd enjoy seeing it," Rosaline said.

"Is that a good thing?" Matthew asked as he finished up with his bow tie.

Samantha continued to carefully run her hands over the fabric. "These tuxes start at around twenty grand. A custom one can easily run double that or more."

Matthew had to admit it looked damn good on him. He liked that it mostly hid his metal collar and shackles. "Well, then, I'll make every effort not to rip it."

Rosaline's eyebrows scrunched together. "You better not rip it."

The side door to the room opened and the High King entered. Matthew's jaw nearly hit the floor.

Gone were his usual robes and he was wearing a grey tuxedo that complemented the pale color of his eyes and hair. His fingers were covered with his usual rings but he also wore ruby cufflinks, and attached to his lapel was a ruby brooch with a golden tail wrapped around it, representing his house symbol.

The most eye-catching change were his incubus horns. There were two sets. The first set started at the top of his forehead and twisted upwards with a slight bend back before curving up again and ending in sharp points. Those babies would scrape at the top of door frames if he wasn't careful.

The second set of horns came out from behind the other. They followed the curve of his head, arching up and over his skull then down his back. They were insanely huge, and all four horns were dusky gold at the base and lightened to gleaming golden tips. Intricate metal jewelry wrapped around the base and twisted down the length. If his horns were this impressive, Matthew wondered what the fuck he looked like in his full incubus form.

But right now, he looked like a mix of classic and modern royalty. Matthew found himself unable to look away.

A warning growl from Prescott reminded Matthew that he needed to be on his knees. He lowered himself and Samantha—a little out of place in pj's—did the same beside him.

"Is he aware of the protocol and the task you have for him?" Malarath asked Rosaline, while giving Matthew and Samantha the hand signal to stand.

"I was about to go over it," she said. "Matthew, I need you to appear before Queen Agleea and Lord Ennius. They'll need to move their thrones out of the way and add a chair. You aren't to tell them that the High King is on his way. They'll figure it out but it's better to build the excitement. You'll be kneeling to the right of the High King's throne once it's all set up."

The High King adjusted a cufflink. "I had thought your vampire completely dominated you, pet. It pleases me to see your incubus come through."

It took a moment for Matthew to realize he had been smiling as Rosaline told him what to do. Presentation was paramount for the incubi and it was rare that Matthew got to peek backstage, and he found himself enjoying it.

A chirp came from Prescott's arm. "We're ready."

Matthew wondered how they'd be getting to Virginia. He hadn't seen a leystone when he went through the tower. When he was in New York the first time, he was teleported into a location blocks away from here. The vampires weren't able to destroy that stone nor the one at Queen Agleea's estate.

Samantha grabbed Matthew's hand. "This part is so cool."

He looked down at her. "What part?"

She said nothing but tried to drag him over to the window. He looked up for approval before moving. Rosaline waved him over. Outside, the sky had darkened and the moon was rising.

Malarath placed his hand on the window and outlines of green runes appeared across it like some sort of magical heads-up display. He closed his eyes and muttered a few words in a language Matthew couldn't identify.

Magic surged, electrifying the air. Then—suddenly—it felt as if his body was being compressed and pushed into a single point. And as abruptly as the feeling started, it stopped.

The view outside the window changed. They were no longer in New York. Far below was a snow-covered forest with a castle nestled among it. It looked miniature from a hundred stories up. This was Virginia and that castle belonged to Queen Agleea. Malarath had teleported the *entire fucking tower*.

"Jesus," Matthew forced out. He had forgotten to breathe in enough air to speak so the sound came out squeaky.

Prescott and Rosaline laughed at his reaction. He looked at them in disbelief. Beside him, Samantha started vomiting into a vase.

"That vase is fifteen hundred years old," Malarath said as he straightened his sleeve.

"Ah, so it's new compared to you, Master," Samantha said between heaves. Matthew ran his hand down her back to comfort her.

Malarath smiled. "Let us go."

"*Let's*. Contractions won't kill you, Didi, I promise," Rosaline said, gathering up the bottom of her dress and walking towards the door.

"Very little could kill me. I still do not like them," he said following her.

"Will you be okay, Sam?" Matthew asked. She held up her thumb and heaved out a 'have fun'.

Matthew stood in the corner of the elevator on the ride down, while Prescott called in for a hunter to collect Samantha from the King's room and for someone to clean the vase. Rosaline couldn't keep still, as if she was going to burst at the seams if she stopped moving.

Malarath ran his hand down her neck and she calmed.

"I'm sorry, Didi. I've been looking forward to this my entire life." She stepped into him and kissed the bottom of his jaw.

"You will enjoy it."

Matthew noticed Prescott fidgeting with his bow tie, only to stop once the elevator doors slid open.

A whole mess of hunters were waiting in the lobby, including three members of the Argonauts. Matthew assumed Hiroto was around but hiding somewhere. Prescott ignored his team as they ribbed him about his missing beard.

Ezra and Ophelia were there, waiting with winter cloaks and shawls for the High King and Lady Rosaline. In formal wear, they looked like children playing dress up.

"Go now, pet."

Matthew paused for a moment. "Are the vamp traps—"

"Mother Mary, we ain't new at this. The ones in the main door have been disabled," one of the Argonauts said. He was a big, bald man who wore a set of massive silvered gauntlets. In Chicago, Matthew had been punched across a roof by him—it hadn't been fun.

Not waiting for a reprimand, Matthew pushed power into his speed and left them in a blink.

He ran through the snow, dodging hunters that were on patrol. If they saw him, they didn't have time to react. Behind him, the tower disappeared, and before him the stone castle rose six stories. Gargoyles lined the roof.

Inside were thousands of heartbeats—whatever Rosaline did to ensure the ball had a large attendance, it had worked.

Matthew passed the leystone and the immaculate snow-covered gardens, lit by ornate lamps and festive strings of light. He weaved through the incubi standing at the front door, zipping through the corridor to the main ballroom.

Behind him the first reports that a vampire was on the premises came through the hunters' comms. By the time dispatch finished issuing the report, Matthew would be where he needed to be.

He pushed aside thick velvet curtains and entered the immense ballroom. The grandeur had overwhelmed him the first time he'd seen it, and he felt the same now. The ceiling was six stories, covered with a scenic mural; the walls lined with impressive art. Packed balconies overlooked the floor.

Every incubus and human companion were dressed to the nines while hunter commanders patrolled the edges in their leathers.

Matthew had forgotten it was near Christmas—he had lost track of the nights—but the decorations that adorned the estate were a spirited reminder. Strands of garland ornamented each banister, an absurdly large Christmas tree was against one of the walls of the room, instead of wine there was eggnog—spiked, judging by the raucous laughter coming from the balconies—and warm candles scented the air with their waxy fragrance.

Slow notes of music reached him as he went to the center of the dance floor. Matthew faced a stone platform that was at the back of the room. On it were three thrones. At the top was the golden throne meant for Malarath, even if it had gone unused for centuries, and a few steps slightly below were two other thrones. On them were Queen Agleea and her consort Lord Ennius.

Queen Agleea was Malarath's granddaughter, and now that Matthew had met the High King he could see some similarities. She shared his sharp features but she had dark hair, not gold. In her incubus form she had teal eyes, but right now they were light blue. She wore a blue and green ball gown tonight.

Lord Ennius still had his goatee, but his hair was loose tonight, falling free. He was shorter than her, and slender, but his demeanor was one that was every bit worthy of being her consort. They were both extremely old and powerful incubi, and Matthew remembered how young they had made him feel the first time he had seen them. He didn't feel so young anymore.

Matthew stilled. The music resumed at a normal pace and incubi waltzed around him; it took them a few beats before anyone processed that a vampire had appeared in the center of the ballroom. Once they did, the orchestra came to a grating halt, nearby incubi panicked, running from Matthew, and hunters pulled their weapons.

Three bolts flew at him. He caught them, the silver sizzling his hand.

Hunters moved in, surrounding him, and the entire ballroom fell deathly silent.

"Do you have any idea—" Matthew said as he dropped the bolts, they clinked against the wooden floor, "—how fast Lady Rosaline would kill me if I got holes in this tuxedo?"

"What are you doing here, Matthew?" a deep voice asked from behind him.

Matthew turned to face High Lord General Tarrick.

Twenty-Two

Matthew swallowed as his silver eyes met the hard, purple gaze of the general. Tarrick's black, fully regrown horns with purple tips were out and he was holding up his clawed hand in a command to stop the hunters from any further attack.

He looked as if he had started his transformation into his incubus form when he sensed a vampire and halted it when he realized it was Matthew. He had shifted his size just enough that his tux stretched tight against his body, emphasizing each of his muscles.

Tarrick narrowed his eyes. "I asked you a question."

"Yes you did, Lord General." Matthew turned away from Tarrick, earning him many questionable glances from the surrounding incubi and hunters. "Queen Agleea. Lord Ennius." Matthew bowed to them. "Your thrones need to be moved out of the way and a second chair needs to be placed to the right of the golden throne."

"It is good to see you again, Matthew, but I am not in the habit of being ordered around by a vampire."

"I'm not the one who issued the order, Your Majesty, I'm simply a messenger."

"Wait—" Tarrick said from behind him, already piecing together what was happening. His comm beeped, interrupting him. He pulled an earpiece from his pocket and stuck it in his ear.

"High Tower is outside," Tarrick reported.

Whispers rose through the crowd. The energy of the room shifted as thousands of incubi began to understand what was about to happen. Disbelief, excitement, nervousness—a whole spectrum of emotions rippled through each and every one of them. Even the hunters began to buzz with anticipation. Incubi began to shift, horns and glowing eyes coming to the fore.

The chatter through the hunters' comms grew excited. Orders were issued for new placement assignments, extra sweeps, even an order to re-engage a few vamp traps that they'd found disabled. Matthew guessed he wouldn't be leaving until they let him.

"My grandfather hasn't moved the palace in a century," Agleea said as she stood. Ennius mirrored her movements and stood next to his queen. "Is he actually going to join us?"

Before Matthew could answer her, he felt the temperature in the room drop.

"I am." Malarath's cold voice filled the space.

At the top of the grand stairs opposite the thrones stood Malarath in all his pageantry and splendor. Rosaline stood to his right while Ezra and Ophelia stood behind him.

The incubi fell to their knees. All of them. From the ones in the topmost balcony to Queen Agleea, they prostrated themselves. Even Tarrick dropped to his left knee. The hunters on duty were the only ones who stayed up, but they still bowed.

Since Matthew's task hadn't been completed, he pushed power into his speed and in about five seconds, he had the two other thrones off to the side and added a second chair. And then, like a good little pet, kneeled beside the golden throne.

The room remained silent as the High King descended the stairs. Rosaline stayed slightly behind him as he passed his kneeling people. Pheromones, broadcasting desire, emanated from the incubi, so damn thick Matthew wondered how the humans—both hunters and companions—in the room could bear it.

Peeking up with their glistening eyes, the incubi watched every vainglorious movement their High King made as he crossed the ballroom and came to a stop before Agleea. He held his hand out to her. Still kneeling, she took it and kissed the top along the rings, then kissed his palm when he exposed it to her.

He pulled away and continued, climbing the steps of the dais and taking his throne. Rosaline took her place on the much smaller chair beside him. Ezra and Ophelia stood behind the throne, ready to attend any of the King's needs.

"Rise, my people," Malarath said with a small lift of his hand.

They all stood, facing their King, watching him like they were starving and he had the only damn steak around. Matthew couldn't help himself as his eyes drifted to Tarrick. He looked more collected than the younger incubi around him, but even he wasn't immune to the High King's presence, his gaze fixed upon his monarch. If Matthew hadn't felt the power Malarath held over incubi he would have found their blind desire downright creepy.

"Queen Agleea—" Malarath said. Agleea stood near the base of the stairs, the area around her cleared, except for Lord Ennius who stayed a few steps behind her. She looked thrilled and not at all upset that she had been kicked off her own throne in her own castle.

"Your Majesty," she said with a smile.

"—your estate looks exquisite this time of year and you're running your territories quite skillfully. I'm pleased with the way they're thriving under your leadership."

Matthew's head snapped up. Those were contractions. He watched as the High King shot a sly smile at Rosaline, who seemed equally as surprised as Matthew. The rest of the incubi hadn't noticed the exchange.

"You honor me, Grandfather."

"I must offer you my congratulations."

Agleea tilted her head slightly. "Congratulations?"

"On your pregnancy."

Agleea put her hand on her stomach. She didn't mask her surprise. She hadn't known she was pregnant. Lord Ennius grabbed her elbow and the two of them smiled at each other. Hushed whispers made their way through the crowd.

"I look forward to meeting my great-granddaughter. If she's anything like you were, I don't envy your task of raising her."

Agleea feigned offense with a wave of her hand. "I wasn't that bad."

"You were a terror. Do you remember the time you stole the Imperator's armor and tried to capture a centaur while wearing it?"

She laughed, as did a few older incubi that had either been there or knew the story. "I remember. I was banished to my room for months. I still don't think the Imperator's forgiven me." Her eyes flickered to Matthew, then back to Malarath. "Speaking of, I'm surprised he's not by your side."

Malarath smiled, and Matthew was a little thrown by it. Since he had sat down, the High King was warm, charming, engaged. It terrified Matthew how effortlessly he could deceive everyone. How warm he was in the spotlight of his grand production, no one noticing the mask he wore.

"I have the night off," Prescott said from somewhere in the crowd. The incubi turned and parted.

Prescott stood with his arm resting on Lily's lower back. She looked gorgeous in a sleek black gown that went well with her horns and striking blue-silver eyes.

Judging by the whispers, many incubi had never seen Prescott out of his armor, let alone sans beard. And with a few exceptions, no one had known the two of them were together.

"Before you get any ideas of trying to relive your youth," Prescott said, "my armor is so well hidden, I don't even think Hiroto could find it."

Laughter rose from the gathering, and some of the apprehension in the atmosphere disbursed.

Malarath said something to Agleea in a language Matthew didn't know and, at Agleea's command, the orchestra continued playing and the ball resumed.

Around the room, Matthew overheard hushed gossip. The High King showing up with a vampire kneeling at his side, news of Agleea's pregnancy, and the Imperator with Lord Teleclus' ward were all juicy topics of conversation.

God, incubi loved their drama.

Rosaline brought people before the King to speak with him. Most of the interactions were boring as hell. 'Oh, High King, you're the best.' 'Why, yes, I really am. Now kiss my wrist my subject.' Not that they actually said that, but they might as well have.

Matthew hated that he had to kneel here, watching the ball from a distance. His incubus side cried out, wishing to be part of them. He wanted to dance, laugh, talk...touch.

The worst part was seeing people he once considered friends: Hunter Commander Silva; Lord Vassu; Tarrick's daughter, Lady Talena...

Tarrick's sons Tane and Tarquin were also here. Hell, all five of his sons were here. Matthew had never met the other three personally but they were easy to spot—they looked a lot like their father.

Seeing Tane only served as yet another painful reminder that he was a slave. And, as if he knew the effect he had on Matthew, the fucker smirked up at him like he had won something. Matthew suppressed the urge to race over and slap him.

He was surprised when he briefly saw Commander Cullip, wearing his doublet, missing his left arm. He didn't see Lady Dennith in attendance but if Tarrick was here, she would probably be back at Ashwood running the war.

Matthew did his best not to stare, but he found himself watching Lily as she danced. She was flawless. Whenever she'd glance up at him, he couldn't find it in him to meet her gaze. He didn't want her to see him this way. After a while, she dragged Prescott away and disappeared. Matthew wondered if she left for his sake or hers?

As the night went on, he studied the incubi, watching them in a way he never had before. They touched each other far more often than humans or vampires did. They stood just a few inches closer to each other than what was socially acceptable among humans, enjoying being in each other's space.

He watched as lovers caressed one another, careful touches through the hair, down the face, and the back of the neck; soft kisses and a mutual exchanging of energy.

Matthew ached for that. He wanted to be touched by someone who wanted him for more than just feeding or lust or control. He wanted a lover to talk with again and to listen to what someone had to say.

God, he missed Devak.

Hours into the ball it became harder to watch or listen to the conversations.

The yearning in his belly welled up and he kept his head bowed and eyes to the ground, not wanting to see them anymore. He knew this would be hard for him, but this was terrible.

Malarath dropped his hand to Matthew's neck and stroked it, forcing him to calm. Matthew hated it and yet he was thankful for it.

"Do you see how they desire you, pet?" Malarath's voice pulled him from his thoughts.

It took Matthew a few seconds to realize that it was just the two of them on the dais. Rosaline was off dancing and Ezra and Ophelia were across the room preying on some hapless incubus.

"I don't think it's me they desire, Master."

"Hm." He nodded a direction with his head. "Look over there—"

Matthew saw a warrior succubus across the room who was gawking at him. "—and there." Matthew followed the King's gaze to an incubus who was currently dancing but kept glancing up. "He has been hard since the moment he laid eyes on you. There are many more if you look."

Matthew studied the room. The High King was right. He saw incubi watching him all over the place. "Are you sure it's not just you affecting them, Master?"

A low chuckle came from Malarath. "I am sure. I am unattainable for them. But you—the tamed vampire demigod—might be in their grasp. They seek to please me and in return hope that I will reward them by giving you to them for a night."

"Is that—" Matthew stopped himself. He was going to ask 'Is that something you would do?' but that was a silly question—of course the High King would. "Is that going to be expected of me, Master?" he asked instead, hoping it wouldn't be. He might long to be among them, but he didn't want to be their whore.

"You do not enjoy the idea?" Malarath asked, almost as if he couldn't understand why Matthew wouldn't be jumping at the chance to fuck his people. Matthew's hip began to ache. Malarath stroked Matthew's head. "There is no need to feel such anguish, young one. You should desire such a thing. My people could teach you much and you could feed on them."

But Matthew couldn't even stand Rosaline touching him and he actually cared for her. He felt so torn inside. His incubus wanted one thing, his vampire another. And it didn't help when both stirred each time he spotted Tarrick. Desire would hit him, then guilt that it wasn't Devak, then hate for every shitty thing Tarrick had done to him. Had Tarrick even thought about him in the year since he had been recaptured? Probably not.

When the High King stopped his petting, Matthew realized that Malarath had been studying him, reading his emotions.

"Come with me, pet."

The High King rose and Matthew trailed after. Incubi bowed as their king passed by. Matthew overheard dozens of conversations speculating where the High King was going, the most common consensus was that he was taking Matthew somewhere to fuck him. Malarath didn't help quash the rumor when he paused before leaving the ballroom and said, "Lord General Tarrick, accompany me."

Tarrick broke away from his dance partner and fell in line behind Malarath as they left the ballroom and entered a private corridor.

It was extremely awkward being so close to Tarrick again. The two of them followed the High King in silence—Matthew with his head stooped and Tarrick with confidence a few steps ahead.

Matthew didn't pay attention to where they were heading until they were in a room together. The room was large. Nice, but nothing special. Definitely not somewhere they would put the High King if he was staying over. Tarrick's scent of night and earth was all over it— this had to be where he was staying.

Hunched over, trying to make himself small and forgettable, Matthew stood out of the way of the two of them.

Malarath's eyes fell upon Tarrick. "High Lord General."

"Your Majesty," Tarrick said with a slight bow.

"You have lost many battles lately," Malarath began. His kind facade gone, leaving him as cold as ever.

"Yes, I'm working on—"

Malarath cut him off, hardly in the mood for any explanations. "I had planned to publicly punish you for your recent failures and for lying to me."

"Your Majesty, I've never—"

A surge of power rolled through the room. Matthew had only ever felt anything close to it when Devak had released his aura, and this was stronger. Much stronger.

Matthew took several steps away from the High King, expecting him to lash out at Tarrick...but that didn't happen. All Malarath did was stare at Tarrick, his golden eyes harsh upon him.

Tarrick bowed his head. "It was a lapse in judgment. It won't happen again, Your Majesty."

"No. It will not."

Tarrick stepped into the High King's space and began to kiss Malarath's jaw in a submissive gesture.

Malarath grabbed the back of Tarrick's blond hair and held him in place. "I have a task for you, and if you complete it I will forgive you. If you fail, I will strip you of your position and wealth, and banish your children so that you will never see them again."

Tarrick looked…pained. "What must I do?"

Malarath released him and walked out of the room, pausing at the doorway to say, "Fix my pet."

Twenty-Three

Matthew watched Tarrick stare at the door for a moment, then gathered himself as the influence of the High King's presence waned. He straightened out the sleeves of his tuxedo and his eyes fell to Matthew, who wanted to shrink away under his scrutiny. This was Rosaline's plan? Bring in Tarrick to fix him? What a terrible idea. Tarrick had tricked him and broken his heart. He would never make the mistake of trusting him again.

Matthew stood still, keeping his head down.

A tablet sitting on a desk dinged. Tarrick picked it up and read something in silence, then set the tablet down.

"What needs fixing, vampire?"

Vampire. Matthew flinched. He hadn't expected Tarrick to be cruel. The incubi had won. He was their slave, he'd do whatever they told him to. There was no need for it.

"Answer me," Tarrick's deep voice commanded.

Matthew opened his mouth to speak but found it too difficult. Desperate for support, he studied Tarrick. But the incubus general stood rigid, his face pitiless. Matthew sucked in a breath of air and tried again. "I'm turning into a ghoul, Lord General."

Tarrick stood motionless for a moment and Matthew looked back down at the ground. He couldn't bear the malice directed at him.

"Show me."

Matthew's hands trembled as he untucked his shirt, undid the bottom few buttons, and lifted it. The rotting flesh had reappeared during the party. Healing it away lasted less and less each time.

"How far down does it go?" Tarrick asked, speaking with the clinical distance a doctor might have.

"Top of my thigh, Lord General."

"And how long ago did it appear?"

Matthew wasn't sure how much time had passed. "I don't know, Lord General, a month or two ago I think."

"No matter, I'll find out later. Sit down, Matthew."

Matthew started to sit.

"On the bed," Tarrick said before Matthew's butt hit the floor.

Matthew felt like a fool as he went to the bed and sat.

Tarrick grabbed the desk chair and sat, facing Matthew. "How much do you know about ghouls?"

"The Imperator showed me one, Lord General. I know that they were once vampires who have, as he explained it, lost hope."

"Stop calling me 'Lord General' every sentence, that's getting annoying."

Matthew's lips pressed together tight. Was he supposed to follow what Tarrick said now? He didn't want to break a rule. "Have I done something to displease you, Lor—" Matthew stopped himself, but it felt wrong.

Tarrick leaned back in his chair and rubbed his hand along his chin. His face softened and he sighed. "No, Matthew. Being admonished by my sovereign is not my favorite experience. Having my children threatened less so." Tarrick began to undo his bow tie. "I can't do anything about you right now until I know more."

Matthew closed his eyes and bowed his head. He really didn't want to tell Tarrick everything he had been through the last year.

"Relax, Matthew. I'll wait on the reports and talk to Prescott tomorrow. I can guess the basics anyways."

Just thinking about the pain and loneliness caused his hip to ache again.

Tarrick sat forward. "Your emotions are all over the place right now. Will you let me wrap a hold on you? It won't be a sexual one, just one to steady you a little."

"You can do whatever you want to me, I won't fight it."

Tarrick said nothing for a few moments, watching Matthew. "I saw Lily here tonight," he finally said. "Which means she knows that you are alive. Undead anyways."

Matthew looked up and offered a small smile at the mention of Lily. "Yeah, she, uh, was pissed at the Imperator about something and barged in when I was training with him. We got to talk for a little bit."

Tarrick stood and slipped off his tux jacket. "That must have been hard for you."

Matthew rubbed at the shackles under his sleeve. "I didn't want her to see me as a slave."

Tarrick disappeared into a walk-in closet to hang up his jacket. "I doubt she even noticed," he said from the closet.

Matthew touched his heavy iron collar. "It's kind of hard to miss. And it sort of sucks that she's dating the man that tortures me."

"For what it's worth—" Tarrick said as he sat back down, his bow tie was loose and the first few buttons of his suit were undone "— he treats her well. Teleclus wouldn't let him near her if he didn't." Tarrick laughed to himself. Matthew had forgotten how seductive his laugh sounded. "Jason is a Greek and Teleclus is a Roman, and they've never gotten along. I was astonished to hear that he allowed it to happen at all. My guess is that Lily didn't let him have much say in it. She really is your daughter. Headstrong and stubborn."

Matthew smiled. Their conversation had turned easy; familiar, like old friends catching up. He cherished the warm feelings, even if they were false, produced by the subtle hold Tarrick had slipped on him.

"If you want me to remove it, I will. But I think it will help you. Just for tonight," Tarrick said.

"Why even give me the choice?"

"I know how much you hate having a hold on you and you've clearly had enough pain as of late." The tablet on the desk beeped again and Tarrick leaned back and grabbed it. "It seems I'm moving into High Tower. I have a lot of work to do to make it happen. I've set out some clothes in the closet that will fit you. Go change. Hang up your tuxedo, I don't want to see it on the ground."

Matthew nearly laughed as he went to the closet. Tarrick was such a neat freak and he knew that Matthew was something of a slob. Inside, on a small table, was a folded t-shirt and black pajama bottoms. They were a little tight on him but still comfortable. He briefly considered leaving his socks on the floor, but self-preservation won and he put them in a basket.

When he came out, Tarrick had pulled the chair back to the desk and was already working on the tablet while talking into a phone. Matthew could hear both sides of the conversation.

"How long do you think you'll be there?" a harsh voice belonging to a female asked. Dennith. Tarrick's right hand.

"I'm not sure. Plan for a while. The King's not happy with me,"

Tarrick said as he pointed at the bed. Matthew went and sat down.

"Will it be Talena or Tane running the household?" Dennith asked.

"Neither. I'd like Darius to run it. I'm going to send Tane to Russia to learn under Tarquin."

"And Talena?"

"She's going too." Tarrick did not sound happy about it.

"Good. She's a warrior—you can't keep her away from the fighting forever."

"I know," he said with a heavy sigh. "I'll send you a list of orders in the hour. I'll need them completed by sunrise."

"I'll get it done," Dennith said. There was a short pause then, "How is he?"

Tarrick looked over at Matthew. "We'll talk tomorrow," he said and ended the call. "There are some books on the side table or you can watch TV if you want, it won't bother me."

Matthew didn't feel like reading and he hadn't watched TV in a decade. It no longer interested him.

"Get under the sheets," Tarrick ordered when he didn't move.

Matthew slipped under the covers and pulled the silky sheets up around him. Tarrick didn't say anything else to him as he went back to work. Matthew watched as he issued orders via his phone or comm while receiving updates and reports from the war. He seemed to be doing a million things at once and he handled each of them with ease.

The hold that Tarrick had on him grew stronger and Matthew smiled. He hadn't felt this warmth in a long time. Not since before Devak's death. As he watched Tarrick work, he let himself pretend that he had never been turned into a vampire. That he and Lily went through their transformations unhindered and they were accepted into incubus society. That he got to spend those last few years with his wife before cancer took her.

That he and Tarrick had met under different circumstances, fallen in love, and had a normal, healthy relationship.

If he had been a warrior, he'd fight under Tarrick's command. If he had been a social incubus, he'd work to improve the wealth and influence of his household, freeing Tarrick to spend more time on the war. Or maybe Devak would have made himself known, and maybe the pleasure guardian would have been his first male lover.

Matthew spent hours lost in the fantasies and a feeling of peace enveloped him as he drifted off to sleep.

When he woke next it was daytime and he was in some sort of metal container that reminded Matthew of a pod-like coffin. The lid was propped open and Silva was standing over him. She had her hand on his hip. His shirt was pushed up, but she wasn't looking at him.

"You really think you can get him back from this?" she asked someone Matthew couldn't see.

"I'm not sure. The High King had him locked up alone for a long time. He's in bad shape and he doesn't trust me," Tarrick said from somewhere in the room.

Cullip looked over the edge of the pod-coffin thing. "Hey, Matthew. It's been a while."

Silva looked down. "Shit, how long have you been awake?"

Matthew offered them a sleepy smile. "Since you started touching me, Commander Silva. You check out my dick yet? I have a nice new piercing in it."

She scowled at him.

"I know you want to," he teased. "Go ahead, Commander."

She rolled her eyes and pulled down his shirt to cover him back up.

"I got these too." Matthew scraped his tongue along his teeth so that the bars of his piercings hooked on them. "Doesn't really make up for the missing fangs though."

Silva pushed up his lip and cussed when she saw the metal canines. "When are you getting the report on what was done to him?"

"Should be here soon. I'll send you a copy," Tarrick said. Matthew still couldn't see him.

"And hello, Commander Cullip." Matthew tried to move his hand but he couldn't during the day time. "Sorry you lost your arm. Prescott took mine but it regrew. Hurt like a bitch."

"Yeah, it didn't feel all that great. You saved my life that day, I never got a chance to thank you. And for getting Ascelina to release me from the compulsion."

"Yeah, that was shitty of her." Matthew's eyes flicked to Silva. "Not that I'm one to talk, I guess."

Tarrick looked over the edge and placed his hand on Matthew's chest. "We're moving you over to the tower now. Go back to sleep,

Matthew."

"Okay, Lord General." He wouldn't have been able to stay awake much longer anyways.

****

Samantha slept curled up in Matthew's arms when he woke. Her subtle scent of parchment and vanilla comforted him...as did the smell of night and earth. Matthew shot up, pulling Samantha into him to protect her.

He was in the tower, which was back in New York, in a room on one of the upper levels based on the view of the city. The room was huge, with heavy dark wood furniture and deep reds. Matthew lay in the center of a king-sized bed with silk sheets.

Sitting at a large desk with two laptops open and reading on a tablet was Tarrick. He wore suit pants and a white dress shirt, the top buttons open. He glanced over the top of his tablet, unimpressed, then went back to his task.

Samantha woke and rubbed her eyes. "Where are we?"

"My room," Tarrick answered, not looking up.

"Why?"

"Because I moved you in here." Tarrick's phone rang and he answered it. "Now is a bad time," he said to the caller.

"Father—" Matthew heard Tane's voice on the other end.

"The decision has been made. You're going to Russia."

There was a sound akin to a growl that came through the phone, then an angry 'fine' and the call disconnected.

Samantha pushed away from Matthew and went over to Tarrick. She crossed her arms and narrowed her eyes at him.

Tarrick set his tablet down. "May I help you?"

"Stand up," she ordered.

"Samantha..." Matthew said as a warning as he got out of the bed as well.

"It's alright." Tarrick said as he stood, wearing an amused grin.

Samantha walked around him, carefully studying his body. When she completed her lap, she returned to Matthew. "Do you want me to like him or hate him?" she asked.

Samantha was strange sometimes. "Um," was all Matthew got out.

"I'll hate him for now." She shot a glare at Tarrick. "You call me Samantha or Oracle. Where's Jet?"

"Playing with Asper outside." Asper was a gargoyle from Tarrick's estate. Maybe Tarrick's familiar, but Matthew wasn't sure how all that worked, nor was he sure how gargoyles played.

Samantha growled. It wasn't deep or really menacing but Matthew put his hand on her shoulder to stop her anyways. Her fangs came down and she grabbed his arm.

"No feeding," Tarrick said before she was able to sink her teeth into flesh.

"But, I haven't eaten since I threw up everything yesterday."

"No feeding," Tarrick repeated as he buttoned up his top buttons. He grabbed a tie from the desk.

"Now I really don't like you."

"Somehow," Tarrick said as he tied his tie, "I think I'll live. Both of you have clothes waiting in the bathroom. Go shower."

Matthew pulled Samantha into the bathroom with him. It was luxurious, worthy of a high-ranking incubus. The shower had multiple showerheads and places to sit, and there was a separate huge spa tub.

"Ooooh, it has jets for bubbles," Samantha said, running over to the tub. "Do you think he'll be mad if we take a bath instead?"

"Yes. Go shower."

She pouted as she stripped and got in. The water was warm as soon as it turned on. Before Matthew removed his clothes, he tried to heal away the rotting skin but it didn't work. He balled his fists and tried again.

Still nothing.

Samantha, wet and dripping, grabbed his arm. "I already know, you can stop hiding it from me."

"I'm sorry," Matthew whispered.

"You only have to be sorry if you actually turn into a ghoul. If you do, I'll be so freaking pissed off. Now come on."

Matthew stripped and joined her in the shower. She looked over the skin for a moment then averted her eyes.

"Are you happy at all?" he asked, as he lathered up.

"Sometimes. I'd rather be with vampires than with people who want to kill them." She tossed him a loofah. "But...not everyone here is the same. There are some nice people. And the High King doesn't treat me like he treats you."

She turned on the rest of the showerheads, creating a lot of noise. "Are there cameras in here?" she whispered. Her hearing wasn't sensitive enough to pick up the buzz of a camera.

"No," Matthew whispered back. "But there could be hunters."

Samantha looked around. "There's not, I can sense them. They don't know that though."

Matthew cocked his head slightly and she smiled at him. She got up on her tiptoes and whispered in his ear. "I will see you become what you're meant to be."

"What does that mean?"

Samantha smiled up at him. "You are the Prince of princes."

Twenty-Four

As much as he tried, Matthew wasn't able to pull any more information from Samantha.

She 'didn't know yet'. Or so she said. Matthew always got the sense she knew far more than she let on, but kept things from him for some strange reason.

Showered, dried, and dressed, Matthew and Samantha exited the bathroom.

"Follow," Tarrick said, tucked a tablet under his arm, and marched out of the room. He led them down several levels.

"Are we going to see the minotaur?" Samantha asked when they got off the elevator, passing through the security doors.

"No." Tarrick did not elaborate.

The room they entered was small with one opening that had a metal hallway that went in two directions. Matthew glanced inside and could see many different passages.

A maze. The entire floor was one gigantic maze.

No wonder Samantha asked about a minotaur.

"I thought you might enjoy hunting with your child," Tarrick said to Matthew. "There's a human in the maze. You can kill it or not, compel it or not, it's up to you." Tarrick pointed to a small cage near the door. "Put the human or body in there when you are done with it. Once you are finished here, Samantha is free to do whatever it is she does all night. But, Matthew, you are to return to my room."

Tarrick left, not waiting for any comments.

Matthew grabbed Samantha's shoulder. "Is this something you want to do? Last time we tried to hunt it didn't go all that well."

Samantha bounced up and down. "That was forever ago. I want to try but I don't think I want to kill them." Her fangs and claws came out and she looked up at him with red eyes.

"Well then, what are you waiting for?" Matthew's irises turned red. "Go hunt the human."

She tore off into the maze. Matthew stayed behind her, letting her do the tracking. They hit several dead ends but eventually she found her prey. A male, somewhere in his twenties.

She froze, keeping around the corner so the human couldn't see them. She stalked him for so long that Matthew wondered if maybe she had changed her mind about feeding. He didn't mention it or rush her. If she didn't want to do something, she'd let him know. Besides, he was enjoying spending the time with her.

When the lost human sat down, defeated, she waved her hand to shoo Matthew away. He had no idea what her plan was but he went around a corner to hide.

"Hello?" she called out.

"Uh, hello?" the human called in response.

"Hey! I thought I was alone here. Where are you?" Samantha's lie sounded natural, her voice sweet with just the right hint of worry.

"Keep talking, I'll come to you," the male said.

"Oh, uh, I'm not sure you'll want to do that."

"Why?"

"Because I'm not human and you might be scared of me," she said. Matthew wondered where she was going with this. If this were his hunt, he would have scared the human so he could give chase—fear provoked his vampiric nature.

"What are you?" the man asked.

She ignored his question. "What did you do to end up in here?"

"I...betrayed someone. What are you?" he asked again.

"I'm a vampire."

"Are you going to kill me?"

Keeping out of sight, Matthew could hear her on the move. She must have revealed herself to him because he gasped. "P-please don't kill me."

The scent of the human's adrenaline pumping was driving Matthew crazy. Unable to help himself, he ran behind the human. It'd been so long since he'd been allowed to hunt. He stayed quiet, not alerting Samantha's prey to his presence. She stood just a few feet in front of him.

"Show me your neck," she said, looking into the male's eyes, and drawing power from the bond. Even still, her compulsion would only last a few minutes at most.

The human's breathing slowed and he tilted his neck. Samantha bounced on the balls of her feet, excited that she had managed to compel someone for the first time. Matthew loved seeing her happy. She pressed into the human's body and wrapped her hands around him to keep him in place, then sank her fangs into his neck. Matthew could feel her pleasure and nearly groaned watching her feed. He'd give anything to have his fangs back right now and join her.

After a few pulls of blood, Matthew yanked the man away from her. She stood in a blood haze.

"More," she said.

"We have all night, you have to make him last."

She blinked hard, shaking away the effects of feeding.

The compulsion began to wear off and the male's fear skyrocketed. Matthew looked him in the eyes. "You think you're alone in this maze, go try to find a way out," he said, compelling the human before releasing him.

He waited until the human was far from them, then had Samantha go for him again.

The two of them spent the night repeating the process five more times before the human was low enough on blood that taking anymore would put him in danger. The final time, Matthew compelled the human to forget what happened while he carried him to the cage.

Spending all night hunting but not feeding left him hungry as hell. Even his soavik was bothering him.

"That was fun," Samantha said as they stepped on the elevator.

Matthew nodded in agreement. "What are you doing the rest of the night?"

"I'm going to be taken to the High King for some vision thing. Don't worry about it." Samantha leaned into him and he hooked his arm around her. "I miss Devak," she said with a heavy sigh. "Do you think that at the end of it all you and me will get that house together?"

Matthew squeezed her tighter. "You're the one that sees the future, you tell me."

"The knife in my back hurts," she said, her voice sounded different; distant.

Matthew watched as her eyes turned all white.

"The eyes in the dark. Ruin will walk the earth. The unbinding binds us all."

Samantha was gone. Replacing her was a young woman hounded by visions she couldn't control. Matthew grabbed both of her arms and held her tight so that she wouldn't hurt herself. She struggled against him. "The Pit is unsealed but the god cannot leave."

The elevator doors opened and standing on the other side was Prescott with a team of hunters. "We'll take her, Matthew."

He desperately wanted to stay with her and started to protest but Prescott shot him a hard glance, letting him know that she was going with him no matter what. He released her and took a step away. A hunter put soft leather cuffs on her wrists and connected them behind her back.

"Remember, Matthew, this isn't my first oracle. She won't be hurt," Prescott said.

"Your flower will wilt," Samantha mumbled to Prescott.

He ignored her. "The elevator will take you to the Lord General's room."

Matthew watched the team of hunters take her away as the doors closed. He thumped his head against the wall as the elevator began to move.

He felt so helpless. All he wanted to do was protect her and he couldn't do shit.

When he entered Tarrick's room, the Lord General was working at his desk. Matthew bowed and waited by the door.

Tarrick snapped his two laptops shut. "Samantha will be okay."

Matthew nodded, still worried.

"You don't speak much anymore," Tarrick said as he stood.

"No," was all Matthew could think to say.

Tarrick came around the desk and leaned his butt against it, crossing his legs at the ankles. "Or cuss."

"You didn't like my cussing anyways."

"Now that it's gone, I kind of miss it." Tarrick's deep blue eyes perused Matthew's body, starting at his face and falling lower. He licked his lips and smiled. "It's not the only thing I miss."

Matthew became extremely self-aware. He wasn't sure what to do with his hands and his body felt too big. He awkwardly pressed his arms into his sides. "What are you doing, Lord General?"

"Flirting."

"Why?"

"I thought it would be fun."

Matthew looked down at the hardwood floor and said nothing. He wasn't going to let Tarrick get to him. He couldn't go through that. Not again.

"Did you enjoy hunting with your child?"

"Yes. Thank you for letting us do that."

"Hungry?"

"Yes."

Tarrick said nothing else. Matthew wasn't sure if he had to ask for blood or not. He wasn't sure if there were new rules to follow. The rotting skin ached and his face twisted.

"You don't have to ask," Tarrick said, reading Matthew. "You can take what I offer you."

Matthew waited for blood to be offered. Since he couldn't smell any in the room, he expected a hunter to show up any moment now with his cold blood. Stale. Gross. Old.

He didn't expect Tarrick's hands to turn into claws, nor did he expect Tarrick to raise a clawed finger to his own neck to cut a thin line along the skin. It started at the back and trailed nearly to his collarbone. A stripe of red appeared as blood collected and dripped out.

The smell of it was irresistible, hitting Matthew like a drug. It was Tarrick's scent of night and earth intensified. Matthew's vampire side came rushing forward. He barely had the self-control to stand still.

"Why would you do that?" Matthew asked, his voice strained.

"Why do you think? I desire you—"

God. Matthew's whole body shuddered as he watched blood pool and drip down Tarrick's neck and onto his crisp, white dress shirt, the bright crimson staining the collar.

"—and you desire me," Tarrick said; low. Seductive.

Matthew took a step away but he couldn't pull his eyes off Tarrick. He watched his pulse beat under the skin. "No," he forced himself to say. "Not anymore."

Tarrick tilted his head ever so slightly to expose more of his neck. "No?"

Closing his eyes, Matthew tried to block out what was happening.

"No. You were right, I never loved you."

"Who said this was about love?"

"No," Matthew repeated. He wanted to say 'this has always been about love' but couldn't get the words out.

"Open your eyes."

Matthew obeyed and his gaze fell to Tarrick's neck once more.

Tarrick removed his tie at a leisurely pace and unhooked the top button. Matthew's leather pants grew uncomfortably tight. Why did Tarrick have to be so damn good looking? Matthew couldn't help but stare at his warrior body, layered with hard slabs of muscle that flexed and stretched with each disciplined movement. It was so un-fucking-fair.

One corner of Tarrick's mouth pulled up into a sly half-smile. "You've always enjoyed my body."

This time Matthew found the words. "It's never been just about your body. Not for me."

"Are you sure?" Tarrick asked, watching Matthew struggle.

Maybe he wasn't as sure anymore. Matthew checked to make sure there was no hold on him. There wasn't. All that was here was raw attraction. And hunger. And blood.

His gums itched as phantom fangs longed to emerge.

Tarrick raised his claw again and made another cut, this time across his collarbone. Blood seeped out, red blooming across his shirt. "You can take what I offer you," he said, repeating the rule.

Matthew couldn't hold back anymore. In an abrupt burst of movement, he crossed the space between them and pushed Tarrick down on the desk, pinning his body and grabbing him by the jaw, forcing Tarrick's head back. Matthew ran his tongue along the cut on the collarbone, licking up each incredible drop of blood. The moment he swallowed, he began to feel lightheaded, the intoxicating incubus blood enhancing every sensation and setting every synapse ablaze.

Matthew gripped Tarrick's chin tighter and turned his head so that the long cut along his neck seeped more blood. He moaned as he dragged his tongue across Tarrick's skin several times, to get every drop of blood he could before the skin knitted closed, healed by vampire saliva.

He stopped himself just short of sucking on the bloody shirt.

It took him several moments to recover. When he did, he realized that he had been grinding his erection against Tarrick's thigh.

Matthew scrambled away from the desk. Tarrick sat up, wearing a pleased smirk across his face.

A million emotions rushed through Matthew. Tarrick was insanely sexy, and terrifying, and confusing. His heart hurt.

The general said nothing as he toed off his shoes, letting them fall to the ground. Then he unbuttoned his shirt, one agonizingly slow button at a time.

Biting the bottom of his lip, Matthew watched the unhurried reveal of more and more of Tarrick's skin. It was flawless, but an illusion projected by the incubus. Matthew had seen the battle scars hidden by a glamor. Truth be told, he preferred the scars but either way he was a remarkable sight.

The incubus peeled off his shirt and slid off the desk. He sauntered over and slipped his hand around Matthew's neck, pulling him into a kiss. Matthew surrendered to it and whimpered as Tarrick's warm tongue entered his mouth, controlling every movement.

Without breaking apart or relinquishing his controlling grasp, Tarrick guided the two of them onto the bed. They fell onto the mattress and Tarrick rolled to his back, maneuvering Matthew above him.

To the outside observer, it might have looked like Matthew was the one in charge here: he was bigger and the one on top, but nothing could be further from the truth. Tarrick controlled everything—he always had.

Matthew let out a small whine as Tarrick broke the kiss, and watched as the incubus ran his claws over his own pec, leaving behind five deep cuts.

Unable to resist, Matthew lapped up the crimson liquid one cut at a time. When he was done, there was another bleeding wound across Tarrick's upper abdomen.

He grabbed Tarrick's hips and pushed him into the center of the bed so that they were no longer halfway hanging off. Then he lowered his head to Tarrick's chest and breathed in deep, taking in his alluring scent before he kissed along the wound, blood staining his lips.

When the cut on the abdomen healed, Matthew nipped and sucked at Tarrick's skin, working his way up his chest. Every dip, every muscle, worshiped.

"Mm, you never could resist me," Tarrick said, letting out a gasp of pleasure as Matthew nipped at his neck.

Matthew propped himself up on his arms and knees, then swallowed hard, looking down at the half-naked incubus below him. "Please give me my fangs back," he begged, the words already out before he even realized he was asking.

Tarrick brought a hand up and ran it over Matthew's hair. "I can't, Matthew. You aren't mine."

Matthew closed his eyes; the incubus blood had his mind swimming. Tarrick ran his claws over Matthew's chest, pressing hard enough to cause pain but not enough to break the skin. With his senses heightened, every touch was agony twisted with pleasure. Matthew wanted less; he wanted more.

The scent of fresh blood filled the air. He opened his eyes to see fresh cuts along the apex of Tarrick's hip, trailing down the V. His yearning grew as he scooted down and licked the wounds. Tarrick's hard sex tented his suit pants.

Matthew wasn't able to wait anymore: he needed to see him. All of him.

He tried to undo the button, but his long claws weren't nimble enough to unfasten it. Out of frustration, he sliced open the material and yanked Tarrick's pants and underwear off. The incubus' heavy cock bounced up and rested on his belly.

Matthew ran his tongue down the length of it, pressing his piercings against the smooth skin of the shaft.

"Devil, you feel so good," Tarrick moaned. His eyes turned from deep blue to a dark purple as he watched Matthew, who sat back on his haunches and stripped his shirt off. "Stand," the incubus ordered before Matthew could return to his cock.

Matthew hopped off the bed and started pawing at his own pants.

"Stop." Tarrick's intense eyes raked Matthew up and down. "Control yourself and finish undressing."

Sneering, Matthew flexed his claws. Tarrick tilted his head slightly, as if waiting to see if Matthew would challenge him. Matthew didn't. His claws became fingers and he removed his boots and leather pants, his hard dick bobbing as he freed it. A pleased croon came from Tarrick, who crawled over and grabbed the base of Matthew's rod and pulled it to his lips.

The warm sensation of entering Tarrick's wet mouth nearly sent Matthew tumbling to the ground as pleasure rocked him and his knees buckled. He gripped Tarrick's shoulders to brace himself.

"Oh god," he managed.

Tarrick's tongue flicked his piercing, sending vibrations down his shaft to his balls. The points of Matthew's claws dug hard into Tarrick's shoulders, piercing his flesh. With a clawed hand, Tarrick grabbed Matthew's hip while he pushed his mouth down on Matthew's cock, bringing all of it into him.

Matthew throbbed, his body on fire, and his mind felt like it floated away, unable to form a single coherent thought.

Tarrick pulled off him, the cock leaving his mouth with a slurping pop, and he dragged Matthew by the jaw down to the bed. This time Tarrick was on top. He rubbed their cocks together and began to secrete a smooth, silky substance that wet both of them.

Matthew's world narrowed down to only the velvety hard member rubbing against him. This was all he was now, just a single point of infinite pleasure.

It ended when Tarrick pushed his knees apart and dragged his dick downwards across Matthew's balls, towards his entrance.

As he pushed the wet tip of his big shaft against Matthew's hole, Matthew's brain began to work again and reality came crashing back to him. The effects of the blood haze lessened, and he realized that Tarrick was about to fuck him.

Tarrick.

The man who lied.

The man who used love as a weapon.

The man who served the High King with unquestioning loyalty.

The new jailer, brought in to fix the broken vampire. He doubted Tarrick even wanted the job. This was just another act to gain Matthew's compliance. And in the end, everything would be ripped away from him.

Again.

Matthew wanted to stop but he didn't move. He'd let Tarrick, the High King, or the Imperator do whatever they wanted to him. He wouldn't fight anymore. He had too much to lose. Samantha. Lily.

His body tensed and he leaned his head back on a pillow, trying to block out what was about to happen, hoping that Tarrick would take what he wanted fast.

Tarrick stopped. "If the pain of me entering you is too much, I'll prepare you."

Being a vampire, the burn wouldn't bother him for long. "No, Lord General, it's fine."

Tarrick placed one hand on Matthew's chest, and ran the other down the patch of decaying skin. "I've misread you. This is too much, isn't it?"

"You can take whatever you want from me, Lord General. I won't fight. I'll do what I'm told. I'll be good."

Tarrick ran his hand across Matthew's chest and shoulders, stroking him in a soothing pattern. His face softened with concern. "Matthew, that's not what—" he stopped, took a moment to think, then said, "Yes, Matthew. You haven't fought me once and I've read the reports, you haven't lost control in a long time. You've been a good boy, and you're doing the right things to protect your daughters."

Hearing those words gave Matthew an immense amount of relief. Tension released from his muscles and he sank deeper into the bed, spreading his knees farther to give Tarrick better access to him.

"No," Tarrick pushed back slightly, letting Matthew's legs fall. "This wasn't about me using you."

"What else would this be about?"

Tarrick took a deep breath and his eyes faded from purple to blue. "I was hoping to feed you. And maybe have some mutually enjoyable sex in the process."

Matthew scooched up a little to lean against the headboard. His arousal waned, his dick rested heavy on his thigh. "I don't need to feed sexually to live. I hardly notice the pain anymore."

"But the pain is still there, correct?"

Matthew nodded slowly.

"The pain is likely contributing to your melancholia. To the ghouling. You have to feed. It doesn't have to be off me. Rosaline is willing to feed you, or there's feeders—both human and incubi—here in the building. You can choose from one of them if you wish."

Matthew really didn't want to do that but maybe it wouldn't be so bad with a human. Or an incubus he didn't know personally. And it might be better if he got to choose his partner himself. Maybe.

Tarrick got off the bed and picked up his ruined clothes. When he disappeared into the bathroom, Matthew redressed and straightened the bed.

When Tarrick emerged, he was fully clothed in a dark blue suit, this one had a fitted vest under the jacket. He looked good. He always did. Matthew stood beside the bed, his head turned down slightly as he waited for instructions.

"Take a seat, there's something we need to discuss," Tarrick said, pointing to the bed. As Matthew sat, Tarrick leaned against his desk and crossed his arms.

"I'm never going to apologize for what I did to you," he started. Matthew's heart sank a little. "It was my duty to break you and keep you in line. Back then, you were just an anomaly, a mystery I was trying to solve. I didn't even consider the possibility that you had been sired by a god." Tarrick paused and rubbed his forehead. He took a deep breath in before continuing. "But...I really did believe you'd be able to find a place among our people, and I spent a considerable amount of time and resources trying to convince others of the same. You think that I don't care about you, but that isn't true.

"I've lost three mates, and I'm a thousand years old, I don't allow my heart to open at any rate that would be considered reasonable to anyone else...but every time I'm around you, you affect and surprise me in unexpected ways. I enjoy your company. I say all this with the knowledge that you won't believe a word because I deceived you."

He looked down at the ground for a moment as if he was deciding if he should tell Matthew something. "When I was captured by you, you never erased my memory about turning Samantha."

"But—" Matthew had thought for sure he had.

"I feigned the memory loss because you would have killed me if I hadn't. And after the battle, when I came back home, I omitted that from my report to the High King because you saved my son's life during the battle against the demons. I wanted to spare you the anguish of seeing your child killed. I didn't know that she had retained her oracle powers."

Tarrick's face twisted in a rare, honest expression. Despite their past, it pained Matthew to see him suffering. "If you turn into a ghoul, I'll lose everything important to me. I'm going to do everything in my power to prevent that from happening. I need you to fight, Matthew. And you need to know, you aren't fighting alone."

Tarrick put his phone into his pocket and scooped up his tablet. He walked to the door to leave, pausing only to say, "Rosaline will take you down to the feeders. She'll be here soon." The door slammed behind him and Matthew was alone. Confused.

"Fuck."

Twenty-Five

Matthew watched the shimmering city as he waited for Rosaline. It had to be at least two or three in the morning at this point, and he wondered just how much of the tower was awake right now. Warrior incubi tended to keep night hours so they could be on call to fight vampires if needed, but he wasn't sure about other incubi and the humans that served them.

The door opened and Rosaline entered. Her normally perfect eyeliner was slightly smudged, her lip color faded, and her dress wrinkled as if it had been on the floor and she had tossed it back on. Even with the minor imperfections she looked wonderful. Her dark purple dress clung in all the right places, showing off her soft curves.

She smiled when she noticed him staring at her.

Matthew remembered to bow.

"Looks like we've both had a long night," she said with a hint of amusement.

He nodded.

"Well, come on," she said, walking from the room, her hips swaying with every step. "Do you know what you want?" she asked when they got on the elevator and it began to move.

Matthew looked at her wide-eyed. "What I want?"

"What kind of feeder you want. Male, female, human, incubus, what?"

Matthew clenched his jaw and looked down. "I don't really want to do this at all."

Rosaline looked up slightly and said, "Stop." For a split second, Matthew thought she was talking to him but then the elevator came to a halt. Whoever was watching this on the cameras stopped the elevator remotely since Rosaline couldn't use the runes. "And turn the cameras off."

There was a pause, then a voice came out of a speaker. "Lady Rosaline, I'm under orders to—"

"Hunter, I will have you thrown from the corps if you do not turn the cameras off. Five minutes, then you can turn them back on."

Matthew heard the cameras and mics power down. "They're off," he told her.

"You don't want to feed? Bullshit."

"Rosaline, I—"

An angry sound of frustration came from her, shutting him up. "You're an incubus. One that is hungry and unsatisfied. And for once I want you to turn off your damn brain and give in to your nature."

The normally sizable elevator felt incredibly small right now. He swallowed hard, not wanting to talk about this, or even talk at all right now. What had just happened with Tarrick was still playing through his mind.

Rosaline stormed at him. He backed away until he hit the wall.

She pressed her fingers into his chest. "You're an incubus. Start acting like one and fuck me."

Matthew froze for a moment. Rosaline always had a way of making him feel wanted...part of his people. With her, he could forget his problems.

He placed his thumb and index finger gently on her chin, tilting her head up as he leaned in. As delicate as a butterfly landing on a flower he brushed his lips against hers. She was tender with her response, not pushing him, not taking or demanding anything from him.

He broke away and ran his hands over her body. Caressing her skin, her curves, her lips...

"No," she said, her green eyes grew dark as she studied his face. "Save this love making stuff for Tarrick. I want it hard."

Matthew growled. The monsters inside of him wanting to take her. He gave into them, grabbing her hair and pulling, forcing her to expose her long neck. His teeth scraped along her skin.

"More," she breathed out.

He squared his body, his frame was huge compared to hers, and forced her to walk backwards until she was the one pressed against the wall. Still gripping her hair tightly, he slammed their lips together in a heated kiss. A feverish desperation took hold and Matthew couldn't get enough of her.

"Matthew...*yes*," she moaned breathlessly into his mouth.

He slipped his hands under her ass and pulled her higher as he worked his lips down her body, giving attention to her collarbone and upper chest, licking her cleavage as deep as her dress would allow. He was greedy in his desire.

Her breath shortened and low whimpers escaped her.

She clawed her hands over his arms and shoulders, feeling him through his tight shirt. He liked the way it felt, like she was worshiping his muscles, that his body pleased her. It was such a difference from Tarrick's touch, which was usually an aggressive domination of masculine control instead of fiery exploration.

With frantic need, he shoved her higher against the wall, dropped to his knees before her, and guided her legs over his shoulders. She gave a small yelp at the sudden change in position.

"Gods be praised, I want you so bad," she said as her fingers squeezed his ears then slid back behind his head, running over his short hair. Matthew pushed the bottom of her dress up around her hips and pulled her lacy underwear to the side to give him access to her.

Keeping hold of her hip with one hand, he brought the other down and spread her folds apart with his fingers. She was already glistening, the scent of her driving him crazy with need.

He had to taste her.

Unable to wait any longer, he leaned in and ran his tongue from her warm opening to her clit. She tasted divine, the way only a succubus could: sweet, tangy, and addictive. Gasping noises escaped her as he played with her clit, his mouth eager to bring her to climax.

Experimenting, he twisted his tongue slightly and aligned one of his piercings with her nub, rubbing it against her. His efforts were rewarded with a loud moan and a tight squeeze from her hands.

God, he wanted to see her body writhing with pleasure that he had brought her. He wanted to see her lose all control and, for a few moments, he wanted her to belong to him. He continued to swirl and flick her bud, falling into a pattern that would bring her close. With his free hand, he slipped two fingers into her core. She thrust her hips, riding his hand as he ate her out.

Both of them were so lost in the moment neither one of them noticed the cameras turn back on or the elevator beginning to move. It wasn't until the doors opened and the scent of seven newcomers assaulted his nose that Matthew came out of his haze.

With his face still pressed into her crotch, he began to growl. He pulled away just enough to turn his head and glowered at the group. His eyes red with anger. How dare someone interrupt this. Rosaline didn't move, she stayed with her legs on his shoulders and made no effort to cover herself up.

Standing just outside the elevator was an incubus that Matthew had seen at parties but had never personally met. Some forgettable lord from California who he couldn't care less about right now. Behind him was his team of hunter bodyguards, the commander of the team dressed like a cowboy.

Matthew's animalistic growl grew louder and he curled his lips, flashing his teeth. He wished he had his fangs.

The lord took a step backwards and the hunters went for weapons.

"I will take the next elevator. Unless—" The lord's voice was unsure but his eyes turned from a dark brown to a glowing green and he licked his lips, watching Matthew, "—you would like another."

Christ, incubi were shameless.

Rosaline waved her hand to shoo him away. "I will see you at dinner tomorrow, Lord Reval," she said, her dismissal clear. Matthew wondered if 'dinner' was food, since he knew that incubi still had to eat a little, or if it was some sort of sexual feast.

Disappointed, Lord Reval bowed. The doors slid shut but the elevator didn't go anywhere.

Rosaline put her hands on Matthew's cheeks as he looked up at her. Her breath hitched just a bit. He closed his eyes and forced them to return to their normal silver coloring, then looked back up at her again.

"Sorry," he said, knowing that it was still hard for her to think of him as a vampire.

She squeezed her long legs around his shoulders, holding him in place. "You're extremely talented with your tongue. If you have plans on stopping I might wrap a hold on you and force you to finish me because I don't want this to end."

Matthew chuckled, her warm thighs rubbing against his jaw. "Would you really?"

She squeezed tighter then relaxed her legs. "No. But you'd be leaving me extremely unsatisfied."

"Well, I can't have that." Matthew pushed his fingers deeper into her as he leaned in and licked her heat, slow at first, building passion up once more.

He almost hated to admit how much he was enjoying every moment of this. Part of him regretted shutting down around Tarrick... the sex would have been incredible. If only he could turn off the part of his brain that distrusted him.

But Tarrick wasn't here and right now all that mattered was Rosaline. Carefully, he began to feed from her, pulling golden strands that shed from her body into him. She smiled her approval and tilted her head back against the elevator wall behind her as his speed increased.

Satisfied purrs came from deep within his chest—it had been so long since he'd fed like this and he had forgotten how truly enjoyable it could be. She tasted incredible. He wanted more. The desire to feel her climax against his mouth drove him into a frenzy and she responded by clawing at the wall behind her, her chest heaving and heartbeat increasing as she neared the point of shattering.

"Oh, Matthew. Mm, please— I'm—" She didn't finish as her body hit the apex of bliss and began to tremble. Matthew moved his fingers in and out of her faster, hitting the pleasure point inside of her, all while he kept the rhythm of his tongue to draw out her orgasm as long as he could.

Her moans slowed and Matthew slowed with her, careful not to cause pain to oversensitive skin. When she finished, her body turned to jelly as she slumped against him. He pulled his fingers out and kept her up by grabbing her hips. He kissed the inside of her thighs, then carefully maneuvered out from under her to stand, but still held her up so she wouldn't fall.

"That's a good start," she said with a satisfied sigh.

"Start?" Matthew asked with a raised eyebrow.

She reached down and ran her hand along the clear outline of his cock, which strained against his leather pants. His hips bucked. It had been forever since he'd had sex with a woman and the idea of sinking into her made his dick throb.

He gripped her hips tighter and waited, unsure if she was ready to go again. He got his answer when she unbuttoned his pants and pushed them down past his hips. His length burst free and twitched as she grabbed it, her small hands making it look huge.

She cupped his full balls.

"It's been awhile, hasn't it?" she asked, massaging his sac.

He answered her question with a grunt and rolled his eyes back into his head as she stroked him and played with his piercing.

"Well?" she asked, her eyes held a wicked gleam. "Are you going to fuck me, or what?"

Faster than she could see, he grabbed her and had her against the wall again. This time he positioned her legs around his hips and lined up his cock to her entrance, then waited for her to catch up with what had just happened.

She gasped at first, then laughed and pressed her stiletto heels into his ass to bring his hips closer to hers. Matthew wished she was naked, so that he could watch her breasts heaving and kiss her navel, but the urgency of their desire outweighed the need to disrobe.

He plunged into her, and he stopped breathing as her slick core enveloped his rod. He would have moaned but he had no air in his lungs. Instead, his face twisted, lost in the ecstasy of feeling her body wrapped tight around him.

She pivoted her hips upwards, draped her arms around his neck, and grabbed on tight. With his hands on her ass, he moved her up and down on his dick, thrusting into her with burning need.

Her hot breath licked his neck, swirling around the cold collar, and her heart rate increased with every frantic thrust. He loved being inside of her warm body. Connected. One.

He grabbed and squeezed her round ass cheeks, playing with them as she rode him.

"Harder," she moaned.

Her wish was his command. His thick rod pounded into her as they both worked towards release.

She arrived at hers first, biting his earlobe hard enough to bruise it and crying out as her body trembled. Her muscles flexed around his length as he continued to pound her.

Matthew was close and, god, he wanted this more than anything right now. Every sense he had was overwhelmed by her. She tasted sweet and salty from the sweat they had worked up. Her scent of rain and apple blossoms filled his nose, her skin felt warm and supple to his touch, her moans the most pleasing melody in his ears, and her beauty staggering.

Rosaline was perfect.

Matthew's balls drew up and his shaft thickened as he hurdled to release.

Then a rule came to him: *no coming without permission.*

Fuck.

A fraction of a second before it was too late, Matthew pulled out of Rosaline and deposited her on the ground. He backed away and squeezed the base of his cock, then gripped his balls as hard as he could to send pain shooting through him. It worked—barely. He was still close but he managed not to orgasm.

"What the Pit are you doing?" Rosaline asked, standing up. Her face a mix of post bliss and anger.

"I…I'm sorry. I'm not allowed to come."

Rosaline let out a flurry of angry words in a language Matthew didn't know. "That's one of the rules?"

He nodded. Ashamed. He tucked himself back into his pants and zipped them up.

"You can come when you're with me," she said.

Matthew wasn't sure he could. Rosaline noticed his hesitation and another string of angry words came from her but they weren't directed at Matthew. "I outrank the Imperator. Tarrick does also, even if Prescott doesn't act like it." They might outrank him but they weren't the ones who forced him to eat silver, or caged him. Rosaline softened. "Would you feel more comfortable if I had him or Didi tell you this?"

Matthew nodded again.

Rosaline placed a hand on Matthew's abdomen and scanned him. When she seemed satisfied he had indeed fed on her, she pulled away. "Alright. I'll clear it up by tomorrow and then we'll continue this. I owe you an orgasm."

"You owe me nothing, my lady."

Rosaline's lips pulled up into a scheming smile. "Fine. Then you owe me. I was cheated out of watching you come and tasting you while you did. If it wasn't so late I'd make it happen tonight but I'm exhausted and you don't look much better."

She was right, he wasn't much better. The night had him spinning with emotional turmoil.

Every time I'm around you, you affect and surprise me in unexpected ways. I enjoy being near you. Tarrick had said. It only served to confuse Matthew more. He wasn't sure what he felt anymore. What he wanted. His future was too uncertain. He had lost too much recently.

At the very least, it seemed Tarrick had been sincere in his motives to stop Matthew from turning into a ghoul. It had been kind of him to let him hunt with Samantha. And to send Rosaline up. He cared for her a great deal.

The elevator began to move again.

"What are you thinking?" Rosaline asked.

He wouldn't have minded talking about everything with her but not with unknown people watching through the cameras. "I was thinking about how bad my balls are aching."

"So I shouldn't run my hands over your beautiful incubus cock?"

Matthew shuddered. "You're mean, my lady."

She laughed; it was both playful and cruel at the same time. The doors opened and Matthew was on the floor to his room. Rosaline pressed a kiss onto his cheek. "You are one of us, Matthew. There's a place for you, don't lose hope." He wished he shared her sense of optimism but he couldn't. She pulled away, giving him permission to leave.

When Matthew entered his room, Samantha was on the bed waiting for him. She looked exhausted, as she usually did after a night of vision assaults.

Jet—in his dog form—lay in the corner of the room; a grey and white striped cat curled on top of him.

"Um," Matthew said.

"That's Asper."

"Seriously? Tarrick's gargoyle is a cat?" Matthew really shouldn't have been surprised. At least they got along. He sat down beside her and stroked her arm. "How are you feeling?"

"Sleepy. It'll take a while for my brain to sort out what I saw."

Matthew kissed her on the forehead before he went into the closet to change into some pajama bottoms.

"Father?"

"Yes, darling?"

"What does being in love feel like?"

Matthew paused halfway through taking off his pants. "Uh, well. It's like…you're alive inside. Like everything is brighter…and more frightening. Love is caring for someone so much it hurts because it makes you vulnerable. Lasting love is hard work and compromise, but it's worth it. Why do you ask?"

She didn't answer but when Matthew came out of the closet he noticed that she was trying to hide a smile. Come to think of it, her emotions had been all over the place lately…almost as if she was falling for someone and wasn't sure about it.

How had he missed this?

"Who is it?" he asked. If it was someone in the tower it couldn't be good.

She shrugged, acting innocent. "Who is what?"

"Who are you falling for?"

"No one. I've had a lot of offers is all. I haven't taken any."

Matthew was relieved. "Good. I'd hate to accidentally kill someone."

Samantha scowled at him, and he winked at her.

"Maybe I should sleep in my own room tonight," she said in a playful huff and started to push off the bed.

Matthew grabbed her and pinned her down. "Nope." He shifted so that they were spooning and kept his arms wrapped around her.

"Do you think the Lord General will let us hunt again?" she asked once she had wiggled to a comfortable position.

Matthew brushed her brown hair from his face and tucked it behind her ear. "I don't know. I hope so."

Sunrise was still a few hours away. But he enjoyed resting beside Samantha in thoughtful silence. It had been a long night.

The next was even longer.

Twenty-Six

Samantha was missing from Matthew's arms. He shot out of bed looking for her.

"Your sired child is unharmed," Tarrick said.

Matthew was in Tarrick's room, on top of Tarrick's bed. The general was in his incubus form: wings, hooves, pointed ears, horns, claws, glowing eyes, tail—the whole bit—but he hadn't grown in size yet. He looked…impressive. Matthew's balls twinged with a reminder they still existed. Matthew ignored them.

Silva stood in front of Tarrick, wearing winter hunting attire, with a heavy black cloak and thicker leathers. On her hips hung her folding crossbow, along with stakes, colorful vials of liquid, and throwing knives.

She placed a bluish-purple iridescent armor breastplate on Tarrick's chest. At five-foot-nothing she had to reach up to hook it over his shoulders. If he were his full height of seven-eight, she'd have to get a stool.

Silva uttered some magic words and the breastplate unfolded into full armor, covering his body. He leaned over and she put armor on his horns.

"We don't have all night," Silva said, finishing with some straps. "Get dressed, Matthew."

Matthew looked to Tarrick who pointed at a compression suit draped over a chair.

Matthew was in the suit and standing next to Silva in a heartbeat. The custom-made compression suit had no right sleeve, allowing his tattoo to be exposed, and a glove on his left hand covered all but the tips of his fingers, so that his claws could form unhindered.

Tarrick stood up straight and spread his wings. Silva attached armor strips on top of them while he adjusted his right gauntlet. "Hiroto thinks he's tracked the body hopper demon but our normal methods of detection aren't working. You're going to help track it tonight."

"I still can't believe it made it to the upper levels," Silva said, walking around Tarrick, making sure everything was in place. Then she grabbed a leather chest piece that was resting on the floor by the desk.

While Tarrick triple checked his armor in the mirror, Silva brought the chest piece to Matthew. "Arms out and lift your feet one at a time."

Matthew did what he was told and Silva raised the armor to his chest. She spoke a word and it expanded around him, encompassing his entire body except his head and tattooed right arm, which had pauldrons and his shackle, but was otherwise bare.

His left arm, however, was plated and had two black leather straps that stretched across his chest.

Silva secured the leather straps in place.

The dull hum of magic buzzed around him and it felt as if the armor plugged into his collar, drawing power from the Night Stones.

Judging by the way Tarrick's eyes drifted over Matthew's body, he must have liked what he saw. "Come see," he said and stepped out of the way of the mirror to make room.

Matthew looked at himself. The armor was black with metal rivets. The leather straps across his chest made his shoulders look insanely broad. A spiked tasset covered the top of his thighs. Below it, the leather armor went all the way down to his feet, forming into heavy boots.

The pauldrons were most impressive: the sides looked like gargoyles' faces and the top had sharp metal ridges. A thick gorget protected his collarbones and went all the way up his neck, covering his lower jaw. He turned his head from side to side and found the armor moved with him like a second skin.

Cloth strips covered his ass, crotch, and sides.

Wanting to see, he brought his vampire side forward. His long black claws and crimson eyes added to the powerful semblance. He looked like an evil dark lord: menacing and threatening. Matthew wouldn't want to face what he saw in the mirror on the battlefield, and he'd only look more frightening when his exposed arm was bleeding and he had Bloodreaver in his hand.

An approving sound came from Tarrick. "You like it."

"Yes, Lord General."

"Prescott and I debated if we should cover your right arm but we worried it'd interfere with summoning the weapon. We can adjust it later once we have more time."

Tarrick walked around Matthew, inspecting every inch of him. "Your armor isn't as protective as mine but it'll stop most projectiles, including bullets and most weapons, unless they're blessed or magical, but the arm guard can block those. Use it like a shield. Like the Imperator's armor, it'll move with you, and you should be able to run at full speed without any problems. We designed it to complement your fighting style."

Matthew wasn't sure what to say. 'Thank you' felt like it might be right but he didn't really feel like thanking a captor for armoring him so that he'd be better at killing people he didn't want to kill. Demons though...he didn't have an issue with killing demons.

Silva's comm beeped. "They're assembled and waiting for us in the lobby."

With no further delay, Tarrick marched from the room, and motioned for them to follow with a flick of his tail.

Matthew marveled how easily his new armor shifted around him as he walked. It felt as if it wasn't even there.

"There's a hook on the belt," Tarrick said. "When we let you summon your weapon, you'll keep your shackle there. If you fail to put it back on when we tell you to, you'll be disciplined. Understand?"

"Yes, Lord General."

In the elevator, he glanced over at Silva who was studying him. He missed being close with her but he had betrayed her trust when he had tricked her and compelled her to do something against her will. She hadn't forgiven him, nor had he forgiven himself. Since then, he made it policy to not compel friends if he could avoid it. He didn't even like commanding Samantha around, even though she was his sired child.

"You're right, he doesn't talk much anymore," she said.

Well, that's slightly humiliating. Everyone had been calling him out on it, but he didn't have as much to say anymore. The less he opened his mouth, the less risk of punishment.

"He's not allowed to talk unless addressed. Matthew, you don't have to wait to be addressed to give a report tonight. And, I do outrank Prescott and won't give you any order that goes against the High King. You won't be punished for following my command."

Rosaline must have told him what had happened the previous

night. It wasn't much of a surprise given how close they were.

"Okay, Lord General."

The doors slid open and the Argonauts were waiting there, except for Hiroto, who was likely hiding in the shadows or off tracking the demon.

The group assembled consisted of Tarrick, Silva, Prescott, himself, and three others he had faced in battle but didn't know personally.

Tarrick motioned to the bald hunter who had on those massive gauntlets. He didn't wear thick armor on his chest, rather just a shirt to cover the green glow of his runes. Matthew would bet money he'd go shirtless if he could get away with it. He had a poorly set crooked nose, bald head, a mean grin, and oversized muscles. He looked like a brawler through and through. "This is Commander Nellis, 'Mac' for short. He's based out of Queen Cathail's household in Ireland."

Nellis grunted at him.

Tarrick motioned to a cowboy-looking hunter. The guy was a walking stereotype with boots, trench coat, hat, two small six-shooter-looking crossbows attached to his belt—the whole nine yards, right down to his silver spurs. "This is Commander Lock, he's in California under Lord Reval...whom you met last night."

Lock chuckled and Matthew glared at him, but Lock didn't stop smiling or seem in the least bit intimidated. If he was in charge of protecting the only incubus to still have territory in the vampire infested California, then he had to have nerves of steel.

"And this here is Commander Vikström, we call her 'Vik'."

"Hejsa!" she said with a friendly wave and slight Swedish accent. She had blond hair and large blue eyes. Her hunter uniform looked like something a blacksmith would wear with a heavy apron. She smelled like soot and chemicals. Slung over her shoulder was a massive grenade launcher. "I faced you last year. I hope we get to fight again. I've adjusted my grenades and you won't be able to throw them back at us anymore." She patted her huge weapon as if it was a child.

"You know they'd be more effective if ya didn't tell him," Lock said with a slight drawl in his voice. Matthew wondered how old he was. Hunters could have extended lives, it was possible that he actually lived on the American frontier.

Vik smiled and shrugged. "I just wanted to give him a proper warning."

The group followed Tarrick out of the lobby.

"Vik serves King Hindrik in Sweden. Although he might be looking to replace her since she burned down half his castle," Tarrick said with a smile.

"It wasn't my fault, General!"

Tarrick laughed. "It was, but I don't really think he'd ever replace you even if you did cost him a small fortune." Vik looked relieved. "But I think he's going to build you a new lab a few miles away." Tarrick continued as he marched outside. "Hiroto will meet us there, and Silva is just filling in as their sixth until the Imperator finds a new member."

Prescott waved his hand as if annoyed by that topic of conversation. "Maybe if you told Cullip to stop crying about his arm and rejoin his team…"

"You tell him. It's your team. Personally, I'd rather keep him at Ashwood."

"We're doing fine with five anyways. We don't even need Silva here tonight—no offense, Commander."

Silva, who was in front, stopped, and the entire group nearly toppled on her at the abrupt change in pace. "None taken, but the last time I left the general's side he was kidnapped by vampires." Her eyes flicked over to Matthew, "I'm not going to let that happen again."

"Demigod and a guardian," Matthew said under his breath.

Everyone looked at him. He forgot hunters had enhanced hearing too. Oops.

"Why don't you repeat that, Matthew? Little louder this time." Her hands dropped close to the stake on her hip.

Matthew looked to Prescott and Tarrick. He didn't want to get in trouble for speaking without being addressed. Tarrick nodded permission and Matthew took a deep breath. "You said he was kidnapped by vampires, Commander. But he was kidnapped by a demigod and a guardian."

Silva narrowed her eyes at him. "A *vampire* demigod and a blood guardian who served the *vampire* god of blood. So. Vampires."

Well, Matthew wasn't about to correct her about Devak being a guardian of Ilertha…but he guessed they were both vampires in a way. He gave her a slight bow, conceding the point.

Prescott grabbed Matthew's left arm and slipped a comm under the armor, then stuck an earpiece in his ear. "You read the protocols for using this?"

"Yes, Imperator." The book had been dry as hell but he had it all memorized.

The group piled into two SUVs. Matthew was with Tarrick, Silva, and Lock, who drove. The rest went to the second car.

While they drove, Matthew's eyes drifted out the window. He watched as they passed by humans, and then he looked up at the moon. It was nice to be out of the tower and he wished he was allowed to go into the city, even if he had to go under guard.

He felt Tarrick watching him and lowered his eyes to the ground, worried that maybe he shouldn't long for things anymore.

"How did you know where to find the Lord General?" Silva asked and Matthew looked over at her, unsure of what she meant. "When you captured him, how did you know he'd be at that church?"

Matthew looked to Tarrick who said, "I've deduced two possibilities: one, that the vampires have a spy that gave away my movements that day or two, your oracle child told you."

"It was Samantha," Matthew said in confirmation.

"She has to be physically close to someone to see their future, doesn't she?" Silva asked.

"When Devak and I kidnapped you, she was under your feet. I hid her in the ground."

"Seriously?" Silva sat back in her chair and crossed her arms. "Deceit comes to you far easier than anyone gives you credit for."

Matthew looked back down at the floor. It stung him to hear her say that. He wanted to apologize but she'd never accept it. Stubborn woman.

The rest of the short drive passed in silence and within a few minutes they were at the brick building that housed the leystone in New York. Teams of hunters patrolled the building, keeping to the shadows.

Silva handed Tarrick his weapon—a kanabō with silver spikes—and Matthew shifted a step away from it, following the others.

The inside of the building looked like an abandoned office with boarded up windows. There was a large stone with runic symbols in the center of one of the empty rooms.

"Matthew," Tarrick said as the group gathered, "if we get into a fight, you're allowed to drink blood if you need it."

Matthew blinked slowly at Tarrick. "I don't mean to offend, Lord General, but it's going to be a messy affair without fangs."

"Oh," Prescott said. "I have something for you for that." He held out his hand, summoned in a straw, and held it out to Matthew.

The Argonauts burst up laughing. Matthew tried to look pissed off, but it was actually kind of funny and he couldn't help but crack a small smile and shake his head.

Prescott touched the stone and in a flash they were in a new location.

Matthew smelled the demon at once. Wait. No. Demon*s*. Plural. Lots of demons.

Twenty-Seven

"Seventeen," Matthew said.

"What?" Prescott asked.

"Seventeen demons, Imperator."

He memorized the layout of the area in an instant. They were in some sort of warehouse. The leystone was covered by a canvas tarp and hidden among boxes.

Around him, the hunters' eyes glowed green as they activated their runes that let them see in the dark. Warrior incubi had okay night vision. It wasn't quite what vampires had but Tarrick would be able to see well enough.

"Where?" Prescott asked.

"Close," a young-sounding voice said. Hiroto appeared beside the group, crouched on a box. His red mask was pulled over his face and his cloak covered his head, but he looked like he was smiling under there. "They have a stable portal open. But it's small, only lesser demons can get through it. Although I've only counted sixteen."

Nellis rolled his shoulders and cracked his knuckles. "Mother Mary, how did they open a portal to this realm?"

Prescott said some words in Latin. Matthew couldn't translate them but he was pretty sure the Imperator was cussing.

"We'll investigate once Matthew gets it closed. Did you see if there were other body jumpers, Hiroto?"

Hiroto hopped off his box and sniffed the air. "I can't be sure."

"Alright, we'll handle this like Millina Ridge. Matthew you'll hang back with Tarrick until I give you an order." Like a well-oiled machine, the Argonauts began to fan out. Even Silva fell into place with ease.

"Imperator?" Matthew asked, stopping them.

"I don't want to hear complaining," Prescott growled.

"Uh, no, quick question. How do you actually kill a body jumper?"

"Easy," Vik said, her voice friendly as ever, "keep it from finding a new body for two minutes or trap it in a body and kill its host. Oh, or you can kill its anchor body but those are nearly impossible to find. If you want to destroy the jumper for good, you need to use a blessed weapon but sending it back to the Pit is usually fine. It takes them a while to crawl back out."

"Right. Okay. So, another quick question, what do we do if it's inside the Lord General?"

All six hunters turned and looked over to Tarrick, who hadn't moved. Sweat beaded his face and his eyes were unfocused, fighting hard against some internal battle they were not privy to.

Matthew had noticed that Tarrick had been uncharacteristically silent since they had teleported in. At first, he thought that maybe he was letting Prescott run this show, but he'd never known Tarrick to just passively stand aside when he could be giving orders. And he *knew* he had smelled seventeen demons, not sixteen.

"Shit," Silva said.

Tarrick grinned, his teeth sharp and demonic. His eyes clouded over with an oily blackness. He charged at Silva but she teleported away before the kanabō could meet its mark.

Vik aimed her grenade launcher while Lock pulled his six-shooter bolt throwers out, both ready to fire.

"Non-lethal," Prescott ordered.

"You cannot bring me down unless you kill this body," the creature hissed.

"Yeah, but we can knock you out just fine," Nellis said, bringing up his fists for an attack. Prescott held up his hand to stop them. The hunters had the creature surrounded. Matthew had his claws out. It couldn't take them all and it knew it.

The demon using Tarrick like a meat suit looked at Matthew and smiled. "She had us convinced you had died at birth. I've already told the others you live. They're coming for you."

Great. Now demons wanted his ass also? Matthew sighed heavily and added this information to the 'this sucks' pile of his life. "Awesome. Tell the demons to get in line. How about you get your black cloudy ass out of the Lord General?"

It laughed. Matthew pushed power into his speed and pushed the demon against a wall. This thing might be wearing Tarrick but it didn't possess his abilities or intelligence. It hadn't expected Matthew to move so quickly, nor pluck the weapon from his hand with ease. It had no idea what Matthew was capable of.

"Leave his body and do not enter anyone here," Matthew commanded, compelling the demon. He could feel the demon struggling against him but it wasn't strong enough to fight both Tarrick and Matthew at the same time. It threw back Tarrick's head and swirling mist poured from Tarrick's mouth. It rose into the air and escaped through a vent in the ceiling.

Tarrick's body spasmed, and Matthew grabbed him before he fell to the ground.

"That was unpleasant," Tarrick said, gathering himself. "We need to find a way to prevent that from happening."

"The last time we fought demons we never found a good way to deal with body jumpers, but that was two thousand years ago."

"Well, they know we're here now. I'll have an update in two," Hiroto said and teleported away to gather intel.

Without waiting on an order, the hunters took up positions around the warehouse. Tarrick reclaimed his weapon and took up a spot by the door.

Matthew felt useless. He wasn't part of this team and didn't know how they did things. Without orders, he just awkwardly stood where they left him. He expanded his senses slightly. Besides the demons, he could smell a water source nearby and lots of wood, but more than a forest—stacked timber maybe. It was chilly and the windows had a layer of frost on them. Snow piled on the ground outside and he heard an owl hooting in the distance.

The scent of surrounding warehouses, oil, boxes, rats, and metal drifted across his nose. He was in northern US or Canada but wasn't able to pin the location down.

"What are you doing?" Tarrick asked.

"Trying to figure out where we are, Lord—" Matthew didn't finish his title when Tarrick glared at him.

"Outside of Saskatoon."

"Isn't that vamp territory?"

Lock laughed from his position of watching out the second story window. "Don't worry your pretty head none. We'll protect you from the big bad vampires."

It took everything Matthew had not to roll his eyes, a habit he picked up from Samantha.

Hiroto's voice came over the comm. "Three more just came through the portal and it looks like they're getting ready to receive even more. We need to stop it now or call in backup."

Prescott responded, letting him know they were on their way. The hunters moved out, leaving Matthew alone with Tarrick.

"Do you know what the demon was talking about? Why they would want you?" Tarrick asked.

Matthew closed his eyes and rubbed his forehead, his head aching. "I haven't a clue. I'll ask the next one I compel, but if I had to guess the answer is going to be something along the lines of *'you're a demigod and I want you to bend over for me'*."

His comment was met with silence. He shouldn't have said that. It was out of line and he'd probably pay for it later, but he was frustrated right now. Being so close to nature, to night, to a human population only a few miles away…he wanted to go run and hunt and fuck.

Only a few steps away from freedom and he knew he'd never taste it again. Even if he knew how to remove the collar—and get Samantha out safely—it'd be followed by the Judge coming to kill him.

His armor suddenly felt like a prison, and his hip started to hurt.

Tarrick grabbed Matthew's elbow, the touch warm. "This is a bad time for you to fall apart, warrior. Stay with me."

Matthew nodded. He could keep it together. The pain on his hip lessened.

Tarrick opened his comm to listen in on the Argonauts. They were picking off demons one at a time with surgical precision.

The scent of blood reached Matthew's nose. Demon and hunter. The comm chatter became a little more frantic and Matthew's tattoos turned scarlet at the edges in anticipation of a fight. He rubbed his arm. "Going to send me in, coach?"

"In a moment. Let the hunters do their job and soften them up a bit. Right now you'd get in the way." Tarrick was calm as ever, as if he hadn't just been possessed by a demon. Nor did he seem to mind sitting on the sidelines while his hunters worked.

Matthew began to pace. Tarrick's eyes never left him and he wore a cocky half smile on his face as if he knew something Matthew didn't.

"Don't you—" Matthew started, then fell quiet. He hadn't been addressed and he wasn't giving a report.

"If you have questions, ask."

"Don't you find it convenient that the demons set up so close to a leystone?"

"No. Magic powers the leylines. They're tapping into it to keep the Pit portal open. That's how Hiroto found them."

"Aren't you worried this will become an incursion?"

"Sure. But it takes a lot of power to make a portal big enough for a pit commander to come through. Guardians can do it. Samantha can do it with your blood. Powerful spirit witches or covens can. But demons we're seeing here aren't that powerful."

"We've cleared enough demons, send him in," Prescott's voice said over the comm.

"Go," Tarrick ordered.

Matthew didn't wait around. As he ran out of the warehouse he heard Prescott say, '*Sa'nile*' and his left shackle fell off. He caught it and attached it to his hip as blood began to pour out of his now red tattoos. Bloodreaver formed in his hand as he ran to another warehouse. The pungent scent of oily blood and the three dead demons lying in the street told him this was the right place.

He didn't bother to use any of the doors. He burst through the side wall, a cloud of concrete crumbling around him. There was a humanoid demon with a thorny body launching spikes at Vik, who was up on a walkway returning fire with grenades.

Matthew sunk Bloodreaver into the demon's back, cutting clear through its torso. He grabbed the demon's body and flung it into a different demon; a huge son of a bitch, descending upon him.

The lumbering demon hissed as spikes pierced his chest. White and green light flashed as Hiroto teleported onto the demon's shoulders and sank his dual daggers into its neck, while Lock appeared at its side and unleashed a flurry of silver bolts into its rib cage.

The hunters had that one covered.

Around Matthew, the warehouse was a mess: greasy demon blood smeared everywhere, their bodies in pieces, and smashed boxes littered the ground. In the center, there was a tear in the air itself, just large enough for a single humanoid to slip through it—the portal.

At the far side of the building, Matthew spotted Nellis. His chest was ripped to shreds but that didn't slow him as he punched a demon with a sickening crunch and sent it crashing into a wall. It hit hard and slid to the ground. Matthew was on it before it had a chance to move, hacking the demon into pieces with his axe.

Silva hid behind Nellis, using his body like a shield as she popped out and fired bolts at demons.

Prescott combated a demon who also brandished a sword with equal skill. The others seemed content to let the Imperator fight without interference.

The sound of clinking metal drew Matthew's attention. He looked over in time to see a grenade bounce along the ground. A horned demon with a bastard sword emerged from the portal. Matthew surged at it and tossed the grenade into it as it exploded, painting everyone with bits of the creature. Except Vik, who dodged into a room that overlooked the warehouse floor. "That was awesome," she said.

"You're paying for my dry cleaning," Nellis said to Matthew, brushing demon skin away from his open wounds. Silva teleported away and swapped to her daggers. She sliced the front of a demon then retreated before it could respond. She repeated the process several times, slowly cutting it to death.

There were seven demons left but only three that Matthew could see on the floor. Some were retreating.

"The portal, Matthew," Prescott said, his sword piercing deep into the shoulder of the demon he was fighting. The demon screamed and twisted around. This one had a thick tail, and it smacked Prescott in his legs, sending him toppling over.

Blood. Bloodreaver whispered to him.

Matthew was on the demon before Prescott could recover. The demon blocked two attacks but Matthew was faster and landed the third. Bloodreaver fed him energy, making him faster, stronger. He could feel his eyes filling with blood and becoming crimson orbs.

He didn't want to close the portal. He wanted more demons to come through for him to fight. He got his wish when three more demons joined the fray.

Matthew smiled.

"*The portal,* Matthew," Prescott repeated.

Matthew growled at the Imperator and flashed his teeth.

"You don't want to do that. My bite is worse. Close the portal. Don't make me repeat the order again."

That sobered Matthew. He was letting Bloodreaver affect him too much.

A grenade came flying at the three demons that had just entered the room. Matthew dodged behind a shelf to avoid the blast...but this grenade was different. It exploded into a thick, sticky web, trapping the demons. The Argonauts descended on the stuck demons, felling them with ease.

Disappointment came from both Bloodreaver and Matthew. He should have rushed out but he was trying not to be reckless. Prescott was pissed enough as it was.

Before he could move to the portal, something slammed into Matthew's side and he went toppling down. A four-armed demon landed on his chest and began to claw to him.

The demon scratched at Matthew's eyes, trying to gouge them out. Matthew released his axe, it turned into a puddle of blood, but before he could try to overpower the creature, it slumped dead on top of him. Silva was standing over him, and a silver bolt stuck out of the demon's spine.

She motioned her head to the portal. Matthew pushed the demon off him and ran to finish his task, avoiding the sticky shit on the ground.

He reached out and touched the swirling black mass. Before he had a chance to close the portal, a wave of nausea hit him and he was no longer in the warehouse.

He was in the Pit.

Twenty-Eight

Surrounding Matthew was an army of demons. Hundreds of thousands, maybe more. Rivers of lava flowed around them and a jagged, unforgiving outcropping jetted from the ground like sharp teeth.

Massive pit commanders lumbered around. There were fat, round demons that looked like they were full of bile, demons that looked almost human, others that looked like monstrous animals, and every type of dreadful combination in-between.

Standing on a rocky cliff-side was a tall man who looked like their leader. He was thin and wore armor. His eyes and hair were pure black and his features were handsome: perfectly structured high cheekbones, full lips, and thick lashes.

He smiled at Matthew and it made his skin crawl.

None of the other demons reacted to Matthew's presence, and it was then that he realized he wasn't actually in the Pit but rather viewing it through the portal.

"Demigod," the thin man said. He had to be half a mile away and Matthew could hear him as clearly as if they were standing next to each other. "Join us."

"Yeah, I'll go ahead and take a pass on that one," Matthew said.

The man's smile dropped and large black wings unfurled from his back. He took to the air, flying to the portal and landing gracefully in front of Matthew.

He reached out and touched the portal, mirroring how Matthew was standing on the other side. The temperature dropped several degrees.

"You are incredible," the demon said. "Tell me your desires and I will fulfill them."

"Um. How about…no."

"Are you certain? Serve me and I will give you anything you wish." He motioned to Matthew's collar. "I can set you free."

Matthew laughed. "For the low, low cost of bowing down to a demon? Really, I'm good. But thanks."

"Serving me would be rewarding." The demon looked as if he wanted to reach out and touch Matthew. "I will care for you and all your needs, sate all your hungers. Unlock powers beyond imagining. What stops you from taking it?"

Samantha and Lily. Also, demons. Of all the lots he wanted to throw in with, demons were down at the bottom of that list.

"My reasons are my own. Who the fuck are you anyways?"

A cruel smile lifted on the alluring demon's lips. "I am Mazarus. Tell Prescott an old friend says hello, I can sense him out there. Oh, and let him know that one day his soul will be mine."

Matthew staggered as a hand ripped him away from the portal, which closed behind him. The warehouse reappeared around him and Tarrick—in his full fucking incubus form, well over seven feet tall— was holding his arm so tight it bruised.

"What just happened?" His voice was deeper and harsher than normal as he snapped Matthew's shackle back on his arm.

Around him, all the other demons were dead and Matthew noticed black blood on Tarrick's weapon. The hunters were holstering and sheathing their own weapons.

Matthew looked to Prescott then back to Tarrick. "Who is Mazarus?"

"What?" Prescott said, not hiding his shock.

Tarrick squeezed Matthew's arm tighter. "How do you know that name?"

"He introduced himself to me."

"You saw him? He's alive?" Prescott asked, taking an agitated step forward.

"Yeah. Tall guy, sharp features. I would have mistaken him for an incubus if it wasn't for his black eyes and the army of demons he had around him. His scent was kinda familiar..." a thought occurred to Matthew "...actually really familiar...jasmine...is he—"

"Yeah," Tarrick said. "He's the High King's son. Presumed dead long before my time."

"Well, he really doesn't like you, Imperator. He wanted me to tell you that your soul will be his."

Prescott scoffed. "That little brat is welcome to try and take it."

"Two thousand years in the Pit, he's not what he once was. Who knows what power he's gained in that time, don't underestimate him," Hiroto said, crouching on a shelf. Matthew hadn't noticed him until now.

"Let's get the fuck outta here," Nellis said with this thick Irish accent. "I have demon bits where they don't belong."

"I second the motion," Lock said. "My wife is going to be mighty angry that I missed dinner." Someone made a whip sound and Lock grinned. "You've seen my wife, right? I'm happy to be whipped by her."

Tarrick began to shrink back to his normal size, his armor adjusting with him. As the group returned to the leystone, the hunters playfully recounted how badass they were in that fight, the stories already taking on new, epic lives.

Matthew found himself enjoying listening to them. It was clear they were all comrades—even Silva knew them well. Loneliness tugged at his heart.

Tarrick glanced back at him. Matthew had been trailing behind but picked up the pace a little so they wouldn't think he was up to something.

"You have fifteen," Prescott told his team when they were back in the tower's lobby. They all teleported away. Except Silva, who stayed with Tarrick.

"Roshambo?" Prescott said to Tarrick.

Tarrick shook his head and walked to the elevator. "No. I'll give the report. But if he kills me, say some nice words at my funeral."

"I'll just—" Silva started.

Tarrick pointed to the space beside him. "You're my commander. Come."

"But I have demon all over me…"

Tarrick ignored the complaint, and she followed. The two of them entered an elevator and were gone. Matthew stood, still waiting for some command from Prescott.

"Well, come on," he said, waving Matthew onto a second elevator. "Why did I have to repeat the order for you to close the portal three times?"

"I'm sorry, Imperator."

"I don't want apologies, I want you to tell me why you didn't follow the order the first time."

Matthew traced his tattoos with his fingers. "I haven't been in a battle in a while, Imperator. As a vampire I enjoy killing, but coupled with the weapon…it's easy to lose control. I wanted to kill more before I closed it."

Prescott glanced at his tattoos. "Alright. I'll start training you how to resist it, but you're not going to enjoy the process. And if you make me repeat myself again, you'll enjoy that even less."

They got off on one of the hunter levels that had separate staircases connecting several floors. Prescott led Matthew into a locker room. He grabbed Matthew's armor at the chest and said a few words. It collapsed in on itself and he set it down on a bench. "You'll be responsible for keeping your own armor clean. I'll send someone to teach you how when we have some down time. Go shower and meet me in the cafeteria in ten."

Prescott teleported away and Matthew stripped out of the compression suit. He didn't dally in the shower and when he got out, there were clothes waiting for him.

Dressed, he went up two flights of stairs to a large cafeteria that hunters used. The lights were low and it was empty.

Matthew sniffed the air. He smelled incense and cherries. "Hiroto…"

He had been standing behind Matthew, stalking him, and Matthew hadn't even noticed. His cloak and mask were missing; his damp, fuzzy white fox ears perked up. "Hmm? What?"

Matthew shook his head. "How long have you been watching me?"

The fox offered a mischievous smile. "A while. I wanted to catch a glimpse of your ass. For the record, it's a fine one."

Matthew chuckled.

Hiroto winked at him. "Did you have fun tonight?"

Fun? Not really. It wasn't all terrible though. Getting out of the tower was nice. He enjoyed seeing things he never had before, and thanks to an enhanced memory he could bring up the location anytime he wanted. It was useful for filling lonely days. "I enjoyed killing the demons."

Hiroto motioned to a chair for Matthew. "Sit."

Matthew sat in the chair but didn't let himself get comfortable, knowing he would have to get back up as soon as Prescott entered. Hiroto jumped on the table and sat cross-legged in front of him. He grabbed his knees and wiggled his body a little. "So, when we gonna fuck?"

Matthew chuckled.

"Don't laugh. I'm killer in the sack. I'll even top you if that's the only way you want it."

Oh god. Thinking about Hiroto topping him had him chuckling harder...not that he wouldn't be down to try but the fox was half his size and like a third of his mass. The image of a climber scaling a mountain came to mind.

"What the fuck are you two talking about?" Nellis asked, attaching his gauntlets to his hip. It was the first time Matthew had ever seen them off. The hunter was in a tight, white muscle shirt that was about two sizes too small and dark pants. Matthew started to stand but Hiroto pushed his shoulders down. He stayed seated.

"I was trying to get laid," Hiroto said.

"You want to be fucked by the vampire? God almighty, you're such a faggot."

Matthew's eyes bugged out. He'd never heard a hunter talk that way—and certainly not around incubi who didn't really care what gender they fed from. Some had preferences but in a pinch, food was food.

Hiroto wrinkled his nose. "I'm not the one that's constantly downing vamp blood to take care of those nasty diseases you keep picking up from whores."

Nellis shrugged. "I can't help it if I like my woman a little dirty."

Jesus, that man was disgusting.

"Catholic slut." Hiroto said with a laugh.

"Lickarse dog."

"Ugly shit drip."

"Maggot cock."

A groan came from the door. Lock was standing there in civilian clothes: a button-down flannel shirt, jeans, a big belt buckle, cowboy boots; he had no weapons and even his runes were invisible. "You two at it again?"

Nellis took a seat on the other side of the table, across from Matthew. The chair creaked under his weight. "You're just jealous Hiroto likes me the most."

"Keeps me up every night," Lock said as he took a seat next to Matthew. He kicked out another chair and rested his boots on it. "Where's the others? I want to get going."

Hiroto shrugged. "They'll be here soon."

Matthew wasn't really sure what was going on but he suddenly felt really uncomfortable with the casual way the three Argonauts were sitting around him. He felt like the odd one out.

Prescott teleported in, still in his armor but clean, and Matthew stood and bowed. Prescott motioned for him to sit back down.

"Where's Vik?" the Imperator asked.

"Fashionably late," she said as she rushed in. In one hand, she held a towel that she was rubbing her sopping wet hair with, in her other she held a wine bottle full of blood. She shook the bottle. "I misplaced it, took me a few to find it."

"We're always waiting on the woman folk," Nellis said.

Silva teleported in. She hadn't had time to shower but she had removed her outer cloak, leaving her somewhat cleaner. Demon blood still smeared her skin. Vik tossed the towel at her and Silva began wiping herself off.

"How angry was he?" Prescott asked as he went to a cabinet and grabbed a stack of whiskey glasses and a bottle of bourbon.

"I don't know. He just sat there. Didn't move. Dismissed us after the report."

Prescott cussed in Latin as he slid a glass in front of everyone, even Matthew, and began to pour. There was one extra glass at the head of the table. "I'm going to have a shitty night."

Vik opened the bottle of blood and poured it in the empty glass in front of Matthew.

"You want me to stay around, boss?" Lock asked.

"Nah. I got it."

Tarrick entered the room. He was out of his armor and in a suit. Cleaned and showered. Matthew had no idea how he'd managed to do so when Silva was still dirty. Matthew bowed but no one else bothered to. Tarrick didn't seem put off by it.

With the glasses poured, everyone grabbed their glass, even Tarrick. Matthew looked down at his. Hiroto bumped his shoulder. "You fight with us, you drink with us."

Matthew grabbed his glass of blood. Everyone stood.

Prescott raised his glass into the air. "To our brothers and sisters who have served in their last mission, may their souls find peace among the gods. For the rest of us, may our days get easier and our lives longer."

They tipped their glasses and drank up. Matthew smelled his glass—it wasn't just blood, there was something else in there too.

"Stop being a puss, drink it," Nellis said as he wiped his mouth.

Matthew knocked the glass back in a gulp. It tasted amazing and he wished he had sipped it instead to make it last.

He noticed Vik studying him with intense scrutiny. "Do you like it? Describe how you feel," she urged, pouring him more.

"It's good," Matthew said, savoring the taste this time. When he had emptied it, she poured more.

As soon as he was done with the third glass, it hit him like a freakin' train. His whole body swayed and he dropped to the ground with a thud. His mind was swimming and he felt like he was floating. He looked up to see everyone staring down at him.

Whatever this shit was, it felt as if he had done ten shots one after the other. He raised his hands in front of his face and waved them. His fingers were blurring and he couldn't stop laughing at how funny they looked.

"Did you get my vampire drunk?" Tarrick asked.

Vik cheered with an excited, "Yes!"

"That shit is amazing," Matthew said. "What's in it?"

"Oh you know, a little bit of incubus blood, and normal blood, some foxglove extract…a few other special ingredients. I've been waiting forever to test it out but no one will loan me a vampire."

"Because you keep killing them," Tarrick said. "And I need them to train hunters, not for your unreliable tests. And especially not to see how drunk you can make one."

"It's how we progress, General," she said with a humph.

Matthew had previously thought Vik sort of a cute woman with a touch of crazy but now he was leaning more towards psycho scientist.

Hiroto grabbed Matthew's arm and pulled him up. "Let's get you seated."

Matthew stumbled into a chair.

"I think I'll dilute it a little more next time," Vik said, studying her bottle.

Matthew shook his head. "Nah. This is great." He really was enjoying the feeling. It had been…over ten years—*Fuck, really?*—since he had been drunk. "You know, if we weren't in a big ol' war, you could sell this shit to vamps and make a fortune."

Nellis took his seat again. "We should just give it to them, be easy to pick them off if they were all shit-faced."

"Alright, those of you with other responsibilities—or wives," Prescott said, looking to Lock, "go ahead and take off. Reports by noon tomorrow."

Lock gave a nod to the group and teleported away.

Silva turned to Tarrick. "I'm going to go check in with Ashwood. I'll be back in a few hours. If you plan on leaving the tower I better know about it, General."

Tarrick waved her away. "You're dismissed, Commander." Silva disappeared in a green flash.

"That pretty young succubus of yours around tonight, Imperator?" Nellis asked. Matthew narrowed his eyes at the big Irishman. "'Cus if you're going to be busy with the King, I'd be happy to feed her."

Oh fuck no. Matthew wouldn't let that dirty motherfucker within a mile of Lily.

He let out a roar, leaped up over the table, and was driving a fist into Nellis' face before anyone could react. The two went tumbling over the chair and across the ground, throwing punches at each other.

Matthew only stopped when his arm shackles snapped together behind his back. He tried to get up to kick Nellis but his ankles became bound too and he toppled back to the floor.

Nellis pushed himself up. "What the fuck is your problem?"

"Lady Lillian is Matthew's daughter," Tarrick said from his seat, relaxed and taking another sip of his drink.

There was a pause as the new information was processed.

Nellis broke the silence. "Seriously, how is that possible?"

"I fucked her mother," Matthew said flopping on the ground like a fish.

Hiroto bust out laughing.

"How come you didn't tell us, boss? I thought she was an orphan," Vik said when the laughter died down.

"I didn't know until recently. And it's still classified information." Prescott looked down at Matthew, less than impressed, "You done fighting?"

Matthew stopped flopping. "Yes, Imperator."

"Devil," Tarrick said, "stop saying 'Imperator' every time you address him."

"It's a rule," Prescott said.

"It's annoying. I'm changing the rule."

"Fine. Matthew, you can use 'sir' instead. But I prefer 'Imperator'. *Olyar.*"

Matthew's shackles broke apart from each other. He stood up and took a chair again, glaring at Nellis.

"You want to go again? I'm down," the hunter said, patting his gauntlets and wearing a shit-eating grin on his bruised face.

"No more fighting. And no more quips about Lily," Prescott said. "And Matthew, Lily would never sleep with Mac, you have nothing to worry about."

"I don't know a single succubus that would actually sleep with Commander Nellis," a sensual female voice said from the door.

Matthew stood up and bowed to Lady Rosaline.

Then he vomited all over the table.

The hunters jumped away as Matthew puked up blood.

"Yeah, I'll dilute it next time for sure," Vik said.

"Is he okay?" Rosaline asked, covering her eyes and nose.

Tarrick leaned back in his chair. "He's drunk."

Rosaline scrunched her face with disgust as she looked at Matthew again. "I had plans for him tonight."

Hiroto grabbed a wet towel and handed it to Matthew. "No wonder he turned me down."

Matthew shook his head and wiped his mouth off. "I don't see why the plans have to change, my lady."

Rosaline looked at the messy table and nearly gagged. "No, I think we can wait."

Matthew adjusted his pants. His balls had stopped being blue and had turned to purple at this point.

Hiroto laughed so hard he had to take a seat, and everyone turned to look at Matthew.

Matthew groaned. "I said that thing about my balls out loud, didn't I?"

Tarrick nodded in confirmation, but was otherwise unreadable.

Matthew wanted to crawl under the table from embarrassment. "Shit. I'm sorry. This stuff…I don't think I should drink it again."

"Nah, have some more. The night is young. None of us have passed out yet and we need to have at least one more fight," Nellis said, pouring himself more bourbon. "And you, my lady, should join us and I'll give you a long list of all the succubi that I've bedded. It might surprise you." He winked at her.

"You're such a dog," Vik said.

But Rosaline looked intrigued. Unable to pass up some juicy gossip, she slid into a chair. Nellis poured her a drink.

"That reminds me," Prescott said. "Lady Rosaline and General Tarrick can give you permission to come."

Yay. Sex.

Hiroto leaned over to Rosaline and whispered. "You should give him permission to get off with me."

"Not until I get mine," she laughed.

Matthew went about wiping up the mess he'd made. He had to stop a few times to steady himself. At one point, he ignored the conversation and began following the tiles on the floor to see if he could walk a straight line. He couldn't, but it was fun to try.

He caught Tarrick watching him. Matthew smiled at him.

"Enjoying yourself?" the general asked, leaning back and sipping on his bourbon.

Matthew fought off the urge to take a seat in his lap. He closed one of his eyes and cocked his head to the side. "You're really cute."

Tarrick chuckled. "Am I?"

"Not like Hiroto cute, he's adorable—"

"I really am," Hiroto said, his ears flicking about.

"—or like Lady Rosaline cute, she's beautiful—"

"Why thank you, Matthew," she said.

"—but like...hot. Masculine."

Prescott groaned and stood. "I think it's time we put the big vampire to bed before he makes too much of a fool of himself."

"No, no, let him talk, boss. This is gold," Nellis said, downing another glass in a single gulp. "Before too long he'll be going through a list of every lover he's had and I know a few people in this room that wouldn't mind hearing it."

Matthew sat down in a chair next to Tarrick. He tried to be sneaky and scoot it closer but it made a loud grinding sound as it dragged across the floor. Tarrick raised an eyebrow. "Oops," Matthew said, then looked to Prescott. "You don't need to put me to bed. I'll behave. Cross my dead heart."

"Fine but—"

Matthew didn't hear the rest of what Prescott said. Intense pain rippled through the bond. Samantha was hurting.

Matthew pushed power into his speed and was out of the cafeteria and at the elevator in a fraction of a second. He began to claw at the elevator doors. "Let me in, let me in."

The four Argonauts that were still around teleported behind him. Vik had a stake, while Nellis was slipping on his gauntlets. Neither

Hiroto nor Prescott bothered with a weapon.

"I know you're drunk but this is a poor escape attempt," Prescott said.

"It's Sam. She's hurting. Please," he said and scratched at the door, leaving deep grooves in the metal.

"Hiroto, go check on her," Prescott ordered as Tarrick and Rosaline joined them. Hiroto teleported away.

"What's going on?" Tarrick asked, frowning with displeasure as Matthew scratched up the tower.

Matthew grew more frantic. "Is she being punished? I have to get to her."

Prescott pressed a rune to call the elevator. "Calm down, Matthew."

Matthew didn't calm. He *needed* to be with his child right now.

"Dispatch—" Hiroto's voice came over the comm, "—we need a doctor sent to room 8902, one that specializes in vampires. Imperator, I think you should let Matthew come up here. Something is happening to his daughter, I'm not sure what. I've never seen this before."

Matthew let out a desperate whine. Finally, the elevator opened and he zoomed inside. Calmly, Prescott, Tarrick, and Rosaline got on as well. Vik and Nellis teleported away.

Rosaline touched Matthew's arm in an attempt to comfort him. He growled at her. Tarrick pulled her away, putting himself between the two of them. "He's moving more on instinct right now. Vampires get wild when their children are in danger. He'll calm once he sees that she is okay."

When the elevator finally arrived at his level, he was through the doors before they fully opened. He blew past Vik and Nillis, and didn't stop to open the door to Samantha's room. Instead, he knocked it off the hinges and burst inside.

Samantha was lying on the bed. She was naked but wrapped in a bed sheet clutching her stomach and screaming.

Hiroto was in the room along with Gavyn, who had pants on and nothing else, his colorful tattoos covered most of his skin.

Matthew scooped Samantha up and retreated into his room with her, slamming the door behind him. He sat on his bed with her cradled in his lap and stroked her. Matthew poured power into the bond to try to take her pain away but it didn't work.

He sliced open his wrist and shoved it in her mouth but she didn't drink. He wasn't sure what else he could do.

A scent crossed his nose. Gavyn. Matthew could smell the hunter all over her. Samantha had sex with him.

Rage filled him. He left Samantha on the bed and ripped away the door between the rooms.

"That door should have been strong enough to stop him," someone said.

But Matthew didn't register it as he barreled down on Gavyn and grabbed the hunter by the neck. "What did you do to her?"

"Nothing," Gavyn managed to say as he choked.

"Matthew." Tarrick's commanding voice drew his attention. "Release him and regain your control."

Matthew wanted to snap Gavyn's neck but that wouldn't help Samantha, and he needed to be with her right now. He released the hunter. "You fucked her."

Gavyn clenched his teeth. "But I didn't do anything to her. We had sex. It wasn't anything out of the ordinary. I mean, it was amazing, but—"

Matthew slammed his fist into the wall sending plaster everywhere. It shut Gavyn up.

"Was this her first time?" Tarrick asked.

"Yes," both Matthew and Gavyn answered. Matthew snarled at him.

Tarrick motioned to Matthew's hand. "Put your claws away, Matthew."

He couldn't be serious right now. Matthew was too revved up to put his vampire guise away.

"*Now.*" Tarrick's face grew dark as if daring Matthew to challenge him.

And Matthew, for whatever reason, couldn't. Not when Tarrick ordered him like that. It had always been that way and Matthew never knew why.

He closed his eyes and tried to think of pleasant thoughts. It took a few moments but his claws melted back into him and his eyes returned to silver.

Tarrick left the room and came back with Rosaline, who looked shaken, and led her into Matthew's room where Samantha was writhing on the bed.

"She's going to scan Samantha. Will you be able to handle it?" Tarrick asked Matthew.

"Yes. Only her though."

Rosaline pushed the bed sheet aside. Samantha hissed at her. "Sam, honey, I'm just going to scan you."

Matthew slipped onto the bed and pulled Samantha into his lap. He held her upper body still to prevent her from lashing out at Rosaline in her confused state.

"You can do it now, she won't hurt you. I won't either." Matthew was feeling a little better, knowing that Rosaline might be able to help.

Rosaline put her hand on Samantha's stomach and closed her eyes. "Ilertha help us," she gasped and looked to Tarrick.

"Tell me," Tarrick said.

"She has soavik glands growing on her blood pouches."

Matthew's heart sank. "But she wasn't an incubus. Before I turned her, she wasn't an incubus."

"You're right, she wasn't an incubus," Tarrick said. "Only humans can be oracles, but losing her virginity triggered a latent ability she got from you. At least, that's what I suspect is going on."

A human wearing a white coat and a stethoscope around his neck arrived. Prescott entered along with the doctor.

Tarrick held up his hand to stop the doctor and addressed Matthew. "We're going to examine her but you're too dangerous right now. I'm sorry." Tarrick nodded to Prescott.

"*Olipsus*," Prescott said and Matthew was out like a light.

Thirty

Hunger rippled through Matthew. Blood, sex, death. He needed to feed all three.

His four blood pouches and his soavik were empty and Bloodreaver stirred below his skin. A month or more had to have passed since he was knocked out. The scent of jasmine told him he was in the High King's room long before he opened his eyes.

Matthew fully woke and pushed himself off the pallet he was laying on in 'his area' of the room. Samantha, the only other occupant, was sleeping, dressed in casual clothes, on Malarath's bed.

Matthew started to go to her but froze mid-step, hovering his foot over the wooden floor. He set it back down on the tiles in his torture zone. He couldn't leave it without permission.

A frustrated growl came from him and he began to pace. His leather pants and cotton shirt felt bigger than normal and his collar hung heavy on his neck. While he waited, he noticed that the artwork in the room had been changed to portraits and scenes featuring incubi, but everything else was the same.

Well into the night, Samantha still hadn't woken and Matthew was worried. God, he wanted to go over there and hold her.

The door opened and Tarrick stepped into the room. He said nothing to Matthew and a moment later Prescott joined them. Matthew bowed to them both and knew their arrival heralded the coming of the King.

Low and behold, the temperature dropped and His Majesty entered his room. Ezra and Ophelia were behind him but he shut the door in their faces, leaving them outside. Matthew went to his knees and lowered his eyes, trying not to think about how hungry he was… how wonderful Prescott's heart sounded, beating blood through his body…how sexy Tarrick looked in his grey uniform and tall, polished boots…how much he'd love to sink his axe into Malarath's face.

Malarath crossed his room and sat on the bed next to Samantha. He stroked her face.

Jex Lane

The edges of Matthew's tattoos began to turn red. He wanted to pry the High King away from his daughter but he knew that'd only lead to terrible pain. His body trembled as he stayed put.

Malarath nodded to Tarrick, giving him permission to speak.

Tarrick motioned to Samantha. "We're keeping her sedated right now but she's well."

Relief swept through Matthew.

"Since the moment I found out what you were," Tarrick continued, "I had hypothesized that any child you sire might end up with some incubi abilities. We knew that she was sneaking around with a hunter but didn't stop it because we wanted to see what would happen. She went through a transformation of sorts. She has the glands but not a full soavik. Like you, she won't need to feed on sex to live but they'll ache when empty. Lady Rosaline has already taught her how to feed correctly."

Matthew was happy that Rosaline had been the one to help her, like she had with him.

"We've done some tests. She can nudge emotions through touch but that seems to be the extent of her abilities. She can't wrap a hold on someone, and took on only one physical trait: her eyes are now silver, like yours."

Matthew looked over at Samantha. The King's cold, judging gaze was on him, and Malarath kept his hand on Samantha's face, like he was claiming her. Matthew should have looked away, showed deference, but he was irritable and angry that they had kept him unconscious for so long—away from her.

"My pet is defiant tonight," Malarath said. His hand moved down Samantha's body, over her breasts and stomach, then rested on her hip.

Matthew bit back a growl and tore his eyes away, looking down at Tarrick's boots. "Are you going to harm her, Master?"

"Why would I do such a thing, pet? She is far more valuable to me than you are." It was good that she had made herself valuable to him. That would keep her safe. "Although…she does not yet wear my mark." He looked to Prescott. "See to it that she does. Same place as her sire's."

Matthew balled his hands into fists. The silver from the brand left on his skin for days hadn't been that painful for him, but for her it would be excruciating.

She didn't deserve the pain. Rage tore through Matthew and he lost it. "I have no idea what Devak ever saw in you," Matthew spat out in anger. Devak had loved this man for centuries, maybe longer, and Matthew couldn't even begin to imagine the two of them together. His guardian had been devoted, loving, and compassionate. The High King possessed none of those traits. He was cruel, manipulative, and he sure as shit didn't care about his people, except to draw upon them for power.

Matthew blinked hard. What the fuck had he just said? Even if the thought crossed his mind, he shouldn't have said it aloud. No. *No*...the High King had a damn hold on him. It melted away his barriers and sense of self-preservation.

"Devak? Your dead guardian? Why would I care about his opinion of me?"

Matthew snapped his mouth shut tight and didn't open it. He couldn't risk the High King finding out who Devak really was.

"Answer the King's question," Prescott said.

Matthew kept his eyes down and didn't say a word. Maybe he should lie...but with a hold on him, he didn't think he could get away with it.

When he said nothing, Tarrick backed away as Malarath stood and came before Matthew. "I thought I had broken you of this stubbornness, pet. What is it that you are hiding from me that you would risk more torture, or even pain upon your daughters?"

Still on his knees, Matthew's gaze shot upwards, and the back of Malarath's hand struck his cheek. He went sprawling down to the tiled floor. A deep bruise formed on his face. Fuck, he was strong. When he tried to return to his knees, Malarath's foot came down on his chest, pinning him in place.

"It gets much worse from here, Matthew. Answer his damn question," Prescott said. Beside him, Tarrick stood silent and expressionless. For the first time ever, Matthew thought he looked...small.

Unable to think of any other way of avoiding this, he swallowed hard and locked eyes with the High King. "Devak was your companion, Master."

The King removed his foot. "No, pet, your guardian was never my companion."

Prescott rubbed his hand over his stubble, a habit he was used to doing when he had a full beard. "Why do you think he was the High King's companion?"

"He told me, Imperator. And I saw a memory."

Malarath's interest was piqued again. "What did you see, pet?"

"A battle in ancient Greece. You were riding on a black dragon. The vampire queen moved around you like a swarm of bats. Devak stood alone against your army...and decimated it as the Sanguine Dominar."

Malarath's gaze moved to Prescott who shook his head. "That's impossible. I fought the guardian, it wasn't Apep. He looked nothing like him, talked nothing like him. There's no way it was him. I would have known."

Apep? Was that Devak's real name?

"Do you fight the same after twenty-five-hundred years? It was him. His body was changed by a god." Matthew tried to snap his mouth shut but the words were flowing against his will. He couldn't shut up no matter how much he wanted to. The hold on him was growing stronger, tearing apart what little free will he had. And worry set in that Malarath was about to find out his mother's identity.

"You never came for him, Master. After the Queen turned him, you abandoned him for power...to become the High King. The throne was more important to you than your love for him. This endless fucking war we're locked in is all about your vengeance. Thousands of years of you seeking to take from the Queen what she took from you...but *you* made him what he was, not her. And in the end, you were the one who took his life. You fucking hypocrite."

"Matthew, shut up," Prescott said.

He wished he could. He howled in frustration, his chest arching off the ground as the High King's eyes bore into him. "It wasn't her fault you lost him," Matthew growled. "You let him go. He was watching over me my whole life and he never once came to see you because of how bad you hurt him. It wasn't until me that he found love again. I loved him and your Imperator killed him. Now he's gone forever and it's *your* fault."

Matthew reveled in his words. It felt so good to lash out and hurt the King, to get some revenge for all the shit he had been put through. His eyes burned red with anger…then sanity returned to him…followed by terror as he realized what he'd said.

He looked over at Samantha. God, please don't let him hurt her.

An eerie silence filled the room. Malarath stilled. Not a single emotion crossed his face, but the temperature dropped so cold that Matthew could see Tarrick and Prescott's breath, and the windows frosted over. The edges of the King's blue eyes burned with a gold ring.

"Leave." The word dripped with a venomous danger. Matthew wasn't sure who the High King was talking to.

Tarrick went to the bed and scooped Samantha up, cradling her in both his arms.

"Matthew, come," Prescott said and marched out of the room. Matthew pushed himself up and backed away from Malarath, leaving the room as quickly as he could.

Both Prescott and Tarrick were pensive. If Matthew didn't know better, he'd think they were both frightened. Prescott hit the bottom rune—to the zoo.

Halfway down, Prescott lifted his head to the camera, "Cut the cams." Unlike with Rosaline, there was no argument as the elevator stopped and the cameras went dead.

Prescott paced back and forth, glancing up at Matthew then muttering something in Latin. Tarrick was silent, trying to piece something together.

"Aau'Apep," Prescott started, "wasn't just the High King's companion. He was his mate—the only mate the King has ever taken. I don't even think Mal has fucked anyone since the day he killed Apep—or Devak, whatever the fuck his name is now—two and a half millennia ago. I'm telling you this, Matthew, so that you understand just how much Malarath loved Apep, and how much you just fucked up. The last time I saw him this angry he walked into a human town and destroyed it."

Fuck. "Will he hurt Lily?"

Prescott rubbed his chin. "I don't know. I'll do what I can to protect her."

"And Sam?" Matthew touched Samantha's hair.

Tarrick looked down at the unconscious vampire in his arms. "I'm going to send her and Rosaline to my estate for a while. If she's out of his sight, he might not direct his wrath at her. Imperator, transfer the Misfits to Ashwood. They're due for their rotation as instructors."

"You're going to allow the oracle to continue her affair with Gavyn?" Prescott asked.

"She has to feed now and I get the feeling she'll be more stubborn about it than Matthew." Tarrick fell silent for a moment then asked, "Is this war only about punishing the vampire queen over a lost mate?"

"Does it matter how the war started?"

Tarrick gripped tighter onto Samantha, the way a caring father would. Matthew wished he'd hand her over but it didn't look like Tarrick would relinquish her if he asked. "I've lost eleven children and three mates to this war. It matters to me."

"Why? What would it change? Unless you wish to step down from your position."

Tarrick's shoulders squared up. "Do you question my loyalty?"

"No. But it sounds as if you're questioning it," Prescott said crossing his arms.

"I'm not. I never have. Not once. I'm loyal to him and the incubi."

Prescott looked down at Samantha, then back to the general. "It's not just revenge on the Queen. It's territory, hunting, wealth. Vampires are murderers and if their population gets too big, it puts the entire supernatural community at risk. You know this."

Matthew didn't believe that propaganda. In the few short months he had spent with the vampire lord Ascelina, he had learned that vampires were good at self-regulating their numbers and making sure they didn't draw human attention when they fed.

Hell, unless the vampire was young and without a sire, they rarely killed the humans they fed upon. And it wasn't that they didn't want to—god knows, their vampire side desired it—it was just that thousands of humans dying each night from blood loss wouldn't go unnoticed.

Tarrick pressed his lips together and took a deep breath through his nose. "Bryson asked for terms of surrender last week. The High King rejected my recommendation that we take it. He won't accept anything but their eradication. They're turning reckless as they grow more desperate. We risk exposure. If this isn't just about vengeance, he would have accepted surrender. Or approved my plans to move into Russia and end this."

Prescott said nothing for a moment, then spoke, slow at first as if considering his answer. "You are a third my age, Tarrick, and you haven't witnessed all that I have. I've watched Malarath bring his people back from the brink of extinction three times: Once when the Sanguine Dominar nearly wiped us out. Again when the demons attacked. And last when the dragons decided they wanted to rule everything and tried to enslave us. He was a general long before your great-grandmother was born. He knows what he's doing. Trust your King."

Tarrick's face showed no emotion but his grip on Samantha was tight. He nodded to the Imperator but said nothing.

The elevator began to shake and groan. Matthew looked around.

"I told you he was angry," Prescott said. "The magic of this tower is tied to him."

"Let me off," Tarrick said. "I want to get Rosaline and Samantha out of here. Lily is with Teleclus?"

"Yes." Prescott hit a rune and the elevator opened. Matthew's heart sank as he watched Tarrick leave without saying another word, taking Samantha away from him, even if he was thankful that Tarrick was watching out for her.

Prescott was silent as he took Matthew to his cage and placed him inside, then left.

Alone, dread filled him.

✳✳✳✳

Nearly a week passed and no one came to see or feed Matthew. The building around him shook like an earthquake on occasion. Sometimes it was so strong he worried the entire tower might come down.

The first few nights, Matthew spent the time recalling memories and playing through them, but eventually his vampire took over and prowled the cage hoping to find blood.

He grew weaker each night and his rotting skin ached.

On the sixth night, Matthew felt the tower teleport. Wherever it had moved to was closer to sunrise than it had been in New York, but it was still nighttime.

Prescott appeared and opened the cage. "Follow me," he said, and led Matthew out of the zoo, past the lobby, and outside.

A grassy field sprawled out for miles in each direction. Before him was a fortress. It was old, the grey stones crumbling apart with age. Matthew could feel powerful magic surrounding the area for miles, keeping it hidden from human eyes.

Prescott marched Matthew through the field. The High King—wearing robes of crimson and a crown—stood in front of a tilted, flat stone, large enough for a person to lay on. There were rusty chains at each of the corners.

Prescott teleported away and Matthew went to his knees.

Malarath stood regal and tall, his crushing golden gaze fixed upon Matthew. "This is where I killed him."

Thirty-One

Matthew's eyes drifted to the stone. Devak had died three times: first when he became a vampire, then when the High King had taken his head, and last when Prescott and Hiroto had poisoned and stabbed him. The High King was responsible for all three deaths in one way or another, influencing the events that led to Devak's demise.

Malarath motioned for Matthew to stand and once he was up, began to circle like a predator stalking prey. It made Matthew uneasy. He could feel the fury rolling off the King.

"You said that you do not know what he saw in me," Malarath began, his voice even and dangerous. "I am power and beauty. My beloved enjoyed the life I gave him, the prestige, the wealth, the command. He was my mate throughout the centuries and I gave him everything he craved. You had him for a few months and you think you can even begin to compare."

Matthew didn't respond. Malarath was right, he hadn't known Devak for long, and who knows how their relationship would have grown; changed.

Malarath stopped inches away from his face. "What could he have possibly seen in you? You are weak and pathetic. Hardly even worthy to be a pet, let alone touch him."

Wincing, Matthew took a step away from the King...or tried to. Malarath grabbed his shoulder to keep him in place. Golden claws emerged and dug deep into Matthew's skin.

Matthew snarled. He was so damn hungry that the pain was bringing his control to the edge.

The High King's other hand came down on Matthew's face with a slap, leaving behind five deep claw marks across his cheek.

Matthew lost it. He was sick of not fighting back, sick of being a slave, sick of being helpless. And fuck, he was hungry. Claws out, he swiped at the King's arm, cutting through his robe and soft flesh. The scent of strong blood filled the air, overwhelming him and driving him wild with need.

He lunged at Malarath's bleeding forearm, but before his lips could touch the scarlet liquid, Malarath slapped his other cheek. This time he sent Matthew tumbling to the ground.

From the grass, Matthew watched as Malarath began to change into his incubus form. The wound on his arm mended faster than he'd ever seen any other incubus heal before. The double set of long, golden horns grew from his head, the color matching his eyes. His ears became long and pointed and his skin took on a lustrous, almost glowing, quality.

The lacing of his robe popped as his body grew, adjusting around him. He was still slender, but he was easily three or four feet taller than Matthew now. The soft boots he wore tore away as his feet turned to hooves, his ankles bending backwards.

Behind him, massive wings unfurled and expanded. The moonlight shimmered off gilded tips.

The immense power Malarath wielded radiated from him like rays from the sun and hit Matthew like a tidal wave, almost physically pinning him to the ground. The High King was magnificent and terrible in his full incubus form. A monster unlike any other.

A sense of self-preservation dwarfed Matthew's hunger. He needed to get away.

Now.

He pushed himself up and stumbled back. He made it three steps before the High King had a hold on him, controlling his mind and body. Matthew struggled against it but he was helpless, frozen in place.

Matthew closed his eyes. Whatever was about to happen next, it would hurt.

He felt Malarath's clawed hand wrap around his neck, just above his collar, and pull him over to the stone. His body didn't resist.

"Please...Master," Matthew said, and opened his eyes again as Malarath pushed him down onto the slanted stone. It was hard and cold against his back. He knew it was too late for any pleading to have an effect but he couldn't help himself, he was scared. No. *Terrified.*

"You are nothing," the High King whispered in his ear. "You dare think you were worthy of him?"

Matthew's muscles shook as Malarath grabbed the waist of his leather pants and ripped them from his body, exposing him to the night air. He did the same with Matthew's shirt, leaving him only in his boots, the shreds of his clothes discarded to the side.

Matthew struggled but he didn't stand a chance against the High King's power. He tried—fuck, he tried—but his body refused to move. He was trapped inside himself, sprawled naked on the rock, arms and legs spread apart.

The High King grabbed one of Matthew's legs and pushed it up, forcing his hips to pivot forward.

Malarath moved the front of his robe aside, revealing his massive cock—thick and veiny, an oversized exaggeration of what a cock should be—that grew hard as he looked down at Matthew.

Oh god.

Matthew couldn't believe what was happening. "Master, please, don't. I beg you, please."

His cries were ignored as the King moved closer, the weight of his body pressed onto Matthew. He wished Malarath would flip him over. Being face to face was too intimate, too close while being dominated in this fashion.

"I'm sorry," Matthew whispered in desperation.

A deep growl came from Malarath as he lined up his thick cock to Matthew's hole.

Fuck.

There was no way Matthew could take that thing. And the High King hadn't bothered to secrete any gel. Matthew couldn't focus enough to force his own body to do it.

It is time you saw the true face of your mother. His sire's words echoed in his mind. *She is revealed through her people, just as I am through mine.* Is this what his mother was? Evil.

Malarath began to work his cock into Matthew, pushing hard against his hole, then past the muscles there. "Please, Father, help me," Matthew cried out, and when there was no response he added, "Please...anyone."

As the cock slid in deeper, he felt his body tearing apart. To his horror, his own cock responded, growing hard. It was either the High King's hold or an automatic response of his body, but it wasn't because Matthew was into this. There was nothing enjoyable happening here.

Matthew's eyes glazed over and he took his mind away from the situation. He was being violated in the worst way and he didn't want to have this seared into his memory forever.

"No," the High King hissed. His hot breath hitting Matthew's still-wounded cheek. "You will know every moment of this."

"Master...please. I loved him, I didn't want him to die. You're right, I was unworthy of him."

Malarath began to thrust and built up a ceaseless, pounding rhythm. Every time Matthew tried to let his mind escape elsewhere, the King pulled him back with a word or by digging his claws into his body, leaving long gashes behind.

Matthew wasn't sure how long the King was on him, in him, using him, but it felt as if time had stretched to eternity. And finally, when the King expended himself deep within Matthew, he was relieved that it would be over soon.

Matthew felt his own body responding to the sex creature's orgasm and he had one of his own. It wasn't pleasing, just an uncontrollable physical response. But even still, shame washed through him as he felt his cum land on his torso.

Finished, Malarath removed himself and wiped off using the shreds of Matthew's shirt. His incubus side melted away and he returned to his normal height. He looked down at Matthew with cruel eyes.

"He was everything," he said, then walked away from the stone, leaving Matthew helpless and covered in blood, cum, and tears.

High Tower wasn't close, but it was so large that it loomed oppressively above him. Matthew struggled to move, but he had no energy left.

The horizon began to glow and he wondered how painful burning in the sun would be. What would happen to him once he died? Would his soul go to his sire? Would his sire spend the rest of eternity torturing him for being such a disappointment? For being so weak. Would he get to see his wife again?

Feelings of misery drowned him. He wasn't strong. He had failed to protect those he cared for. He was nothing.

A sweet voice wrapped around him. "You are everything, my prince."

Thirty-Two

Devak. His skin bronze. His dark hair was a little longer now but not by much. He was in his usual cotton outfit with leather laces.

No.

Not Devak.

A hallucination.

Devak was dead.

"You are strong, my prince. You survived long years alone, you left your family behind to protect them, and you still strive to keep them safe. In your life, you've faced many storms and survived them. You will survive this."

Matthew tried to speak but he was too weak, too overwhelmed, to open his mouth. Devak ran his hand over Matthew's brand. His warm fingers felt so good. Tears fell down Matthew's face.

"You're powerful. You have it in you to fight him. Stop thinking like a vampire and start thinking like an incubus."

Matthew had no idea how to stop him. Malarath was too powerful.

"He's shown you his weakness," Devak continued.

His people...Malarath drew his power from his people. They worshiped him because they were tied to him. But what if they weren't? What would happen if they turned against him? Then he'd just be a normal incubus. An ancient incubus, but one that could be killed.

A small thread of hope weaved through him.

But...he was about to die. The sun was going to kill him. The sky began to turn a light purple and the stars faded away.

Devak smiled down at him, his eyes warm and friendly. "I love you, my prince." He leaned down and kissed Matthew's forehead.

The hallucination faded away. Matthew tried to call out. He wanted Devak back, even if he wasn't real. He *needed* him to stay right now. He *needed* someone.

In his delirious condition, Matthew slowly realized that there was another incubus standing next to the stone. Matthew struggled to get away from it. He couldn't take another one in him. It was already too much.

"Still yourself, young one," a deep voice said, soothing him. "I'm not going to harm you."

Tarrick wrapped a warm blanket around Matthew's body and scooped him into his arms, cradling him. With Tarrick in his incubus form, Matthew felt small against his chest, but found it comforting. Safe.

Tarrick crossed the grassy field and brought Matthew back into the tower right before the sun broke the horizon. Matthew didn't fall asleep. He couldn't. He wanted to, god, he wanted the sweet release of nothingness but it didn't come to him.

He couldn't move or speak in Tarrick's arms but he watched his face. Tarrick looked down often, as if checking to see if Matthew was okay.

When they entered the general's room, Tarrick lay him down on his bed, leaving him wrapped tight in the blanket.

"You should be sleeping," he said, sounding genuinely worried. Maybe it was just a trick so that Matthew would trust him again, but right now he didn't have the faculty to figure out Tarrick's motivations.

Tarrick frowned and left Matthew's field of vision. Water began to run, and when Tarrick returned, he was dressed only in tight underwear.

"I'm going to bathe you." Tarrick removed Matthew's boots, unwrapping him from the now-dirty blanket, and carried him into the bathroom. He entered the filled spa tub, setting Matthew down next to him. Using soap and a washcloth, he began to clean Matthew everywhere. When his hand got close to his ass, Matthew struggled to move, to speak or beg him to stop.

"I'd like to clean you out," Tarrick held up an enema nozzle. "I'm not going to harm you. I'll be quick. Can you blink once if that's okay?"

Matthew didn't blink for a while. He didn't want anyone near him, even Tarrick...but he also didn't want the High King's cum sitting inside of him. The very thought of it turned his insides.

Tarrick didn't rush him, waiting patiently for the answer. Matthew blinked once. He felt the metal nozzle enter him, some pressure from water, then release.

Tarrick drained the water in the tub and cleaned Matthew out twice more before he was satisfied that Matthew was fully washed.

With tender care, the incubus general dried and dressed Matthew. He placed Matthew on the bed then disappeared for a short time. When he came back he had returned to human form, but instead of his normal suit, he was in pajama bottoms and a shirt. In his hand, he carried a bag of blood.

He pushed the tube to Matthew's mouth and squeezed the bag. Matthew didn't really feel hungry anymore, but his body responded to the blood on instinct, swallowing it. He began to feel a little better, at least physically, as his body repaired itself.

After three bags, he could talk again with some effort.

"Sam—" Matthew said, his voice scratchy.

"She's fine. As is Lily."

The two of them sat in silence for a while. "If you aren't going to sleep, would you like me to read to you?"

"No."

Tarrick looked…a little lost as to what to do next.

Matthew, having never seen Tarrick like that before, took pity on him and asked, "How bad is the ghoul wound?" Matthew had felt it creeping across his body but it had been the least of his worries at the time.

"It's spread. It's covering most of your lower body now. Would you like me to wrap a hold on you? It'll help you rest."

"No. Please no."

Tarrick sighed. "What can I do for you?"

Rewind time…rescue him… "Can you touch me?"

"Are you sure?" Tarrick asked.

"Yes." Back when he was a firefighter—before becoming a vampire—he had taken a few classes on how to interact with victims of different crimes, including rape. He knew oftentimes they didn't want to be touched…but Matthew wasn't a human, he was an incubus and he needed the connection right now to ground him.

Tarrick slipped into bed and folded his arms around Matthew, pulling him into a spooning position. Matthew felt…nothing. Empty. Like someone had scooped his insides out and had forgotten to put anything back. Tears leaked from his eyes but it didn't feel like he was crying. They seemed to escape on their own.

And he stayed like that for hours. Until, finally, he could actually feel Tarrick wrapped around him and the sun-filled room came into focus.

"Why am I not burning?"

Tarrick kissed Matthew's shoulder and he could feel a smile cross the general's face.

"What's so amusing?" Matthew asked.

Tarrick sat up and rolled Matthew over, pulling him onto his lap so they could look at each other. "I knew your curiosity wasn't lost. I've missed your questions." Tarrick ran his hand over Matthew's short hair, stroking him. "The magic of the tower is woven into every inch of this place, even the windows. Vampires won't burn here."

They were silent for a while, then Matthew said, "You never raped me. All the shit you did to me, you never actually raped me."

"No. I never had to." He stopped stroking Matthew's head, and pinched the back of his neck, above the collar. Matthew wasn't sure why he was grabbing him there but eventually he released him then resumed stroking.

"Why did you grab me like that?"

Tarrick ran his fingers down Matthew's cheek. "It's something we do to young incubi to make them behave. It triggers a submissive response for those who haven't been through their second transformation. I didn't mean anything by it."

"Yes, you did. Everything you do is on purpose."

"Alright, you caught me. I was hoping it might help you sleep. You could use the rest."

"He didn't need to do it. I'm obeying. I'm his slave. He had a hold on me. I didn't mean to say those things about Devak out loud. He forced it. Why would he force it?"

"Shhh. Get some sleep."

"He didn't need to take me that way. I already made the choice to submit, to be his weapon. I'm giving him what he always wanted from me."

Tarrick tilted Matthew's head and looked down at him. "I think—" He fell silent and his eyes flicked to a camera in the room, so subtle no one watching would have seen it. After moments of silence, he spoke. "I think he already knew about Devak."

"This was just a stupid incubus manipulation? Why?"

"I don't know. And I'm not in a position to question it." Tarrick's arms tighten around Matthew.

"I don't believe you. You know."

"He's ancient, and sometimes his moods and motivations can be... erratic. I'm not sure why on one hand he's going out of his way to keep you alive, stop the ghouling, and on the other..." Tarrick trailed off for a moment. "My King has spent the last few millennia unable to resolve the feelings he had for his dead mate. A mate that ignored him when he returned, and instead fell for you. Tonight happened because Devak chose you, not him."

"Do you think he'll do it to me again?"

"I don't know, but—" Tarrick paused, his eyes searching Matthew's face, "—you should prepare yourself for that possibility."

Save me, Matthew wanted to say but he knew Tarrick wouldn't. He was loyal to his king.

Matthew couldn't do this anymore.

He couldn't be a pet.

He couldn't be submissive to a master that took away all sense of hope.

He had to do something.

Fighting the King directly wasn't an option. No, this battle had to be a slow corruption. Underhanded sabotage. This battle he had to fight with careful plotting and patient subversion.

Laying there in Tarrick's arms, Matthew decided he was going to play their stupid fucking game and he would play it better than any other incubi could.

He was going to destroy the High King if it was the last thing he ever did. He was going to turn his people against him and he'd start with Tarrick.

Matthew must have drifted to sleep at some point because when he opened his eyes next it was nighttime. And the tower was back in New York.

Tarrick hadn't moved from his spot, his arms resting over Matthew, who was curled up in his lap. Matthew looked up at him.

"Hungry?" Tarrick asked. He was able to make the most mundane words sound charming.

Matthew wasn't sure if he was asking about blood or sex. He was hungry for both but…he couldn't have sex right now. The violation of his body was too fresh.

"For blood," Tarrick said, probably sensing his distress.

Matthew watched Tarrick's muscles shift around as he got out of the bed to retrieve his phone from the wooden desk. It rang the moment he touched it.

Tarrick checked the number but didn't seem to recognize it. He answered the phone with an authoritative, be-quick-about-it, "Yes."

"I want to talk to my father." It was Samantha.

"How did you get this number?"

"Um. I'm an oracle. Jeez, my dad said you were smart."

Tarrick scowled and tossed the phone to Matthew who caught it midair.

"Sam—"

"What happened?"

Matthew thought about lying to her but she'd eventually see it in a vision. He sat up on the side of the bed, letting his feet touch the floor. "The High King had sex with me. I didn't want it."

A quiet growl came through the phone.

"Don't be upset. I'll be okay. How are things with Gavyn?" Matthew could feel a rush of giddiness through the bond…followed by guilt. "I want you to be happy, sweetheart. Don't feel bad for being happy. Is he a good guy?"

"He's one of the best men I've ever met. I should have told you about him but…I thought you would command me not to see him anymore since he's a hunter. I wasn't sure…I couldn't see what would happen."

Matthew wished she hadn't hid this from him, and on some level thought maybe he should be angry, but he couldn't bring himself to feel that way towards her. Not right now anyways. "You don't have to keep things like that from me. Hearing about your happiness pleases me."

"Did they tell you our eyes match?"

"They did. I can't wait to see them."

"Can Tarrick hear me?" she asked.

Matthew looked up to Tarrick, who didn't confirm one way or the other. But he knew the general could hear her. Warrior incubi had sensitive ears, he just liked people to assume he couldn't. It gave him an advantage. "Yeah, he can."

"Good. 'Cus I'm about to tell you something that you both need to know but he won't be happy about it."

"Sam—" Matthew started.

"You two need to trust each other. It's the only way you'll survive. You need each other right now."

Trust Tarrick? How could he even begin to do that? Samantha had never been wrong before but he had been cut deep. A few years ago, Matthew would have jumped at Tarrick like a puppy seeking approval, but now…now he wasn't sure how he felt.

He looked at Tarrick, who waved his hand in a dismissive motion as if what he had just heard was ridiculous, and sat down on the chair behind the desk.

"I have to go now. They just found out I stole the phone and they're going to take it from me. I love you. And Jet says hi."

"Love you too, and scratch his head for me." The line went dead. He tossed the phone back to Tarrick, who set it down and put his hand on his chin, studying Matthew. He *was* smart and he wouldn't really have dismissed what Samantha said so quickly but he didn't look like he'd address the issue.

Tarrick's phone rang again. "Darius," he answered.

"General, I apologize for the vampire. We're not sure how she got a hold of the phone." Darius was a social incubus that was part of Tarrick's household. Matthew had some interaction with him in the past but not much. The incubus didn't like Matthew, although Matthew couldn't recall ever slighting the male.

"You don't need to worry. I'm not angry," Tarrick said.

An audible sound of relief came from the other end of the call. "Do you want me to punish her?"

"Yes."

Matthew stood and balled his fists. His eyes bore into Tarrick. Tarrick shot Matthew a harsh look and held up his finger as a warning for him to stop.

"I'm not sure what I should do...I've never punished a vampire before," Darius said.

"How would you punish a young incubus for disobeying?"

"Send them to their room. Give them a few days alone to reflect on their misdeed."

"Then you have your answer. Don't starve her of blood but keep her from Gavyn while she's punished."

Relief washed over Matthew. She was getting a slap on the hand, not tortured. He sat back down as he listened to Darius give Tarrick some updates on the estate—most were mundane, or even downright boring (who the hell cared if Lady So-and-So had acquired new artwork for the ballroom?) but to Tarrick's credit he stayed engaged and showered his praise upon the young incubus who was running things in his stead.

"Your control has improved," Tarrick said when he ended the call. "There was a time you would have just attacked me when you got that upset."

Matthew tried not to feel thrilled by the compliment, and yet he was. Pathetic for sure, but he could use the kind words right now.

"What's expected of me?" Matthew asked. "I mean...am I training tonight or going back to the cage, or...something else?"

"I've had no new orders from the King. Until I receive some I'm still in charge of you. I'm going to take it night by night."

"May I...may I return to my room and have some time alone?" Matthew wasn't sure Tarrick would honor the request but he needed some time to think. Time to plan. He didn't want to be around anyone right now.

"Alright."

Tarrick stood from his chair and Matthew followed him to the door. Silva stood guard right outside.

"Take him to his room and get him some blood. Matthew, if you need anything just ask in the cameras and the request will come to me."

Matthew took a few steps down the hall, following Silva, then he stopped. He wanted to thank Tarrick for taking care of him. For pulling him off that rock, for his kindness when cleaning him, and for not pushing him right now.

But he couldn't find the words and anything he tried to say caught in his throat.

He reached out and touched Tarrick's arm. Silva's hand lowered to the weapons on her belt but Tarrick held up a hand to stop her. Matthew took a step in and began kissing Tarrick along his jawline.

Tarrick tilted his head to allow Matthew more access. After a few moments, Matthew pulled away. He wasn't sure why he had done that but he had needed to.

Tarrick placed his hand on Matthew's shoulder and squeezed. "My warrior." Matthew's heart swelled. God, he loved it when Tarrick called him that. "Go with Silva."

Matthew bowed slightly and followed the hunter commander down the hall. When they entered the elevator, he took up a spot as far away from her as possible. She watched him as he lowered his head. Matthew had resolved to stop being a scared pet but right now he didn't feel strong. His resolve came and went in waves.

"I would never wish what happened to you upon anyone," she said.

Matthew looked at her. She knew. Of course she knew. The whole tower probably knew by now...hell, most of them had probably seen it happen right outside their windows. The High King had raped him out in the open.

Silva made a slicing motion at her neck. The elevator stopped and the cameras turned off. It seemed Rosaline was the only person they gave shit to for requesting that to happen. But it made sense. She was valuable and not a hunter. She couldn't defend herself against Matthew if he chose to kill her.

"Tarrick's in danger."

"Why?" Matthew asked.

"The order was to leave you out there and let you die."

Tarrick had disobeyed a direct order from the King? No one disobeyed the King. Not ever. "Why would he do such a thing?"

"Why do you think?"

"I don't know."

Silva stared at Matthew like he was an idiot. Maybe Tarrick did care for him…but enough to break rules? That was something he hadn't even done to save his own daughter when she had been captured by vampires.

"He should have left me."

"I agree."

Matthew rubbed his chest. The words hurt, even if she was just agreeing.

"Not because I want you dead, but because you've already decided to end yourself. You're about to become a ghoul, I don't think there's anything we can do to prevent that."

She was right. But now he had something to live for: stop the King at any cost.

"Is there anything I can do to help the general?"

Silva shook her head. "If there is, I'm not sure what. I just wanted you to know the risk he put himself in to save your undead ass."

Silva pressed her thumb against a rune and the elevator continued its journey. "By the way, your daughter is somewhat creepy."

Matthew smiled, knowing she was talking about Samantha, not Lily. "Why? What'd she say to you?"

"And I quote: 'Death blooms into life and love.' Which she followed by some inappropriate comments about going black and not coming back."

Matthew stifled a laugh. "Just ignore her. She had a crush on Bryson and she's fucking with you." Before the vampire general became a vampire, he was a hunter and Silva's lover. Until recently she thought that he was dead.

Silva raised an eyebrow. "I thought you stopped cussing."

Matthew looked down and shrugged. It was easy to be himself around her, it always had been. That's why the loss of her friendship had hit him so hard. "Apologies."

"Doesn't bother me."

They didn't talk the rest of the way to Matthew's room. Once inside, Silva teleported away, returned with blood bags, and left again.

After drinking, he sat down on the only chair and began to plot. He spent the night working through how he was going to present himself from now on; how he would act around others, including the King.

He'd have to be careful. He couldn't appear to be rebelling. Outwardly he'd have to play the role of perfect slave while he looked for opportunities to work against the King. That is, assuming the King wouldn't reissue the order to kill Matthew…but he wasn't dead yet. He had to believe he had some time left. And he needed to find out why Tarrick would risk everything to save him.

Just before sunrise, he had decided on a plan.

Matthew looked up at a camera and rubbed his tattoos. "Prescott said that he would train me how to resist my axe. I was wondering if he was still going to do that, and if it could be sooner rather than later? It hurts and it's only getting worse."

It wasn't a lie. Bloodreaver was hungry. But more importantly, he needed a way to win over the incubi people by doing the one thing he was truly good at—fighting.

He couldn't simply be a weapon on Malarath's leash. No, that made him look too weak. He had to convince the incubi that he was fighting for them—that he wanted to destroy vampires.

He needed to be their hero.

A champion.

He needed to be on the one team that every hunter looked up to, and every incubus gossiped about.

He needed to join the Argonauts.

Thirty-Four

Matthew woke to pressure on his chest.

When he opened his eyes, Hiroto's face hovered above him. His mask and cloak were missing but he still wore a ninjaesque hunter outfit.

"Morning!" he said, far too cheerful.

The sun had just set for fuck's sake. Matthew needed a damn moment.

"You know I've had a really shitty week, right?" Matthew said rubbing his face.

"Yep. Terrible." Hiroto moved down Matthew's body and lifted his shirt. He pressed his finger hard into the rotting skin. "And would you look at this? Just awful. I thought you might want to talk to someone."

Matthew grabbed Hiroto's hips, picked him up, and deposited him beside the bed. "Not really, no." He scooted out of bed and grabbed some clothes off the floor.

"Nope, wrong outfit. Get your workout stuff," Hiroto said, sitting cross-legged on the mattress like a child.

"Are you going to help me with my axe?"

Hiroto drew his two daggers and spun them, displaying practiced skill. "Mine have a nasty cost too: they also like to end lives. Prescott thought I'd be the best to train you."

Matthew nodded to the daggers. "They have names?"

"Murder and Mirth. Don't ask me which is which, they lie to me all the time." Hiroto sheathed them as Matthew went to shower. Matthew spent a long time scrubbing himself and even still he felt dirty. Hiroto didn't rush him.

When he came out of the bathroom wearing his workout clothes, Hiroto was frowning.

"Have I displeased you?" Matthew asked.

"I was hoping you'd change out here." A sly smile crossed the fox's face.

Matthew chuckled despite himself.

"Sure you don't want to talk about anything? I have big ears meant for listening." His white ears both pointed in Matthew's direction.

"Thank you but…I don't want to think about it right now."

Hiroto's eyes pierced into him as if he wouldn't take no for an answer.

Matthew sat on the bed next to the kitsune. "Look, I'm his slave. My body is his. There's nothing I can say or do that's going to change that. There's no point to dwelling. I'd rather focus on what I can do right now, which is learn how to get this damned weapon from taking over my mind every time it's hungry."

His words were for the sake of whoever was watching at the other end of the cameras. He had no doubt this would be reported back to the King.

He wanted Malarath to believe the rape had made him compliant. Which was a little ironic because if he hadn't been violated, he might have spent eternity falling deeper into submission, but not anymore.

"Alright, come on then." Hiroto led Matthew to a workout room. Prescott met them there, removed the shackle, then left. They started by summoning the axe and dismissing it repeatedly. It got tiring but Matthew didn't complain.

"How long have you been a hunter?" Matthew asked, summoning his axe for what felt like the millionth time.

"I was in the first class of hunters. The corps itself is only four centuries old. Before that everything was a little more disorganized. Humans were hired as bodyguards by individual houses and armies raised based on need."

"Do you enjoy being a hunter?" Matthew dismissed his axe. A pool of blood was collecting on the floor below him, and he grew hungrier each time he summoned the weapon.

"Yeah. I like both my teams." With the exception of Prescott, each of the Argonauts also had a personal team they led to protect the respective incubi they served. Matthew had seen Hiroto's other team: all assassins.

"It must be nice to belong to something, to have some sort of purpose. I miss fighting with hunters," Matthew said, hoping Hiroto would pick up his subtle hint. He stopped summoning in his weapon. "I need blood if we're to keep going."

Hiroto paused for a moment, as if trying to decipher Matthew's intentions. He nodded then said, "Keep summoning your weapon until you can't anymore."

"If I do that, I'll lose control. It'll take over."

"I know. That's the point."

Matthew frowned. "I thought you were nice."

A wide grin crossed Hiroto's face. "You've never trained under me before."

Hiroto must have been some sort of sadist because he forced Matthew to summon and dismiss his weapon a few dozen more times before Bloodreaver took over. Matthew lost control and the next thing he knew he was on his back with Hiroto's two daggers in his chest.

"I'm back," Matthew said.

Hiroto removed his daggers and tossed a blood pack at him.

"You made it to a hundred and twelve times before it took over. Do it again but make it to a hundred and twenty. It'll be five lashes for each one you fall short."

Matthew groaned.

"Prescott warned you that this wouldn't be easy. And this is just the beginning. Wait until you see what I have planned after you get up to two hundred."

Matthew groaned even louder and Hiroto laughed.

He made it up to one-sixty before sunrise and somehow managed to avoid getting whipped. Matthew returned to his room exhausted, but it felt good that he had made progress. He collapsed into bed and fell into a deep sleep.

Thump.

Matthew tried to move as a wave of pleasure woke him, but it was still day and his body didn't want to respond. With effort, he opened his eyes to see Tarrick sitting on his bed beside him. He had on a grey suit that went well with his blue eyes.

"You were having a nightmare. Screaming. You weren't waking."

Had he been? He couldn't recall what he was dreaming about. "Daymare," Matthew said.

Tarrick wasn't amused. Samantha would have appreciated the joke.

"I just wanted to make sure you were okay."

"I'm fine." Neither of them believed that. "Why did you disobey the King and save me?"

Tarrick's Adam's apple bobbed up and down as he started to answer then fell silent with a swallow. Eventually he answered. "It's rare the High King loses control but it can happen. I believe that he still has plans for you and I didn't want him to regret a command issued from a place of rage. Once he's calmer he'll either be grateful for my actions or he'll order me to end you and then probably kill me." He smiled and added, "I'm hoping it's the former."

Disappointment welled up within Matthew. Silva had made it seem like Tarrick had another reason for saving him...

"I might hold off the training with the axe. It's too much for you right now," Tarrick said.

Matthew's heart sank even more. "Please, General, let me keep training. I need something to focus on."

"Alright, fine, but if your nightmares get worse I'm stopping it. No complaining."

Matthew could accept that. "When do you think Samantha will be back?"

"I'm not sure. The King isn't holding audience with anyone, not even the twins have seen him. Until I find out his mood, it's too risky here for her. Expect her gone for a while."

That was a long time to be away from his bonded child but he'd endure if it kept her safe.

"When she's finished with her punishment, I'll set up a nightly video chat so that you can talk to her."

"Thank you."

Tarrick rested his hand on Matthew's shoulder. Finding comfort in it, Matthew closed his eyes and began to drift back to sleep.

Tarrick waited a few moments then stood. Matthew struggled awake again. He didn't want Tarrick to leave but he was too sleepy to speak anymore. He wrapped his sorry excuse of an incubus hold on the general, who looked back at Matthew.

"I can't stay, my day is a busy one." Disappointed, Matthew removed his hold and shut his eyes. He was surprised when Tarrick didn't leave and instead sat back down next to him and placed his hand on his chest. "Would you like to come and sleep in my room? I have a few meetings but I can do most of my work from there."

Matthew's eyelids fluttered as he struggled to keep them open. Yes. Yes, he wanted to sleep in Tarrick's room. He didn't like sleeping alone in the best of circumstances and now...now he needed to be around someone, even if Tarrick sent his emotions into a constant state of confusion. He blinked once.

Tarrick's lips pulled up into a seductive smile. "Go back to sleep, I'll have you moved."

Matthew drifted back to sleep for a while but woke a few more times. Once when he was in the elevator, laying on a gurney. Hunters surrounded him. Guess that's how they moved him around. Another time he woke on Tarrick's bed and listened to him issuing orders into his comm—a pack of shifters causing trouble in Georgia and he was sending hunters to check it out. The final time, Tarrick was sitting beside him reading on his tablet.

"Everything is okay, sleep," he said without looking up. He placed a hand on Matthew's head and stroked it. Matthew felt so weak inside. He shouldn't need to rely on Tarrick...someone who betrayed him... and yet, even knowing that, Matthew needed it.

Tarrick put his tablet down. "You are the most stubborn vampire I know and the only non-lord that can wake during the day. It's quite annoying." Matthew tried to smile but only the corners of his lips twitched, causing Tarrick to smile. "You keep fighting the sun and maybe in a few centuries you'll be able to walk around. But right now, you're young and you need to rest both your mind and body. Sleep."

His last word was an order that Matthew didn't dare disobey. When the sun finally sank below the city skyline, Matthew woke to find Hiroto crouched on his chest again.

"You know my bed is just as comfortable as the general's. It's a little smaller but that makes it better for cuddling."

Matthew chuckled.

"Don't listen to him," Tarrick said, still sitting next to Matthew, wearing a fresh suit and reading a report from a folder marked 'priority'. "Hiroto sleeps in a nest and all your limbs would be sticking out of it."

Hiroto shot a mocking scowl at Tarrick. "I like my nest. It's comfortable and safe. Matthew would love it too if he gave it a chance."

Matthew scooted himself up. Hiroto gracefully rolled off his chest, bounded over Tarrick, and landed on his feet beside the bed.

"Come on, let's go," Hiroto said, clapping his hands together to speed Matthew along, "We're going to make Bloodreaver your bitch."

"Go easy on him tonight, Commander. And no more threatening to whip him."

"Aw, I wasn't really going to whip him, General…unless he wanted it for fun," Hiroto said with a wink.

"Whipping for fun?" Matthew asked as he left the bed and stripped off his shirt to change. "Who would actually want to be whipped willingly?"

Tarrick's eyes grew dark and he sat up a little straighter as his gaze drifted across Matthew's chest. "It can be quite pleasurable if the right person is doing it."

Well, that was something Matthew couldn't imagine being into. He'd had enough of being whipped.

Matthew noticed both Hiroto and Tarrick were watching him with a hungry intensity that made him a little uncomfortable. He moved his arm to cover his rotting skin and looked around. Spotting fresh workout clothes set out for him on a chair, he pushed power into his speed and changed faster than they could see.

"I'm ready, Commander."

Both Tarrick and Hiroto looked disappointed. Hiroto grumbled and saluted to Tarrick as he moved to leave. "Well then, come on."

The training went on for a week. The kitsune didn't follow Tarrick's orders to go easy on Matthew, who would end each night hungry and exhausted. But, Matthew had a feeling the fox pushed him intentionally, giving him a needed distraction.

Hiroto would keep him out training until about five minutes before the sun rose, when he'd return to Tarrick's room, shower at record pace, and collapse into bed. He still woke a few times each day, and each time Tarrick would rub Matthew's chest or squeeze the back of his neck, encouraging him back to sleep. With the training, they didn't have much time to talk but slowly he began to feel a little better.

Matthew rose one night and there was no Hiroto sitting on him… and Tarrick wasn't in his room, but Prescott stood beside the bed with his hands clasped behind his back. His face was somber and there were deep bags under his eyes. It looked like he'd had a hard day.

"Get dressed," he said motioning to Matthew's clothes. "The High King has summoned you."

Matthew had tried to prepare himself mentally for facing the High King again. He was determined to stick to his plan and felt sure he could pull it off…but, fuck, he couldn't stop his hands from shaking.

Malarath had ordered him dead and at any moment someone might carry out the order and kill him. Matthew had to convince him he was a pet worth keeping.

That idea alone made him cringe.

Prescott walked him to the elevator in silence, but didn't join him. When the doors opened again, Matthew was surprised he was on the spa level, not the floor with Malarath's room.

Once he was through the security doors the scent of jasmine hit him and he lost what little nerve he had. Only the thought of more punishment for failing to appear got him moving.

He stepped into the room. The High King stood facing the large pool, his back to Matthew.

Matthew fell to his knees and leaned forward, his hands and head pressed on the floor.

Ezra and Ophelia were attending the King, undoing the laces of his dark robe. Malarath waved them away. They moved off to the side and kneeled, adjusting their sheer robes to perfection.

Malarath turned and said nothing as he studied Matthew. While he endured the scrutiny, Matthew noticed the lingering, faint scent of night and earth…Tarrick had been in the room recently.

Finally, the High King spoke. "Remove your clothes, pet."

Matthew's hands trembled as he stood and removed his shirt. It took him a moment before he moved onto his shoes and finally his pants. He kept his eyes down the entire time, unable to look at the King.

Malarath spread his arms out. "Attend me."

A lump formed in Matthew's throat and he had to swallow hard a few times before it went down. He crossed over the ornately tiled floor and stopped just short of Malarath. He had watched Ezra and Ophelia enough to know what to do. Starting at the laces on his side, Matthew began to untie them. He didn't rush, going the same speed the twins did.

His hands wouldn't stop trembling as he worked the silk free. He came around the front and untied the ribbon that held the front of the robe closed. Before he could finish, Malarath reached out and grabbed Matthew's neck above his collar.

Matthew dropped his hands and went still.

If he was going to do this, he had to start now. Perfect pet. Perfect slave.

Matthew took a step into the High King. "Master," He leaned into Malarath's pale neck, the blue veins below his skin visible. He brushed his lips just above the collarbone. "How can I please you?"

Pheromones scented the air, coming from the twins, who were watching with wide eyes, their desire thick. Matthew hoped he wouldn't have to fuck them, but he was committed to this now and whatever shit he had to crawl through he'd do it.

And when Matthew held Malarath's heart in his hand, all of this would be worth it.

The twins both looked to Malarath with a silent plea to join in. The King ignored them as he released Matthew's neck and slipped out of his robe, revealing his lithe, graceful body.

"Bathe us," Malarath said as he entered the large pool.

'Us'? Matthew wasn't quite sure what he should be doing. Ezra and Ophelia stood and disrobed. Ophelia grabbed Matthew's hand and dragged him into the water until he was about waist high, while Ezra grabbed a floating tray full of everything they could possibly need to bathe someone.

Ezra dipped a washcloth into the water to wet it, then put some gel onto the cloth and rubbed it over the High King's body. The soap dripped down over his subtle muscles.

Ophelia did the same with her own washcloth and began to rub it over Matthew.

The smell of the body wash was…familiar…like fragrant oil…like Devak.

A great sadness welled in Matthew's chest. Violating and owning him weren't enough? Now the High King had to torment him as well?

Matthew's brain shut down and he grew distant.

"Pet—"

Matthew raised his eyes.

"—do you find the scent pleasing?"

Fuck him. Matthew bit the inside of his cheek in an effort to keep control, but he couldn't help his eyes from turning red. Ophelia took a step away from him.

"Forgive me, Master."

"Forgive you? For what, pet?"

"For the way I spoke to you. For displeasing you, Master." The words stuck at the back of his throat. The only thing Matthew was truly sorry for was that he wasn't strong enough to kill him yet.

An evil smile crept across Malarath's face and he held out his wrist.

Matthew carefully grabbed the back of Malarath's forearm, then leaned in and kissed the King's fine skin.

"Enough," the King said, his voice hard as he pulled his arm away from Matthew. Only sounds of bubbling water echoed around them as the twins attended them.

When they were finished, Malarath exited the pool and Matthew trailed after him. The twins dried them both, before they were dismissed. The scent of their disappointment hung in the air as they scurried away.

Malarath glared at Matthew. "I ordered your death."

"I know, Master. A hunter told me."

Malarath reached out and tugged at his collar. Matthew stumbled forward, stopping just short of falling into the High King. "I should remove this and let the Judge end your miserable existence."

"Give me a chance to prove myself to you, Master."

"You have had many chances and you have failed them all, pet. You are a wretched creature with a rotting body. What use do I have for you?"

Matthew gripped at his decaying flesh, trying to hide it, but it was too far spread now. "Let me fight for you, Master. I'll prove my worth."

"You would kill vampires, your friends, your people in my name?"

Yes, he'd kill them. Ascelina, Gwenyth, Emilia, Stolus, even Bryson. It didn't matter. After the King was dead, the vampires could repopulate. Their sacrifices might be unavoidable.

It was a cold but calculated decision, one that tore at him, but he was resolute in his goal. "I'll kill anyone you tell me to, Master."

"You would kill Samantha on my order?"

Matthew lowered his eyes and shifted his weight back on his heels as if it would put distance between him and the King. "Master, I-I couldn't."

Malarath's hand tugged at the collar again, bringing Matthew nose to nose with him. For a moment, it seemed he might remove the collar and end everything, but instead he released Matthew. He held out his hand, produced thick gel in his palm, and smeared it across Matthew's chest.

It was unpleasant and Matthew had no clue as to why he did it. Some sort of incubus thing he never learned about?

"Dress and leave my sight, pet."

Matthew wasn't sure if it was okay to use his speed but he did, tossing on his clothes, and was at the end of the hall waiting on the doors to open in no time at all.

When he got on the elevator, he leaned against the wall and let out a heavy sigh of relief. He hadn't been raped again, he hadn't been asked to fuck anyone, and he was alive for now. He considered that interaction a win.

The elevator took him to the floor with Tarrick's room. He stepped through the security doors and into the hallway were the Wardens, the team of hunters led by Silva, Tarrick's personal guard, stood.

"What the fuck are you doing here, Matthew?" Silva asked.

Matthew pointed behind him. "Um, I was brought here by the elevator. I don't have any say in where it brings me."

Silva looked up at the cameras. "He shouldn't be here."

A loud crash came from inside Tarrick's room.

"Hell's bells," Silva cursed.

"What's going on? Why could I hear that? I thought his room was warded?" Matthew asked.

"He destroyed the runes," one of the other hunters said.

"Go to your room, Matthew," Silva ordered.

Another crash.

"What the hell is happening?"

"I gave you an order," Silva said, all furious five feet of her standing between Matthew and the door.

Matthew bowed and backed up to the security doors, but before they had a chance to open a loud wail came from Tarrick's room. It sounded so helpless; pained.

If Silva wasn't going to tell him what the hell was going on, he'd find out for himself. He surged forward, weaving past the hunters, and slipped into Tarrick's room, shutting the door behind him.

He immediately regretted his decision as a side table went flying into him and splintered apart as it hit his chest. A wood chunk impaled him, coming dangerously close to his heart. He pulled it out and growled at his attacker, but stopped when he saw the state of the room. Everything was smashed or destroyed.

There were claw marks in the artwork, the bed, what was left of the furniture...Paper reports littered the room, and laptops and tablets were shattered on the ground. Part of the wall itself had holes in it.

Standing across from him was the High Lord General in his huge incubus form, hunched over, and crazed. Shreds of a suit clung to some of his skin but he was mostly naked. Atop his head, his horns were gone and all that was left were small, jagged stumps as if they had been ripped off him.

Tarrick roared and stalked towards Matthew.

Thirty-Six

Matthew had about two seconds to decide what he was going to do. He could run out but that'd mean dealing with an extremely pissed off Silva. He could fight but he didn't want to face Tarrick while he was in his full incubus form—both of them would end up hurting each other. Or, he could try submitting.

He sunk to his knees and dipped his head in a passive bow as Tarrick stalked towards him. The incubus leaned over and sniffed the air near Matthew then snarled. He reached down and pulled Mathew up like a doll.

"Mine," he growled and carried Matthew to the partly destroyed and tilting bed. Setting him down, he sniffed the air again. A heartbreaking howl came from Tarrick. "Mine," he repeated.

Tarrick dragged his claws across Matthew's chest. At first Matthew thought he was going to hurt him but instead, Tarrick shred the front of his shirt and peeled it off, then used the remnants of the material to frantically wipe Matthew's chest.

Understanding came to Matthew. This was the High King's doing. He must have taken Tarrick's horns just before summoning Matthew as punishment for saving his life. Then the fucker put his scent all over him, knowing he would return here.

Tarrick began to hump Matthew's leg and his black wings with purple tips spread out behind him, fluttering with excitement. His large cock dug into him hard. "Mine."

That seemed to be the only word the general was capable of uttering in his current condition.

He grunted, hot air coming out of his nose, and began to rub his hands all over Matthew, producing gel and coating his skin with silky trails. The scent of night and earth overpowered him.

Matthew gripped Tarrick's broad shoulders and held on. He laid back and let the Tarrick-monster do its thing.

He let out a hiss when Tarrick's tail slipped under the waistband of his pants. The hiss turned into an unbridled moan when the tail coiled around his cock, massaging it to stiffness.

A pleased hum came from Tarrick, who seemed elated to be satisfying something that was 'his'. He crawled up Matthew, his knees straddling each side of Matthew's hips. Heavy balls rested on his stomach and Tarrick stroked his own thick erection.

When Tarrick's tail slipped lower, a cold dread began to well inside Matthew's chest. He didn't want the feeling—fought against it—but there it was, spreading through him.

Tarrick stopped.

"Don't enter me...please don't," Matthew said, having no idea if the creature would understand.

Tarrick looked Matthew over, then the tail retreated, wrapping back around his cock and squeezing.

That was okay...Matthew could handle that. The dread melted and he moaned as the tail worked him, sliding it up and down his trapped cock. It felt like the best damn hand job he'd ever had. He thrust his hips forward and arched his back.

Matthew's body twitched and loud moans escaped as he drew closer to release. Desperate to ground himself, Matthew gripped muscular thighs and squeezed hard. Tarrick slowed, keeping Matthew near the edge but not letting him topple over. It was agonizing pleasure and Matthew wasn't sure he could handle much more of it.

"Please," he begged.

Every touch became electric, his skin tingled, and Tarrick's powerful aroma put his senses into overdrive. The Tarrick-monster grinned and tightened his tail. The intense pressure brought Matthew so close that any friction would set him off.

Whimpers of frustration fell from Matthew's lips. "Tarrick, please." He moved his hips, trying to create friction—trying to get off—but the massive creature on him didn't let him move. "Yes. Fuck. I'm yours. I'm yours. Let me come. Please."

Tarrick's eyes raked Matthew's body and a low rumble came from his chest. He began to twist his tail. It was all Matthew needed. He coated the inside of his pants with his milky seed, his body convulsing under the incubus.

Tarrick stroked his own cock faster and his own orgasm followed. Matthew's release had felt good but Tarrick's looked like something else altogether. Wave after wave of his thick cum painted Matthew's chest and face. And when he had finally finished, Tarrick rubbed his seed into Matthew's skin.

Matthew stilled and let Tarrick mark him; claim him. He found himself enjoying this. He let himself pretend that he belonged to Tarrick. Foolish. But a nice fantasy.

When Tarrick finished smearing his spunk all over Matthew's chest, he collapsed on the bed and wrapped his arms and legs around Matthew's body in a possessive grip. Matthew began to purr as he shifted into Tarrick, letting himself be completely enveloped.

A sigh of satisfaction came from Tarrick and he drifted off to sleep.

Well…great. It wasn't that late into the night and Matthew was sticky and caged under a resting Tarrick-beast. He'd kill for a bath right now but he wasn't about to try to slip away and risk waking the monster.

About ten minutes passed when a green outline of light appeared in the air and a hunter teleported in. Cullip. Wearing his fitted black leather doublet and armed with his full complement weapons. He even had on his mask that looked like a skull.

The hunter pulled off his mask and set it down on what was left of Tarrick's desk.

"He's made quite a mess in here," Cullip said, stroking his greying goatee as he looked around.

Matthew tried to pull a sheet up over his chest but Tarrick's body had him locked in place.

"Stop that," Cullip said. "You don't want to wake him. It's better if he sleeps the *calsanic* off."

Matthew sighed and gave up. Cullip had probably seen worse anyways. "Calsanic?"

"Incubus word. 'The craze'. It's sort of the incubus equivalent of a blood rage. It can be triggered by intense desire, loss, hunger, or a handful of other things."

"Like losing one's horns?"

"Yeah, that'll do it for him. Horns are a pretty big deal for most incubi but the general has always been particular about his. All our years together and he's never told me why. I've always chalked it up to vanity, but this feels like something else…" Cullip walked over to the side of the bed and ran his fingers over the stumps that were once Tarrick's horns. "Damn it."

"What?"

"I don't know for sure—I'm not a witch—but I think they've been sealed. Won't regrow until the magic is removed. No wonder he's so upset."

"Will he be like this for a while? I'd love to take a shower..."

Cullip laughed. "You're the one who decided to disobey Silva. Now you get to live with those consequences."

Matthew frowned. Oh well. Being held by Tarrick felt nice anyways. "Why isn't she the one in here?"

"She called me. The general and I are closer. Incubi are less likely to attack friends when they lose it."

Cullip sifted through the wreckage in the room and found a stool that had managed to survive Tarrick's wrath. He set it up right before the bed and took a seat.

"Staying?" Matthew asked.

"For a little bit. I just want to make sure the general remains asleep."

Matthew studied Cullip, and realized he didn't actually know much about him.

He knew that Cullip was the current headmaster for the Ashwood VHA, that he was on the Argonauts until he lost his arm, and that he was just over five hundred years old. But beyond all that, he didn't know much about the man. During their training, he had always been serious, sticking to the task at hand; never one for small talk.

"How did you become a hunter?" Matthew asked since it seemed they would have some time together.

Cullip raised an eyebrow.

"Well, how did you meet Tarrick I guess...because you're older than the Hunter Corps..."

"You always were so damned chatty."

Matthew smiled at him. "I guess we could sit here in silence and stare at each other."

Cullip shrugged. "That's fine by me."

Defeated, Matthew stilled but after about five minutes he began to grow restless. He started to shift about a bit, testing the limits of how far he could move. Maybe he could just wiggle out, shower, and come back.

"You're going to wake him," Cullip said, "and he'll probably try to mark you again."

"That's fine by me," Matthew said, narrowing his eyes at the hunter.

Cullip ran his fingers over his goatee. "Alright. If I tell you how we met, will you stop fucking around and let him sleep?"

"Deal."

"I was a Spanish conquistador."

"Seriously?"

"Yes. I came from a poor family and practically grew up in the streets. I thought becoming a conquistador would give me the opportunity to make something of myself, but I never found the riches or the prestige I hoped for. When I hit my forties, I was a washed-up drunkard. The sixteenth century wasn't exactly kind to humans as they aged.

"One night I was in a local tavern, drinking to forget some of the shit I had done in the name of God and country, when this man walked in. He had such a presence that every head turned. The man ignored us, his attentions set on the tavern keeper's daughter. She was young and due to enter a monastery soon. I watched the man seduce her. And when she left with him, I went after them with the intention of defending her honor."

Cullip laughed at himself, at the man he had once been. "He took her out back and that's when a vampire attacked. Without even considering what I was fighting, I pulled my sword and rushed the son of a bitch. I was out of my league when it came to vampires. Still, I tried…the vampire was about to kill me when the man turned into a massive demon and ripped it apart.

"I didn't know what to do. I thought the devil himself had come to take my soul…I fell to my knees, repenting, and the creature laughed at me. 'Would you like a job?' Those were the first words Tarrick ever said to me. I had impressed him by facing the vampire instead of running from it. Once I had calmed down, it didn't take him long to convince me to come work for him. The gold he offered me helped…I was greedy back then.

"He shipped me off to Prescott for training and after a few years I returned to be the general's personal bodyguard."

"Why don't you go back to it? I mean, being his commander and rejoining the Argonauts…"

"I've already upheld my end of the deal, no more questions."

Matthew huffed.

"Alright, fine. Silva is young for a commander but is extremely capable. She needs the experience. If I came back, it would displace her and I want the general to have another commander to rely on besides me. As for the Argonauts, it really is the arm." Cullip motioned to his missing limb.

"They're the best of the best and I'm slower now. I'm still good, but not at their level. Prescott turns a blind eye because we're battle brothers, but if he took a step back he'd see that I'm not the person for the job anymore. And, most importantly, I enjoy training new hunters. In a way, I get to shape the future of the entire Hunter Corps. It's incredibly fulfilling."

"I can understand that," Matthew said. "Having a place in something bigger than yourself." He sighed and looked at the heavy shackles on his wrists.

"You've always wanted that, haven't you?"

Matthew nodded. "Sometimes I wonder what I'd have been like if I was human and had been trained to be a hunter…"

Cullip chuckled. "I've read your file. You'd have never been tapped."

"Really? Why not?"

"Too much of a family man. You liked your stable, happy life. Hunters need to place duty above personal comfort. They're often victims of vampires looking for revenge, not frat boy firefighters."

Matthew had hardly been a stereotypical 'frat boy' but he understood Cullip's point. He would never have left Lily or Alyssa to go be a hunter. Even if he could come home, the job would be too demanding.

Cullip picked his mask back up. "You'll hold up our deal and let him sleep?"

"Yes, Commander."

"I go by 'Headmaster' now."

"Yes, Headmaster."

"You better. I'm going back to Ashwood. Good luck." With a glow of light, Cullip left.

Outside the room, Matthew heard Cullip report to Silva that Tarrick was sleeping now. It dawned on Matthew that those hunters had heard everything that had happened inside…embarrassing. Ah, well.

Matthew scooched around a little to try to get more comfortable, then settled in for the night. And the day…and into the next night. Tarrick slept halfway on top of him the entire time, keeping him caged. A few hours into the new night, Matthew had had enough of being gross and sticky.

Despite his deal with Cullip, he pushed Tarrick off him.

Tarrick woke and growled, his purple eyes flashing in anger.

"Stop it," Matthew ordered. "You're done with this shit."

Tarrick lunged at Matthew to grab him again but he was across the room before he could even come close.

"Listen to me, I don't know why losing your horns has thrown you into such a state but you need to pull yourself together," Matthew said. Tarrick stalked at Matthew, but every time he came close, Matthew dodged him. "You're the High Lord General, you need to start acting like it. You're better than this."

Apparently, Tarrick wasn't hearing him and grew increasingly more frustrated each time Matthew evaded him. Matthew finally sighed and let himself be caught.

Tarrick picked him up and brought him back to the bed where he pinned Matthew again. Matthew looked up into Tarrick's eyes, he had to get through to him somehow.

Over the last ten years Matthew had lost his wife, his guardian lover, and his freedom. The incubi wanted to use him to kill vampires. The vampires wanted to use him to kill incubi. His sire abandoned him—not once but twice now. His body decayed around him, and not long ago he was raped. Tarrick throwing a fit over his horns seemed… petty…but Tarrick didn't need a side by side comparison of whose life was shittier—he needed compassion, someone who cared for him and didn't belittle his pain.

"Tarrick, please, you've handled worse, you can handle this. You're a warrior and a protector. Not just of your family but your whole people. And they rely on you and need you. You're their rock. Having your horns removed is terrible…and I know you'll lose some social standing, but you're the most intelligent person I know—you'll gain that back. It's not as bad as you think it is."

Tarrick stopped.

Matthew could see the struggle in his eyes. He put his hands on Tarrick's face. "Come back."

Tarrick looked down at Matthew. He blinked hard several times, trying to regain control of himself. His irises returned to a deep blue color and his body began to shrink. Wings folded away, tail retracted, ears rounded, hooves became feet, and claws became soft fingers.

He held onto Matthew for a moment then he released him and rolled to his back, closing his eyes. A few bits of shredded clothes hung off his otherwise naked form.

Tarrick eventually opened his eyes and looked around. A deep frown crossed his face as he saw the mess. "Cullip was here?" he asked as he inhaled deeply.

"Yeah. He came to make sure you were okay but went back to Ashwood. Silva and her team have been outside for the past night and half. I don't think she's left to sleep."

"She let you in here?"

"Do you really think she'd do that? She doesn't let me do anything anymore. Truth is, I'm hiding from her," Matthew said with a slight smile.

Tarrick let out a chuckle, then he turned serious as he studied Matthew. "Did I take you against your will?"

"You don't remember what you did?"

Tarrick shook his head. "No. The memories will return in time but...no. I can smell myself all over you."

"You spent a while rubbing your lube on me, which is gross by the way, and you came on me but I let you do it. You didn't rape me... you actually took care of me." He was a little embarrassed that he had enjoyed it so much. Even crazed, Tarrick was a sex god.

Tarrick reached over and put his hand gently on Matthew's jaw. When Matthew looked up at him, Tarrick brushed his thumb across his lips. "I'm glad I didn't hurt you."

Matthew wasn't sure what to say. The two of them lay in silence for a while until finally Tarrick gently squeezed his shoulder. "Let's go shower."

"Yes. God, yes." Matthew got off the bed while yanking his boots off and stripping out of his pants, the insides of which were covered in dried cum. He dropped his clothes on the floor and nearly sprinted to the bathroom.

Making it to the shower first, Matthew twisted the knob to get the water flowing out of the six showerheads. He didn't bother to test the temperature and scalding hot water ran down his body, heating him. He loved it. The only other time he felt this warm was the few hours after feeding on a human.

He missed being warm all the time. It was one of the reasons he enjoyed sleeping next to incubi—their bodies ran hot. And Devak's ran even hotter…

Fuck, he missed Devak.

Tarrick opened the glass door to the large shower, adjusted the knob to a reasonable temperature, and joined him. Using a washcloth, Matthew scrubbed himself raw. He caught Tarrick ogling him once. A brazen smile crossed the general's face, who then went about his business.

Matthew eyed the tub. Showers were great and all but now that he was clean, he wanted to relax. Without a word, he exited the glass shower and turned on the tub's water, settling down in it while it filled.

He felt eyes upon him and when he glanced back, Tarrick had a scowl on his face. Matthew laughed as he realized that he had dripped water all the way from the shower to the tub and that's what upset him.

"You just destroyed your entire room and you're mad at me for getting water on the floor?"

"It would have taken you no extra effort to grab a towel," Tarrick muttered.

Matthew laughed again. He spotted some bubble bath sitting on a vanity at the back of the bathroom. He stood and stretched his body a little to show it off and ensure that Tarrick was looking at him. He then marched across the bathroom, soaking wet, to grab the bottle of blue liquid.

Tarrick growled as he watched Matthew drip water absolutely everywhere.

Matthew winked at him then strutted back into the massive tub, dumping the entire contents of the bottle into the water.

He was being a defiant little shit but he enjoyed pushing his boundaries with Tarrick. The general would yank back on his chain if he took it too far, but for now he was letting Matthew get away with it. If he didn't know better, it almost seemed like Tarrick enjoyed his more playful nature.

"Your ghoul patch has shrunk," Tarrick said from the shower.

Matthew moved the bubbles away to look at it. Tarrick was right. It wasn't much, but had shrunk a bit. Maybe because now Matthew had focus…a goal, a mission.

He smiled, leaned back into the seat, and closed his eyes as the water finished filling. The floral scent of the bath gel filled the air, relaxing him. The shower turned off and Tarrick slipped into the tub, sitting opposite him.

The two men relaxed in a comfortable silence.

"I never wanted to be a general," Tarrick said, breaking the stillness.

Matthew opened his eyes. Tarrick leaned back, his arms outstretched on the edges of the bath. Matthew fought the temptation to scoot over there and sit in his arms.

"Really? I find that hard to believe." Tarrick was too good of a general to imagine him doing anything else.

"I was a social incubus my first transformation, not a warrior."

Matthew's jaw dropped. Tarrick? Social? He didn't even like parties. And he was a skilled warrior…built like one too. Matthew didn't even know it was possible for incubi to change. He thought once they'd hit their first transformation they became a warrior or social and that was it.

"Everyone in my family was a warrior. My mother was already the High Lady General when I was born, all my siblings were warriors, and even my human father was a fighter who served her."

Tarrick was like Lily in that regard; her mother had been human. Only one parent needed to be an incubus for the child to become one, there were no half breeds. At least not when they bred with a human.

"But I ended up a social. I was a disappointment to my mother… she saw me as something that needed protection. I resented her for it and rebelled by taking no interest in her war. I was like any social incubus, I wanted to own businesses and build wealth and power. I wanted my own household before my second transformation—which is almost unheard of by the way. New houses can only be formed with permission from the High King and it's not something he allows often."

Tarrick smiled, lost in a memory. He took a deep breath of the warm, scented air.

"When I was around ninety I had met most of my goals, I didn't own a household yet but I had many businesses that made me extremely wealthy and popular. I was at a party one night and it was attacked. I was useless, couldn't even handle a sword correctly, but there was a warrior there…Gerhardt. He was old and strong—my mother's right-hand actually. I had ignored him most of my life but watching him fight…he was magnificent. He faced a dozen vampires and he killed them all. And I knew I had to have him."

Tarrick laughed and shifted slightly, bubbles sticking to his chest. "I was young and he was out of my league but when I want something, I get it. He became my first mate. I had no idea how serious the war was back then. He told me stories but it all felt so distant. Parties and sex and wealth were all I cared about. I was a young fool…but he liked that I was something that the war hadn't tainted. That when he came home, he could leave it behind."

He stopped his story for a few minutes and looked upwards, his eyes not really focused on anything. Matthew said nothing, knowing Tarrick would continue when he was ready.

"He died in a vampire ambush trying to save an incubus family. That was the night the war was no longer distant for me."

Tarrick rubbed his forehead.

"I had to do something. I begged my mother to teach me to fight but social incubi aren't built to fight vampires. My father took pity on me and taught me how to use weapons. I spent my days training and my nights sneaking out looking for vampires to kill. The first time I faced one I nearly died…but I kept at it, and once I found the names of the vampires that killed my mate, I attacked their stronghold alone. It was a slow process, took all day and night, and by the time the sun rose again they were all dead. Lords and all.

"The High King was so impressed with me that he gave me the

castle I had cleared and assigned a dozen warriors to me. I finally had everything I had ever dreamed about but it felt so empty. When I went through my second transformation, I emerged from it a warrior incubus. It didn't take long for me to become a general after that."

Tarrick stood and grabbed a nearby towel. He dried himself off, wrapped the towel around his hips, and began to walk out of the bathroom, pausing at the door.

"Gerhardt loved my horns—they were his favorite part of me," he said without looking back, then he left, shutting the door behind him.

Matthew sat in the bath for a while to give Tarrick a little time alone. The story he'd just heard broke his heart. This fucking war…everyone was bleeding from it.

He didn't think it was possible to hate Malarath more than he already did, but he found himself seething.

Matthew got out of the tub and dried off. Having no clothes, he wrapped the towel around his hips. He was about to walk into the room when he heard Silva's voice. He froze and hid behind the door.

"Come out, Matthew," Tarrick said. "She won't hurt you."

Matthew felt a little embarrassed that a human who was maybe 110 pounds soaking wet had him cowering. He peeked out the door to see Silva standing before Tarrick. She didn't look mad but even still, Matthew retreated. "It's okay. I'll wait in here until she's gone."

"Get out here," Tarrick ordered, not playing around.

Matthew came out. Tarrick was already dressed in a suit and just finishing putting on a burgundy tie. A set of clothes waited for Matthew on the bed. Leather pants…fuck, when Rosaline returned, he needed to talk to her about this leather fetish she seemed to have.

Matthew took the long way around the room, keeping maximum distance from Silva, and snatched his clothes. He dressed while she gave a report to Tarrick.

"I've arranged a new room for you. It's ready now. And Darius is sending over a full wardrobe, it should be here by morning. Both Lady Rosaline and Headmaster Cullip have requested that you call."

"Alright. I won't be going out tonight. Go get some sleep."

"Yes, sir." Silva saluted then teleported from the room, but not before casting a hard glance Matthew's way.

"Lord General," Matthew said, once she was gone, while tossing on his shirt. All the cameras and listening devices were broken, giving them a rare moment of privacy. And the hunters in the hall had left with Silva. A new shift would no doubt be up here soon.

Tarrick straightened his tie and ran his fingers through his dusty blonde hair, setting it in place. "Yes?"

"I need your help. The High King is going to kill me. And I find myself not wanting to die despite…" Matthew gripped the area where the ghouling flesh was. "…despite what's happening to me."

"I am already trying to help you. That should be obvious."

"I know. I need more, I need to make myself invaluable to him. And the only way I know how to do that is by fighting. I never wanted to be a weapon…and now I need to be more than that. I need you to put me in the field."

Tarrick studied Matthew for a moment. "I need permission from my king to use you in that capacity."

"I know you can get it."

"Your confidence is misplaced, I'm not in his favor right now."

"You'll get permission. My confidence is justified—you know how to play the game."

Tarrick lifted his eyebrow upon hearing the compliment then rubbed his jaw, thinking. "You understand what I'll have you doing? You'll be back fighting your own people again and this time there's no reward for it."

So long as he could make himself a topic of conversation, there'd be plenty of reward.

"I understand. And yes, I'll kill whatever you want me to."

Tarrick narrowed his eyes. "Last week you wanted to die. You're raped and now you want to live? To fight?"

"Yes."

"I need to know why before I put my people at risk by letting you near them."

Matthew wasn't sure if he should tell Tarrick the truth or not. He needed help. He also needed to plant the seeds of doubt. Samantha had told them that they needed to trust each other…and this seemed as good a time as any to start. But it seemed so risky. If Tarrick was tricking him again, Matthew was dead. But he was dead if he didn't. He really had nothing to lose anymore.

"Malarath is a terrible king."

"Those are treasonous words, Matthew."

"But true. He's only king by virtue that he's the most powerful, not because he's good for his people. He checked out centuries ago. You practically rule in his stead. He might have been a great king once, but he's not anymore.

"You might have the vampires on the run for now, but Samantha wouldn't have woken the dragons if she didn't think that they could do a lot of harm. It's only a matter of time before they really join the fight. And the vampires can hold out for a while more. There could easily be a peace but he won't allow it. Because he's not a good king. And you've known this for a long time."

Tarrick said nothing. He clasped his hands behind his back. "It doesn't matter what kind of king he is, he's my king and I am loyal."

"Why?"

"Why am I loyal?"

Matthew nodded.

"It's hard to explain to someone who has not finished their transformation. Incubi are connected in some way I've never fully understood. He's our leader, our head, the one that gives us direction. I've served him my entire life and won't stop now."

"You're wrong. I do understand. I've felt that connection too. I've actually seen it, it's…divine fabric that ties you to him and gives him power. But it's by the choice of the people. That power can be taken away."

Tarrick fell silent. Matthew wished he knew what he was thinking. God, he was an inch away from facing death. All Tarrick had to do was end this conversation and report it to Malarath and it'd all be over.

"You see the fabric because you are Lysandros' son? That's an ability you have?"

Matthew flexed his hands into fists a few times. He wasn't sure he could trust Tarrick with this but if he didn't lay himself bare right now, Tarrick would never be swayed. The loyal incubus would sacrifice his own children, his lovers, his holdings, even his own life at the King's command. But what would he do for his goddess?

"I see the threads that tie the incubi to Malarath because I am Ilertha's son."

An uneasy laugh escaped Tarrick. "No, Matthew."

Matthew said nothing.

"No, Matthew," Tarrick repeated.

Again, Matthew said nothing.

Then Tarrick began to process the pieces he had. It was a while before he spoke again. "I refuse to believe that you are my goddess' son."

"No? The evidence is there. The Blood God didn't turn me at random. He picked me because I'm a demigod and he knew I'd be powerful. He hates my mom by the way, called her *the whore*. Samantha has grown soavik glands on her blood pouches. Everyone keeps saying Lily is strong for her age—it's because she's the granddaughter of a goddess. No other incubus has silver eyes like I do. And she used to sing to me…a nursery rhyme that you yourself told me is about a boy who is lost and one day reunites with his family. I'm pretty sure the song is about me."

"That's not enough for me to believe you are my goddess' son." Tarrick slipped a phone out of his pocket. "But I have an easy way to verify." He raised the phone to his ear. "Send Dawn to High Tower. My old room. I need her immediately. And don't send any hunter teams to this level until I request them." Tarrick ended the call.

"Dawn?" Matthew asked.

"You will see." As they waited, Tarrick watched Matthew, making him feel tight in his own skin. Whoever this Dawn was, his future rested in their hands.

A few minutes later, there was a knock on the door. A woman entered. She was a hunter with blonde-reddish hair. She had high cheekbones, a soft chin, and small nose that would have made her look friendly if she wasn't wearing a don't-fuck-with-me-right-now expression. Her leathers hugged her tightly, almost as if they were an under layer to some missing armor. Matthew recognized her as a hunter cadet that he had trained with a few years ago, but she smelled different now. Like death. Something had changed.

"A demon…" Matthew said.

"*Vigr,*" she said as she snatched the air and a spear appeared out of a swirl of smoke. She pressed the spear tip against his cheek. It wasn't silver but it tingled his skin.

"Call me a demon again and I'll remove the top of your skull and drag your soul to Hel."

"*Dawn.*" Tarrick used her name as warning to back off.

Dawn took a step away from Matthew and let go of her spear. It disappeared into a puff of shadowy smoke. "Apologies, Lord General.

I take exceptional offense to being called a demon."

"What is she?" Matthew asked. The cut on his cheek already stitching together.

"She's a valkyrie."

Matthew blinked once, slowly. "What?"

"It's complicated."

Matthew stayed silent, waiting for more explanation.

Tarrick sighed. "Valkyries are servants of the god of war. She enjoys being a hunter, so we've come to an agreement. She stays and I have access to a divine being. It has come in handy more than once."

Dawn nodded, her eyes glued to Matthew. "Why have you summoned me, General?"

"Is Matthew Ilertha's son?"

She clenched her jaw. "Yes."

"Wait—" Tarrick clearly hadn't been expecting that response, "—he's Ilertha's son?"

"Yes, General. But you should know it is likely Malarath will kill him if he finds out. I suggest you not tell him."

"Why would the High King kill him for such a thing? He worships Ilertha as well."

Dawn scoffed. "If you say so, sir."

"Then who does he follow?" Tarrick asked.

She shrugged. "I don't know. Not my god. And not Ilertha."

Tarrick put a hand on his broken desk, leaning into it. "Do you know who his father is?"

Dawn paused, looking Matthew up and down. "No."

Matthew took a step at her. "If you know, you have to tell me."

"I don't know."

Matthew didn't believe her. He grabbed her shoulders, ready to compel the information from her. She glared at him but didn't try to escape his grasp. "Ilertha is the sex god. She fucks everyone and only she could tell you for certain who your father is."

"Let her go, Matthew," Tarrick ordered. "That's all I need from you, Dawn. You're dismissed."

Once Matthew released her, she turned to Tarrick. "General, if you are going to fight demons again, I should be at your side."

"If I need your expertise I'll assign you to the mission."

"Yes, sir." She looked disappointed as she teleported out.

"How long have you known about your mother?" Tarrick asked.

"Since we removed Devak's curse and he told me that he was a guardian of Ilertha, not the Blood God."

Tarrick's eyes darted back and forth, putting together pieces. "That's why he fled the battle when the blood guardians showed up. They would have killed him otherwise."

"Yes." Talking about Devak made Matthew's heart ached with longing for his dead guardian.

"I wonder if it was Prescott's weapon or the poison from Hiroto's daggers that killed him in the end..."

Hiroto had said something similar. "Why would that matter?"

Tarrick ignored his question. "You're going to try and kill the High King, aren't you?"

"Yes. Are you going to tell him?"

Tarrick shook his head. "What you're really asking is, 'Am I going to betray the incubus king I've been loyal to for a thousand years to protect you, the son of my goddess?'"

"Yes."

Tarrick pulled his phone from his pocket. "Send a team up here to escort Matthew back to his room." He hung up and said, "I can't answer that right now. I need time."

Matthew wanted to ask how much time but he knew this wasn't a decision that could be rushed. And it was one Tarrick could never recover from if things went bad. He only hoped that Samantha was right...that he could trust him even though every part of him was screaming that this was a terrible idea, that he shouldn't have told him anything.

Matthew sensed a team of hunters teleporting into the hall outside. He went to the door but stopped short of opening it. "Whatever you choose to do, you should know that you were wrong, Tarrick. You once told me my feelings for you were just lust...an obsession...a lie... you were wrong about that. I do love you, even though I shouldn't. Even though it confuses me sometimes."

Without bothering to look back he left the room, knowing a response wouldn't come from the general.

Thirty-Eight

Matthew spent the next few nights alone in his room. He passed the time by reading dry-as-shit hunter training manuals. It amused him that Prescott himself had written several of them.

A new reinforced door separating his room from Samantha's had been installed and, to his disappointment, locked. He was hoping to sneak in and grab a few fiction books.

The chest piece of his armor was displayed on the stand in the corner. He ran his fingers over it, feeling the slight shock of magic pulsing through it. It really was remarkable armor and he felt like a badass in it. He wondered if he'd get a helmet...he should have a helmet.

One night, a tablet was sitting on his side table when he woke. He'd never really used one—they'd become popular after he had been turned. It made him feel dated but he fiddled around with it for a few hours and got the basics down. He found it had an app loaded on it that taught languages, specifically Russian. And it had a game where he swapped jewels around. He spent way more time playing than he cared to admit.

When Prescott appeared in the room without announcement, Matthew scrambled to hide the app as he rose and bowed. The Imperator looked less than impressed.

"You have five seconds to change into your compression suit," Prescott said and grabbed the armor chest off the stand. By the time he turned around, Matthew was already changed. Prescott hooked the armor over Matthew's chest and activated the magic. The armor expanded and wrapped around him.

"What's going on, Imperator?" Matthew asked, snatching a comm from the air as Prescott tossed it to him.

"You'll see. When did you eat last?"

"Few days ago. The last time I trained with Hiroto." Matthew wasn't sure why the training had stopped, if it was the High King's doing or Tarrick's, but at least he wasn't caged.

Prescott motioned for Matthew to follow him and the two armored men walked down the hall to the elevator together. The two hunters standing guard saluted as Prescott as he passed. He nodded back and raised his comm to his mouth. "I need a half gallon of blood in the lobby."

When they arrived at the lobby, the rest of the Argonauts were waiting for them. They were securing weapons and double checking the belts on their leathers, prepping for a battle it looked like.

A hunter appeared with a large bag of blood. "Down it fast," Prescott said. Matthew did. "You remember how to get to the stone?"

"Yes," Matthew answered, wiping blood from his lips.

"You have thirty seconds to meet us there. Don't let a human see you. Go."

Matthew really wanted to know what was going on now. They were going to let him run around New York alone? But, he supposed, there wasn't much of a risk of him escaping. The collar no doubt had a tracker on it and they knew he'd never abandon Samantha, even if she wasn't currently in the tower.

He pulled energy from his blood pouches and sprinted out the door. The city went by him in a blur and he didn't stop until he was standing next to the stone. Having teleported, the Argonauts were there waiting for him when he arrived.

Prescott touched the stone and they teleported to a shabby building with no windows, and the only exit was a thick door. Holding up his six-shooter crossbow, Lock opened the door and looked outside.

"It's clear," he said.

Matthew followed the team out. They were in the middle of nowhere; a massive snow-covered field that had trees surrounding it.

"Where are we?" Prescott asked Matthew.

"I don't know, sir, I've never been here."

"Best guess."

They were about eight hours closer to dawn...the snow... "Somewhere in Russia, Imperator."

"Yes. There's a town five miles north of here. Think you can keep up with us?" Prescott asked. Hunters had a limited range on their teleport and if they weren't familiar with the area they had to see where they were going, so they wouldn't be going too fast. And Matthew could easily follow their scent if he lost sight of them.

"Yes, sir."

The hunters teleported away and Matthew took off after them. He hadn't taken into account how hard it was to run in armor in the deep snow, but he managed to keep up by changing his strides to leaps and hopping over the drifts. He felt ridiculous but it worked. Behind him, the building disappeared as he passed through a veil that kept it hidden.

As they approached the town, the hunters stopped teleporting and continued on foot. Without saying a word Matthew fell in behind them, and it wasn't long before he knew why they had stopped tele-porting: vampires.

Lots of vampires.

Prescott held up his hand and the team waited in silence.

A vampire was coming their way. The hunters disappeared leaving Matthew exposed and alone, without any sort of instruction.

Dicks.

It'd be nice to know what was going on here.

A female vampire dropped down from the roof of a derelict con-crete building. She looked young, maybe seventeen when she was turned but, judging by the power that radiated from her, she wasn't a young vampire. She crouched and sniffed as she studied the grove of trees the hunters were hiding in.

She called out something in Russian. Matthew didn't know enough yet but he guessed it might have been 'who's there?' or 'show your-self.'

Fine. This vampire would sense Matthew soon enough—he had to act. If he got punished for it, oh well.

Matthew appeared next to the vampire. "Do you speak English?" he asked, tossing her a charming smile.

She gasped, not expecting his speed. "Da."

For a moment, he considered killing her. She wasn't weak but he could rip her throat out before she could stop him. However, doing so would cause her body to decay and the scent would draw others. And, more importantly, he didn't want to kill her.

He looked into her eyes. "You checked out this area and found nothing here. Move along."

As she struggled against his compulsion, he gently touched her face and pushed her emotions, making her want to trust him.

Nodding, she surrendered to him and wandered off, her eyes passing by Matthew as if he was no longer there.

Matthew returned to the trees where he knew the hunters were hiding, even if he couldn't see them. Hiroto returned from scouting, and the team reappeared.

"There's a pack of six wolf shifters guarding the outside," the fox reported. "Inside has eleven armed human thralls, six more unarmed, and five vamps, one's a lord. There's eight patrols in the area and our intel was correct: they have a safe room."

"Where's Zakhar right now?" Prescott asked.

"Top floor, second room from the left of the western corner."

Prescott motioned to Vik, who pulled out her cell phone. She brought up a picture of a vampire and showed Matthew. The man was plain-looking, with a thin nose and big ears. Matthew thought if he threw on some glasses, he'd look like a stereotypical science geek.

"Here's the deal," Prescott said to him, "we need to take this vampire—Zakhar—alive. We can't fight our way in because they'll have him in that safe room before we could get him out."

"And I ain't wantin' to fight this whole place," Lock said.

Nellis flexed his gauntlets. "I still think we should. Sounds fun."

"Hush," Prescott said. "Matthew, since it's a vampire owned building and you don't need to be invited in, you're going to jump in, grab the vamp, then run back here with him. We'll cover the escape."

"I'm taking him back to the stone, sir? Won't the vampires just destroy it once we're gone?"

"Yeah, but getting him is more important than one leystone in the middle of nowhere Russia. With this many vamps around, they'll be finding it soon anyway."

"Can I have my axe, Imperator? Or, you know, any other weapon…"

"No. Do what I tell you to and you won't need it."

Crash into a room, grab a vamp, run away…should be easy enough.

"The building is three blocks over," Hiroto said. "Salmon colored."

"Any other questions?" Prescott asked.

Matthew had a bunch. Why was this guy important? Why were they using such a snatch and grab tactic? It seemed so risky and there'd be vamps all over them chasing them down once Matthew nabbed the man. He could outrun just about any vampire…except the snow slowed him, he'd have a struggling lord in his arms, and some vampires could fly. But he'd figure it out. He always did. "None that are relevant, sir."

"Go now."

Matthew took off, weaving through buildings to dodge patrolling vampires. An uneasy tingling sensation pricked at the back of his neck. Something was off.

On his way to the building, he rounded a corner and almost ran smack into the back of an armed human. He froze. The human hadn't seen him. Matthew backed away unnoticed and slipped through a broken window of an abandoned building.

Taking the human wouldn't be an issue normally, but making any sound or drawing blood would alert every vampire in the area. He couldn't risk it. A few other humans came patrolling through but eventually moved on.

He exited the building and, with greater caution, finished making his way to the three-story pinkish-orange building. It was teeming with vampires, shifters, and humans—far more than Hiroto had reported. The vampires roaming outside looked like fighters, most armed. The werewolves were mercenaries, not a friendly pack. And the humans could pass as special forces.

Matthew saw the room he'd be aiming for. His plan was to pour energy into his legs, go crashing through the window, grab Zakhar, and retreat.

He was getting ready to jump when he sensed something else. Lords. Fuck. Five of them. Shit. No wonder he felt uneasy; their auras pressed at him.

There was no way Hiroto would have missed them…

Oh. Of course. This was a fucking test. Unless they needed to close portals, the Argonauts could handle something like this on their own.

Prescott wouldn't be putting Matthew on a mission—or testing him—unless the High General had done something.

Matthew smiled to himself.

Tarrick had given him his answer—he was siding with Matthew.

Tarrick was going to stand against the High King.

Samantha had been right, they had to trust each other now.

A strange warmth Matthew rarely felt anymore bubbled in his chest.

Well, he sure as hell wasn't going to bash through a building filled with people who would kick his ass and have him running like a coward. If he had to pass this test, he'd do it the incubus way.

He'd make a show of it.

Thirty-Nine

Matthew returned to the grove alone after he had finished executing his plan. If the hunters were there, he couldn't see them. He shrugged and began trekking back to the stone.

"What are you doing?" Prescott asked, appearing before him.

"I was going to wait for you by the stone, Imperator," he said.

Prescott looked behind Matthew. "Where's Zakhar?"

"Yeah. About that, sir. Hiroto's information was a little off."

An exaggerated gasp came from the trees. *"Never,"* Hiroto said.

Prescott sighed. "Alright team. We'll come back and clean up this place tomorrow when the sun's up. Let's get Matthew back."

The trip to the stone, and then to the tower, passed in relative silence. Prescott sent his team ahead and rode in the elevator with Matthew.

"I told Lily what Malarath did to you," he said as he pressed a rune to take them to one of the hunter floors.

Matthew's chest sank. "Did you have to, sir?"

Prescott removed his helmet. "Too many people saw it happen, by now the story has spread through the entire community. It was better she heard it from me first. She handled it okay. She's tough."

"Is she? I could talk for days about what she was like as a child, but I really don't know what kind of woman she's become. I've missed too much of her life. Sir."

"She's a survivor. It's made her hard but she's young enough to not have lost her idealism. She's perfect." A small smile crossed Prescott's face not at all meant for Matthew.

The way his voice grew softer as he talked about her, it was clear he deeply cared for Lily. Matthew didn't like the idea of Prescott with her, but he was happy she found someone who cared for her. Someone who could keep her safe.

"Do you think she'd ever want to see me again, sir?"

"Yes, she's been asking. But the High King isn't permitting it right now."

That was that then. "Can you tell her—" Matthew wasn't sure what he wanted to say. Tell her he loved her, that he missed her, that he was sorry...

"I'll tell her," Prescott said, apparently knowing what Matthew wanted.

"Thank you, sir."

The elevator doors opened and Matthew followed Prescott out of the elevator, into a conference room located in one of the hunter sections of the tower.

The team took a seat around the oval table. Prescott, who stood at the head of the table, motioned for Matthew to sit as well.

Hiroto, sitting opposite Matthew, pushed down his mask and smiled at him.

"Hiroto, you'll start," Prescott said.

The kitsune stood. "We could use someone as fast as he is. He was able to keep up with us just fine, even if he can't teleport. His ability to compel would be helpful for interrogation, and his ability to erase memories would be good for clean-up. He's also a gargoyle commander. It'd save us having to break out the busters each time one gets frisky. Because of his weapon, he needs to fight from time to time anyways, Matthew might as well be with us where we can keep an eye on him. He'd round out the team, it's a yes from me."

Hiroto smiled at Matthew again and sat back down.

"Vik," Prescott said.

She pushed her grenade launcher from her lap onto the table as she stood. "I like the idea of having a vampire on the team. Hiroto has better eyesight and hearing but vamps have a better sense of smell, so long as they remember to breathe, and Matthew can sense demons. Also, I wouldn't mind using him to test out new toys. The Lord General is so reluctant to give me any vampires and they never cooperate. My only reservation is that he uses a melee weapon. It's hard enough getting grenades in there with you and Mac. With three it'll be rougher, but I have a few ideas on how to adjust. Yes, I'm okay with him on the team."

Great. She wanted him because he'd be her guinea pig. Oh well, at least he was two-for-two so far. Matthew wondered if the whole team had to accept him or if majority rules. Or maybe Prescott had the final say and he just wanted input.

She took her seat again, and Prescott motioned to Nellis who didn't bother to stand. "I like the guy, he can throw a punch, even if he can't hold his liquor worth shit. But tonight, instead of trying to carry out his assignment he bitched out and returned to us. That pisses me off. No. I don't want him on the team."

Matthew couldn't blame him. He wondered if the sun had gone down in Russia yet. It had been close to dawn there.

Nellis leaned back into his chair, and Lock stood and adjusted his belt. "I don't trust him. He's killed more than a few of my friends," the cowboy said.

Hiroto fidgeted as if he wanted to say something but he kept his mouth shut.

Lock held his hand up to Hiroto to settle him down. "Yeah, Hiroto, I read his file. I know the circumstances ain't so black and white, that doesn't mean he didn't rip them apart. And what if something happens to either of his daughters when he's in the middle of a mission? Or if his axe takes control of him? I don't like the idea of havin' to watch a teammate over my shoulder. But I'd be willing to see him through a trial period. Give him a chance to prove me wrong. I'm abstaining until then."

Prescott took a deep breath. "Sorry, Matthew. I'm sure you figured out that tonight was a test to see if you'd be a good fit for the Argonauts, but it's an all or nothing decision on this team."

"What about you, Imperator?" Matthew asked, wondering what his answer would have been.

"You wouldn't have gotten this far if I didn't already approve you for the team." Prescott rubbed the stubble on his chin then crossed his arms. "Something strange has happened in the last few weeks. Four different people have independently mentioned that you'd make a good sixth member.

"I think that you're more incubus than people give you credit for. You want to be on this team and you've been dropping hints around. I found the idea interesting. Your skill set is one the Argonauts has never had before. You don't come without your challenges but we can overcome those. You're trainable and, when you're not busy losing control, you can follow an order."

"Four, sir?"

"You don't know which four people came to me?"

"No." Matthew had hinted to Hiroto and Tarrick but he wasn't sure the other two.

Prescott motioned to Hiroto. "Our fox likes the idea of having another nonhuman with us. The Lord General wants to use you back in the field, he pointed out I could babysit you better if you were on my team. Headmaster Cullip said something in passing. And Samantha."

Cullip? Really? That was surprising. And Samantha? Of course she'd try to help him but he hadn't expected it. He should have.

"She was insistent that you'd be joining the team soon. Saw it in a vision or something. But oracles can misinterpret things, especially when it's someone close to them. She probably saw you fighting alongside us in some battle and took it to mean you—"

A hunter teleported into the room interrupting him with a quick salute. "Sir, you need to see this." He grabbed a remote for the screen that took up most of the wall behind Prescott. A Russian news report came on along with live footage from a helicopter, filming a charred town leveled and smoldering. The sun had risen there.

Matthew could only pick up a few words from the report but the gist of it was that a military munitions storage had blown up a few minutes ago. It wasn't clear if there were any casualties.

Prescott turned back to Matthew. "What did you do?"

"I—"

"Imperator," A female voice came from Prescott's comm. "This is Commander Reshetilov, I serve Lady Eesla.

"Go ahead, Commander," Prescott said, not taking his eyes from Matthew.

"Something really...strange...uh, is happening. Two werewolves just showed up here carrying a bag. It has a vampire in it and they're insisting that they deliver it to you and only you."

"One moment, Commander." Prescott put his comm on mute.

A wide grin crossed Matthew's face. "You're right," he said to Nellis, who was glancing between the news footage and Matthew, "It'd be really fucking shitty if I didn't carry out the mission. There was a time I would have rushed into the building weaponless, tried to face the lords and the other vamps without a second thought. And it would have been a mess.

"None of the werewolves had on contacts to prevent me from compelling them, so I compelled a couple to bag Zakhar as soon as the sun rose and the rest blow the munitions depot I smelled nearby."

Matthew couldn't have risked compelling the humans since they were enthralled to vampire lords, who would have been able to sense the loss of control. But the wolves... As far as Matthew knew, he was the only vampire who could compel other supernatural creatures. Well, his sire too, but that hardly counted.

Prescott turned his comm back on. "Commander Reshetilov, the wolves are under a compulsion right now. Take them into custody and cage the vampire. I'll be there sometime tomorrow to claim them. Once you have them secure let dispatch know and we'll release the compulsion."

"Yes, sir." The comm cut out.

"I change to a yes," Nellis said, grinning while he watched the burning town.

Prescott flicked off the screen and pointed at Matthew. "One year. That's your trial period after which we all get to vote again. There's a few things you need to understand. You aren't a hunter or part of the corps, you'll be unique in that regards. You're still a slave. You break my rules, I'll punish you. And, since you are a reflection of me, it'll be worse than it's been in the past."

Worse? Worse than eating silver? Being whipped? Starved? Put in a cage? Awesome.

"The High King's orders trump any others. If he wants you and we're on a mission, you leave the mission. I expect you to be fluent in Russian by the end of this month. If you aren't out with us, you'll be training. How far is he with the axe?" Prescott asked Hiroto.

"We're starting to get there. Maybe a few more months and it won't be an issue unless he's starving. It might be decades before he fully masters it and can tap into all its power."

"As long as it's not taking him over, that's fine. You might want to take a temporary leave of Lord Kōki, you'll be here most nights working with him."

"Can't wait." Hiroto shot a sly wink to Matthew.

"Oh, two more things. One, that ghoul patch grows at all, you're out. And two," Prescott summoned in a small box and tossed it to Matthew. He opened it, inside was a brass ring that sparked of magic...a motherfuckin' daylight ring. "Welcome to the Argonauts."

Forty

Being an Argonaut was exhausting. Well, at least training to be an Argonaut anyways. Over the next three weeks, Matthew mostly worked with Hiroto, who forced him to stay awake during the day so he could get used to the daylight ring (again). He didn't get much sleep, and when he was allowed to sleep he crashed hard and fast.

Hiroto hadn't been kidding when he had implied that he was a strict trainer. He ran Matthew ragged, taking him to the limits of his control and expecting him not only to keep away a blood rage, but to stop the axe from taking over his body. He also refused to let Matthew go outside and stand in the sun. Hiroto was huge into discipline and schedule while training; he wouldn't allow anything to change from his rigid plan.

The little fox was evil.

Well, not really. Matthew knew Hiroto was being hard on him to help him in the long run. It was needed if he'd have any chance of staying on the Argonauts…but still, he missed the fun, I-want-to-fuck-you fox that was replaced by the serious, do-it-ten-thousand-times-until-you-master-it fox.

In addition to training with Hiroto, Matthew had to squeeze in learning Russian. And study all the hunter rules. What took humans years to master he had to do in a few weeks. It wasn't exactly easy.

The only thing Matthew had to look forward to was when Samantha called him on his tablet. The first time she called, he wasn't sure why his tablet was making such an awful sound but he pressed the persistent green button and her face appeared. Her irises were a striking silver now, and with her brown hair it almost looked as if they were truly related.

After she made fun of him for holding the camera wrong—all she saw was his forehead until he tilted it down—they got to talk for ten minutes. And every night from that point on they had ten minutes of video calling.

He savored every second of that time, even if she insisted that they only speak in Russian to help him practice. Sometimes having an all-seeing oracle child was annoying as shit. He would have rather just spoken to her in English since their time was so limited but he did it her way. Her Russian was near-perfect.

Matthew learned that she was getting along with the people at Tarrick's estate for the most part, and things were going okay with Gavyn. Her boyfriend met some resistance since hunters sleeping with vampires was a huge violation of their rules, and every hunter had their own opinion on the matter—which they weren't shy in sharing.

Every night when their talk ended, he missed her more and more. The distance was killing him.

During training, he never saw Tarrick. He knew the general was still in the building, he'd smell his lingering scent from time to time, but he never came down or let Matthew sleep in his room. He was probably angry at him for putting him in that position.

Whatever the reason, Matthew found himself longing to see him, even for a few moments. He wished he had Tarrick's restraint and control when it came to emotions; it would make everything less complicated.

Matthew crashed into bed early one night, around six p.m., hoping to get a few hours of sleep before Hiroto harassed him some more, but no such luck. The moment he closed his eyes he saw a white flash through his eyelids and he felt the fox land on his chest.

Matthew groaned and put a pillow on his head. "Go away."

"Up."

Matthew groaned again and threw the pillow at Hiroto, who backflipped out of the way and landed crouching on the edge of the footboard.

"You know," Matthew said, "I actually have to get sleep even with a daylight ring on, right? It's not just a free pass to be awake all the time—" Hiroto tossed a bottle of blood at him. Matthew hadn't been getting all that much blood lately. "What'd I do to earn this?"

"There's an attack in progress. That vamp you bagged, Zakhar—they're trying to get him back. He's a pretty big boss in Russia."

"You should have led with that. Where's the attack?" Matthew ripped off the cap and downed the blood as fast as he could.

"Sweden. We were keeping him in King Hindrik's castle. That's where it's happening."

Hiroto grabbed Matthew's armor from the stand and hopped back onto the bed. Matthew was in his compression suit in a moment and stood before him, arms out. Hiroto hooked it over him and activated the magic, expanding the armor.

"That's where Vik lives, right? She's the commander there."

"Elevator." Hiroto said and disappeared with a flash of white light.

When Matthew made it to the elevator, Hiroto pressed the button for the lobby.

"Yeah, she was there when the vamps started their attack like ten minutes ago. They've already blown the outer walls and some have made it inside."

"Is the Lord General there?"

"Yep. And the rest of our team. We weren't going to call you in since we haven't done any team training. But…the High King ordered you to the fight."

"Really?"

Hiroto nodded.

"I wonder why," Matthew said.

The elevator's doors opened. "Stone," Hiroto said and disappeared again.

Matthew was out the doors and crossing blocks of New York in seconds.

"Rumors are already flying that you might have joined the team," Hiroto said when Matthew arrived. "If he doesn't act soon his reveal won't be as impressive."

"Ah, *the show.*"

Hiroto laughed as he pulled up his red mask to cover his face. "I call it *the spectacle.*"

Damn it. That sounded cooler.

"Prescott's going to have to take off your shackle, I don't have that ability." Hiroto put his hand on the stone. "Follow our lead and listen for the Imperator's orders. Don't go ahead of us. Remember that we need to work as a team here. You aren't a solo fighter anymore."

"Got it." Matthew flexed his long, dark claws and his eyes turned red.

"Oh, and, not many know you're fighting for us. Since the vampires can overhear our comms nothing has been said yet. The call will go out as soon as I teleport us in, but don't be offended if some hunters take shots at you," Hiroto said and activated the stone.

With a green flash, Matthew was in Sweden. He was inside a large, undecorated room of a brown-stoned castle or estate—or so he assumed. Incubi loved their castles. Surrounding him were dozens of hunters that had also just teleported in. Weapons immediately turned on him.

"Be advised that the vampire Matthew is fighting with the Argonauts. Do not attack him," a dispatcher said over the comm.

That didn't stop eight bolts and two silver tipped arrows from coming his way. Most hit his armor and bounced off harmlessly, but he had to catch two before they went into his head.

"I should have a helmet," he said to Hiroto, dropping the bolts. He was thankful that his armor covered his neck, which was one of the easier kill spots on a vampire, but enough damage to the brain and he wouldn't be waking up ever again.

"Stop shooting my teammate and move out," Hiroto yelled at the hunters who seemed generally confused by Matthew's presence. Hiroto might have been small but he had a frightening visage decked out in his assassin gear, and the hunters did as he said.

A nearby explosion rocked the castle, sending bits of dust flying into the air. Hiroto teleported away and Matthew went running after his scent. He cut through hallways, filled with dead bodies and blood, both human and a few incubi. The vampires that had breached the castle had been pushed back out.

It sounded like they were trying to get in again. Matthew headed to the west end where he also picked up Prescott's scent.

He was almost to the front doors when Hiroto yelled, "Stop!"

Matthew came to a screeching halt inches from the doorframe. Hiroto emerged from the shadows and motioned to a decaying vampire's body, then touched a runic symbol that was carved into the frame, draining it of power.

"Thanks," Matthew said, disappointed he missed the rune. It was a dumb mistake. One that could have gotten him killed. But the smell of blood and the energy of the battle outside made him excited…and sloppy. He closed his eyes and centered himself. He couldn't risk losing control. He needed to be smart right now.

"Let's go," Hiroto said and teleported outside.

Matthew followed more cautiously this time, relying a little less on instinct and a little more on his training. Frigid air hit his face as he exited the castle. He had never been to Sweden before and now he wished he had taken the time to visit.

The view before him was breathtaking—in his case, quite literally. The castle was located low on a mountainside. Laid out before it was a flat valley with a now-frozen river cutting through it. Jagged snow-covered peaks surrounded him. Above him, more stars than he had ever seen in his life, blanketed the night sky.

Matthew could imagine spending time in the valley, passing the night studying the stars or running along the river, tracking animals. The only thing that would make it perfect would be a small human population to stalk and hunt.

His fantasy was quickly shattered by the reality of a battle happening around him.

One of the wings of the castle looked as if it had been under repairs, but now crumbled as a fire raged, filling the air with thick smoke. The electricity had been cut and flares lit the grounds so that the hunters and incubi could see. There were calls to get generators running.

The vampires' attack was genius. If they had tried for a frontal assault, they would have been slaughtered, the castle near unassailable from that angle. But the vampires came through the back of the mountain side, tunneling through the ground and emerging from the rear.

They had set up trenches and mounds of dirt to protect themselves. Whoever had moved this quantity of earth had to be extremely powerful. Matthew could sink into the ground and make tunnels with time, but he couldn't make anything this large or intricate.

The vampires also had witches with them, teleporting their forces in and creating their own protective barriers.

But perhaps the most shocking to Matthew was the presence of humans. He had seen them use thralls but never at this level. There were hundreds of them. All armed like a fucking military force, which was strange because the incubi had long ago found magical ways to counter modern weaponry.

Hunters had runic shields that would automatically form when a high-speed projectile came at them, and homes had protective wards that stopped missiles or bombs from reaching their target. But hunter runes had limits, and after a few minutes of taking a full barrage of bullets, their shields would go down and they'd have to fall back and wait for it to recharge. And the castle's defenses meant shit if a bomb went off from within the ward.

The vampires knew this and were sending in suicide bombers. From a distance, Matthew watched as hunters shot down the humans, but one made it through and an explosion blasted the area, sending bodies flying and leaving behind a deep crater in what was once a back garden.

Jesus. This attack was a slaughter on both sides.

An incubus warrior fell to the ground and almost hit Matthew on his way down. The incubus rolled and got back to his feet, scowling at the vampire lord that had ripped one of his wings in half. The vampire sneered and flew off to fight a more threatening foe. The warrior raised a weapon to Matthew but lowered it when he saw who it was. He sneered and turned to fight a new target on the ground.

Matthew rushed after Hiroto, who hadn't bothered to wait for him. They ended up on the front side of the castle where Tarrick had set up his command between the front door and a still-standing section wall.

Several warriors stood guard, while human dispatchers worked on military grade laptops, and hunter teams teleported in and out, relaying information or getting new orders.

The battle was a chaotic hurricane with Tarrick—armored and in full incubus form—standing calmly in the eye, directing the storm.

The Argonauts were there as well, but Matthew's attention ripped away from them when he sensed vampires nearby. A few feet away actually. He looked around, but with the overwhelming smells of the battle he had no idea where they could—

Matthew surged forward at Tarrick, who moved to a defensive stance in response to the charge. A foot in front of the general, Matthew reached down into the ground and grabbed a vampire by its neck, plucking it from the dirt like a weed, and threw it up into the air. An ear-splitting shriek came from the creature as its wings emerged and it tried to fly away, but the hunters were already riddling it with bolts.

Matthew grabbed a second vampire. This one tried to fight him, sinking lower into the ground, out of his reach, but Matthew split the dirt apart, revealing a tunnel. He jumped in to attack and midair he heard Prescott say, *"Sa'nile."* Bloodreaver formed in his arm as Matthew came down on the vampire, slicing it from neck to hip. With a second swing, Matthew dismembered it for good measure.

A spray of blood coated the entire mobile command center. Tarrick wiped it out of his eyes with a look of pure annoyance.

Matthew grimaced. "Sorry, General."

"We're moving inside to solid ground," Tarrick said to the command support around him, ignoring Matthew. "Where's my GPR?"

"The one at the castle was destroyed. We're bringing in new devices now," a dispatcher said while scooping up her laptop and slinging a pack over her shoulder as the entire operation began to move inside.

Matthew picked up his shackle, attached it to his belt, and jumped out of the hole, landing next to Hiroto. "What's GPR?" he whispered to the fox, not wanting to piss anyone off.

"Ground-penetrating radar."

"Oh."

"Didn't you read the weapons and devices manual?"

God damn it. "It was that or learn Russian. It's next on my list, I swear."

Hiroto laughed. Oh good, now that they were in the middle of death and mayhem, he was back to being a fun-loving fox.

"Argonauts—" Tarrick said as he moved into the castle, "—flank the west side. See if you can't get into their tunnels and scatter their leaders."

Prescott acknowledged the order and teleported away, along with the rest of the team. Matthew went running after them. Man, having magic to move around must be awesome.

On the way there, he saw a group of human thralls keeping a team of hunters pinned down behind a boulder. He altered his trajectory slightly and charged at them. The thralls opened fire with their machine guns. Bullets bounced off Matthew's armor, but one hit him in the forehead. He went tumbling to the ground as the bullet went through his skull.

Ouch.

He focused on healing and was back on his feet before the humans could do any real damage.

Blood. Bloodreaver whispered to him.

"Yeah. Yeah. You'll get your fill."

Matthew swung his axe deep into the humans' soft flesh, slashing them apart. He was so used to fighting monsters that it was almost laughable at how easy these thralls went down.

He would have felt bad for them but they had shot him in the head and that pissed him off. With the humans lying in pieces on the ground, he took off again. He heard confused remarks from the team of hunters behind him, wondering why the hell Matthew was back on their side.

"What took you so long?" Prescott asked when Matthew ran up. The rest of the Argonauts looked peeved too. They had been waiting for him about a quarter mile from the battle, up the mountainside. There wasn't much foliage, mostly rocks and snow.

Matthew pointed to his forehead. "I was shot in the head. Then I killed—"

Prescott held up his hand to silence him. "Hiroto sensed some vamps near here. Find us a way in. Once we're in, be quiet. The moment any of us make a sound, they'll be onto us."

Matthew put his hands on the frozen ground. He sensed a tunnel twenty feet to his left, walked over to the area above it, and pushed the dirt open to form a hole.

Prescott jumped in first, followed by Hiroto and Lock. Vik handed her grenade launcher to Matthew and went in. Nellis shoved him aside and went after her. Matthew followed, closed the hole behind him, and handed the grenade launcher back to Vik. She smiled as a thank you.

Hiroto was already gone, scouting ahead.

Prescott motioned for the group to follow him. The tunnel was cramped and crude, bending around boulders. Every now and then the passage would widen or get so small that he and Nellis had to crab walk sideways to squeeze through. There were also false branches that lead to nowhere.

The team paused as they all heard a group of vampires approach.

Nellis grabbed Vik and ducked into a side passageway with her. Prescott and Lock backtracked to a wide section and all of them disappeared from Matthew's view.

God damn. Trying to fit in with a team of hunters that had completely different abilities wasn't easy. Matthew leaned against the wall and sank into the dirt as vampires passed by.

When he stepped out, the team was already down the hall, not waiting on him. He was starting to get a bit frustrated, feeling like a leashed dog they were forced to take out because mom said so rather than a useful squad member.

Matthew gripped his axe and trailed after them.

From above them, Hiroto dropped down and made hand motions to indicate that the vampire command center was a hundred feet ahead. There were four lords inside, three regular vamps, and six humans. Russians, judging by the voices Matthew heard. He was relieved that Bryson wasn't here. He really didn't want to kill him today.

Matthew had no idea what their plan was as they neared the command room. The Imperator alone could take on a vampire lord or two…in open quarters. But four lords in a small area would just swarm him and rip his armor off. And there was a slight problem—it was sealed.

Prescott motioned for Matthew to make an opening on his command. Vik raised her grenade launcher and took aim. Matthew couldn't help but feel a little uneasy about her choice of weapon in such a cramped space, but he didn't have time to dwell on it as Prescott gave him the signal to go.

Matthew opened a hole in the wall and Vik rapid-fired grenades into the room. He closed the hole and explosions caused the tunnels to shake, followed by pained screams coming from the sealed command center. The Argonauts teleported into the room. Matthew started to make a hole so he could join them but a cloud of silver dust came bellowing out of it.

Well. He wasn't going in there. It'd boil his skin and blind him, making him too much of a liability. It sounded like the other Argonauts had it under control anyway. The humans had died in the first concussive blast. The regular vampires went down with the silver and second explosion. The lords were fighting but they were hampered by the silver and unexpected ambush.

Matthew sighed heavily.

Blood. The axe whispered.

"Yeah, I know the feeling," he said to it, wanting to get into the fight. A fucking battle was going on outside and instead of being part of it he was leaning against a wall, doing nothing but opening dirt holes. Matthew: born of the sex goddess, Ilertha, sired by the Blood God, Lysandros, wielder of Bloodreaver, Harbinger of Ruin, and dirt mover *extraordinaire*.

"Prince—" a voice said with a thick Russian accent. He looked down the hall to see a brute of a Russian vampire with a flattop haircut. He also had pink scars down the side of his body, as if he had been badly wounded recently and was still healing.

"*Vikentiy*," Matthew growled.

Forty-One

Vikentiy. Betrayer. Large motherfucker with a stupid military buzzcut hair.

Matthew gripped his axe and began to stalk down the narrow hallway towards the big vampire.

Vikentiy didn't wait for Matthew to get to him. He jumped and moved the dirt above him to get away.

Matthew surged after him. Dirt crashed down as Vikentiy collapsed the ceiling. Matthew roared and forced the dirt away from him as he crawled out of the tunnel.

By the time he got to the surface, Vikentiy was flying in the air; his large grey bat wings flapping impressively behind him.

"Prince—"

"Don't call me that," Matthew growled. With no ranged weapon, he was helpless to do anything but look up at the flying creature. "Only one person may call me that and he's dead because of you!"

"Then I saw it wrong? You aren't fighting alongside those who plunged the sword into his chest?"

Matthew huffed and paced back and forth below Vikentiy. Prescott or Hiroto were just tools—instruments—used by the High King.

"Come down and fight me," Matthew yelled up at him.

Vikentiy shook his head. He had a sword sheathed and a gun at his belt but he didn't draw them. "You are stronger than I, Prince."

Out of frustration, Matthew grabbed a rock and chucked it at Vikentiy, who swooped out of the way.

"I know they are forcing you. We will find a way to free you. I swear to you."

"Keep your damn oaths. They aren't forcing me, I asked to fight. And if you were to find a way to free me, the first thing I would do is cut off your head. Samantha might not blame you for what happened, but I do."

Vikentiy looked confused. "You belong with us, you are the strongest of us, sired by our god. Surely you want to be free again."

"My Sire doesn't give two shits about me nor I him. I belong to the High King now. And if you ever find a way to free me, I will go back to him."

A distant explosion drew both their attention.

The Russian unsheathed his sword and flew off to rejoin the battle, slowing only to say: "You were supposed to be our hope."

Matthew tried not to let the words affect him, pacing back and forth as he waited on his team. But he knew that his plan to kill the High King would mean becoming hated by vampires. It was a price he couldn't avoid paying.

The Argonauts weren't long, teleporting through the hole he had left behind. A light coating of silver dust covered all of them and most had minor scrapes and bruises. Nellis had a few bite marks on his arm that he was healing by drinking vamp blood.

"If he's staying on the team, I need to rethink silver grenades," Vik said.

Matthew growled at her. The sounds and smell of the battle still raging in the distance had him on edge. It took everything he had not to join the fight and begin cutting people apart. Prescott, wearing a horned helmet that covered his entire face, made a 'cut it out' motion with his hand. Like a good little pet, he stopped.

"We're going to flank the back-west side of the battle," the Imperator said.

Fucking finally. A fight.

The team teleported down the mountainside and Matthew went full speed after them. He didn't wait on Prescott's go ahead. When he got to the first group of vampires, he laid waste to them. They didn't even see him coming and didn't stand a chance.

The axe fed him energy. Each time it tasted blood it made him faster and stronger. It was a snowball effect that seemed to have no limits. Dozens fell to him.

A vampire lord swooped down from the sky to try to stop Matthew's onslaught. The vampire slammed into him and sent him tumbling down the battlefield. Hunters scattered but two didn't get away in time. Matthew felt them expire the moment his body crashed into them, the force of impact too strong.

Soaked in blood, he got up and charged the lord for a counter attack.

The vampire prepared to launch into the air to gain an advantage, but before it could jump, Nellis teleported behind it and punched it square in the back, sending it soaring in Matthew's direction. Matthew held up his axe and sliced it along its belly.

It fell to the ground—still alive and clutching at its chest, already healing its wounds.

Matthew descended upon the creature and ripped out its heart with a thunderous roar.

He let loose his aura, so that the vampires would know the death and destruction he would bring upon them.

The vampires in the area around him began to retreat...*as if he would let them.*

Matthew squeezed the now-decaying heart and tossed it to the ground. He tore through a group of humans that began shooting him, killing them with ease, then gave chase to the vampires, who were falling back to the witches for protection.

"Matthew, form up on me," Prescott said from across the battle-field.

More. The axe whispered.

God, he wanted to give himself over to it. Both the axe and his predatory instincts wanted to chase the runners down.

But Hiroto's rigid training had worked. He could resist it. And this wasn't about killing as many as he could, he was here to win over the incubi.

Matthew tore himself away from the chase. He hopped over the rubble of what was once a thick stone wall, ran through what was left of the gardens, and rejoined his team, who were busy holding silver chains around a female lord. She hissed at them, and a loose chain whipped around as she fought them.

Matthew ran in and grabbed her jaw. "Stop resisting them and sur-render."

One of her arms was free and she swiped at him, taking off half his ear with her claws. Matthew repeated his order, this time in Russian. He also nudged her emotions and pulled power from the axe to force her into submission. Her body slumped as her will fell to him.

"Do you want me to order her to fight, Imperator?" Matthew asked as he touched his ear and clenched his jaw when pain rippled through him. Why the fuck had he touched it? Ow.

"No," Prescott said, "we're taking this one alive for interrogation. Once she's secure you can release your compulsion."

Vik slapped some thick silver shackles around her wrists, while Hiroto chained her legs. Another team of hunters came to take her away.

Matthew forced himself to keep an indifferent expression. He didn't want anyone to know that his soul ached for the vampire lord. He knew what fate awaited her...one worse than death.

"Would you like me to try to catch another one to fight for us, sir?"

Prescott took off his helmet and looked across the battle. The vampires were falling back. The witches, who Matthew had avoided because magic always messed him up, were covering their retreat. He shook his head. "No. This is over. We'll let the other teams do the clean-up."

From under a pile of rubble, Matthew heard a low moan. Hiroto heard it too and rushed over to move the debris away. Other hunters in the area joined in.

Matthew forced his axe to return to his tattoos and lifted some of the bigger rocks.

Under was a male warrior incubus with bluish coloring on his horns and wings. He was in bad shape, his heart failing and his body broken. Vik leaned in and kissed him but he wasn't responsive. Damn it. Matthew could heal him but blood energy alone might not be enough and he hadn't fed on sex in a while.

He grabbed Hiroto, ripped off his mask, and pulled him into a kiss. Surprised, the fox struggled against him for a moment, then he wrapped his arms and legs around Matthew as he gave into what was happening.

Matthew's hands slid under the fox's ass to keep him in place and he began to feed on the strands of sexual energy. His incubus side called to him as he slipped his tongue into Hiroto's mouth. He was rough but the fox responded with careful, gentle swipes, almost as if waiting for permission for more.

When they finally ripped away from each other Hiroto was panting. He turned his hips upwards, pressing his erection into Matthew's stomach. His irises had changed, expanding to fill his entire eyeball with a long slit down the middle—his fox eyes. "Wow," he gasped.

Matthew caressed Hiroto's cheek and set him down. He went over to the dying incubus and pressed his lips into his, forcing what he had just taken from Hiroto into the warrior. He laced some of his blood energy in with it for good measure.

The incubus moaned and clamped onto the back of Matthew's head as he took over the feeding. When he had consumed everything Matthew had in his soavik, which wasn't much, Matthew pulled away and let the hunters take care of the now stable incubus.

He might have considered staying lip locked for a little longer but he didn't want to risk the warrior coming to his senses and finding a vampire kissing him. That'd be bad for everyone.

"I'm sure there are other incubi around here you could heal if you need more juice," Hiroto said with a wide smile.

"We'll let the medics handle them. We've been summoned back to High Tower," Prescott said.

Disappointed, Hiroto scrunched his face. He had a streak of blood down his right cheek. Matthew motioned to where it was. "You have some blood here."

Hiroto laughed. "You're one to talk."

Matthew looked down at himself. He was coated in congealed blood, decaying bits of flesh, and what he thought might have been a chunk of liver.

Prescott reported the team's status and plans to dispatch.

"High Lord General Tarrick will be returning with you. General Tarquin is taking over the clean-up," a dispatcher responded.

The team walked to the stone instead of teleporting; Matthew assumed it was for his sake.

Vik slung her weapon over her shoulder and looked around at the smoldering castle. It looked as if every ounce of happiness had been sucked out of her. "Do I need to come, sir? I should stay and help King Hindrik with this mess."

It wasn't a surprise she wanted to stay, this was her home after all. Her hunters were hit the hardest.

"Yeah, the order came from the High King, but I'll try to get you back here as quickly as possible," Prescott said.

Lock dropped back and fell into a stride with Matthew as he holstered his two crossbows. "Did ya mean what ya said?"

Matthew looked at him. "About what?"

"That ya'd come back even if you were freed?"

"You heard that? I thought you were busy fighting."

Lock tapped the comm on Matthew's wrist. "Your comm was open to our team. Dispatch and the command center would have heard it too."

Matthew wanted to smile but he forced himself to frown as if he was disappointed. Of course he knew his comm had been on, he was the one who set it that way. He wanted the other hunters to hear what he said to Vikentiy. He needed to start building trust with his team and the incubi as a whole. If dispatch heard him, it wouldn't be long before someone slipped what he said to an incubus, then the rumors would begin spreading like fire. The incubi were wonderfully predictable when it came to gossip.

"Yes. I meant what I said. I'd be recaptured eventually, anyways, and the Imperator has made it pretty clear he can do worse to me than he already has. I don't really want to find out what that means."

Prescott looked back and he tipped his head in confirmation then continued leading the team to the stone.

"And the vampires are losing anyway. Even if I wanted to, I can't turn that tide alone."

Lock nodded in agreement but didn't say anything.

Before Matthew entered the castle, he surveyed the battlefield. It was busy with incubi forces helping the wounded, and hunters sweeping the area to make sure there were no hiding vampires. Confused humans, left behind and no longer compelled, wandered around. Bodies littered the ground and bloodstained patches of snow red.

He turned away and continued walking with the team.

Hiroto bumped Matthew's arm. "You know, if you ever want to make out again sometime…"

"Oh for fack's sake," Nellis groaned. "You'll rub ye tiny wab on anything, won't ye?"

"Something's bothering him," Hiroto whispered to Matthew, "his accent has gotten thicker."

Nellis waved his gauntleted hand as if to brush off Hiroto's words.

Hiroto bounced past Nellis and stood in front of him. Nellis didn't stop walking, and Hiroto had to backpedal to avoid being ploughed over. "Aw, did Matthew kill more than you? Does that bother you?"

Matthew wasn't sure how many he had killed but he really didn't want to get into a pissing contest. He didn't mind it so much with Tarrick's youngest son Tane, whom he hadn't seen on the field tonight, but it'd just be trouble to have one with Nellis. All it took was one of them to reject him from the team and he was out.

"I swear to my great God I will punch your wick arse through this wall," Nellis said and raised a fist.

"Enough," Prescott said, and that was the end of it.

The team entered the leystone room. It was busy in there with hunters and incubi teleporting in and out. Tarrick was waiting for them, still armored but back in his human from. Silva stood by his side, holding his kanabō, which was nearly as long as she was tall.

Tarrick had wiped off the blood from his face but some still stained his hair and chest plate. Compared to Matthew though, he was sparkling clean.

Now that they weren't in the middle of a fight, Matthew bowed to him.

"You fought well, Matthew," Tarrick said. "You cleared most of the western side. Their retreat was because they didn't think they'd be able to send in anyone that could stop you and they feared you were going to begin raging."

Matthew beamed at the compliment. He then realized he was standing there smiling like a fool and looked away.

"You didn't know that you were the reason they withdrew, did you?"

"No, General."

"If you had been aware of your surroundings and paying attention, you would have heard what the vampires were saying to each other."

Ouch. Matthew thought he had done well. He had stopped every time Prescott had ordered him to, even when every part of him wanted ed to fight on. He took a step back as if he had been slapped.

"He did okay considering the short amount of time he's been training with the axe," Hiroto said.

"No, the general's right," Matthew said, "I should have heard it. I'll work on it."

"Good." Tarrick motioned to Matthew's shackle. Matthew hid his resentment as he snapped it on. "Let's go."

Prescott activated the stone and with a flash of green light they were back in New York.

It was time to go face the High King.

Time for *the spectacle*.

Forty-Two

The Argonauts, General Tarrick, and Silva exited the elevator and headed to the throne room. Tarrick led the way, followed by Prescott, then the rest of the Argonauts with Matthew in the back.

Heavy boots stomped hard against the marble as the group marched through the plush waiting room, down the hall, and through the impressive doors. Silva—her presence not required—waited outside.

A wave of power hit Matthew as he entered. The throne room was filled with incubi—kings and queens that ruled over different areas of the world.

Matthew recognized them all from pictures Rosaline had shown him, and a few he had seen in person at the various parties he had been to back when Tarrick was his captor.

All of the incubi were incredibly handsome; each was a flawless example of authority and strength. There was no question they were monarchs. And yet every one of them was loyal to Malarath, their threads solidly linked to him.

The only non-royalty incubus in the room was Lord Teleclus, who Matthew had the feeling could be a king if he desired it, and Lily, standing by his side.

God. What was she doing here?

The throne room was dark, lit only by the lights of the city and the glow of three massive televisions that were displaying footage from the battle that had just taken place.

It was the first time Matthew had ever seen footage of himself fighting. He was a terrifying sight to behold in his vicious-looking armor and pale skin splattered in bright red blood.

He watched as he swung his axe, taking off a human's arm, then followed it up by slicing off a vampire's head. Blood sprayed everywhere.

Matthew watched himself smile, lost in the pleasure of killing. He hadn't remembered smiling like that. It was perverse...and yet, a part of him he couldn't ignore.

Matthew watched as he got knocked across the battlefield. Camera footage came from one of the hunters who hadn't moved out of his way quick enough. A nauseating crunch came through the speakers as the hunter died when Matthew's body hit him.

The footage changed to Matthew ripping out the vampire lord's heart and roaring to the heavens. His eyes had turned completely red in that moment of ecstasy.

A gasp came from Lily and she covered her mouth with a hand.

Teleclus grabbed her shoulder and pulled her into him, turning her away from the gruesome images.

Prescott had said she was tough, and Matthew believed him, but it was one thing to be strong, it was another to watch your father rip his enemies' insides out and revel in the pleasure of it. It saddened him that she had seen him that way.

From atop his throne, the High King gave a signal and the playback paused. The lights turned on in the room, and the TVs automatically pulled back into the wall and disappeared behind panels.

Tarrick and the Argonauts came forward and dropped to their knees.

Tarrick stood.

"You honor me, Your Majesty," Tarrick said with a slight bow. Matthew couldn't help but notice every other incubus had glowing eyes and horns out and, while Tarrick's eyes were purple, his lack of horns was noticeable.

King Ngai of South China came forward. "We still lost many," he said. His light purple eye belied his concern. "Are our own estates at risk?"

Tarrick eyed King Ngai as if he was an annoyance. "We're at war. Your estates are always at risk." Tarrick clasped his hands behind his back. It almost seemed he took the stance so that he wouldn't reach out and slap sense into the incubus king. "To alleviate some concerns, I already have a team working on counter-measures, including a new early warning system. I'll have it deployed as soon as possible."

"How did they tunnel so close without notice?" Malarath asked.

"I am not yet sure, Your Majesty."

"Your speculation."

"There are only two vampires who can make tunnels that quick and thrall so many humans at once. I've made sure that Titus is... occupied. Which leaves only one other possibility."

Malarath leaned back, displeased. "You did not see *her* though?"

"No, Your Majesty, we didn't. But...if the Queen was the one behind this, it might mean—"

Malarath held up his hand. "I am aware of the repercussions." He sat thoughtfully for a few moments, then his eyes slid to Matthew.

"The Argonauts may rise, except my pet." Matthew stayed on his knees while the rest stood. "Warrior," Malarath said to Prescott, "how was he tonight?"

Prescott shifted his helmet from one arm to the other and glanced back at Matthew. "He did well. He followed orders. There's room for improvement, of course, but I anticipated it given his age and training. If I'd known you'd throw him right into it, I would have made team training a higher priority. That's scheduled for next month."

Malarath sat quietly for a while. No one else spoke, waiting for the High King to address them. "He is my pet and my weapon," he said to the other monarchs. "I will field him so that he may destroy those whom stand against me. But I will hear your concerns."

There was an eruption of sound as different kings and queens voiced their objections to using Matthew. It was nothing surprising. "We don't need him, we're winning anyway." "He's a vampire." "Can he be controlled?" "Will he betray us again?" "He's too unpredictable."

Most of the kings and queens were just being cautious. They would follow Malarath's orders despite concerns. But there was one King— Leomaris, a large, severe-looking incubus that ruled the Midwestern United States and Northern Mexico—who glared at Matthew with a seething hatred. His hatred only seemed to grow as the discussion went on.

"King Leomaris," Malarath said. The rest of the room fell silent. "Do you have something to add?"

"It is an abomination, Your Majesty. A mockery of everything we are. You should kill it."

"Should I?"

Leomaris' face softened a little and he bowed to the King. "I did not intend for that to sound like a command, Your Majesty. It's just...this creature was turned by the Blood God, who stands against our god-dess. What if the god returns? What if we have to face him as well?"

"The god will not return for him. Even if he did, Lysandros does not concern me. I have dealt with gods before."

Jesus. Could the High King actually take on the Blood God? May-be he had tricks Matthew was unaware of. People spoke of 'rules of this realm' all the time but he didn't know what they were. Maybe Malarath did.

Leomaris looked back at Matthew and his anger laced with a deep sadness. "He killed my daughter."

Shit. His child? Matthew had no idea who she would have been but he had killed a few warrior succubi along the way. Most he couldn't remember because he lost control...

Malarath stood and descended the dais. He came to stand next to Leomaris and put his hand on his shoulder. Leomaris leaned into the touch and dipped his head in reverence.

The High King brought his mouth close to Leomaris' ear and with a low voice said, "You have served me loyally for many centuries. You have always carried out my commands without issue. I reward that. You may kill his child if it will help ease your pain."

Matthew's head snapped up. "What?"

"You would let me end the oracle?" Leomaris asked.

"No, Master—" Matthew tried to stand only to find himself pushed back down to his knees by Prescott. Matthew's eyes went red. He'd fight them to try and save Samantha. He'd fight them all. He didn't care what the consequences were. He couldn't lose her.

Malarath ignored Matthew's pleas. "No, the oracle is far too valu-able. He has another daughter." He waved his hand over to Lily.

Every set of eyes fell to Lily. Her eyes widened, but she stood brave. She didn't try to run or retreat into Teleclus, who stayed by her side.

"Please, no—" Matthew let out a cry when Prescott's fingers gripped so hard into his shoulder his bones fractured.

Leomaris looked from Lily to Matthew and back. "Lady Lillian is Matthew's child? She's not an orphan as we were told?"

Lily closed her eyes for a moment then reopened them. They were no longer bluish-grey but rather pure silver, the same as Matthew's. Whispers ran through the gathering. Most found the revelation incredible.

"She is of his seed. You have my permission to end her life, and after you will accept that I have broken my pet and that he serves me now."

"You can't—" Matthew shut his mouth when Prescott looked down at him with hard eyes, a silent command telling him to shut the fuck up. Why wasn't he protecting Lily? Didn't he love her?

Matthew looked to Leomaris. He focused on the threads that tied him to the High King. He noticed they were weak, as if his anger had caused him to become out of sync. Then, as Leomaris made his decision, it bound itself stronger to Malarath.

"I don't wish to harm Lady Lillian for the sins of her father. I trust in your rule as always, Your Majesty."

Is that all this was? Another fucking manipulation? A game? Lily another piece on the board that Malarath moved so Leomaris would stay loyal to him?

But, if someone as devoted as Leomaris could break away and threaten Malarath's power, that gave Matthew hope. If the threads that bound them together could be broken in anger, then he was going to use that against him.

Leomaris began kissing the High King's neck. Malarath allowed it for a few moments before brushing him away and returning to his throne. His gaze fell to Matthew again and he did not look happy.

"Grandfather." Queen Agleea stepped forward. Her ornate green dress clung to her body, she showed no signs of pregnancy yet. "You've heard our concerns but many of us believe that having Matthew fight for us will bring an end to this war far sooner than we could have ever hoped. I have always championed it and, even though he escaped for a time, it is clear he is yours now. I look forward to a time when we can walk in the night without fear." She put her hand to her stomach. "To a time when our children will not know the terror of vampires."

Several kings and queens nodded in agreement. Matthew felt thankful she spoke because he was pretty damn certain he was about to be punished for speaking without being addressed.

With painful release, Prescott removed his hand from Matthew's shoulder.

"Your Majesty," Prescott said, "may we be dismissed? Vik would like to get back to her home and her hunters. We were going to join her to help with the clean-up. And we could all use showers."

Malarath nodded. "You may go, warrior. Lord General, you are dismissed as well, along with Lord Teleclus and his ward. My pet will stay." He motioned to the pillow on the floor beside his throne. Despite being caked in blood and dirt, Matthew rose and took his place by the High King's side.

The next few hours passed without much incident. Matthew was studied by the other incubi often. They had a vast range of emotions concerning him; some loathed him while others didn't bother to hide their attraction. Maybe there was something sexy about a large, blood-soaked vampire kneeling at their ruler's feet, but Matthew didn't see it.

"Some of your hair is missing," the High King said at one point.

Matthew reached up and felt the back of his head, and sure enough there was a bald spot where the bullet had exited. "I was shot, Master. I can force my hair to grow but it'll grow everywhere."

"Do it. I will have it removed again."

Damn. Matthew was kind of hoping he wouldn't have to be totally hairless from the neck down anymore. Oh well.

After hours of listening to kings and queens discussing shit Matthew couldn't care less about—politics, territory disputes, population numbers—he was finally dismissed back to his room.

When he got there, Silva was waiting for him. She had showered and cleaned.

"Commander," he said, nodding to her.

She grabbed his chest armor and removed it for him. "You need to clean this before you go to sleep."

"Oh. I don't know the correct way to do it. The Imperator said he'd send someone to show me how but things got a little crazy."

She shook her head. "Go shower, then I'll show you."

Matthew showered and dressed into pajama bottoms. Silva was waiting for him with a bag of cleaning materials for his armor. She also had some blood, which he drank greedily. He wished he could have fed during the battle but no fangs made that nearly impossible.

He forced his body to begin regrowing his hair. It'd take the night to make it long enough where it could be cut evenly.

Silva expanded his armor, then explained how to care for each part.

Matthew enjoyed her direct teaching. She expected him to do it right once she explained something but didn't yell if he got it wrong. Instead, she corrected the mistake and told him to do it again.

"How come they didn't invite you to be on the Argonauts?" Matthew asked as he scrubbed the arm plate.

Silva bit her bottom lip, as if deciding whether or not she wanted to answer.

"I mean, you're talented enough. I saw you fight with them back when we faced those demons, you were able to keep up. You're good at fitting in with a team...I'm not so much."

"There's a few reasons. One is that I'm a new commander and all of them, except you, have been commanders for decades. Also because of my history with Bryson. They feel it might sway my judgment."

"Ah. You know he asked about you."

Silva looked conflicted for a moment. "No. Don't tell me. I might have to kill him one day and I don't want to know. The man I loved died when he was turned into a vampire."

"Is that what you think? That when we become vampires we change?"

"Yes."

"If that's the case, then why do I care so much about Lily? It's easier to think we're mindless monsters when you spend your nights killing us but that's not the reality. Everything is more intense and we crave blood, but I'm not much different than how I was when I was a human."

"I've read your file, you're completely different. Besides, you just spent half the night slaughtering vamps and now you're trying to convince me I should like them?"

Matthew laughed. "No. Sorry. I'm a hopeless romantic and a hypocrite. There's a part of me that dreams of a world where peace reigns and you and Bryson could be together." He set the armor down on his lap. "But my dreams don't matter. I will serve the High King."

It wasn't only incubi Matthew wanted to turn away from Malarath, it was the hunters too. They were deeply integrated into the incubi society. They served as protectors, lovers, and friends. He wanted to plant seeds in Silva's mind. Maybe her love for Bryson would be enough to pull her away from all this when the time came.

"I saw you fighting tonight," she said. "I was with my team a little south of you. You've grown more powerful than I think anyone expected. It impressed the hell out of a lot of hunters."

Matthew rubbed his tattoos. "Yeah, well, my weapon feeds me. The more it kills the stronger I get."

"I'm not just talking about your raw strength. Your technique has improved quite a bit."

He had Devak to thank for that. When they had trained together, his guardian focused on improving his speed and it paid off. "When are you going to get around to yelling at me for disobeying your order when I ran into Tarrick's room?"

Silva smiled.

"I'm serious. I'm really tired and I'd like to submit a formal request that you hold off until I've had a chance to sleep."

She laughed and put the leg guard she had been cleaning back on the rack. "If I was going to yell, I'd have done it already. I'm not happy you disobeyed me but you helped the general that night. And I'm not the one who punishes you. It was reported to Prescott, and if he didn't do anything about it then you're in the clear. Now, get to sleep."

"Yes, ma'am," he said, and she teleported from the room.

It felt nice talking to Silva again without the guilt trips or feeling terrible for his actions. Maybe there was a small possibility he could fix what he had broken between them.

It had been an incredibly long night, but as Matthew settled into his bed, contentment filled him. Tonight, his plan to become desired by the incubi had moved forward in his direction. They would see a warrior vampire incubus that they would lust after. And soon, he would begin turning them against their king one-by-one.

He'd have to start at the bottom, with incubi that weren't close to the King, so that Malarath didn't notice until it was too late. Then Matthew would end him.

Matthew felt the sun rising outside. He slipped his ring off and fell into darkness, smiling.

Forty-Three

Matthew overslept for once. With the ring off, he should have woken the moment the sun set but he was lost in a pleasant dream. Devak was alive…wearing only an apron and baking cookies. Which was a little strange since neither of them could eat said cookies. Still, they smelled nice.

When Matthew felt a hand on his chest he tried to shoo Hiroto away.

"Can't training wait a few hours? I'm having such a nice dream…" he mumbled and turned over.

"But if you don't wake now, we'll miss the show," a deep, sexy voice said.

Matthew's eyes snapped open. Tarrick was standing by his bedside wearing a dark suit and holding up two tickets to a play. Unsure of what was going on, Matthew stared at him like an idiot.

"You've been given the night off for good behavior. We're going out. Your clothes are over there. Get dressed."

"But…I'm being allowed out?"

Tarrick flashed a devious smile. "With me. And a bunch of hunters, but just ignore them. You've never seen New York before, have you?"

"Just some side streets and out the windows. But you know that."

"I do. I'll wait for you in the lobby." Tarrick slipped the tickets into his suit jacket and left.

Matthew couldn't believe the High King was letting him out. Nor could he believe that he was going to spend the night with Tarrick.

Still, whatever the hell was going on, he wasn't going to pass up the opportunity to see the city.

It only took Matthew a few minutes to get ready. He briefly paused, naked in front of the mirror. His patch of rotting skin had shrunk down to an area about the size of his palm. Matthew healed it away and hoped it'd stay hidden for the night.

He also ran his fingers through the hair on his head. It was longer now; how he liked it. Long enough to style or leave messy and it'd still look okay. He rubbed his face and thick stubble scraped his fingers. Then he traced his fingers down the hairs that ran from his navel to his cock, which had a small nest around it. Yep, he liked this look on him. It made him feel masculine.

He only wished he could hide the High King's brand on his hip or remove the piercings. He actually had gotten used to them and he had to admit the cock piercing did feel good...but they hadn't been his choice to get.

To his displeasure, a suit had been laid out for him. He really hated suits but if that's what Tarrick wanted, he'd deal with it. Besides, even Matthew would never go to the theater in jeans. The sleeves and pant legs did a well enough job of hiding his shackles and there was a scarf to cover his collar. He looked almost normal.

Not wanting to waste any more time, he hurried to the lobby.

When he exited the elevator, Tarrick was just finishing giving some instructions to Silva who saluted and teleported away. He smiled at Matthew. "You wear that suit well."

An exhilarating rush of tension and excitement filled Matthew's chest. He suddenly felt self-conscious. Not sure what to do with his hands, Matthew adjusted the sleeves a little. "I, uh, thanks. You too. Your suit that is." Oh god. *Shut up*, he told himself.

Tarrick slipped on a long wool coat and put on black leather gloves. "Let's go, I don't want to be late."

Outside, there was a limo waiting and Tarrick opened the door and motioned for Matthew to get in. They slid into the back seat and sat so close their elbows bumped.

The limo pulled away from the tower.

Matthew was confused. So far, Tarrick had complimented him on his looks, held open the door, and was now sitting unreasonably close in the spacious limo. He could have sat anywhere.

Matthew grew a little nervous. "Are we on a date?"

Tarrick chuckled. "I do not date."

"Alright. What is this, then?"

"I want to show you the city. I know you enjoy exploring new places."

Matthew wasn't entirely convinced but, still, he was excited to see more of New York from the ground level. He leaned over to the window and watched the buildings as they drove by.

Life buzzed around him; the feeling intoxicating.

The limo came to a stop a few blocks from Broadway and the driver opened the door for them.

"We have a little time. Let's walk the rest of the way," Tarrick said as he got out of the car and led the way down the street.

Bright lights and colorful posters besieged Matthew's vision. It was wonderful. The sound of cars, beating hearts, street performers, and the excitement of life all sounded like sweet music to him. It had been so long since he had been under the night sky, among people.

Overwhelmed by it all, he froze.

Tarrick, walking ahead, hadn't noticed he lost Matthew until he was twenty feet away. He looked back over his shoulder and cocked an eyebrow. Matthew didn't notice, lost in the enchantment of the world around him.

It wasn't until Tarrick came back and grabbed his hand that he felt grounded again.

"Are you alright?" Tarrick asked.

"I'm sorry, General. It's just...all the people...and..."

With a careful touch, Tarrick ran his hand through Matthew's hair. His buttery-smooth leather gloves felt so soft. "Steady yourself, young one. You can handle this."

Matthew took a deep breath. He could handle this.

"You've grown your hair," Tarrick said.

"Yeah, that bullet I took left a bald spot. The High King said I could regrow it but he'll cut it again."

"Shame. I like it longer."

Matthew smiled. "Me too."

"If you're going to let yourself be shot in the head, you need a helmet for your armor."

Matthew raised up his hand with a 'See? You get it' motion. "I wouldn't say I 'let myself be shot,' but I do want a helmet."

"I'll see about getting one made. Now come on, we're behind schedule." Tarrick, who hadn't let go of his hand, pulled Matthew along through the crowd of people towards a busy theater.

It was then that Matthew noticed a hunter for the first time tonight. She was wearing street clothes and blended with the crowd, but he recognized her as someone from Silva's team. After seeing one, it was hard for him not to try to spot them all. He saw a few more blending in with people, but there were some in their leathers, moving in the shadows.

It amazed him that the hunters went unnoticed among so many humans.

"They aren't really necessary but I'd be setting a poor example if I ditched my bodyguards every time I went out. Not that Silva would let me," Tarrick said, noticing how Matthew was scanning the rooftops. "New York is one of the safest cities for incubi. Other than when Ascelina helped you escape, we haven't had an attack here in a century."

"Because the High King lives here?"

"That. And too many humans. Most vampires still don't want to risk exposure. It's also home to the best hunters I have. Not to mention I spend many resources keeping this place safe. It's good for my people to have a city they can walk around in without fear."

Tarrick motioned his head at a couple coming their way. It was a succubus that Matthew didn't know with a human on her arm. Her human was absorbed in her every word and she seemed equally as smitten with him.

It wasn't until they came much closer that she went pale and nearly tripped over herself when she saw Tarrick. She recovered gracefully. The male thought she had stumbled on her stilettos and chastised her for wearing ones that were so tall.

Tarrick smiled warmly at her and she nodded respectfully, then moved on. She hadn't even noticed Matthew.

"Who was that?" Matthew asked.

"Her name is Deanna. She's a houseless incubus, not even thirty yet. She's never seen me in person before."

"Ah, so no one important."

Tarrick yanked Matthew's arm, spun him around, and pressed him against the dirty wall. His eyes grew dark. "Each and every one of them is important."

"I'm sorry, General." Matthew went limp in Tarrick's grasp. "I didn't mean it like that. I'm just so used to being around the who's who of society that it's easy to forget that most incubi aren't ladies or queens or rich as fuck. I didn't mean she was worthless."

"Good," Tarrick said, accepting the apology. He pulled away from Matthew and retrieved the tickets from his pocket. "I think you'll enjoy the play. Let's go."

Matthew was disappointed that Tarrick was no longer holding his hand, but he did notice the heads of every woman and many men turning as Tarrick walked by. He couldn't blame them.

Inside the theater, they checked their coats and headed up a set of stairs—Matthew trailing behind, his eyes drifted down to the general's incredible ass. When Tarrick glanced over his shoulder, Matthew adjusted his sleeve to hide his ogling, but he knew he'd been caught by the way Tarrick was grinning.

They entered a private box with two plush seats. Matthew sat down, then went about memorizing every detail of the theater. It was old and picturesque with gilded wood carvings, nouveau artwork of naked ladies, and stained glass. Crystal chandeliers hung above the audience.

The orchestra was finishing tuning their instruments. Matthew spotted a few hunters in the crowd but they belonged to other incubi whom he also spotted. Not all of them were in private boxes, some sat with the general audience.

"You should save your excitement for the production itself," Tarrick said.

"I can't help it. This theater is beautiful. It's places like these I think about when I'm caged. I can recreate the memory and drop myself in it to pass the time. If you told me we had to go back now, I'd still be thankful you showed me this."

For the briefest of moments, Matthew thought Tarrick looked remorseful, but it passed as quickly as it came. "I'm thrilled you're enjoying yourself."

The lights dimmed and the curtain opened.

The show itself was wonderful. Matthew hadn't seen a play since becoming a vampire and it was a completely different experience than when he was human. Every pitch change in the music was heard, every subtle motion of the actors was seen, even the reaction of the audience became as important as what happened on stage.

The play was a historical musical with a hip-hop score, yet still had traditional Broadway elements weaved into it. Matthew found it fascinating.

When it ended, Matthew joined the standing ovation and felt so energized that he wanted to bound about like a child.

"I see you enjoyed the production," Tarrick said once the applause died down and the audience began to disperse.

"Yes. Thank you for bringing me." Matthew couldn't wait to tell Samantha about it. He wanted to go into every detail of what he had just seen.

"You're welcome. Come on, let's get out of here." Tarrick cut through the crowd—or more accurately, the crowd seemed to part before him—and led Matthew back into the limo that was waiting for them outside.

"Are we returning to the tower?" Matthew asked when he got into the limo.

"No. The night is young. And I think you'll enjoy the next show more than this last one."

Matthew looked out the window as the limo began to move. "You're taking me to another theater?"

Tarrick laughed, his dark blue eyes glinting with amusement. He took up a spot opposite Matthew and pulled a box out from under the seat. "For you."

Now he was getting gifts? This not-date sure felt like a date. Matthew opened the box and nearly cried when he saw what was inside.

Jeans.

Honest-to-god jeans.

"Don't get too attached to them," Tarrick said. "They're for tonight only. Change."

The box had a long-sleeved shirt as well. Matthew began using his speed to change, taking off the suit jacket and tie before starting on the shirt buttons.

"No," Tarrick commanded. "Slow." The general settled into his seat and spread his arms across the back, waiting for the show. He looked so damn powerful sitting there, and his authoritative presence was downright sexy.

Matthew swallowed hard and tried to ignore the twitch his cock gave. He continued to unbutton his shirt, slowly this time, revealing more and more of his body. He slipped out of his shirt and Tarrick made a quiet sound of approval.

Matthew felt a little uncomfortable with being put on display, but hearing Tarrick's desire was hot as hell and made the discomfort worth it. He slipped out of his shoes and finally unzipped his pants.

The low roof of the limo made taking them off a little awkward but Tarrick didn't seem to care. When he pushed them down, his dick popped free, half-hard and lying heavy against his leg. It hadn't been his choice to go commando, but he didn't mind so much now.

He felt the edges of his irises burn red as he looked at Tarrick, who said nothing while he watched Matthew redress.

When Matthew had worked his way into the jeans and t-shirt, Tarrick produced some boots for him, along with a beanie, gloves, and a new knitted scarf.

"I don't want people to know you're a vampire," Tarrick explained when Matthew studied the new items. "Nor do I want them to know I'm the Lord General." His body began to change as he shifted his glamor. Tarrick's hair turned from dusty blond to dark brown, and his eyes from blue to brown as well. His strong facial features softened slightly and his skin turned a bit darker, giving him a Mediterranean look. Sexy but it felt wrong.

Matthew knew that Tarrick hid scars he had collected over his years of being a warrior, but he had no idea how drastically the incubus could change his look. "You only glamor your scars normally, right? I mean...you look like you?"

Tarrick nodded and motioned to his body. "It takes a lot of energy to keep a glamor like this up. Most incubi don't have the ability. Hiding scars or changing eye color is significantly easier."

Matthew pulled on the beanie and slipped the gloves on. "It's a shame you hide your scars. I like them."

"I think I could lose most of my limbs and you'd still like me."

Matthew wrapped the scarf around his neck, hiding his collar. "Depends...would you still have your cock?" If this was a date—and he was damn sure it was no matter what Tarrick said—then he sure as fuck was going to flirt.

"I don't need my cock to pleasure you."

"No?"

"No."

"Prove it," Matthew said, issuing a challenge. One he hoped Tarrick would answer by sliding over next to him and using his hands or mouth in creative ways.

But Tarrick didn't do that. Instead, he wrapped a hold around Matthew so abrupt and hard that he had no time to try and break away from it. His whole body turned on, and he felt as if he was at the edge of an orgasm. Without even realizing he was doing it, he arched his back against the seat, pressing his now rock-solid erection against the inside of his jeans. A loud moan escaped his lips.

As soon as it started, it was over and the hold was gone.

"Jesus fucking Christ," Matthew panted. Tarrick sat unmoving with a smug look on his face. "That's not fucking fair."

Tarrick shrugged. "You're the one who challenged a thousand-year-old incubus. You have no one to blame but yourself."

Matthew looked down at the bulge in his pants. "Now I'm going to be hard for the rest of the night."

Tarrick's gaze followed Matthew's and the edges of his irises turned purple. "Perhaps we can do something about that later." He leaned forward and added, "If you desire it. You haven't fed—truly fed—in a while, have you?"

Matthew looked away. "You already know the answer to that."

"I do." Tarrick placed a hand on Matthew's knee. "You should start feeding again. Not just for the sensible reason of stopping your soavik from hurting—I know it hurts no matter how much you ignore the pain—but because you could use the extra edge the energy will give you during a fight. Or use it to heal my warriors. Although Hiroto certainly didn't mind feeding you."

Yeah, Hiroto *had* enjoyed the kiss. And to be honest, Matthew had as well.

"It's been difficult...to even think about sex...you know, since..."

Tarrick squeezed his knee. "I know, young warrior. I have a few ideas that might help you. We'll see if we have time to try them out later."

Matthew was a little worried. When Tarrick had gone into monster-mode, Matthew had enjoyed what had happened but what if he was asked to do something he couldn't yet handle?

As if sensing his distress, Tarrick spoke. "I know trust between us is fragile at best, but I won't make you do anything you aren't ready for. At least not tonight. I give you my word."

Matthew set his gloved hand on Tarrick's. "Okay." He was giving him his trust, just for tonight, and he prayed that it wouldn't end in pain.

The limo came to a stop down a dark alleyway. When Matthew got out of the car, he could feel a magic veil somewhere nearby. His brain told him that this area was dangerous and that he should just keep walking on by. That was the magic, of course, working to keep humans away.

Tarrick took the lead and went to a battered door. It looked like it was the exit to a Chinese food joint. He grabbed the handle, paused for a moment, and glanced back at Matthew. A wide grin spread across his face.

"What?" Matthew asked, wondering why the fuck they were here.

"I just can't wait to see the look on your face is all."

"Yeah? The food smells good but I've been on a liquid diet for the last ten years…"

Tarrick opened the door and disappeared. Not 'went through the door and was inside the building'. No. He *disappeared*. Matthew could no longer smell or hear him. Beyond the doorway was nothing but darkness.

Matthew reached out and put his hand through. It felt tingly.

"By all the gods in the heavens…Matthew, just *go*," Silva said, teleporting in behind him. Matthew had almost forgotten they had a hunter team trailing them.

He grumbled at her and walked through the doorway.

The same nauseous feeling he got when teleporting rolled through him as he emerged on the other side of the magic-portal-door-thing.

Matthew gasped at what he saw.

He stood in what looked like an old European town with a narrow cobblestone road lined with shops complete with thatched roofs. People packed the busy road, rushing around, chatting, laughing…

There were incubi of all ranks but there were also witches, shifters, gargoyles on the corners of houses…and creatures that Matthew had never seen up close before. His jaw dropped as a fucking troll went lumbering by him. It was easily thirteen feet tall, grey, ugly as shit, and wearing only the bare minimum of tattered clothes that could be considered decent.

Three tiny orbs of light darted past Matthew's face and he watched them pause in front of a woman who smelled like seawater. The light orbs dimmed slightly and looked like small humans with transparent wings. Faeries. Real faeries.

The woman they were talking to—at least Matthew assumed the high-pitched squeaky noise they made was a language of some sort—had bluish skin and when she moved she shimmered.

The signage for the stores were written in a language Matthew couldn't read, but he could guess what they were based off pictures. There was a potions shop, a reagent vendor for witches, a shop that sold food in strange colors—Matthew had never seen a white apple before but there it was—and a blacksmith who was busy working. He looked like a freaking dwarf with a half-burned beard and a body wider than tall.

And this is just what Matthew could see from where he entered. He could sense that this place was huge—extending for miles.

A supernatural city.

Matthew spotted Tarrick's glamored form leaning against a lamppost with his hands in his pocket and a knowing smirk painted on his face.

"Welcome to King's Borough, Matthew."

Forty-Four

Behind Matthew, Silva and her team entered King's Borough and melted into the crowd. There were other hunters, but most looked as if they were off-duty.

Matthew forced himself to stop gawking and join Tarrick. "I was shot in the head last night and it wasn't nearly as mind-blowing as this."

Tarrick looked pleased.

"That blue woman, what is she?" Matthew asked.

"Sea witch. If you make a deal with one, never break it—their scorn is unending."

"Does she actually live in the ocean?"

Tarrick rubbed his chin, amused. "Yes. And if you happen upon a mermaid don't listen to her lies. They'll say anything to steal men away to breed with them."

"Sounds like personal experience," Matthew joked.

Tarrick laughed. He pushed himself off the lamp and began down the road.

"Wait, *have* you fucked a mermaid before?" Matthew asked, keeping himself at Tarrick's side.

"I'm old, Matthew."

"But…what about trolls? You haven't fucked a troll before have you?"

"I'm old, Matthew."

"Ew. Really? What about a centaur?"

Tarrick glanced at Matthew.

"God damn. Is there anything you haven't fucked? You know what, never mind, I don't want to know." Matthew took a step to the side as three massive wolves went running by him. "I wonder what mermaid blood tastes like," he mused.

Tarrick stopped walking. "Careful what you say, there are ears everywhere. I don't want people knowing what you are yet."

"'Yet'?"

"Yet." Tarrick began walking again, leading Matthew down the main street but keeping to the side so as to not draw attention. When they took a turn down another street, a thick curtain of pheromones blasted Matthew's senses.

They had entered what he could only describe as the red-light district. There were humans, shifters, and, of course, scantily dressed incubi of both sexes showing off their goods and hawking their wares, which in this case was their bodies.

A succubus approached Matthew. She had generous breasts, and leaned over slightly, giving Matthew an excellent view of her cleavage. "You and your companion looking for a third? I promise neither of you will be hungry by the time you're finished with me."

Matthew wasn't sure what to say to her.

"We're eating later, darling." Tarrick grabbed Matthew's arm and pulled him along, leaving the succubus behind them, frowning.

"I really wish you hadn't done that thing to me in the car," Matthew said, adjusting his pants. The pheromones were driving him crazy and every incubus they passed was hot as hell. Matthew eyed a male whose tail coiled around his body, the arrowed tip of it tucked into the front of his pants to draw attention there. He wore only tight fitting pants that showed off his defined V and, with a wink, he promised a hell of a good time.

"You know the feeders in the tower are much higher quality. You should try one."

"I...maybe. Would they—" Matthew became too embarrassed to finish his question and fell silent.

Tarrick pulled Matthew into an empty alcove. His warm body invaded Matthew's space. Even though he wore a different face, Matthew couldn't help but wish they weren't both wearing so many clothes. "Would they what?"

"Would they let me be in charge? I mean..." Matthew trailed off, not ready to voice how fragile he really felt after what the High King had done to him.

"They're trained to fulfill any desire. There are some that are better at submitting than others but the feeders in High Tower are the best of the best. Most would love to spend a few hours being dominated by you."

"And I would be allowed to do that? I'm not allowed to come without permission…"

"You're his pet. He wants to keep you fed but he doesn't want you seeking your own pleasure, which is why the rule is there. I'll tell him you're willing to feed. He might make allowances. Now, come." Tarrick pulled Matthew back into the street. "We're almost there."

They passed by a tavern that was packed with off-duty hunters. Matthew pulled his beanie down further but none of the hunters took notice of him, nor did they give a second glance to the glamored Tarrick.

Every now and then, Matthew saw a vampire ward or trap but Tarrick led them around or Silva and her team disabled them before they passed by.

The deeper they went into this part of the city, the darker the street became, and the creatures rowdier and shadier. He saw at least two fights get broken up by on-duty hunters.

Tarrick led him to a massive building that had a line around the block with people waiting to get in. They walked up to a large bouncer, Tarrick palmed him an absurd amount of cash, and he moved the rope out of the way for them.

The inside was crammed with people surrounding a cage. The scent of blood filled the air and loud cheers nearly deafened Matthew. It was a fighting arena and there was a match going on right now.

Tarrick pushed through the crowd to get ringside. Bodies pressed close to them as people fought for a better view of the action.

In the cage was a massive werewolf in a half-human half-wolf form fighting a wiry looking male hunter. The hunter was unarmed, wearing only hand wraps and fighting shorts. It didn't seem a fair fight to Matthew—werewolves were stronger than hunters, and they had better senses. Not to mention they healed faster.

Matthew was proved wrong when the hunter teleported into the air behind the werewolf and landed a series of blows into the back of the wolf's ribcage. Matthew could hear the bones breaking. The hunter didn't let up. He teleported again—this time to the side—and drove his heel into the werewolf's jaw.

The wolf howled and swiped blindly at the hunter; his claws caught the human's calf and blood went flying. Cheers and boos erupted around them. Matthew felt as if he was drowning in the energy of the room. And he loved it.

He began cheering as well. Although, he didn't care who won so long as the fight was a good one. Watching a hunter go toe to toe with a werewolf was incredible. Matthew didn't normally get to see the hunter runes uncovered, and watching them surge with green light when the rune drew upon power fascinated him.

There was a jagged rune near the hunter's left shoulder that had to give him strength because it glowed right before each punch. And before each teleport, a rune with two swirling lines inside of a circle flashed.

The werewolf took aim at that one, trying to disable it by clawing the skin, breaking the circle. He managed to strike the hunter's chest but missed that rune and the hunter disappeared again, reappearing low and on the other side. He kicked the back of the werewolf's knee and it buckled over. The hunter's jagged rune surged a bright green and he pounded his fists into the wolf's face.

The wolf fell unconscious and the fight was over. The referee grabbed the bloodied hunter's wrist and held it into the air. A resounding roar erupted from the crowd.

Cheering and smiling, Matthew looked at Tarrick, who seemed pleased that the hunter had won but was too restrained to allow himself to get swept up in the surging emotions around him.

Whatever, he was missing out.

They watched two more fights. The first was a female match of a warrior succubus versus a naga, a half-snake, half-human creature. The battle was intense but the naga won.

The following fight was between two bear shifters. The men were massive in their human forms but they shifted as soon as the fight started. They were both grizzlies and it was hard to differentiate between the two once fur and blood started flying. Matthew cheered whenever one landed a good blow. It was a long fight. Both had an extreme amount of stamina but eventually one went down.

A witch's duel was on the schedule as the main event. Matthew had never seen witches fighting in such close quarters and he couldn't wait to see what it'd be like.

They had a little bit of time as the cage was set up with wards to prevent magic from flying out of the arena.

"Yet," Tarrick said beside him, removing his gloves.

Matthew looked at him confused.

Tarrick motioned to a group of off-duty hunters on the other side of the cage. *I don't want people knowing what you are yet.* This was the 'yet'. For whatever reason, Tarrick wanted this entire place to know he was a vampire.

"Am I unclear, warrior?" he asked when Matthew hesitated.

"No," he said and pulled off his beanie. "But I really wanted to see the witches."

Matthew looked at the hunters across the way and let his eyes go red. He taunted them with a sneer and watched as their faces turned deadly serious and they teleported away.

A moment later, he could hear calls coming through earpieces. "There's a vampire in the arena." Followed by quick orders of what was going to be done about it. Matthew wanted to add a dramatic 'dun duh duuuuh' in for them.

What happened next was fast. Two teams of on-duty hunters and a handful of off-duty ones teleported in and shoved the civilians out of the way, clearing the area around Matthew. Silver chains flew at him. For a split second, Matthew considered dodging them but it was such close quarters, if the hunters opened up people would get hurt and that'd probably piss off Tarrick.

He dutifully stood still as the chains wrapped around him.

A hunter came at him, stake in hand.

"Oh no, please don't hurt me," Matthew said in an apathetic, monotone voice.

The hunter raised his arm to drive the stake into Matthew's heart, only to find a hand wrapped around his wrist. "Stand down, hunter."

"General—" The hunter took several steps back.

Tarrick's glamor was gone and he was back to looking like himself.

A chain brushed against Matthew's cheek and his skin sizzled. Another group of hunters teleported in and Tarrick raised his hand to stop them from attacking. He then spoke into his comm. "Dispatch, stop sending hunters to the arena. The vampire in question is Matthew and he's with me."

"Acknowledged, Lord General," dispatch said, followed by the order to stand down.

If Tarrick had done this to capture everyone's attention, it had worked. The entire room was watching the events unfold.

Whispers swept the crowd...most of the creatures in this room had never seen Matthew in person before. Hell, the way they were talking, many thought he was just a rumor. Even most of the hunters had only ever seen him from a distance or on recorded footage.

"I swear I'm always untangling you from chains," Silva said from behind him as she began to remove the metal.

Matthew winked at her as she came around his front. "Admit it, you like seeing me tied up."

One of the chains 'mistakenly' brushed against his cheek again. "Oops," she said. Matthew was torn between laughing and growling. He deserved that one but it was painful.

"High Lord General Tarrick—" A heavy man wearing a suit sans tie pushed through the crowd and walked into the clearing. He was human, in his mid-fifties, and looked as if he had spent his youth fighting. Matthew wondered if he was an ex-hunter. "—you are the last person I ever expected to see in my arena."

"Oh?"

"Word is that you don't approve of it."

Tarrick smiled. It wasn't friendly, more like the type of smile a predator might flash right before killing their prey. "If I didn't approve of this arena, Conor, it would never have opened. Nor would any hunter set foot in here, let alone participate."

"In that case, I hope you've been enjoying my matches."

Tarrick looked unimpressed. "They were adequate, but I'm used to watching creatures fight for their lives. It's far more entertaining."

A tight smile stretched across Conor's lips. "If you want death matches, all you need to do is change the law and I'd be more than happy to host them. Besides, you've yet to see the main event."

"I've seen witches go at it before. Lots of flash, not much substance."

Silva finished taking the chains off Matthew. When the last one dropped to the ground, he rolled his shoulders and stretched his neck. Lots of people were staring at him. Most people, actually. Matthew wondered what the hell the general was up to.

"You want to throw him into the ring?" the arena owner asked. If he were a cartoon, Matthew was positive the man would have dollar signs for eyes.

Tarrick shook his head. "You have nothing here that could stand a chance against him."

"Give me a week. I'll find something that'd be a challenge for him."

"If you could find a creature that would challenge him, even I'd be interested in watching. But he belongs to the High King. Any fight he participates in is at His Majesty's pleasure."

"Shame. A fight with him would be the biggest event of the century."

Oh. Matthew figured out what Tarrick was doing. God, this was brilliant. The High King was influenced by his people and if his people wanted to watch Matthew fight, he'd be inclined to approve it. And the incubi here tonight were exactly the type Matthew wanted to influence: the common incubus, the ones who didn't have grand households or endless wealth at their fingertips. They were the majority. Start with them and the rest would begin to follow.

But Matthew hadn't told Tarrick his plans, beyond saying that the High King could be weakened. How did he know? Tarrick always seemed to be several steps ahead of him. And in one conversation, the general had set the stage to turn Matthew into a celebrity. And he had done it in such a way that no one, not even the King, would suspect what was going on.

"Would you and the vampire—"

"Demigod," Matthew interrupted. Conor paused. "You know, because my sire is the Blood God. So...demigod." Matthew didn't like being called a demigod because he really wanted nothing to do with his sire, but he'd bet that the people here had seen plenty of vampire fights—both in the war and in the arena. Building himself up as an epic demigod warrior would play better.

Tarrick said nothing but he seemed to approve.

"Would you and the *demigod*—" Conner corrected, "—care to join me in my box for the final match?"

"No. We're leaving." Tarrick gave some signals to Silva, who once again blended into the crowd. Other hunters saluted as he walked by. Matthew followed him out, trying to look as menacing as possible.

He had no doubt that by the time the story reached the ears of the upper-class incubi, Matthew would have fangs out and blood dripping from his mouth.

Walking out of King's Borough was a completely different experience than walking into it. The sea of people parted before Tarrick. Everyone nodded, saluted, bowed, or even kneeled out of respect.

No one solicited sex this time, but the desire was there. Tarrick could have pointed at anyone and commanded them to start fucking him in the street and Matthew didn't think there was a single person that would have turned him down.

Watching someone with such influence sent an exhilarated shiver through Matthew's body. His incubus side wanted to purr; it liked being so close to power...but his vampire side wanted to rip the faces off everyone who lusted after Tarrick. That side of him was a little possessive.

"I don't believe you by the way," said Matthew when they finally exited King's Borough.

The limo was waiting for them where it had dropped them off. The driver held the door open.

"What don't you believe?" Tarrick asked, getting in first.

Matthew slid in next to Tarrick. "That a witch brawl is all flash. It was the headliner for fuck's sake. No way it's not amazing."

"I'll capitulate that witch duels can be quite the spectacle. Perhaps one day I'll take you to one." Tarrick pulled out his phone and checked the clock on it. "It's not even two a.m. yet. We have time."

"Time for what?"

"Dinner."

Matthew trailed after Tarrick on foot as they walked through a vibrant block filled with loud clubs. It was getting to that time where people found themselves stumbling around drunk and seeking out food trucks.

Tarrick was on the hunt and Matthew watched with fascination as the general's predatory side emerged. The incubus' eyes swept each human he passed, looking for the perfect meal.

They passed a trio of young women who strutted and displayed themselves in an effort to catch Tarrick's attention. Matthew wouldn't have minded feeding from them. "I don't think we'll find any priests down here."

Tarrick looked over his shoulder at Matthew. "Priests might be my favorite meal but I would tire of them if they were the only thing I ate."

"Then what are you looking for? Because we've passed at least twenty people who would love to jump your bones."

Tarrick turned a corner. The establishments on this street were more exclusive and quiet. Matthew saw people wearing lots of leather under their big coats. "I have something specific in mind. It just requires a bit of searching."

"I wish I had my fangs," Matthew mumbled. He'd love to be hunting for blood right now. Even so, this was still fun.

"There," Tarrick said, and nodded towards a young human that came out of an unmarked door. He was slender, much smaller than both Matthew and Tarrick, and cute. His hair was a few inches long and messy, his lips were full and pouty, and his huge eyes were a wonderful light brown.

He shoved his hands in his pockets and kept his head down as if his night hadn't been going the way he wanted it to.

Tarrick picked up his pace to cut the man off. He motioned for Matthew to approach from the other direction.

Tarrick lined himself in the path of the young man and stopped walking. The human ran right into him and bounced off his body.

"Jesus," the male said, scrambling to right himself. "I'm so sor—" He trailed off when he looked up at Tarrick. He froze for a moment, his cheeks turning red. "I didn't see you there."

Tarrick straightened the front of his suit and smoothed out his coat. "Obviously." Tarrick's voice sounded dark and menacing. He took a step closer to the human. "You shouldn't be so careless when walking, kid."

"I'm not a kid…" The human swallowed hard and took a few steps backwards—into Matthew. He gasped as he turned around, his eyes mapping Matthew's large frame.

The poor kid's heart was racing. Tarrick wasn't wrapping any hold on him to calm him either.

He backed away from Matthew only to bump into Tarrick again.

Tarrick scowled. "What did I just tell you?"

"Wh-what do you want from me?"

Tarrick grabbed the man's jaw with his gloved hand and maneuvered him against a wall. Tarrick became a barrier of muscle blocking the boy in. "I want to use your body for my pleasure. I want to pin you down and watch as you struggle to free yourself *and fail*. I want to leave you ruined and wrecked."

Conflicting emotions tore through Matthew. His vampire—and incubus—would love to dominate this kid…but he refused to take anyone against their will.

Tarrick pushed two fingers into the boy's mouth. The human sucked on the leather and *moaned*. His eyelids sagged and his eyes rolled back.

Tarrick leaned in and whispered. "Do you want that?" The human continued to suck on Tarrick's gloved fingers. Tarrick ripped them from his mouth and grabbed the human's jaw again. "I asked you a question, boy."

"Yes, I want that," he said, breathless.

"Name."

"Kyle."

Tarrick smiled and motioned his head to the side. "This is Matthew. You'll call me 'Sir'. Do you understand?"

Kyle nodded, looking desperate to please. "Yes, Sir."

Fuck. Tarrick had complete control over this kid and didn't even bother to use a hold or release any pheromones. It was so fucking hot that Matthew had to adjust his bulging jeans.

Tarrick motioned a finger down the street and their limo pulled up to the curb. The driver got out and opened the door for them.

Kyle's large eyes darted between Matthew, Tarrick, and the limo as if he was trying to figure out who Tarrick was.

Tarrick grabbed the back of Kyle's neck and guided him into the vehicle. Matthew slid in.

"Go sit in his lap," Tarrick ordered Kyle. Matthew spread his legs wide and Kyle timidly took a seat on a leg. Matthew wrapped his arms around his waist and scooted the boy in.

"Where are we going?" Kyle asked, looking around as the limo began moving.

"I own a penthouse not far from here." Tarrick pulled a card from his pocket and handed it over. "This is the address if you'd like to call someone and tell them where you're going."

Kyle took the card and looked at it for a moment. All it had on it was an address. "No. That's okay," he said and slipped it into his pocket.

"The safe word is 'red'. Repeat it to me."

"Red, Sir."

Tarrick nodded his approval. Matthew wondered why Tarrick was bothering to give him a safe word when incubi didn't usually do that. Maybe it was for his sake.

Kyle moved in Matthew's lap, rocking unintentionally on his hardening cock. Matthew bit his lip to hold back a moan and his hands began to wander the human's body.

"Is he your submissive, Sir?" Kyle asked.

"Take his scarf off," Tarrick said. Kyle shifted to face Matthew and untangled the scarf. He pulled it open, revealing Matthew's collar.

The human reached out and touched it. "You make him wear such a heavy one?"

Tarrick met Matthew's eyes. "Personally, I like them thinner but he disobeyed and earned himself that one."

Matthew pushed up the sleeve of his shirt showing off a shackle. "I've earned these ones too."

Kyle touched the shackle. He looked almost...envious. Matthew had never been with a human who craved dominance like this one clearly did. How the hell did Tarrick know this human's desires?

The human traced his fingers along the visible parts of Matthew's tattoos and then continued up Matthew's arm, tracing his muscles. "You don't look like a sub."

"It depends who I'm with."

"Your eyes are so light. I've never seen anything like them," Kyle said when his exploration reached Matthew's face.

Tarrick leaned back and settled himself into an authoritative pose—his arms stretched out and one leg resting over the other. "Tilt your head to the side and let Matthew kiss your neck."

Kyle obeyed. As did Matthew. He pressed his lips against the human's soft skin. The scent of blood rushing below the surface was irresistible, and the feel of the pulsing vein had his missing fangs aching and his cock straining painfully. The loud beat of the heart was a wonderful symphony and Matthew couldn't fight the pull of it.

He sucked at the human's flesh hard enough to leave bruises, and his vampire guise ripped forward. Matthew snapped his red eyes shut, then pulled Kyle into his chest so the kid wouldn't see his claws.

The human loved the rough handling, pressing his nose into the dip above Matthew's collarbone and breathing in heavily. His breath pooled and warmed the cool skin there.

Matthew forced himself to be calm and returned to looking human.

"Good boy," Tarrick said, looking at Matthew. Kyle, most likely thinking it was for him, smiled against Matthew's neck. The limo came to a stop outside of a high-rise.

"Carry him," Tarrick ordered Matthew once they were out of the vehicle.

Matthew scooped Kyle up and slung him over his shoulder. He wasn't gentle about it but he didn't hurt the human.

Matthew glanced around. There were hunters all over: patrolling the street, disguised as doormen, and even one masquerading as a bum. And the high-rise itself was filled with incubi and humans.

The hunters didn't salute when Tarrick walked by because there were humans that weren't *in the know*, but they did nod respectfully.

Most did a double take when they saw Matthew.

They took a private elevator to the penthouse, which consisted of the entire top floor and matched the décor of all Tarrick's spaces: warm and modern with antique touches; dark wood and deep hues of red.

Kyle wiggled in Matthew's arms as he looked around, seemingly blown away by the amount of wealth he was looking at.

Personally, Matthew could take it or leave it. What he wanted from life didn't have a price tag and he had always been fairly modest with his material needs. As long as he had enough money to take a vacation every year and feed and clothe his family, he had been happy.

In the massive bedroom, with windows that overlooked the cityscape, Matthew tossed Kyle onto the bed. The human looked at Tarrick and Matthew, his eyes full of nervous anticipation and desire.

"Come, Kyle," Tarrick said as he walked into the bathroom. Kyle scooted off the bed and padded after him.

A moment later, Matthew heard the shower running and Tarrick came out, shutting the door behind him. He raised his wrist to his mouth. "Silva come in here."

Silva teleported in.

"Take your team and any other hunters on this level and run a sweep of the building. Every floor."

Silva pressed her lips together and her nose flared slightly, angered by the menial task. She bit out a, "Yes, sir," and disappeared.

"Disable any cameras and listening devices," Tarrick ordered Matthew.

Matthew found two: one in an AC vent and one in a lamp. He made short work of them.

Tarrick slipped off his coat and jacket and hung them. "We have a few minutes to speak and after this assume we can never speak openly again. Who else knows about your mother and your plans?"

"Samantha, obviously. And Hiroto. He knows about my mother but not my plans to weaken the King. That's it."

Tarrick tapped his hand against his leg and took a moment to think. "You understand that I have to follow every order that I'm given. That I cannot make it look like I've broken away from the King. If he suspects anything we'll both be killed."

"I understand. I want to know why you decided to help me."

Tarrick took off his cufflinks and rolled up his sleeves, exposing his muscular forearms. With his leather gloves still on, and still in the dark suit, he looked like a hitman: sexy and dangerous. "You were right. The King isn't good for my people, not anymore. He's using us to carry out his revenge. Over the years, *millions* of us have died and I tire of a world full of ceaseless battles. I want to give my children a future that isn't a war. And…you are my goddess' son. I can't ignore that."

"Oh," Matthew said. Those were good reasons, but a part of him had hoped the answer would be 'because I believe in you' or 'because I love you'.

On reading his emotions, Tarrick crossed the room and put his hand on Matthew's shoulder. "We don't have the luxury of a romantic love story. You don't belong to me and I refuse to fall for something that I cannot have. If we are going to do this, we can't afford to be distracted by each other."

Matthew scratched at the area above his heart. Once they killed Malarath, would Tarrick love him then? He couldn't fathom the restraint the incubus had over his emotions. How could someone just choose not to love? It was such a foreign concept.

Tarrick grabbed Matthew's hand and pulled it to his mouth. He brushed his lips against his skin. "Do not take that to mean that I do not desire you."

"But," Matthew said, his voice wavering, "isn't what we're about to do 'distracting'?"

Tarrick pressed into Matthew's body and kept walking, forcing Matthew to back up until his legs hit the bed and he plopped down. The incubus crawled into his lap, his legs spread around Matthew's thighs. "No. This is feeding."

"I—"

Tarrick silenced him by claiming his mouth. The kiss was rough and possessive; everything Matthew wanted it to be. He melted under the weight of Tarrick sitting on him.

Without thinking, he focused on his coiled thread within himself, forced it to unravel, and attached it to Tarrick.

Tarrick sucked in a sharp breath as his eyes turned purple.

Bound together, Matthew felt an overwhelming need to please

Tarrick. He began kissing his neck and working his way up his jaw.

Tarrick pulled Matthew hard into him and his whole body trembled. "No. Matthew. Stop."

Devastated, Matthew withdrew.

Tarrick looked him over. "What was that?"

Matthew whimpered.

Tarrick stroked the back of his neck, soothing him. "I'm not angry. I just want to know what that was."

Matthew rubbed his temple and pushed the fog away. "That was the same fabric that attaches incubi to the High King. A thread. Every incubus has one that is tied to him…it's why he's so powerful."

"He can physically see what I just felt, just like you can?"

"Yes."

"Can he see if I'm no longer loyal to him?"

"I don't know. I assumed you'd just lie about it…"

"I'm not sure I can fake it. I don't even know what *it* really is. My knowledge on gods and the divine is limited." Tarrick sighed. "Subterfuge might not work here. We'll have to snap the people away from him in one big moment."

"How did you know what my plan was?" Matthew asked.

"Your actions made it obvious."

"Did they?"

Tarrick nodded. "Step one, garner my loyalty. Step two, join the Argonauts as a way to reintegrate yourself back into our society. Step three, start swaying the incubi away from the King. But you think too small. You were going to try and win them over one at a time, weren't you?"

Matthew frowned.

"There's no need to be upset," Tarrick said, running his fingers over the back of Matthew's head. "It was a sound plan given your current resources. But something like that would take centuries and the incubi need a new leader or it'll be chaos."

"You?"

"It's the only option that makes sense. They'll never trust a vampire, not even one born of Ilertha." Tarrick settled his ass back on Matthew's thighs as he thought for a moment. He touched Matthew's collar. "This is another problem. I know two witches powerful enough to remove it but I'm not sure what their price will be."

"If it's removed the Judge will find me."

Tarrick looked to the side and clenched his jaw. "Devil, I wish I had known that earlier. This is becoming far more complex than I had envisioned. I didn't expect the collar to be the thing protecting you from the Judge, nor did I know that the King could look at any incubus and see how loyal they are."

Matthew dug his fingers into Tarrick's hips and looked down. "It's not too late for you to stop. It might be safer for your family if you back out now. If you tell the High King what I'm doing, I'll be punished, but I don't think it'll be worse than what I've had—he expects me to rebel."

Tarrick hooked his finger on Matthew's chin and forced him to look up. "If I don't do this, I'm looking at another century of war...three or four if the dragons start fighting. It could be over tomorrow and he won't let it. And...you are the child of Ilertha, our goddess...I've always believed you were sent to stop this war. So, no. I won't back out. We're doing this."

Matthew smiled. "Good."

"Don't attach your 'thread', or whatever you want to call it, to me again."

"Didn't you like it?"

Tarrick moved his hips forward, his massive erection dug into Matthew's stomach through their clothes. "Just the opposite. It was—and I don't say this lightly—better than anything I've felt before. Until I understand it, it's too dangerous. We can't risk the High King knowing."

Matthew nodded in agreement.

The sound of the water shutting off drew both their attention.

"One more thing. I've set the stage for you, but you're the one who needs to make it convincing. You need everyone to idolize you."

"They will."

"Good. Ready for dinner?" Tarrick asked, his purple irises settling back to dark blue.

Matthew looked at the closed bathroom door, the human presumably drying off on the other side. He wasn't quite sure what Tarrick had in mind and it made him a little nervous.

Tarrick squeezed Matthew's arms and pulled him into a heated kiss. He broke away and whispered into his ear. "I won't make you do anything you aren't ready for. If you want to stop, you can at any time."

"You're giving me a choice?"

Tarrick flashed his pearly white teeth as he smiled wide. "Yes. But I know what you can handle. You won't say stop…nor will the human. Now, let's eat."

Forty-Six

The human exited the bathroom, then froze midstride. His eyes wandered up and down Tarrick, who was still straddling Matthew in a domineering position.

"I instructed you to come out here naked," Tarrick said, pushing himself off and squaring his body as he stood.

Kyle looked at the towel around his hips. "Sorry, Sir," he said, his voice barely louder than a whisper.

"Not yet, but you will be." Tarrick stalked to the human and ripped the towel away from him. The human's prick was already rock hard.

Tarrick grabbed Kyle's wrists, dragged the boy over to the bed, and pulled the human over his lap, forcing his butt into the air.

With a resounding *smack,* he spanked him.

"No, Sir, please! I'm sorry."

"Are you?" Tarrick asked and brought his gloved hand down again, this time spanking the other cheek.

Kyle squirmed, trying to get free, but Tarrick kept him in place with a strong grip. There was no way any human could overpower a warrior incubus.

"Yes. I'm sorry, Sir."

"You," Tarrick pointed at Matthew, "go clean that up." He motioned to the towel on the ground. "Then undress. And you," Tarrick looked down at the boy, "are going to take forty more. You will count each one out loud. Are my instructions clear?"

"Yes, Sir. I'll count, Sir."

Tarrick started and each time he brought his hand down, the human cried out the next number. The slaps were light at first, warming him up, then grew progressively harder with each one. Kyle's eyes began to water and his ass cheeks turned a bright red. The scent of his arousal surprised Matthew.

As Tarrick delivered the punishment, Matthew folded the towel, put it back in the bathroom, returned, and undressed. He draped his clothes over a chair and watched the show before him, waiting—

naked and hard—for instruction.

"Forty, Sir," Kyle hissed—his face wet and body limp on Tarrick's lap.

Tarrick rubbed his tight little ass. "That's a good boy. You did well. And look how warm and red you are. Feels good, doesn't it?"

"Yes, Sir," Kyle said. He looked as if he wanted to drift off to another place, but Tarrick cradled the back of the boy's head and turned it so that he was looking at Matthew.

"What do you think of the slave?"

Kyles gaze floated up and down Matthew's body, pausing at his penis. "My god," he gasped. "He's big, Sir."

Matthew gripped the base of his shaft and squeezed. He wasn't enormous to the point where it was painful for his partners, but he was larger than average. Matthew motioned his chin at Tarrick. "If you think I'm big, wait until you see him."

Tarrick pushed his hips forward into the human's stomach. Kyle gulped when he felt the erection…then whimpered.

Tarrick went to his feet, pulling the human up with him. When Kyle was steady enough to stand on his own, Tarrick released him and inspected the human's body.

"Hmm, yes. You're almost perfect."

Kyle fidgeted under the critical gaze, but his prick stood at attention, exposing his need to be mistreated.

Tarrick grabbed Kyle's balls, and squeezed. The human yelped and tried to pull away, but the incubus held him in place, not letting him go.

When Kyle finally accepted what was happening, he stilled. Tarrick pulled out a long, silky pink ribbon from his pocket, wrapped the ribbon around the human's balls, and looped it around the base of his rod, finishing the look with a bow. Kyle's sac pulled tight and his erection grew even harder with the ribbon acting like a cock ring.

"There. What a pretty little cock. Don't you think so, Matthew?"

Matthew thought the bow looked ridiculous…and yet there was something appealing about seeing a dick all wrapped up like a present. And seeing the human get off on the degradation was extremely provocative. "Yes, sir. Very pretty."

Tarrick scooped the human up and laid him face down on the bed.

"Prepare him for me," he commanded Matthew as he loosened his tie.

Matthew crawled up behind Kyle and carefully grabbed his hips, pulled his ass into the air, and ran his hand over the red cheeks, feeling the warmth there.

The human moaned, Matthew's cold hand offering him relief.

Matthew moved his index finger down the center of the boy's ass, and felt the kid tense when his touch grazed over the small pink hole.

Matthew kept going and cupped his balls, giving them a light squeeze before going back up.

Pressing a single digit against the entrance, Matthew wondered if the human would question where the lube had come from, but he looked too dazed to care.

"Use your tongue," Tarrick said before Matthew had a chance to start producing gel.

Matthew glanced back at him.

Tarrick's eyes grew dark. "Your punishment will be far worse than a spanking if you disobey." Matthew shuddered at the warning; hot and dangerous all at once, and made him wonder what Tarrick would do.

But right now, he had no desire to disobey.

Matthew scooted the boy to the middle of the bed and crawled behind him. He leaned in and licked the human's skin, starting at the lower back and moving downwards.

The fluttering hole had the faint taste of soap. He swirled his tongue around the outside, teasing the boy with his piercings and causing him to push back wanting more. But Matthew was going to take his time with this and Tarrick didn't rush him.

He wet the outside—Kyle bucking and moaning with each stroke—then pushed his tongue into the tight channel.

The boy gasped.

"That's good, Matthew. Make him wet for me," Tarrick said, the words oozing from him like liquid sex. He went over and sat in front of Kyle and ran his fingers along the boy's back. "Are you enjoying this?"

"Yes, Sir," Kyle answered with a heavy breath as Matthew continued eating him out.

Tarrick pushed himself up on his knees and unzipped his pants.

Matthew slowed in his task, watching the display over the two mounds of red ass cheek. Kyle had gone silent, watching Tarrick with complete focus.

The incubus was more than happy to be the center of attention for the moment. He opened his pants and pulled out his hard dick and heavy balls. The human gasped at the large package.

Matthew actually felt terrible for the human. There was no way it wouldn't be painful for him.

Kyle's mouth opened as if he wanted to say something but no words came out.

"Do you like what you see?" Tarrick asked.

"Y-yes, Sir," he squeaked.

Tarrick stroked his length. "I'm going to destroy you with this but for now I want you to worship it with your mouth."

Like an eager puppy, Kyle's ass wiggled as he wrapped his lips around Tarrick's glans. The head alone had the boy's mouth almost full, his lips stretched wide. He took in as much as he could, unable to even get halfway down Tarrick's shaft, then pulled off. He licked from top to base and worked his way to the incubus' balls, soaking them with saliva.

If Tarrick was enjoying the blowjob, he wasn't letting anyone know it. His expression was one of indifference, which only made Kyle try harder. Matthew was thankful that every time he had been with Tarrick, the incubus had always acted like he enjoyed it.

This human's needs seemed far different than his own.

But then again, when Tarrick acted indifferent on the battlefield, it only made Matthew fight that much harder, wanting to impress him. Perhaps he and Kyle weren't that much different after all.

Tarrick, who seemed to have no intention of removing the rest of his suit, placed his hand on the back of Kyle's head and took over, directing him where to lick, suck, or lap his cock next. "Use your fingers now, Matthew. Open him up for me."

Matthew sat back and pressed a single finger against the human's tight hole. It slid in with only a little resistance and Matthew added a second digit. He curled them forward, and the human went wild when the fingers pressed against his prostate. He bucked and leaked cum in a constant stream. Tarrick held the human's face against his cock, not letting him go anywhere.

"*Sir*," the human begged, not asking for anything and at the same time asking for everything. He might have come right then if it wasn't for the ribbon around his package.

Tarrick gave him nothing except a firm hand.

Matthew worked another finger in, and one more, stretching the trembling boy.

"That's enough, Matthew. Come stand beside the bed."

Matthew removed his fingers and stood where he was told. Seeing the human with his red ass up in the air and lips wrapped around Tarrick's hardness had his cock and balls throbbing. He reached down to touch.

"You aren't touching yourself, are you?" Tarrick said, his back to Matthew, but his voice a low warning.

Matthew stopped his hand inches from his erection. "Uh, no, sir."

"And if either of you come before I tell you to, my punishment will be cruel."

Kyle whimpered, and Matthew bit back a frustrated growl, his dick feeling neglected.

Tarrick flipped Kyle onto his back and moved between his legs. "Hold him down," Tarrick said as he lined himself with the human's hole.

Matthew stood above Kyle, whose head was nearly hanging off the side of the bed. He grabbed his wrists, crossed them over his chest, and held them in place with one hand while pressing down on his shoulder with the other.

Kyle's tied up prick leaked on his skinny abdomen while Matthew's bobbed in the air, just inches above his mouth. The human's tongue darted out, trying to lick the underside of his rod. Matthew was tempted to lean down and let him, but he resisted the urge, fearing Tarrick's wrath.

Tarrick pushed into the human, going inch by inch. Kyle gritted his teeth and his face twisted up as he adjusted to the intrusion. Soft grunting noises filled the air.

The sexual energy coming from him began to overpower Matthew's senses. "I need to feed."

"You may," Tarrick said.

Matthew gripped the human tighter and pulled the golden threads of energy into his soavik.

Fuck, he was delicious.

Tarrick's teasing and build up had served to intensify Matthew's hunger and enhance the taste. A gloved hand came to rest on his chest, stopping his feeding. "Slow," Tarrick said. "This is why you need to feed more often. You'll hurt him with the way you're going."

Tarrick was right, he had been drinking in the human like a man who'd just found the only oasis in an endless desert. Kyle looked at the two men above him, confused by their words, but he said nothing.

The general resumed working himself into Kyle, pushing into him until he was fully seated. He began to thrust. Slow. The human's breathing grew ragged and his skin grew hotter.

Tarrick grabbed Kyle's knees and leaned over him. "You like the feeling of my enormous cock stretching and filling your small hole, don't you?"

Kyle moaned in response.

Tarrick pushed him up so that his head drooped backwards off the bed, exposing his entire neck to Matthew. "Release him, Matthew, and fuck his mouth. I want to see both of his holes *stuffed* by us."

Jesus. Matthew wanted to see that too.

"Kyle, look at me," Tarrick said.

The human struggled to keep his attention on Tarrick. He tried to lift his head only to let it drop back over the edge of the mattress. His eyelids went heavy.

"Kyle—" Tarrick warned, grabbing the back of his neck and forcing him to meet his gaze.

Kyle focused.

"—grab Matthew's wrist. If it's too much for you, let go and he'll stop. Do you understand?"

Kyle nodded.

"I want you to say it out loud."

"Let go of his wrist if I want him to stop, Sir."

"Good boy." Tarrick released his head and ran his thumb down Kyle's filled erection as a reward.

Matthew set one of his hands on the human's shoulder, and Kyle grabbed his wrist right below the shackle and opened his mouth, waiting for Matthew to enter him.

Matthew didn't have to lean down far, just enough to angle himself correctly, and pushed in a few inches. The feeling of a warm mouth surrounding his sex was incredible. He loved the sensation of Kyle's tongue rubbing the top of his dick instead of the bottom, and when the human flicked his piercing he nearly lost it.

"All the way in, Matthew."

Matthew looked up at Tarrick then back at the boy. "There's no way he can take me."

"He can and he will. You'll stay in him until I tell you to withdraw, or if he releases your arm."

Matthew couldn't see Kyle's face from this angle but the scent of excitement and nervousness surged from the human in waves. He pushed his hips forward, sliding deeper into the boy's mouth until he hit the back of Kyle's throat…then kept going. The human struggled as Matthew pushed past his gag reflex, but he didn't release his grip on Matthew's wrist.

Kyle's neck bulged as Matthew's cock filled it. The outline of his sex inside of the boy looked hot as hell. Matthew thrust, watching the neck swell even more. His balls smacked against the human's face with each push.

"Let him breathe," Tarrick said as Kyle's skin began to turn a bright red.

Matthew pulled out and Kyle gasped for air, his throat sounding raw and ruined. Tarrick patted Kyle's stomach. "That's a good boy, taking him all in like that."

Kyle's only response was to push his chin up and open his jaw wider, waiting for Matthew.

Matthew slid back into the wet mouth and locked himself deep into the warm, tight throat. Each time Kyle swallowed, Matthew couldn't hold back a moan.

Tarrick assaulted the human from the other end, pounding him hard as Matthew did the same. Unable to breathe, no sound came from the writhing human, whose body they were feasting upon.

When Kyle began to struggle, Matthew withdrew. He hadn't wanted to. He wanted to keep going until he exploded into the human's stomach, and honestly, he was close. But he also wanted to please Tarrick and show him that he had some level of restraint…even if Tarrick usually made him come like a teenager who'd just discovered porn. It was a little embarrassing.

He let Kyle take a few more deep breaths then he thrust himself back in, taking him harder this time, building his pleasure.

On the other end, Tarrick held Kyle's hips down while he impaled him. The human looked as if he might shoot his load any moment. The ribbon around his cock seemed to be the only thing holding him back. Tarrick looked as in control as ever—each hard thrust seemingly for the human's pleasure instead of his own.

There was a part of Matthew that wished Tarrick would take his clothes off so he could admire his fantastic body, but there was another part of him that found the suit with leather gloves so damn sexy. It played to his imagination, which was running rampant.

Tarrick locked his gaze onto Matthew's. Unable to look away, Matthew nearly came right then. He almost forgot to let the poor boy breathe; it wasn't until Kyle began to thrash that Matthew pulled out.

The human sucked in three large gulps of air before Matthew filled him again. He was too close to the edge to wait. He expected the human to let go of his wrist, but he held it tight as ever. Matthew could hardly believe that Kyle was willingly letting him do this to him.

"Jesus," Matthew said. "He tastes so good."

Tarrick seemed pleased that Matthew was enjoying the meal he had picked. He pressed down on Kyle's neck and Matthew felt the pressure against his cock. In response, he began thrusting faster, humping the human's throat raw.

Matthew was painfully close. His balls drew up and his length filled. He removed himself from the warm mouth, ready to cum on the human, but was surprised when Tarrick dragged Kyle away so that he was no longer hanging off the edge.

Tarrick motioned for Matthew to kneel beside the human on the bed. Eager and so fucking close to release, Matthew didn't even hesitate. He moved to where he was told to and reached down to stroke himself to completion.

A feral growl came from Tarrick and Matthew stopped just short of grabbing his cock.

"Lord General…please. I'm dying here."

A ravening—almost evil—grin crossed Tarrick's lips as he reached back and slapped Matthew hard across his face.

Matthew's head snapped to the side and instinctively his vampire guise came ripping forward. A guttural snarl escaped him as he flashed his fang-less teeth.

The human was caught between a moan and a shriek, and the scent of terror rolled off him like perfume. But Kyle didn't have time to process everything.

Tarrick's eyes turned from blue to purple. "Come," Tarrick commanded the human as he pulled on the silky bow that trapped the human's cock and balls while continuing to ram against his prostate.

The moment his cock was free, the human sobbed and shot his load hard into the air. The first spasm of white seed splattered his chin and each one after striped his abdomen.

In response, Tarrick began to unravel. Matthew watched as his perfect control slipped in the brief moments leading up to release. The incubus' body tensed as he filled the human.

Thump.

The sensation—along with the aroma of fear, sex, and lust—sent Matthew careening over the edge. Completely untouched, he came on the human's chest, his thick bands of cream joining the already debauched looking skin.

When the haze of his orgasm faded, he sat back on his heels and looked at the boy, who was silent, except for his heart, which was beating fast and hard.

Tarrick continued to slowly rock into him. He scooped up some of the cum and pushed it into Kyle's mouth. The human was petrified, frozen in place.

"Swallow," Tarrick ordered.

Giving the human a task seemed to bring him out of it a little. He swallowed and Tarrick repeated the process until all the cum was pushed into his mouth.

When he was done, he let the human suck on his leathered gloves for a few minutes. "Wipe his mind."

"Everything?"

"Just the end. Let him remember tonight."

Matthew forced his vampire side away, then grabbed Kyle's head to stop him from looking away. "You didn't see anything strange tonight. The sex was fantastic, and you have no reason to suspect we're anything but human."

The human's fear subsided and he began to suck on Tarrick's fingers with new enthusiasm.

"Lie down," Tarrick ordered Matthew.

When Matthew settled down in the bed, Tarrick removed his hand from the human's mouth, scooped him up, and placed him next to Matthew. Matthew pulled the warm human into him and stroked his arm.

Tarrick went to the bathroom and, shortly after, returned with some damp towels. He had already cleaned himself, his pants zipped up and his gloves removed. He handed Matthew a towel before he began wiping down Kyle. Tenderly, Tarrick cleaned the sticky residue from Kyle's chest and between his legs.

When he had finished, he lay on the other side of the human and stroked his belly. "Did you enjoy that, Kyle?"

"Yes, Sir. Can we…maybe do that again sometime?"

Tarrick stroked the human's hair. "Perhaps. But for now, go to sleep. I'll have my people take you home in a bit. Okay?"

"Okay."

Matthew felt Tarrick wrap a hold around the human, who drifted off into a relaxed sleep.

"What's going to happen to him?" Matthew asked.

"Normally, this would just be a night he'd never forget…but a friend of mine is looking for a submissive feeder and he would be perfect for it."

"How does that work? Are feeders taken against their will?" Matthew worried that Kyle was about to become some sort of sex slave.

Tarrick ran his hand over Matthew's arm. "No. They're brought into our world and taken care of. They're paid exceptionally well and want for nothing. Favorites have their lifespan extended. Some become close friends and lovers, or even mates. A human like Kyle would be coveted because of how he tastes."

Matthew ran his fingers down Kyle's side. A soft sigh of satisfaction sounded from the sleeping human. "Did you know he'd taste that good when you picked him out?"

"I had hoped, but even I don't know until feeding begins. I chose him for his submissive nature."

"Well, if he does enter this world, he's going to freak out when he finds out who we are," Matthew said with a chuckle.

Tarrick smiled. "Yes, I suppose he will." Tarrick raised his comm to his mouth. "Commander, come in here."

Silva appeared in front of the bed. She did a double take when she saw Matthew lounging around naked.

"See something you like?" Matthew asked with a wink, motioning to his body. God, he loved teasing her. He wasn't even sure why but he did.

She ignored him. "We didn't find anything during the sweep, General. The building is secure."

"Ah, yes. Thank you."

Silva narrowed her eyes. "If you need privacy in the future, I'd rather you just say so and not send me on bullshit tasks. Sir."

"Watch yourself, Commander, you haven't even begun to see the number of 'bullshit tasks' I can assign to you." Matthew thought Tarrick was angry with her but then he smiled and she shook her head. It appeared he had grown close to Silva since she had become his hunter commander. Tarrick motioned to Kyle. "I want full background on this human. Family, friends, everything you can dig up."

"He was that good, huh?"

"Holst will think so."

"If Lord Holst likes him, he'll owe you quite a bit. He's been searching for the right feeder forever."

"I know. Take him home for now." Tarrick grabbed Kyle's clothes and redressed him with Silva's help. Then she slung him over her shoulders and left with him. It was a little strange seeing a woman who was five-nothing carry him out, but she didn't even struggle thanks to her runes.

Matthew wondered if Tarrick would use Kyle as a way of swaying over whoever this Lord Holst was. He didn't ask since Silva's team stood right outside and there were no wards blocking the sound.

He looked up to find Tarrick standing at the foot of the bed, staring down at him. His eyes had turned purple.

"Um. Should I get dressed?" Matthew asked, suddenly feeling a little exposed despite what they had just done together.

"In a moment." Tarrick continued to stare unabashedly.

Matthew sat up against the headboard and moved to pull the sheet over his hips.

"No," Tarrick said.

Matthew let his hands fall to the side. He wasn't sure what he should be doing. Tarrick watching him like this confused him. Did the incubus want him or not? He cared for him but did it really end there? It was hard to believe when he watched Matthew with such desire.

But maybe Tarrick was confused also. Vampires had killed most of those he loved—falling for one couldn't be easy. Maybe he just needed time to realize his own feelings, the way Matthew had needed time to realize how he felt for Devak.

Then again, maybe Matthew was being an idiot. Tarrick was almost a thousand years old. He probably was telling the truth when he spoke of matters of his heart. Matthew just needed to accept that his love was an unrequited one and always would be.

He sighed.

"I've never had sex like that," Matthew said, wanting a change in topic. "It was really…intense. And thank you for giving him the ability to say no. I know you didn't have to, but I needed it."

"I know." Tarrick's eyes ran up and down Matthew's body, but otherwise he didn't move. He said nothing for several minutes. He just stood watching Matthew.

"I don't understand what's going on right now," Matthew finally said, breaking the silence.

"Me either," Tarrick whispered. He blinked hard once, then broke away and grabbed his suit jacket and coat from the closet. "Get dressed. We're done for the night. I'll meet you downstairs."

Tarrick hurried from the room, leaving Matthew behind, naked and in a state of confusion.

Matthew sat on the bed for a few minutes before moving to get dressed. He spent the time considering what any sort of relationship with Tarrick would be like and he hated all the answers he came up with.

Even if he had hoped that things might change in the future, he had to face the reality that was his situation: he was a slave and he existed at the mercy of the High King. Once the patch of ghouling skin was gone Tarrick would probably return to his estate. Matthew rubbed that area of his hip. He watched as the rotting flesh reappeared. At least it wasn't growing in size.

As he dressed, he decided that he'd just enjoy what he had now. Lately, life had left him broken and in pieces, he hadn't felt very strong. But now he had hope. He *was* strong and he'd prove it to himself. That gave him a small amount of comfort.

We live long lives, Matthew, Rosaline had said to him, and she was right. If he and Tarrick were meant to be, it couldn't be now. He could wait…even if he did long for more.

A small twinge of guilt bubbled up from deep within him. Devak had desired Matthew's love…and Matthew had been an idiot to resist it for so long. He'd give anything to change how that went down. Or to have another day with Devak.

But his guardian was long dead and Tarrick was alive.

Once he had finished dressing, Matthew grabbed Tarrick's tie and cufflinks that were left behind in his rush to get away. He tucked them into his pocket as he headed out.

Silva was waiting in the hall for him.

"Where's the human?" Matthew asked.

"You should be careful, you still aren't allowed to speak unless addressed."

Shit. When he was out with the team or with Tarrick that rule didn't apply, but she was right, it was still a rule. "I'm sorry, commander."

"Personally, I don't care," she said, as she led him into the private elevator. "But you'll be punished if someone overhears and reports it. To answer your question, I had another team take the human home. One of the perks of being a high-ranking hunter is that I can have others do the bitch work...normally."

Matthew laughed. "Still mad he had you do that sweep, huh?"

"I hope whatever you two talked about was important."

"It was."

They were silent for a few moments as the elevator descended, until Matthew asked, "You ever fight in that arena?"

"You really liked watching that, didn't you?" she asked with a chuckle.

He shrugged. "Yeah, it was okay I guess."

She eyed him. "You guess?"

"Alright, it was fucking awesome. Do they have fights like that every week?"

She laughed. "Not every week. And, no, I've never fought. Although they keep trying to get me in the ring. Darragh fights in there a lot. You should ask him about it."

"Darragh? Who's that?" Matthew asked.

Silva shook her head. "You should learn your teammate's names. Mac's full name is Darragh Mac Nellis."

"Oh. Um. I don't know your full name either...or anyone's I guess. I just assumed that hunters only took the one name when they became hunters."

"Julie."

"Really?"

"Yes."

"Julie Silva," Matthew said with a laugh.

"What's so funny?"

"You have such a girly name."

She threw a playful punch into his arm. "Shut up."

The two of them were laughing when the doors opened. Tarrick raised an eyebrow upon seeing them and both fell silent.

Without a word, Tarrick walked outside into the waiting limo, Matthew trailed behind while the Wardens covered the car by watching it from rooftops. Matthew took the seat opposite Tarrick.

"You left these," Matthew said and dug out the cufflinks and tie from his pocket, handing them over. Tarrick made no effort to take them, he just sat there, looking at Matthew.

Feeling a little awkward, Matthew set the items down on the seat beside him. "Have I done something to displease you, Lord General?"

"No."

Silence filled the air.

Matthew started playing with his daylight ring. There was always a faint buzz of magic coming from it but it didn't bother him.

"Where'd this ring come from? I thought there were only four," Matthew asked.

"The High King had it commissioned at the Imperator's request."

"Ah." Devak had told Matthew there was only one witch who knew how to make them. That witch must have been an ally of the incubi, otherwise the rings probably wouldn't be so rare.

"Do you think of him often?"

Matthew gave pause to the sudden question. "You mean Devak?"

Tarrick nodded once.

"I, uh, try not to. It's painful, you know? It's—" Matthew blinked hard a few times and swallowed. "I feel guilty that I don't think of him more, but with my memory, it feels too real…it's too hard. It's the same with Alyssa. I know it's not healthy but…" Matthew rubbed his forehead. His failures—his losses—gnawed at him. He'd do anything to see them again.

"I think of my mates often."

Matthew studied Tarrick, who seemed to be lost in thought, and waited to see if the general would say anything else. He didn't. More silence passed. Tarrick was processing something, and Matthew tried to be patient but it was driving him crazy.

"I had fun tonight…you know…on our not-date," Matthew offered, trying to lighten the mood.

Tarrick's focus returned and the edge of his mouth lifted, exposing a tiny crack in his serious demeanor.

Matthew smiled back at him. "Thank you for—" Matthew stopped talking when dark voices began to whisper in his ear and a surge of power brushed against the edge of his senses. "Fucking hell."

Tarrick sat forward. "What is it?"

"You need to let me have my weapon right now."

"Only the Imperator or the High King can remo—" Before he could finish, the windows of the limo shattered as some sort of concussive blast hit them. Matthew's sensitive ears were ringing.

A flurry of movement erupted around them as shadowy clouds surged through the windows and two demons took shape in the car.

The first was a dark cloaked figure that looked almost human, except sharp spikes covered its body and it had all black eyes. Raising a dark dagger, it lunged at Tarrick.

The general grabbed the demon's wrist and broke it with a stomach-churning *crack*, forcing it to drop the blade. With his other hand, Tarrick plucked the dagger from the air and drove it through the soft flesh of the demon's throat, forcing it upwards into its brain. Black blood leaked from the wound, but Tarrick pushed the demon off him onto the limo's floor before any could get on his suit.

Matthew would have been hella impressed by Tarrick's prowess if he wasn't busy with his own demon. It had appeared inches away from his face and sunk its dagger into Matthew's shoulder.

When the demon hissed at him, strings of oily black saliva clung between its mouthful of sharp teeth.

Matthew swiped at it, but the creature matched his speed, dodging his attacks. It lashed out at Matthew again, jabbing the dagger at his stomach. Matthew didn't bother dodging—he didn't have enough room in the cramped limo—and he wasn't really one for finesse anyway. The dagger barely missed his pouches.

The attack left the demon open and Matthew poured as much energy as he could into his strength and punched the demon square in the chest, sending it into the partition.

The limo swerved defensively then came to a stop.

The demon tried to push itself up but Matthew wasn't going to let that happen. He was laying into it with punch after punch before it could move. Its skin split open and ribbons of black blood painted Matthew's chest and the area around him.

"Matthew," Tarrick said.

Matthew didn't stop, even though his demon was dead.

"*Matthew*," Tarrick repeated, this time with full command behind his voice.

Matthew growled and looked back over his shoulder. There wasn't a single drop of blood on the general. He had already taken off his shirt and was in the process of pulling off his pants, his body growing.

He shook his head. "Why is it that no matter where I bring you, you end up making such a mess?"

Matthew looked down. He was *layered* with blood: his own red blood from his wounded torso, his bleeding tattoos, and black blood from the demon he had just pulverized.

A large mass of something hit the roof of the limo with a loud *thud*.

Tarrick—still transforming into his full incubus form—exited the limo and finished his transformation. The only piece of clothing he wore was a pair of boxer-briefs, the seams stretched to their absolute limits.

Matthew ran out of the car after him and surveyed the area. They were in the middle of a four-lane street surrounded by tall brick buildings. Around them were abandoned cars, and dead humans littered the ground.

There was a faint shimmer of a veil, masking this fight from passing humans and sending them on a detour.

With a glow of green light, Silva fell from the sky, sword in hand, and drove it into the chest of a demon that was lying on the roof of the limo, finishing it off.

"Report," Tarrick said, his voice a few octaves deeper now.

"There were six total," she said, stabbing the demon again for good measure. "Four are dead now. One made a break for downtown. I have my team on its ass now. We lost the other. Argonauts are three minutes out—none of them were in High Tower tonight."

Tarrick looked around. "And the other demon?"

"We lost it but I don't think it went far. They seem to want something from either you or Matthew," Silva said as she jumped off the car and opened the trunk. Inside was a whole cache of weapons and Tarrick's breastplate. She grabbed it, hooked it over his shoulders, and uttered the words to expand it. The iridescent metal caught the street light, gleaming in the night as the armor wrapped around his body.

Matthew couldn't help but stare at the incubus. Tarrick wasn't the biggest warrior of his race but Matthew always found him the most

impressive. One glance at him and no one could mistake him for anything but a leader. His body language was commanding and unassailable. His voice certain with authority.

Even the stumps he now had for horns didn't detract from his
splendor.

Tarrick stretched his extraordinary wings and stomped a hoof
against the ground to shake his armor into place.

In this form, his strength could rival that of a vampire. Memories
of the night he saw the High King's true form came rushing in…the
King was far bigger than Tarrick…and stronger…and merciless…and,
oh god, the pain…. Matthew began to spiral downwards as flashes of
that night filled him. He closed his eyes and stumbled back, crashing
into the side of the limo.

The faint scent of sweet wine and fragrant oil drifted past and a
firm hand came to rest on his shoulder. "Muri," a gentle voice whispered. Matthew opened his eyes to see Tarrick standing over him. He
flinched but Tarrick didn't relinquish his grip.

"Warrior—" Tarrick said, brushing his other hand across Matthew's face, "—I need you to track a demon for me. Can you do that?"

He focused on Tarrick's touch…his breath…his scent…anything
to help him stay grounded in this moment. Tonight had been such a
nice night, he didn't want it to end in despair and sorrow. Tarrick had
given him a task. And, yes, he could do that. He pushed himself off
the car and sniffed the air.

He caught the demon's scent. It was somewhere near—and above
them.

Silva grabbed a kanabō from the trunk but Tarrick reached over
her and picked up a claymore instead. A human using the bladed
weapon would need two hands to wield it but Tarrick only needed
one at his current size.

Matthew couldn't help but think his weapon change was for his
sake. He hated that fucking kanabō. Even after all this time he couldn't
help but remember the night he had been beaten to near death with
it. That was the shitty part of having an almost perfect memory; he
remembered the good and the bad.

"Think you can keep up, old man?" Matthew said, trying to lighten
the mood.

"*Old man?*" Tarrick tossed Matthew a longsword. Matthew winked as he caught it and took off in the direction of the demon. The general followed, his hooves pounding against the asphalt, and said, "You do understand that age gives me incredible stamina, something you struggle with."

Ouch.

Not that he was totally wrong...

Silva teleported in front of them. From a pocket in her cloak she pulled out a handful of thin, inch-long metal bars. They began to glow green in her hand and she tossed them out in front of her.

A veil formed.

Matthew found it fascinating. He had never actually noticed a hunter do that before. He passed her and she watched where he was going, then teleported in front of him again and repeated the process to keep them hidden from humans.

"If you sent your team away, did you kill that demon by yourself?" Matthew asked her.

"Yes. I know how to do my job...*and* I managed to kill mine without getting blood everywhere," she said, tossing out another metal rod at the entrance to the alleyway they turned down.

Matthew looked at himself. His clothes were ruined. He had been hoping he could sneak the jeans back into his room to wear when he was alone...now he mourned their passing.

"I was sired by the *Blood* God. Blood."

"Uh huh," she said, teleporting to the other end of the alley.

Matthew sped next to her. "What does 'uh huh' mean?"

"It means I take back what I said earlier about your technique improving. Stop being sloppy."

Tarrick caught up behind them—his breath rapid but controlled, like that of an athlete. "Is it close?"

Matthew listened. He could hear the whispers. A faint scent of death drifted past.

He looked up. "It's above us somewhere."

"Stay here, Matthew," Tarrick said as he jumped into the air. Silva teleported to the roof of a ten-story residential building.

Matthew huffed and sat down on an overturned plastic bucket. It creaked under his weight. "Yeah. That's okay. The vampire will just chill down in this alley. Alone. Not having fun fighting a demon."

He wasn't alone for long.

Matthew watched as Silva teleported along the building, firing her crossbow in the air. A moment later, a twisting mass of wings and muscle came shooting across the night sky. Tarrick was weaponless and locked in combat with a demon. This one was the most cliché-looking demon Matthew had ever seen; with burgundy skin, wings, horns, hooves... It looked almost like an incubus, but twisted and mean.

The two figures wrestled each other as they plummeted. Tarrick ended up on top. He spread his wings to slow their descent but they still came down fast, crashing into a fire escape. The metal groaned and broke under their weight, sending them rolling down into the alley. They fell on a closed dumpster.

The wind was knocked from Tarrick's lungs and he began gasping for air. The demon recovered faster, standing on the lid and lunging at the incubus. A hail of bolts flew at it; most of them bounced off harmlessly but one buried itself into his cheek.

The demon hissed at Silva and pulled the bolt out.

Matthew lunged at the creature, jumping up onto the dumpster and slamming his body into it. The demon stumbled off the bin but managed to stay upright with a flap of its wings.

Matthew leaped down at it, sword first. He hit its shoulder dead on...and the sword bounced off its skin.

The demon laughed and clawed at Matthew's much softer flesh, slicing him.

More blood.

More mess.

Damn it, everyone was going to make fun of him now. Out of pure vanity, he pushed power into his healing, even though the wound wasn't severe and would heal quickly enough on its own.

The demon licked Matthew's blood from the tip of its claws. "It is true then," it said, its voice dark. "You have been summoned. You will come with me."

"Yeah...nope," Matthew said and lunged at it.

The two went smashing to the ground, rolling one over the other in a struggle to get on top. Claws, fists, and knees flew as their bodies thrashed about.

Matthew somehow got a hold of its wrist and he yanked the demon to the ground beside him.

Before it could get back up, a big hoof stomped on the creature's head, popping it like a watermelon, sending brain matter and viscous black blood all over Matthew's side.

Tarrick stood triumphantly above the demon. He removed his hoof from what was left of the demon's head and gave it a little shake, getting even more shit on Matthew.

"Aw, come on." Matthew sat up, wiping his face with the inside of his shirt. "Seriously?"

Tarrick smirked and shook his leg again, undoing all Matthew's efforts to get clean.

"Now you're just being an asshole." Matthew shot up and ran his bloody hand down the front of Tarrick's armor, leaving a long smear of blood. "I can be one too."

Tarrick caught Matthew's wrist and pulled him in. He leaned down and claimed Matthew's mouth; aggressive and almost ruthless in his conquest. Caught by surprise, Matthew tried to pull away but Tarrick gripped Matthew's wrist harder and locked his free hand behind his head, not letting him go anywhere.

Matthew surrendered and passion twisted inside of him, heading downwards and heating his core.

He felt so small right now. Possessed. Owned. And for once it felt good.

He never understood his attraction to Tarrick. By all rights, he should despise him: Tarrick had deceived him, made him a slave, brought him into this fucking war, and didn't even love him back... and yet...even with all that, he still wanted the incubus general.

He wondered if it made him a weak man for feeling this way.

Matthew wanted more than just this kiss and instinctively he wrapped his shitty little incubus hold on Tarrick. In response, Tarrick brushed his own hold against Matthew. It felt like a feather tickling his skin. It wasn't aggressive or manipulative, it was just there, warm and comforting.

He settled into the kiss, letting Tarrick lead with his aggressive tongue. Matthew wished their hard armor wasn't between them.

"Aw, if I had known there was going to be an epic make out session I would have gotten my ass here quicker," a young-sounding voice said from behind Matthew.

Forty-Eight

A low grumble came from Tarrick's chest as he pulled away from Matthew and glared at Hiroto, who was crouched on a dumpster a few feet away. Mask pulled down, his smile grew wider as he saluted Tarrick.

Matthew was left staggered for a moment before he gathered himself and realized that the rest of the Argonauts—and the Wardens—were all watching them.

Matthew took a step away from Tarrick and straightened up.

"I take it you lost the body jumper," Tarrick said, his body beginning to return to its human form.

"If you had your damn comm on you would have known that, General," Prescott said, pulling off his helmet.

Tarrick shrugged. "It must have been damaged during the fight."

Matthew could see Tarrick's comm unmolested on his wrist. Come to think of it, he hadn't turned it on since he left the bedroom. It was almost as if he hadn't wanted to call for backup or issue orders tonight. Maybe he needed a break from being a general…or maybe he just wanted to fight alongside Matthew for once.

Prescott eyed Tarrick but said nothing about the comm. "I've ordered a team to clean up the veils and—"

Tarrick waved his hand dismissively, cutting him off. "Thank you, Imperator. You can take it from here."

An SUV pulled up. Tarrick, human-sized now, got in the back and motioned for Matthew to follow. Matthew looked to Prescott for a moment, unsure if maybe he should stay with his team, but Prescott gestured for him to leave.

Matthew got in beside Tarrick and sighed heavily as he sank back into the seat. He was getting the SUV dirty but he didn't care.

Tarrick wrinkled his nose. "You smell."

Matthew laughed. "You're not exactly roses right now either." They both looked out the windshield as the driver pulled onto a street. "What do you think the demon meant by saying I was 'summoned'?"

"My best guess is that you've caught the attention of a demon ruler—maybe Mazarus—and they want you."

"The High King's son? Why is Mazarus in the Pit anyways? Or is that something I shouldn't ask?"

Tarrick let out an amused chuckle. "I very much doubt that you would refrain from asking something just because you shouldn't."

Matthew tried to suppress a sheepish grin but failed. He had to admit…ever since Tarrick showed up in his life again, he was back to feeling like himself again.

"And everyone knows the story. Isn't that right, Peters?" Tarrick asked the hunter driving the SUV.

The hunter glanced into the rearview mirror. "Yes, Lord General. Seems every other party I have to guard, it gets brought up."

Matthew raised an eyebrow. He'd been around plenty of parties and it had never been brought up. In fact, in his experience most incubi rarely discussed the High King, and if he was mentioned, it was with hushed reverence. "I think I've been going to the wrong parties," he said.

The edge of Tarrick's mouth pulled up into a half-smile. "Actually, yes. When you were under my care, you rubbed shoulders with the aristocracy, but there's a whole other side to my people you've never had the chance to see. Perhaps one day I'll show you."

The idea thrilled Matthew but he didn't let himself get too excited—the future was too uncertain and out of his hands.

Tarrick turned his body to face Matthew, which should have been awkward considering he was in plate armor, but he managed to make it look effortless. "Mazarus was the High Lord General before my mother gained the title. He led the final stand in the Pit itself and, with his army, held off the demons long enough for the Pit to be sealed. He didn't make it out and was presumed dead."

"I thought—" Matthew paused, worried he might be punished, but curiosity won out. "I thought that the High King hadn't…been with anyone since he killed Devak…were all his children before then?"

"Yes. And the others are all dead now. He doesn't even have many descendants anymore. We all expect him to have another child. A new heir."

"That's what Rosaline wants, isn't it? To give him one?"

"Indeed." A small thread of sadness came from Tarrick and it took Matthew a moment to figure out why: Rosaline would never be on their side. She loved the High King. He was her mentor, her savior. If they killed him, she wouldn't forgive them.

She was one of Tarrick's closest friends and what they were doing would drive them apart in the end.

Tarrick had let Matthew feel that sadness...then he cut off the emotion and Matthew could no longer read him.

Matthew placed his hand on Tarrick's armored thigh. "You know, this was the best date I've ever been on."

"It wasn't a date, Matthew."

"Whatever you say, Lord General."

Tarrick sighed then rested his hand on top of Matthew's and the two spent the rest of the ride back in an easy silence...that is until High Tower came into view and a massive weight pressed down on Matthew. It was his prison and, once inside, he couldn't forget he was a slave; not like he had tonight when he was walking around New York with a man he loved.

But he didn't let any of it show as Tarrick led him to the elevator. He bit back his disappointment when the elevator stopped on his floor and Tarrick dismissed him with a, "There's blood in your room. Have a good night, Matthew."

It wasn't quite the way he had wanted the not-date to end but he could hardly complain.

In his room, he drank the cold blood that was waiting for him, showered, slipped on a pair of boxer-briefs, and was on his bed just before the sun rose outside. Even with the ring on, he still felt the pull of sleep. His body was tired and overworked as it finished healing the wounds the demon gave him.

Matthew looked at his hip; the rotten patch of skin had shrunk a great deal during the night. That meant that Tarrick's job would be done here and he would most likely return to his Ashwood estate.

Pain filled his chest. He didn't want Tarrick to go away.

He reminded himself that he needed to stay focused on his goals. He had a king to overthrow.

If we are going to do this, we can't afford to be distracted by each other.

Tarrick was right.

But Matthew wanted to be distracted by him. He wanted to feel warm arms wrapped around his body. He wanted to hear the general working as he slept. He began to imagine Tarrick's scent and realized he was being a fool. He pushed away the thoughts but the scent didn't fade…it was real.

Tarrick was nearby.

Matthew slid off his bed, silently went to his door and pressed his hand against it.

Tarrick was just outside, standing in the hallway. Then, finally, Matthew heard him back away from the room and head back to the elevator.

Matthew didn't want Tarrick to leave…he opened his door and appeared in front of him, blocking his way to the elevator.

Tarrick came to a stop. His dark blond hair was still wet from showering and he was wearing black lounge pants with a white t-shirt that clung perfectly across his chest. He met Matthew's eyes and his mouth parted as if he meant to say something but words failed him.

Matthew took a cautious step closer, entering his space.

Tarrick's eyes raked over Matthew's near-naked body. He said nothing then pressed his eyelids closed and turned his head away.

He let out a deep breath and, unexpectedly, his glamor melted away. Terrible scars appeared across his body and he had deep bags under his eyes, which opened and drifted back to Matthew's face. He looked worn; exhausted.

Matthew reached up and traced one of the longer scars up Tarrick's arm until it disappeared under his t-shirt. He rested his hand on a muscled shoulder and gave him a reassuring squeeze. "When was the last time you slept?"

"Over three weeks now."

Not since the night he had lost control?

Fuck.

Three weeks was a *long* time to go without sleep, even for an old incubus.

Matthew slipped his hand behind Tarrick's neck and pulled him closer. Tarrick's body relaxed and he rested his head on Matthew's shoulder, melting into him. He was vulnerable, exposed in a way Matthew had never seen before. It was completely un-Tarrick-like and yet nothing felt wrong about it.

Matthew wrapped his other arm around him and pulled him in tighter. "I'd never admit this to either of my daughters, but I think the best dates always end with a shared bed."

Tarrick's body trembled, whether it was a laugh or something else Matthew wasn't sure, but he was unwilling to let Tarrick leave. He grabbed Tarrick's hand and tugged, leading the general down the hall.

Without windows, his room was dark—he hadn't bothered to turn on the light earlier since he didn't need it—but it didn't seem to bother Tarrick, who made his way to the bed and slipped under the sheets. Matthew joined him, pressing against his back so that they were spooning. He wrapped his arms around Tarrick's body and held him tight.

Tarrick's breathing fell into a shallow, rhythmic pattern.

Matthew watched over him, his mind turning. He wanted more of this. He wanted every night of this. And he longed to hear Tarrick say *I love you*, just once.

But none of that was for him. He already knew this and was fixating on what couldn't be.

"Matthew—" Tarrick said, his voice sleepy.

"Hm?"

"I can't sleep if you're doing that."

"Doing what?"

Tarrick slipped Matthew's daylight ring off his finger.

Oh.

Matthew's body went stiff. He struggled against the sun but he wouldn't last long. "Cheater," he said, relieved. His chest rumbled with a happy purr.

Tarrick nestled against Matthew's body. "Go to sleep, warrior."

Matthew didn't know the exact moment sleep took him, but the elation of having Tarrick's body warm him was the last thought on his mind.

Forty-Nine

At nightfall, Matthew woke contented for the first time in ages. He was on his back, Tarrick pressed beside him, his masculine scent of night and earth intoxicating. He muttered something indecipherable and turned, wrapping his arms around Matthew and resuming his sleep.

On the other side of him was another person—his body warmer than Tarrick's. Matthew inhaled the delicate aroma of sweet wine and fragrant oil.

Devak rolled over and also wrapped his arms around Matthew. "He's tired, my prince," the guardian said.

"Then we'll let him sleep." Matthew couldn't be happier. He put an arm around each of the men he loved and pulled them in tight.

Devak leaned into Matthew's shoulder. "I'm sorry I couldn't protect you from Malarath."

"I know you would have if it was possible but…that's right…" A memory came to Matthew: Devak stabbed by Prescott. Devak dying.

Devak was dead.

Matthew squeezed his eyes closed.

And when he opened them, his bed was cold and empty. No Devak. No Tarrick, either. Although his scent still lingered.

He cursed his brain for tricking him. It was cruel that he smelled Devak…*touched him*…only to have him ripped away again. It had been over a year since his death and the pain hadn't dulled.

His hand moved to the empty space where Tarrick had been. He supposed it was too much for a slave to expect a loved one beside him when he woke.

His heart ached and he blinked hard, refusing to let his eyes tear up.

Sliding out of bed, he ignored the bottle of blood and the ring waiting for him on a nightstand, and went to the door that separated his room from Samantha's. Pressing his hand against it, he wished she were here. It had been more than a month since he had last seen her in person and being away from his bonded child for so long wore on him.

His tablet began to ring. He sat down on his bed and answered it.

Samantha's face popped up. "I miss you too," she said.

Matthew smiled at her. She brought him more joy than she'd ever know.

"How was the date?" she asked.

"It wasn't a date…"

She laughed. "It was totes a date."

"Yeah. I know, right? It was amazing." She let him tell her all about it. Well, he skipped the part with Kyle. "Do you think he'll let me fight in the arena?" he asked.

She cocked her head to the side. "Kinda. You'll see."

He sighed. "What's the point of having an oracle for a child if you don't tell me anything?"

"Phhff, I tell you almost everything."

There was movement on the screen and Samantha looked up, over the camera. "I only have another minute. Don't be pushy," she said to whoever was in the room with her.

"Is that Gavyn?" Matthew asked.

She turned the camera and Gavyn was standing there in his hunter attire. His outfit covered considerably less than what hunters normally wore; it was a leather harness that left his chest and arm tattoos exposed. He had a standard silver sword, stakes, and elixirs on his belt.

He nodded respectfully to Matthew then addressed Samantha. "I'm sorry I interrupted, I just wanted to say goodbye real quick before I go on duty. Will you be coming to the party tonight?"

"I don't know yet. But I'll give you a kiss for luck, you'll need it."

"Will I? Why? What's going to happen?"

She gave him a devious little smile.

"I hate it when you do that." He grumbled as she jumped up and tried to kiss him. Gavyn glanced at the camera and nervously turned his head so she caught his cheek. She grunted her displeasure and tossed her tablet face down on a table.

Matthew shook his head as he listened to them make out. A moment later her face filled the screen again. Gavyn was gone from her room.

"I take it things are going well with him?"

Embarrassed, she looked away for a moment and smiled. "Promise me you won't kill him."

"Nope. If he breaks your heart I can't guarantee anything," he said in half jest...but the truth was if Gavyn harmed her, Matthew might have no choice in his actions.

She scowled, then smiled. "It's gone."

Matthew moved his hand to his hip. The skin was smooth there. No more ghouling. "Yes. It's gone."

"We're out of time, talk later."

"Looking forward to it, love you."

The screen went black.

"So, last night was a date?" Hiroto said from behind him.

Startled, Matthew whipped around and clawed the air. Hiroto teleported out of the way and reappeared crouching atop the bookcase.

Matthew forced his claws to recede. "Jesus Christ. How is it that I can't sense you at all sometimes? And I know you aren't using that bullshit rune to mask yourself."

Hiroto pushed down his mask, his eyes smiled as happily as his mouth. "Trade secret."

"Have you been here the whole damn time?"

The kitsune hopped off the bookcase back to the bed. "Who do you think brought the blood?"

The door opened and Ezra and Ophelia entered. Matthew groaned when he saw them.

"You are to—"

"—come with us," the twins said.

"He has training," Hiroto said; all hint of playfulness faded.

"We have orders—"

"—from the High King, *fox*." They said the last word in unison, looking awfully proud of themselves.

"Fine. But I'm coming along."

Their adolescent eyes narrowed and their pink lips pulled tight.

"You are—"

"—not needed."

Hiroto shrugged. "You know the rules, you aren't to be alone with him."

"That's a rule?" Matthew asked, not really surprised.

"More or less. For whatever reason the King values these two, and doesn't want you to murder them."

"Do you think you could stop me if I really wanted to kill them?" Matthew didn't ask out of pride, he was genuinely curious if Hiroto thought he was fast enough to prevent him from snapping one of their necks.

"Hm," Hiroto said. "I think you could kill one and I'd be able to stop you before you killed the other. Then, of course, I'd have to take you down."

Matthew locked his gaze onto the twins and let his eyes burn red. He licked his lips. "Want to test it?"

The twins' eyes widened.

Hiroto pulled his mask back up. "Yes."

In the blink of an eye, Matthew had his hand wrapped around Ezra's small neck.

Two daggers pressed up against Matthew—one aimed at his blood pouches, the other at his neck, angled so that it'd damage his brain enough to stun him while his body repaired.

Hiroto had been right, Matthew could have snapped Ezra's neck just fast enough before the assassin stopped him.

Ezra trembled in his hand as Hiroto pulled his daggers away.

Matthew leaned down and whispered, "Isn't this what you want, incubus? Me touching you? Having my way with you?"

Ezra's fear turned to desire and his body shuddered again.

Matthew laughed and released the small incubus. He could play their stupid games too.

"*He* will hear of this," Ophelia said, her voice her own and not shared with her brother, who was pressing his body into her.

Matthew went to his side table and slipped on his ring. "Is there anything he doesn't hear of?"

Hiroto sheathed his weapons. "Not really, no," he said as Matthew began to drink the bottle of blood that had been waiting for him, downing it slowly to make the twins wait. When he was done, he walked to the closet.

"There is no need—"

"—to dress," they said with a mix of fear and anger.

Matthew ignored them and slipped on some pants anyways. Their small faces scrunched with displeasure but they said nothing else as they led him from the room to the spa floor.

Just as before, he was stripped, showered, and shaved. Hiroto disappeared but Matthew knew he was watching. He had half expected him to stay out in the open and make lewd comments, but maybe the little fox knew how humiliating this was and was giving him some semblance of privacy.

While showering, Ezra and Ophelia both tried to get him to respond to them sexually, pressing their bodies close, rubbing across his privates, even fingering his hole as they washed and shaved him.

He ignored their advances, thankful his dick was obeying tonight, hanging soft between his legs. When they wrapped their holds around him, Matthew growled a warning and they backed off. The High King would probably hear about that too but he'd risk the punishment.

Disappointed, they redressed him in workout clothes. His clothes felt slippery on his freshly shaven skin and he ran his hands through his short hair with a frown.

"Long or short hair, you still look hot," Hiroto said, appearing from behind the shadows of a marble pillar and leading them on to the elevator.

"Thanks, Commander."

"You know, humans have done research and they say petting an animal reduces stress and blood pressure."

Matthew laughed. He could think of a few places Hiroto wanted him to 'pet'. "I have almost no blood pressure most of the time."

Hiroto pointed at Matthew's crotch. "Then how does your cock get hard?"

"I...that's a good fucking question. I have no idea." Great. Now that'd be bugging him all night.

Hiroto pushed his hood back. His soft white hair fell around his neck and his ears popped up. "I think you should try the petting thing anyways."

Matthew reached out and touched the fox's ears. Hiroto leaned into his hand as he stroked the soft fur. Petting them was relaxing and he enjoyed Hiroto's playfulness, but he knew it would be short-lived. Once training started, Hiroto would be an insufferable hard-ass.

Still, he'd take advantage of it while he could.

He was about to ask what type of training they'd be doing when he noticed that the elevator had passed all the hunter levels of the tower. "I thought we were sparring tonight. Are we going out instead?"

"I wish. I'd totally go out on a date with you."

"Sly little fucker, you know what I mean."

Hiroto winked then looked up at the camera. "Someone going to tell me what's going on?"

No answer came through.

"Wait here," Hiroto said, as if Matthew had some sort of choice in the matter.

Hiroto pulled up his hood and vanished in a white glow.

He didn't return and when the doors slid open a minute later, Matthew was relieved he was in the lobby and not down in the zoo.

Hiroto was nowhere to be seen but Prescott and Nellis were all suited up and armed.

Standing in front of them was Tarrick, who was in his uniform: tight black trousers tucked into polished boots that ended just below his knees, a white button up shirt, and a grey wool coat with silver embroidery and shiny buttons. The back had pleated seams with holes that allowed his wings to come out and the pants looked as if they could expand around the waist.

He looked so damn good in the outfit. Matthew imagined Tarrick pinning him against a wall and taking him while wearing it…or maybe tossing him to the ground and keeping him down with a shiny boot pressed on his chest.

Tarrick glanced at him; the edges of his eyes flared purple then faded back to blue. Matthew realized that he might have been throwing out some pheromones, broadcasting his longing.

Oops.

Tarrick pointed to a compression suit draped over a plush purple chair.

Before he could utter the order, Matthew was in it and gave Tarrick a bowing salute.

"We have a mission," Prescott said and tossed Matthew a comm.

Nellis paced across the marble floor and punched one big gauntlet into the other. "A lame ass mission. Why are you pulling us for this shite?" His Irish accent was thick, and he smelled like alcohol and sex.

His fun night had clearly been interrupted.

"Mac, you're not a rookie," Prescott said, his face grim. "But if you've forgotten how to speak respectfully around the Lord General, I'm happy to give you a primer."

The brute mockingly bowed to both Prescott and Tarrick. "Apologies, sirs."

Lock teleported in, his duster billowing behind him as if a wind had picked up. He was holding Matthew's chest piece.

Matthew held his arms out as the armor expanded around him. He buckled the two leather straps of his arm guard over his wide chest and found himself enjoying this ritual of readying for a battle. And he knew he looked damn impressive in the armor.

Looking up, he caught Tarrick eyeing him. He wondered just how long he had stayed in his bed last night. Did he get enough sleep? He looked better but it was impossible to tell with a creature that could influence how others saw them.

"Don't get too excited, we're not expecting trouble," Tarrick said.

"Where's Vik?" Lock asked as he pulled out one of his revolving crossbows, checking the ammo.

"She's always running late, maybe she's the one that needs a primer on protocol," Nellis said, crossing his arms over his chest.

"I'm here, sorry!" she said as she teleported in. She had no grenade launcher but her cloak was bulging out around her. When she moved, Matthew could see that her belt and the inside of the cloak was lined with dozens of small glass bottles, each with a different liquid.

Lock holstered his crossbow and tipped his hat respectfully at her. "Trying the new set-up?"

"Yep, we'll see how it goes."

"I doubt you'll get the chance to test it tonight, Vik," Prescott said. "We're escorting."

"Aw, who?"

"Me," Tarrick said. "Let's go."

There were two SUVs and a limo waiting outside. The first vehicle had half of Silva's team in it. The rest of the Wardens were going to follow by teleporting, covering the caravan from above.

Tarrick got into the limo. Silva was waiting inside for him.

To Matthew's disappointment, Prescott motioned for him to get into the back of a six passenger SUV. Lock got into the driver's seat with Prescott shotgun. Nellis and Vik got into the middle while Matthew had the back row to himself.

"You're awfully quiet tonight, vampire," Lock said as he pulled the car out.

Matthew was surprised the cowboy had noticed. "Oh, uh, no one's really addressed me."

Prescott, with his helmet sitting in his lap looked back. "You know that rule doesn't apply when we're working. What has you bothered?"

God. That list was a mile long. "I'm starting to feel the effects of being away from Samantha for such a long time," he said, picking an issue that wasn't likely to get him in any trouble.

Vik reached back and set a hand on his knee. "You know that she was sent away for her protection."

"Yeah. That's why I didn't mention it. Still miss her though."

Vik nodded and patted his leg before pulling her hand back. "Being away from children is hard but you'll see her again soon. I'm sure of it."

"You have children?"

She looked like she was maybe twenty-three or four max. And he couldn't picture her with kids.

There were several snorts and laughs.

"You all shut up. Yes. I have children. All grown now. Two incubi, four humans. Lots of grandchildren. Many of whom are hunters themselves." She smiled proudly.

Matthew's jaw hung open for a moment. "How old are you?"

There were a few more chuckles.

"Uh, because you don't look old," Matthew said when he realized just how rude he sounded.

She adjusted her cloak, the bottles clinking together as she moved. "Oooh, I stopped counting the numbers a century ago. I'm sure it's in my file."

Jeez.

Matthew wondered if he'd ever met one of her children...or killed any, but he wasn't about to ask. He sat back and rubbed his smooth face. He missed the slight scratch of his stubble. "Where's Hiroto?"

"Scouting ahead," Prescott answered. "Most missions he'll be doing that."

The caravan drove down the freeway, heading out of the city. The streetlights assaulted the car in a rhythmic pattern as they drove.

"Your daughter called me," Lock said, glancing at Matthew in his rearview mirror. He had a few lines around his brown eyes. His skin was tan and he was sporting a five o'clock shadow. The guy looked like he should be in an ad for cigarettes.

"Samantha called you? Why the hell did she do that?" He couldn't think of any reason she'd have to talk to him.

Lock shrugged. "She called me a hypocrite then hung up."

Matthew suppressed his laughter. He had no idea why Samantha would do that but he found it hilarious. His daughter was wonderfully unpredictable. "I'll ask her about it next time I talk to her."

"You ain't no hypocrite," Nellis said, coming out of his brooding a little. But he still kept his arms crossed over his chest.

Prescott raised his wrist to his mouth. "Dispatch, let Darius of House Tarrick know that Samantha has gotten a hold of another phone and please pull all the records for it."

There was an acknowledgement from dispatch and Prescott turned to face Matthew again. "She keeps doing that and she's going to get more than a time out."

"I can compel her to stop if it's that much of an issue, Imperator. But I'd rather not." Matthew really hated ordering her around. She was an adult. A young one, but an adult nonetheless.

"No need. I expect her to obey our orders, same as you. You should warn her that there will be consequences to disobeying."

"Don't I know it," Matthew muttered under his breath.

He watched the cars ahead of him and wondered why Tarrick needed an escort of two elite hunter teams in the middle of their safest city. Was it because of the demon attacks last night?

Movement out of the corner of his eye caught his attention. Hiroto was sitting beside him and Matthew had no idea how long he had been there.

He pushed his red mask down and smiled. "No creepy crawlies inside the building, boss," he said to Prescott.

The caravan took an off ramp and turned into a run-down residential area with lots of apartments and townhomes. They pulled over to the curbside. It wasn't too late, just after nine, and there were a few people out on the street, eyeing the limo and two imposing SUVs.

Matthew watched as two members of Silva's team—dressed in street clothes—dropped veils around the area. He wondered what the humans watching saw. Whatever it was, they stopped looking at the cars and went about their business.

The Argonauts exited the car. They were in front of a six-story apartment building. Trash littered the ground and there was fresh tagging on the wall.

Why the fuck were they here?

Silva held open the door to the limo and Tarrick got out. He adjusted his thick coat. A hunter teleported into the building and opened the door from the other side.

Tarrick walked upstairs, the hunters fanning out to cover the area.

"Matthew, come," Tarrick said without looking back.

Matthew obediently trailed behind, following him into a cramped elevator. Silva and Prescott joined them. No one spoke.

They went up to the third floor, exiting into a long hallway. It was dirty with age but it did look as if people attempted to keep it clean.

"Matthew only," Tarrick said. Silva and Prescott waited by the elevator.

Halfway down the hall, Tarrick knocked on a door. A moment later, it creaked open.

The human, Kyle, was standing there.

Fifty

Kyle's eyes darted between Tarrick and Matthew and his heart began to race.

"Sir?"

Tarrick smiled down at him. "Hello."

"What are you doing here? I can't go out tonight, you should have texted." He glanced at Matthew. "What is he wearing? Is that armor?"

Kyle's voice rose in panic and Matthew wondered why Tarrick wasn't wrapping a hold on the poor kid.

Tarrick pushed past Kyle and entered his home. From what Matthew could see, it was small with a living room, a tiny kitchenette, and two doors leading into what Matthew assumed was a single bedroom and bathroom. The TV was on in the living room and it looked like Kyle slept on the couch. Matthew could sense a woman in the bedroom. Asleep.

The place sort of reminded Matthew of what Samantha had lived in before he found her. Old, desperate, poor.

"Now's not a good time," Kyle said, but made no effort to stop Tarrick, who stood in the living room looking around. Matthew waited at the door.

"Invite him in," Tarrick ordered.

Kyle looked back at Matthew and laughed. "Is this some sort of scene where he pretends to be a vampire? I'm not into blood play—it's a hard limit for me."

Was that why Tarrick had Matthew in the armor tonight? Because he *looked* like a vampire in it, with pale skin against the black leather and metal.

"This isn't a scene but you are correct, he is a vampire, and he can't enter unless you invite him in," Tarrick said.

"Okay, I don't know what this is but you should—"

Tarrick didn't let the boy finish. His wings unfurled and his eyes began to glow purple.

Kyle gasped and stumbled back, slamming into the wall near the door.

God, his fear laced the air so thick Matthew could nearly taste it. His eyes zeroed into Kyle's neck and he watched his pulse move the skin. He wondered if feeding from his blood would be as amazing as feeding from his sex.

Tarrick stood waiting, his wings half-folded behind him only to avoid bumping into furniture.

"W-what are you?" Kyle finally found the courage to say.

"I'm an incubus and he's a vampire. Go ahead and show him, Matthew."

Matthew let his irises go red and he held up his hand; long claws formed from his fingertips.

"Oh my god," Kyle gasped, pressing harder into the wall as if it would protect him. "Are you here to kill me?"

"No." Tarrick stretching his wings a little. "Would you like to touch them?"

Kyle didn't move. He seemed to be stuck to the wall like it was flypaper.

Matthew laughed. "He's not going to bite. That's what I do."

Kyle glanced at Matthew and his eyes widened.

"Come here, boy," Tarrick said, his voice deep and authoritative. The order got the submissive human moving.

He pushed off the wall and with a few nervous steps, made his way to Tarrick. Once there, he reached out and touched the dark leathery wing. The first time he made contact he pulled away as if it had burned him. With a little more courage, he touched it again, running his fingers along a boney ridge.

"Wow," he gasped. Matthew knew how the human felt. He'd had the same reaction the first time he saw Tarrick's wings. Granted, he was tied up in a forest at the time with silver burning him to near death...but it had still been awe-inspiring all the same.

"W-what's an incubus?" Kyle asked.

"Invite Matthew in, and I'll tell you."

"But..." Kyle looked back at Matthew, "...he's a vampire?"

Matthew's eyes went back to silver, his claws retreating. There was no point in scaring the human more than he already was.

Tarrick rested his hand on Kyle's shoulder and squeezed. "He is.

But I promise that no harm will come to you."

Kyle seemed unsure.

Matthew shook his head. "Kid, I had my dick jammed down your throat last night. If I was going to hurt you, it would have been then."

A nervous laugh came from the human. Matthew joined him with a warm chuckle.

"Okay. You can come in."

Matthew strode inside, shutting the door behind him.

"Give him his memories back," Tarrick said, stepping away from Kyle.

Uh. Matthew knew he could take memories but he never knew he could give them back.

Tarrick sighed. "Vampires suppress memories, you aren't really erasing them. Just try."

Matthew placed his hands on Kyle's shoulders and looked into his eyes. "You remember last night as it really happened."

Kyle blinked a few times then took in a few short breaths. "I remember you punched him and his eyes turned red and yours were purple like they are now."

Tarrick nodded. "I am a creature that feeds on sex. You don't have much family, do you Kyle?"

Kyle took a step away and looked at the closed door to the bedroom. "My mom…"

"And not many friends either."

"I have friends."

Tarrick raised an eyebrow.

Kyle lowered his head. "Not many people would miss me if you're going to kill me."

"I already told you that I'm not going to kill you," Tarrick said, annoyed. "I want to offer you a job."

"A job?"

"Yes. Incubi don't always have time to go hunting for food, so we hire individuals to feed us."

Kyle swallowed hard. "Feed you?"

"Have sex with us. One of my friends is looking for a submissive and you'd be perfect for him."

"So…I'd be like a…prostitute?"

Tarrick's eyebrows furrowed. "That's a human term. We call them feeders. Even members of our own species fill the role, although humans are better suited for it. And feeders aren't viewed as some sort of common prostitute or whore." Tarrick lay his hand on the human's cheek. The human melted into him. "You crave domination and the one I'm sending you to will be able to give you what you need, and in return you'll give him what he needs. The arrangement would be mutually beneficial."

"I—" Kyle looked around his shitty apartment. "Does it pay?"

"Yes. You'll get a two hundred thousand signing bonus and a hundred thousand a year, and all medical and living expenses will be taken care of. You may also keep any gifts you are given while working."

"Two hundred thousand *dollars*? Are you kidding?"

"No," Tarrick folded his wings back into his body. "And I've been informed that your mother is nearly crippled by advanced arthritis. We have medicines that might help heal her. It's not a guarantee, but my doctors are optimistic."

Kyle was overwhelmed and it took him a moment to formulate his next question: "Why me?"

"I already told you, my friend is looking for a submissive. You have a good temperament and as far as humans go, you're handling this fairly well." He really was handling it well, all things considered. Tarrick hadn't put a hold on the human once. Tarrick smiled, wide and friendly. "And some humans taste better than others. You taste extraordinary. Are you interested?"

"This isn't a joke?"

"No, this is not a joke."

Kyle pressed his lips together then nodded. "If I say yes, am I signing my whole life over or something?"

"No, you're free to leave once the terms of your contract have been fulfilled. But you do have to agree that you won't tell people that we exist."

Matthew knew that Tarrick was glossing over the part where they would tap his phone and watch what he does to ensure he didn't try to convince humans that monsters were real, but Kyle didn't need to know that right now.

"Yes. I'm interested," Kyle said.

"I'd like you to meet Lord Holst tonight to see if you're a good match."

"Tonight?" Kyle looked back at the closed door again.

Tarrick brushed the human's hair to the side. "You'll only be gone a few hours. If you want, I can call a nurse to come stay here."

"You can do that? This late?"

"Yes. Why don't you go tell your mother you'll be back by midnight and that there will be someone here if she needs help."

Kyle nodded then disappeared into the bedroom, closing the door behind him. Matthew could hear him waking up his mother and talking softly to her.

He seemed like a good kid doing the best he could with little money and a sick mother. Matthew wondered if he enjoyed submitting because he needed to have someone take care of him for once. But maybe it was more complex than that. Whatever the reason, he was happy the kid would be in a better place with the incubi.

Tarrick used his phone to call for a nurse. It sounded as if a nurse was already waiting for the call and would be there in a few minutes.

"Commander Hiroto, please let Holst know we're on the way," Tarrick said.

Hiroto slunk out of the darkest corner of the living room. "In person?"

"Yes. Make an entrance of it."

Hiroto bowed and teleported away.

"I don't know Lord Holst," Matthew said.

"He's a friend."

Matthew waited for Tarrick to say more but he said nothing. "Is that all I'm getting? 'He's a friend'?"

Tarrick's lips twitched as if he was holding back a smile. "I just wanted you to ask."

A low growl formed deep in Matthew's chest and worked its way up his throat. Tarrick's eyes grew dark as if daring Matthew to challenge him.

Challenging Tarrick had never once ended well for Matthew...he backed down.

A pleased sound came from Tarrick.

"Holst is...different. He's wealthy—his holdings put mine to shame—but he cares little about his standing among our people. It's uncommon for a social incubus to behave that way but because he funds most of the war, kings and queens leave him alone and that's how he likes it. He's a master of his own world.

"The non-elite love him. They like that he doesn't feel the need to climb socially and he employs a great many of them or helps them when they are in need."

In other words, Holst probably wasn't strongly connected to the High King…and winning him over meant winning over the people. Matthew chewed the inside of his cheek as it occurred to him that tonight wasn't about Kyle, but rather Holst.

But why call in the Argonauts? And Matthew wasn't sure why he needed to be here for this. Not that he minded—he loved getting out of the tower.

Kyle slipped out of his mother's bedroom.

Tarrick picked up a jacket that was slung over the couch and held it out to the human. "Ready?"

Kyle nodded and put his jacket on. "Should I still call you, 'Sir'?"

Tarrick motioned for them to leave the apartment. "You may call me Tarrick for now," he said as they walked down the hallway.

Kyle noticed Prescott and Silva—both fully armored—at the end of the hall. His step faltered as he eyed Silva's weapons.

Matthew, who took up the rear, rested a hand on Kyle's shoulder. The human looked up at him. "They're Tarrick's bodyguards. They're humans. It's actually kind of neat, witches tattoo them with magic and it lets them do things like teleport around."

"Really?"

Matthew looked up at Silva, who half rolled her eyes and teleported next to them.

"Wow," Kyle breathed out.

Tarrick was waiting in the open elevator along with Prescott, but Kyle paused. No one rushed him. When he was ready, he moved into the cramped elevator. Silva stayed out this time, teleporting down to the ground floor.

"Is Holst, uh, *Lord* Holst—" Kyle corrected, unsure of what he should call him until Tarrick nodded in confirmation. "Is Lord Holst a vampire or an incubus?" Kyle asked as the elevator doors closed and began to move.

Prescott tried to hide a choking scoff that came out from under his helmet.

Kyle shifted away from him a little and into Matthew.

"Why don't you explain that one, Matthew," Tarrick said.

"Vampires and incubi are at war and have been for thousands of years. I doubt you'll ever see another vampire."

"A war?"

"Yes. But you don't need to worry about it. I don't think there's many vampires left in the states. Just stay away from the west coast."

Kyle's eyes drifted down to Matthew's shackle. "When you called him a slave, you weren't talking about some sort of kink thing, were you?" he asked Tarrick.

"No, I wasn't. He's a slave. One that fights for us."

The doors slid open, and Tarrick led them to the cars, motioning for Matthew to rejoin his team in the rear SUV. They piled in and were off, heading to the stone in New York.

"I'd still love to know why he pulled us for this routine feeder bull," Nellis said. He seemed to be in a little better mood but not by much.

"You know how the general is," Lock said from the driver's seat. "I suspect we'll find out once we get to Holst's estate."

Prescott pulled off his helmet and looked back at Matthew. "Do you know what he's up to?"

Matthew shrugged. "I never know anything, sir."

"What's he talking about right now?" Prescott asked.

"Uh."

"Not answering my question is a terrible idea."

Matthew was only hesitant because Tarrick outranked Prescott… but Prescott was his team leader and closer to the High King. The dynamic was dangerous to navigate. Matthew turned out the noise of the traffic and listened.

"Kyle just asked if he'd ever get to have sex with me and the general again. And he was told that it was unlikely to be anytime soon. Now the human's asking how come the world doesn't know that vampires and incubi exist—"

"Predictable shit they always ask," Nellis said.

Prescott turned back in his seat and tapped his fingers on his helmet. Matthew went back to his eavesdropping. He was enjoying Kyle's innocent questions and Tarrick's kind answers.

"Matthew, ask Nellis about the arena," Tarrick whispered in the other car.

What the hell was Tarrick playing at?

"Silva tells me you've fought in the arena, Nellis."

Nellis puffed his chest out a bit. "Yeah? She tell you I have the highest win ratio of anyone that's stepped into the ring."

"Seriously?"

"Wouldn't want to embarrass my team by doing bad, would I?"

"No, I guess not. What about you guys? Have you fought?" Matthew asked.

Prescott scoffed as if it was beneath him.

Nellis shook his head. "You act all high and mighty, boss, but I know for a fact you fought in the gladiatorial rings ages ago."

"Sure. Back when a fight was worth it. None of this caged matched, knock-each-other-out bull."

"*Bull?*" Nellis' eyebrows knitted with anger. "What'd you say you and me go at it next time? No armor, fists only. When you're missing a few teeth, you won't call it bull."

Lock shook his head as he changed lanes. "Careful what ya ask for, Nellis. I don't think it's the Imperator that'll end up with the missing teeth and ya know it."

"How about you, Vik?" Matthew asked before Nellis could respond.

"Nah, they won't let me bring explosives in. 'Too dangerous'."

God, she really was a nutter.

Lock glanced into the rearview mirror and noticed Matthew was looking at him. "I don't need to fight in front of an audience to prove myself. I know how good I am," the cowboy said.

Matthew leaned into his seat and rested an arm along the back.

"You want to fight in the arena," Prescott said. It wasn't a question, but Matthew answered him anyway.

"I always want to fight, Imperator."

Prescott tapped the top of his helmet again, sat silent for a moment, and then said, "It's up to the High King. I wouldn't hold your breath."

Damn.

Nellis spent the rest of the drive recounting his many fights with Matthew only half aware of him; the conversation in the limo took most of his attention. Kyle was asking questions about what life would be like for him, and Tarrick, with expert skill, answered everything in a way that wouldn't scare the human.

Like Nellis had said, the questions were predictable, but it didn't matter to Matthew, he just wanted to hear Tarrick's voice.

Fuck.

He had it bad.

This was bad.

A distraction.

He tried to focus on Nellis but he kept drifting back to Tarrick. His deep, seductive voice resonated through the limo.

Only when they were pulling over, outside of the building that housed the New York City leystone, did Matthew give his full attention back to the big Irishman. He was talking about a match where he fought a tiger shifter.

Matthew sat forward and pretended to hang on his every word. No one seemed to notice he was feigning interest.

When they piled out of the car, Matthew followed behind Tarrick and Kyle since he didn't know the protocols for securing an area. Still, he stayed vigilant even if he didn't sense anything dangerous nearby.

Kyle eyed the run-down building. "What are we doing here?"

"We're going to teleport to Kentucky," Tarrick said, placing his hand on Kyle's neck and leading him into the building.

Inside the barren building, Kyle's mouth fell open as he watched the stone's engraved runes light up with a faint green glow.

Silva opened a white vomit bag and handed it to Kyle. "Everyone loses dinner the first time they teleport. It's normal, and there's no need to be embarrassed about it."

Kyle took the bag from her and held it tight to his chest.

The two teams of hunters (minus Hiroto), the incubus general, and the human all stood close to the stone. Silva touched it and with a green flash they teleported away from New York.

Fifty-One

Kentucky. Well...a concrete room in Kentucky anyways.

The room had a vamp trap around the stone and the single, reinforced door had anti-vampire runes. The leystone on this end looked new—all the runes seemed freshly carved and the stone was polished. Matthew touched it.

The magic made his skin crawl as if it was trying to repel him.

He hated magic. Or was it that magic hated vampires? He wasn't sure.

"Do you like my new setup for the leystone, Matthew?" Tarrick asked, stroking Kyle's hair, who was on his knees heaving into the bag. It surprised Matthew how tender Tarrick was towards the human, treating him as if he was precious.

Matthew yanked his hand off the stone. "Very vampire proof, Lord General."

"A necessity, thanks to you."

Matthew couldn't help but smile. His plan to destroy many of the leystones had been a major blow to the incubi. Although it looked like replacements were finally going up.

Kyle wiped his mouth with the back of his hand as Silva handed him a bottle of water.

Lock had already disabled the vamp trap and deactivated the rune so that Matthew could pass.

"Ready?" Tarrick asked Kyle.

Kyle took a deep breath and nodded.

Tarrick led the way through a second concrete room with the same anti-vampire set up, and finally outside.

Acres of land sprawled before them, covered with a light dusting of snow. On the far side of the expansive lawn sat a two-story white, plantation-style mansion that had warm lights streaming from nearly every window.

Matthew could sense it was full of incubi and humans.

Waiting outside of the bunker that housed the stone, or perhaps guarded it, stood a team of mean-looking hunters. All of them dark skinned, bearing many battle scars. They gave off an aura of don't-fuck-with-us.

"Lord General. Imperator," the team leader said with a salute. He was obviously a veteran hunter, not faltering or letting his eyes linger on Matthew as most did when they saw him.

"Commander Baine," Tarrick said with a nod.

"Lord Holst wanted me to tell you that he'll be a few minutes. He has a…business meeting he's finishing up." A car pulled up for them. Baine held the door open for Kyle and Tarrick. "And personally, I'd consider it a courtesy if you used a phone instead of an assassin fox to announce your arrival."

"Would you now?" Tarrick asked as he sat down in the car and pulled the door shut before the commander could respond.

Baine shook his head as the car pulled away. He turned and looked at Matthew. "The vamp coming inside?"

"Yep," Prescott answered. "Get the wards down."

Baine gave a signal to his team. They teleported away to disable the vampire wards; Baine stayed behind. "I'll have to get the monarch. I doubt she'll enjoy having a vamp in her house. You always have to make my life so damn difficult, Jason."

Prescott chuckled. "This one's on the general. I'm just along for the ride tonight."

"What the hell is he up to?"

"That human with him is a feeder. A gift."

"That scrawny thing? Holst will tear him apart."

Matthew didn't like the sound of that.

A voice came over the comm, reporting that the wards were disabled.

"Go to the front door, Matthew," Prescott ordered, and the teams teleported away.

Matthew ran across the acreage and arrived at the door in a few seconds. Tarrick and Kyle were getting out of the car. Kyle looked at the house wide-eyed. He kept close to Tarrick, nearly bumping into him. Tarrick grabbed his neck again, and the act bolstered the human's resolve, giving him courage like the bravery of a child when a parent was nearby.

Prescott, Kyle, Tarrick, and Matthew waited. The rest of the hunters had fanned along the perimeter of the estate. Prescott removed his helmet and tucked it under his arm, then ran his hands through his dark hair to straighten it. He always looked young to Matthew, but the act made him seem younger.

"This home is owned by a human?" Matthew asked no one in particular. He could feel the boundaries at the threshold that prevented him from entering.

"Yes. Lord Holst's mother," Tarrick answered. "It's kept that way as an extra layer of protection against vampires."

"That's smart," Matthew said. "I'm surprised more incubi don't do that."

"It only works if the human owns the house—we can't just put it in their name on the deed and pretend they own it. It has to truly be theirs, and incubi want to own our own wealth because it ups our social standing. It's rare we trust a human enough to let them have our home. But like I said, Holst is different."

The door opened, and standing there was a human that Matthew had no doubt in his mind was the 'monarch', as the hunter had called her. She looked of Italian descent and somewhere in her late-thirties. Tall with long silky, dark brown hair she had curled at the end. She wore black heels, leather pants, and a corset that made her small boobs look far bigger than they were.

She studied Matthew for a moment. There was a lot behind her dark brown eyes, as if she had lived a hard life and seen everything. If Matthew had to guess, she was far older than she looked; her life extended by an incubus—her son most likely.

"What trouble are you going to get my son into tonight?" she asked. Her entire attitude screamed 'I don't want to deal with your bullshit right now'.

Tarrick bowed—*actually fucking bowed*—to the human. "Lady Carlotta—"

"Don't 'Lady' me. Answer my question."

"This is Kyle," Tarrick said, motioning to the human. "He's a new feeder I think Holst would enjoy. That's all. No trouble, Lottie. I swear."

Kyle squirmed under Carlotta's judgmental eyes. "He looks too fragile for my son. What's the real reason you're here?"

Tarrick shook his head. "He's stronger than he looks. He'll be a good fit. I have no other reason."

"Really? That's why the Argonauts are following you around? Why you sent your assassin to scare my household half to death? And," she pointed to Matthew, "don't get me started on him. I've never once put up with your games. I'm not going to start tonight."

She slammed the door shut, leaving them all outside.

Matthew began to laugh. Other than the High King, he'd never seen anyone put Tarrick in his place, let alone a human.

"You find that funny?" Tarrick asked, stern and humorless.

"I like her."

"Shut up, vampire," he snapped. Holy shit, he was pissed. Matthew took a step away, out of his line of fire.

Tarrick took a moment to let his anger subside then knocked softly on the door.

Carlotta opened the door again and raised an eyebrow.

"Ilertha sings to him."

She looked to Matthew. "Does she really?"

"She used to," Matthew answered, "but not for a long time now. I never found out why she sang...or why it stopped. I must apologize, I'm not sure how I should address you."

Matthew glanced at Tarrick and Prescott for some help, but they offered none.

"I'm addressed as 'High Priestess'."

"High Priestess of Ilertha?"

"Does that bother you, sired son of Lysandros?"

"Not at all, High Priestess. I have no love for my sire. And I was born an incubus." Matthew bowed.

"At least you're charming. And respectful. I like that." She looked to Prescott. "Is he on a tight leash?"

"*Asonda*," Prescott said.

Pain swelled through Matthew, dropping him to his knees and causing his vampire side to come out. He began to claw at his collar while screaming. Prescott said something else, releasing him from the pain.

Matthew stayed on his knees, trying to pull himself together when every part of him wanted to rip Prescott's throat out.

He forced his claws away, but his eyes stayed red. He was too angry right now to turn them back.

"That leash tight enough, High Priestess?" Prescott asked.

"It'll do, Imperator," Carlotta said. "Matthew, sired son of the Blood God, you may enter my home."

Matthew pushed himself to his feet and, in an effort not to glare at Prescott, he checked on Kyle. The human looked drugged out, rubbing himself along Tarrick's side—the effects of a minor hold Tarrick had placed him under to keep him calm.

Carlotta took a step back to allow the group entry. The foyer was beautiful with old wood and cream walls. An impressive set of stairs swept to the second floor. Baine stood on the upper landing, keeping an eye on Carlotta.

A human butler took Tarrick's and Kyle's coats and disappeared with them.

Bang. Bang.

The sound of two gunshots drew everyone's attention.

"Stay put, Matthew," Tarrick ordered before he had a chance to go dashing after the sound.

The scent of blood filled his nostrils and his metal teeth itched. No one else seemed concerned.

A moment later, heavy footsteps approached. An incubus wearing an expensive suit appeared on the landing above—Holst. He had the same dark hair and eyes as his mother, contrasting with his light skin. His face was masculine, cut sharp with a dark five o'clock shadow. When he adjusted his suit jacket, Matthew could smell gunpowder on him.

He looked like a freakin' mob boss.

That is, if mob bosses were hot, young, and sexy.

"Go get that mess cleaned up," he said to Baine, who nodded and teleported away. Then Holst turned his attention to his guests. He smiled as he descended the stairs. "Brother," he said to Tarrick. The two of them grabbed the backs of each other's necks and pushed their foreheads together.

From what Rosaline had told Matthew, Tarrick's blood-related siblings were dead. Matthew got the sense that these two were childhood friends. Perhaps even raised together. Many of their mannerisms were the same: they had the same confident stride, the same seductive smile, and even their bodies were around the same size and build.

Matthew had a hard time believing that Holst was only a social incubus. He looked as if he could fight with the best of them if he had to…and he'd already proven he wasn't shy about killing. Whoever he had shot was dead now.

The two incubi pulled apart. Holst nodded to Prescott, but didn't bow as others did. Prescott, for his part, nodded back and took an unassuming spot in the corner.

"Is there a reason you're supervising, Mother?" Holst asked.

"With him here?" She motioned to Tarrick. "Yes."

"Lottie, I am the High Lord General. Leader of—"

Carlotta cut him off. "Give the speech to someone who didn't change your diapers. I'll give you two your privacy. Just try to keep out of trouble, and send me the vampire when you're done."

As she walked out of the foyer, Matthew couldn't help but lock his eyes on her hips and their slight sway. He wondered what duties a High Priestess for the Goddess of Sex performed.

"He's a hungry one," Holst said. Matthew tore his eyes away from Carlotta only to find himself under Holst's scrutiny. His dominating gaze felt so much like Tarrick's that Matthew couldn't help but get even more turned on. He was thankful his armor did a good job of hiding his growing erection.

"Give him a break," Tarrick said, dropping his hand to Kyle who was half-hiding behind the general. "Matthew only had his transformation a few years ago. You were worse at that age."

Damn it. He'd been throwing pheromones again. Why the hell was he so fucking horny tonight? Actually, he knew the answer. He was still high from the date and wanted a repeat performance. If he couldn't have Tarrick, his incubus side would settle for pretty much anything right now. His incubus was a slut.

Matthew bowed. "My apologies, Lord Holst."

Holst laughed. "You sure like them young. And dangerous. He submits to you?"

"He submits to everyone the High King wants him to," Tarrick said, not really answering the question but not denying anything either.

Holst gave his friend a knowing glance.

Tarrick smirked and squeezed Kyle's shoulder.

For the first time since Holst showed up, he looked at Kyle. "Don't tell me you've brought him here as a feeder."

"Yes."

"He's not my type."

"He is."

Kyle, no longer under a hold, stepped closer to Tarrick.

Holst reached out and grabbed his neck, yanking the human away from the general and holding him at arm's length.

Kyle shuddered and gasped, "Sir."

"You haven't earned the right to call me 'Sir' yet. Undress."

Kyle looked around the brightly lit area. "Here?"

Holst's shoulders squared like a man who wasn't used to having his orders questioned. "Was I unclear?"

"No." Kyle's heart began to race as he removed his clothes. When he got to his underwear, he paused and looked up at Holst, who indicated that, yes, he meant everything.

Naked, Kyle's flaccid cock hung between his legs, and he seemed to be resisting the urge to cover it. To his credit, he kept his hands planted at his side.

Holst reached out and pinched Kyle's nipple. Kyle tried to squirm away, but Holst grabbed his shoulder and kept him in place. He then ran his hands down the human's belly before finally cupping his balls and squeezing.

"I like them bigger," Holst finally said when he was done with his inspection, releasing Kyle. Matthew wasn't sure if he was talking about Kyle's dick or body. Maybe both.

"No you don't."

Holst grumbled. "Fine. I like them to have more fight."

"No you don't," Tarrick repeated.

Holst clenched his teeth. "I do."

"Sure, until you break them. Then you grow bored. This kid isn't that, you'll like him."

"I don't think so. I'm sure you'll find a place for him."

Kyle dropped his head, looking at the ground, and his hands went to cover his crotch. Matthew understood that defeat.

Tarrick didn't seem too disappointed. Maybe Holst rejecting feeders was common. "Suit yourself. Matthew, you can have him."

Have him? "What?"

"You need a feeder. You like Kyle. Seems like a good way to keep you fed. And it'll keep him in New York. It's an ideal situation for everyone."

Matthew glanced over to Prescott, who gave him a 'sure why not?' shrug. "I'll run the idea past the King, but I'm sure he'll approve. He wants to keep you in peak fighting condition…this month anyway."

Matthew went to Kyle and grabbed his upper arm. "Would you like that, Kyle?"

Kyle looked up into Matthew's still red eyes. He trembled. "I thought you were a submissive. A slave."

"A slave to the incubi, yes. A submissive to him." Matthew motioned to Tarrick. "But with others it depends. I've never done the whole dom thing, but I'm sure I can figure it out if that's what you need."

Holst growled. "You'll hurt him if you don't know what you're doing."

"What do you care, my lord? You don't want him."

Holst growled again, this time at Matthew's disrespect. Matthew was relieved when no one made a move to punish him for it.

Matthew grabbed Kyle's arm, forcing the boy to turn as he pulled him into his chest. The human leaned in and smelled the leather.

"Do you like my armor?" Matthew asked, keeping Kyle locked tight in his arms.

"Yes," he said between deep breaths.

Matthew released him. "On your knees. Hands behind your back."

Kyle went to his knees. His cock hardening.

Matthew lifted his boot and pressed it against the human's small package. Kyle moaned, and then whimpered when Matthew pulled away from him. "My boot is dirty. Clean it."

Kyle reached over to grab his shirt.

"With your tongue," Matthew ordered before Kyle made it to his clothes. Matthew had never degraded a person in bed—or anywhere actually—but he was finding Kyle's needy response to be such a wonderful turn on.

The human leaned over, his firm ass in the air, presenting itself; his tight pink hole on display for everyone to see.

Matthew looked up to see Tarrick's eyes turn light purple as he watched, but more importantly, Holst's dark brown eyes shifted to a plum color. It made the two incubi seem even more alike. If Tarrick had dark hair instead of dusty blond it'd be hard to convince Matthew that they weren't blood-related, even if their features differed slightly.

"Fine, I'll try him," Holst said, his voice strained with desire and eyes locked on Kyle.

Tarrick, who was standing behind Holst, grinned. "Are you certain? I don't want to have to find him a new placement a week from now."

"I'll take him," Holst said. "What's your cost?"

Tarrick's grin got wider, showing off his pearly white teeth. "I want to hold an exhibition with Matthew. A fight, but I don't think the High King will approve unless there's enough chatter about it."

"Done."

"Wait one minute," Prescott said. Everyone except Kyle turned to face the Imperator; the human seemed a little out of it, still licking Matthew's boots. "What are you playing at, General?"

"I'm not playing. I just enjoy watching Matthew fight." Tarrick's eyes flared bright purple.

"Then fire up one of the recordings or watch him in the next battle he's in. You're up to something, and I tire of trying to guess what it is. Start talking."

A sound of disapproval came from Tarrick's throat. "You're overstepping, Imperator."

"No, I'm not. He's my team member, and I don't approve of you trying to manipulate the King. I want to know what you're up to—the real fucking reason. Otherwise, I'll do my damnedest to prevent it, and of the two of us, I'm the one the King calls friend."

"I don't think he calls anyone 'friend'."

"General," Prescott said, angry. "I should be on a date right now and instead I'm watching this little twink lick Matthew's boots. You've run into the end of my patience."

"Alright. Fine. The people don't believe that we have enough dominion over Matthew. Hunters don't want to fight with him, and incubi fear that he's going to lose control. Look at what you had to do tonight just to get him in the door. Lottie should not have needed that level of convincing."

Oh right. When Prescott had turned on the collar. Matthew was so wrapped up with Kyle, he had forgotten that he was still pissed about that.

"If they watch Matthew fight for the glory of the High King—see him bending his knee to him—it'll help convince the people that we have control over him. It displeases me to have an army that second guesses my orders. I could do this via parties or have him fuck his way through the court until they feel safe but it'll take too long. This is the fastest way and it doesn't go against the High King's desires."

The truth was that both of them needed the arena match as a first step to win over the incubi, but Tarrick's lie sounded believable. Then again, everything he said sounded believable.

"Then just ask the King for the match."

Tarrick shook his head. "You know how he is with his pets. We need the people to want this first before I ask."

Prescott didn't seem convinced.

"How much time and energy are you willing to put in to make it so that people trust your teammate? Because as it stands, it'll take years. My way will be weeks."

Prescott let his chest fill under his armor as he took in a deep breath. "Alright." He pointed to Matthew. "You better win."

"I hope he does—I want it to be a death match."

"Gods. Fine. I'll start training him for whatever the King wants him to fight."

A moan at Matthew's feet drew his attention. Kyle was still working away at his boot—he'd almost made it to the top of one. Matthew reached down and touched Kyle's head. The human looked up, his lips were puffy and slicked with saliva, and his eyes looked distant as if he was zoning out.

Matthew was a little disappointed that he wasn't going to be getting a feeder for himself, but he didn't expect to be walking away with Kyle tonight. He only made the human lick his boots because he had seen in it a porn once and had a feeling it would get Holst interested.

"You'll get your fight," Holst said. "Just give me a few weeks, and it'll be the topic everywhere."

Tarrick motioned his hand to Kyle, offering him.

Holst swooped down and grabbed Kyle, pulling him into his body. "You're mine now. Do you understand?"

Kyle responded by pressing his body into the incubus. Holst kept an arm wrapped around him.

Tarrick chuckled at his friend. "He's only yours if he signs the contract, and he needs to be back in New York by midnight."

Holst didn't seem concerned. "I'll take care of it. Are you staying? Bourbon?" Holst asked Tarrick.

"Just one. I can't stay long. There were some attacks earlier and I'm needed."

"I miss the days when you weren't a High Lord."

Tarrick laughed. "I don't. Matthew, go find out what Lottie wants with you."

Prescott snorted. "Two guesses."

"Matthew, you have permission to come with her," Tarrick added.

Holst looked back and forth between Matthew and Tarrick, then smiled wide, Kyle still tucked away naked under his arm.

"That's the High King's rule, not mine. Although, it's one I enjoy watching him struggle with," Tarrick said, his eyes holding a sadistic glint.

Matthew frowned. Being told when he could and couldn't have an orgasm wasn't fun. If he had been allowed to masturbate then maybe he wouldn't have a raging erection under his armor right now.

Prescott began walking down a hall. "Come on, Matthew, let's go see what the High Priestess wants with you."

M atthew followed Prescott to the back of the house. Behind him
he could hear the two incubi and Kyle retiring to another room.

Prescott stopped in front of wooden double doors and knocked.

"Come," Carlotta said from the other side.

He pushed both doors open. Inside was a temple to Ilertha: there
was a statue of the goddess in the center, and surrounding it were pillows and lounge chairs. Burning incense and candles lined the walls.
Offerings of gold and jewelry collected at the statue's feet.

The room smelled like spice and sex. Or maybe that was Carlotta,
who was standing with her hands clasped in front of her.

Prescott entered and nodded respectfully at the statue (not something Matthew had expected) then stood out of the way. Matthew
hoped that, if he did end up having sex with Carlotta, the Imperator would at least turn invisible so he could pretend he wasn't being
watched.

Matthew took a step forward and stopped just short of entering
the temple room.

"Ilertha won't smite you if you enter," Carlotta said, amused.

"I know, it's just…" Matthew wasn't really sure what it was. He
hated his mother? The only thing he knew about her was that she gave
him up and sent Devak to protect him. He loved Devak, but he could
have used a mom growing up.

Carlotta motioned for him to close the doors and join her. He did
so. "Would it be too out of place for me to ask why a human is a High
Priestess to the incubus goddess?"

She went to a table and lit a candle that had gone out. "Ilertha
holds many domains. She is goddess of sex, lovers, beauty, pain and
pleasure, guile, fertility, and more. Incubi are her blessed people—a
personification of what she is—but she accepts any who follow her
tenets. Do you worship anyone?"

"No, High Priestess."

"Why not?"

"Uh, well, I went to church a few times, but I was never really sure God existed. And then when I met a god, it wasn't quite the religious awakening I was hoping for."

She considered Matthew for a moment. "When did the singing stop for you?"

"Shortly after my escape. I heard it every now and then but it eventually stopped entirely."

"Do you think it stopped, or do you think you stopped listening?"

"I...don't know."

"Come sit." She motioned to a red, plush ottoman. He did as she commanded. "You're an honest creature, aren't you? Deception doesn't come as naturally to you as it does other incubi, does it?

Matthew glanced back at Prescott. "Bad things happen to me when I lie."

Prescott raised an eyebrow but said nothing.

Carlotta placed her hand on Matthew's cheek and turned his focus back to her. Behind her was the marble statue of Ilertha, beautiful and looking down upon them with a peaceful face.

"Would you like to hear the singing again?" she asked.

"Yes," he whispered.

Carlotta, with her hand still on his cheek, leaned down and kissed Matthew. She was much softer than he expected. He thought she'd be as hard and tough as her attitude. There was a hint of that, but there was something else too: understanding. It was as if she knew what he needed and was offering it to him.

The kiss deepened, and she crawled onto his lap, placing her knees on each side of his thighs.

His hands began to wander, exploring the tops of her legs, then her hips, and finally cupping her ass. He squeezed her wonderful portions, pulling her into him.

She pulled away and touched his armor, running her fingers along the sharp edges. Hushed words fell from her lips and the armor began to fold away into just the chest piece.

"I thought only hunters with runes could do that," Matthew said.

She smiled but didn't explain as she stood and pried the chest piece from his body, setting it on the floor beside them. She knocked Matthew's knees apart with her legs, then scooped her hair into her hand

and turned, exposing the laces of her corset.

Matthew's first thought was to rip her clothes off her, but he didn't want to seem too eager. He also vetoed his body's impatient desire and, instead, forced himself to go slow and sensual, kissing along her spine as he worked her corset off.

A pleased sound of encouragement escaped her mouth and she tilted her head to the side.

The corset peeled away and dropped to the ground. Matthew—growing impossibly hard in his compression suit—looked up at her as she turned. The buds on her dark pink nipples swelled, and he found himself standing and placing his mouth around one. He swirled his tongue around the tips, then sucked in, pinching the skin between his teeth. She gasped at the sensation.

He slid his hands up her body and back down, snaking his way to the front of her pants and unbuttoning them. He hooked his thumbs into the waist and slid them off her hips.

She helped with the last part, taking her pumps off and peeling the pants away. Matthew unzipped the side of his compression suit. Before he could slip it off, she traced the outline of his cock with her hand.

He grunted.

After a few moments of her pawing at his shaft, he rolled his head back to study her. Naked, she was a creature of strange beauty. She wasn't flawless like a succubus: she had the beginnings of wrinkles at the corners of her eyes, she had a few stretch marks around the bottom of her belly right above her dark strip of hair, and her shape wasn't the perfect hourglass ratio that most succubi had.

But Matthew found every flaw interesting. Real.

He could see why incubi liked her. Her confident sexuality was undeniably appealing, and he could hardly keep his hands off her.

"Remove this," she commanded as she tugged at his clothes. This time, he used his speed and was out of the suit and naked before she had a chance to finish a breath. Her smile widened as she drank in his body. His muscles were tight under his smooth pale skin. The only blemishes he had were the High King's brand and the tattoos that snaked their way up his right arm.

His brain picked a hell of a moment to remember that Prescott was standing in the room, but he pushed the thought from his head. It wasn't like the guy hadn't seen him naked—a lot—and chances were if he wasn't here, then the sex wouldn't happen. Matthew wanted the sex to happen. His thick cock raised in attention to prove it.

He hoped the Imperator enjoyed the show.

Carlotta pushed Matthew down to the ottoman and gracefully straddled his legs, her knees wrapped against Matthew's thighs once more. His length pressed against the outside of her heat, twitching with anticipation.

He ran his hands up her back and pulled her into a kiss.

She reached her hand down and stroked his granite-hard rod. Matthew hissed against her, his ass clenched, and his hips pushed forward into the touch.

She lined his sex with hers and lowered herself. Matthew shuddered as her warmth wrapped around him.

He leaned into her neck and began to lick it, the blood under her skin enticing—not that he could get at it without severely hurting her, or being punished.

The priestess began to move, pleasing herself on his body.

"Listen," she whispered in his ear, her breath clinging to his skin.

Matthew tried. He could hear the sounds of the household—servants cleaning, hunters giving routine updates on their positions, another couple having sex in one of the far wings of the house, someone eating something crunchy. He heard her breath shorten each time she fully seated him into her, but there was no singing.

She draped her arm around his neck and pulled him in so that he was looking over her at the statue of his mother. Which might have killed his erection if Carlotta didn't feel so damn good riding him.

"Feed," she said between moans.

Matthew inhaled the golden strands of sexual energy as she rode him, bringing them both close to orgasm.

Then he heard it.

Ilertha's song.

It was so quiet at first, he thought he might be imagining it, but as they fucked, the song grew louder. Sung in the ancient incubi language, it was beautiful and divine. The melody had an otherworldly quality.

Without any permission from him, his eyes stung.

Carlotta continued moving in his lap, her heart rate rapid and her skin heated against him.

She cried out as she reached her climax, and Matthew joined her. His orgasm started slow, the first wave rolling through him like a low boil. The next wave was harder, fervent, shaking both their bodies as his muscles tensed, and he clamped his arms around her.

On the third wave, nausea hit him. His head spun and the world around him turned.

He never made it to a fourth wave. Instead, his body fell back. Carlotta still in his arms, he hit the ottoman and kept going—falling through the material and into the ground itself. Down and down he went. Colors blurred around him, and his stomach leaped into his throat.

When he landed, they were no longer in Kentucky.

Carlotta was in his arms, both of them naked. He sat her down on worked stone beneath their feet and looked around.

They were standing in a crumbling building. There wasn't much of it left, just a few pillars and half walls…and beyond that was fog…and beyond the fog was darkness. Nothing.

"What is this? A mind breech?" he asked Carlotta who was trembling from the cold. He wished he had warmth or clothes to offer her.

"No, this is different."

"Save me," a voice whispered, carried on the wind. Ilertha's voice.

Carlotta went to her knees. "My goddess," she said under her breath as if she couldn't believe it.

"Save me, my son," Ilertha's voice said again.

Carlotta's head snapped up to Matthew. "Her son," she said. It wasn't a question. She was old enough and smart enough to figure it out.

"Please," Matthew said, "Malarath can't know. If he finds out—"

Intense pain tore through Matthew's jaw as the bones there broke and he lost teeth. He closed his eyes and focused on healing.

"Matthew, release her," Prescott ordered.

Matthew opened his eyes. He was back in the temple, his body draped over the ottoman. The Argonauts looked down at him. Hiroto placed his hand on Matthew's forehead.

Matthew tried to ask what was going on, but his jaw was shattered. Nellis had blood on his gauntlet—the fucker had punched him in the face. Why?

"Release her—*now*," Prescott said.

Matthew looked up to see Carlotta still in his arms…he was crushing her, his claws digging into her back. She gasped for air.

He let her go the moment he realized what he was doing.

She took in a sharp breath. Matthew tried to apologize but the words came out jumbled. He pushed his healing, forcing his body to recover as fast as it could.

Meanwhile, Vik handed Carlotta a vial of vampire blood to heal her wounds.

"What happened?" Prescott asked.

Matthew looked at Carlotta with a silent plea: Please. Please, do not tell them who I am.

Carlotta sat up and moved her hips just enough that his softening cock was no longer inside her. She stayed straddling him while her wounds healed. Her eyes were wide as she looked down at him, studying his face like he was the world's biggest diamond on display at a museum.

Vik held out a robe, which she ignored.

"High Priestess," Prescott said, breaking her from her thoughts.

She took a deep breath. "It seems Lysandros doesn't want me anywhere near his son, thinks I might sway him. He sent me a warning. It wasn't Matthew's fault."

"Can gods do that?" Prescott asked Hiroto.

"You doubt my word, Imperator?" Carlotta asked as she moved off Matthew and grabbed the robe from Vik, slipping it over her shoulders.

"No. But I need to know how exactly his sire can influence him."

Hiroto patted Matthew's head. "I don't know all of the Blood God's powers, but he can't compel Matthew unless he comes to this realm personally. But gods can send visions and messages. He can learn to resist them."

"We done here or are we going to stare at his cock all night?" Nellis asked.

Hiroto sighed softly to himself. "It's magnificent, isn't it?"

Matthew rubbed his incredibly sore jaw and sat up. He spat out two teeth that Nellis had knocked out—new molars were already emerging from his gums—then covered his dick with his hand. Magnificent or not, he wasn't thrilled that his entire team was taking a gander at it.

"Get dressed," Prescott ordered.

"Yes, sir." Matthew did as commanded.

Lock pushed himself off the wall he was leaning on and helped Matthew back into his armor.

"Commander Hiroto," Carlotta said, "next time you need to announce that Tarrick is on his way, please use the doorbell."

Hiroto's eyes squished, as if he was smiling under his mask. "Okay. Doorbell."

"I want to see him again," Carlotta said as the team moved to leave.

Prescott turned back. "You'll need approval from the High King."

She frowned. "Nights like this I wish my son was more like his father." Holst's peculiar social behavior must not earn him any favors with the King.

"Yeah," Prescott agreed, "your mate was a good one."

As they left, Matthew could hear Holst and Tarrick laughing about something. He paused.

"Come on," Prescott said, "we've played our part. The general can make it back to New York on his own."

The return trip surprised Matthew. They didn't make him sprint distances, nor did they teleport ahead. Instead, the team walked across the field.

Prescott led the march with Vik right behind him. She was fiddling with her bottles, complaining that she wished they had seen some action tonight. Nellis had scooped Hiroto up and placed him on his shoulders. The fox seemed happy to sit there.

Matthew followed after, listening to their banter, with Lock trailing behind him in silence—perhaps to keep an eye on him.

Hiroto turned around on Nellis' shoulder, facing Matthew. "You upset he broke your jaw?"

Matthew hadn't even thought about it. "No. I'm glad I was stopped before I could hurt Carlotta. But why not just knock me out with the collar?"

The team hesitated.

"You tried and it didn't work?" Matthew asked.

Prescott slowed. "I'm not sure."

"But a fist to the face worked just fine," Nellis said with a smile.

Prescott resumed his pace to the concrete structure. Holst's hunter commander, Baine, and his team were back standing guard.

"Whatcha thinking about?" Hiroto asked Matthew.

"I'm thinking about how much I hate you right now."

Hiroto frowned and the team paused again, eyeing Matthew.

"It's just...how *does* my cock fill with blood if I don't have a pulse?"

Hiroto nearly fell off Nellis laughing. The Irishman had to reach up and steady the fox, holding his waist with his gauntlet. The others joined their laughter.

"I'm serious. I need to know."

Prescott nodded to Baine as the team entered the structure that housed the stone.

"No one's going to tell me, are they?" Matthew asked at the stone. The team laughed again and they teleported out.

Fifty-Three

Training kept Matthew busy.

Two nights after they brought Kyle to Holst, he was sparring with Prescott when he heard a dispatcher over the comm reporting that High Lord General Tarrick would be moving back to Ashwood estate.

Matthew's heart sank. He was expecting it since his wound had healed, but he had hoped it wouldn't happen right away. That maybe the High King would want to keep him close for some other reason.

Prescott used the distraction to cut off three of Matthew's fingers with an axe he was using.

Matthew howled at the pain, dropped his weapon, and backed off.

"You think you're the only one with people they love?" Prescott asked.

Matthew cradled his hand against his chest. "I—"

"What happens in a battle if Tarrick goes down? You going to mourn his loss right then and there? Leave your team vulnerable?"

Matthew had never really given it much thought. In the past, he just raged.

"What you're going to do is file the pain away and focus on your job. Realize that there's time to mourn after, when it doesn't risk the lives of those around you."

Matthew nodded. "I'll work on it, sir."

"Good."

"Was that just a test or is he actually leaving, sir?"

"Both." Prescott offered nothing else as he came in for another attack.

****

A week after that Matthew woke to full lips working themselves across his neck. He let out a pleased sigh and wrapped his arms around the woman kissing him, tangling his fingers through curly hair.

He inhaled rain and apple blossoms.

"Rosaline," he breathed out as she nipped at his neck. He fully woke and released her. "You're back?"

Dumb fucking question. Of course she was back. But Matthew's reasoning skills were currently tied up in his cock.

She sat up and straightened her tight green dress. "It's been a while."

Matthew sat up as well, resting his back against the headboard. "Too long. Has Samantha returned as well?"

"Not yet. We're keeping her away as long as we can. I don't think Didi has realized she's gone. I'm not sure he even realized I was gone."

Was that why Matthew hadn't seen the High King in a while? Was he zoning out or whatever the fuck it was he did?

"Why are you back?"

Rosaline ran her hands across Matthew's chest then rubbed his abs a few times. He reached out and put his hand on her thigh, feeling the silky smoothness of her long legs.

"I wanted to return. And Tarrick asked if I would take you to the feeders. We're still working out the permission-to-come rule. Until we do, you'll need Prescott or I to give you approval each time. Tarrick thought you'd rather it be me than him."

"The general's right, I'd rather it be with you. Don't tell the Imperator this—" Matthew started. Rosaline flicked her eyes to the camera in worry. "—but you are way sexier than him."

Rosaline seemed relieved and flattered, her red lips pulling into a smile. "I think your daughter might argue that point."

Matthew picked up a pillow and tossed it playfully at her. "God, I don't want to hear that."

Rosaline tossed the pillow aside and fussed with her hair. Her eyes dropped to Matthew's hips and she ran her finger along the healed skin. "Sam told me you'd be okay, that you wouldn't turn into a ghoul, but I feel better now that I've seen it for myself."

Matthew grabbed her hand and brought it to his lips, kissing her palm.

"I'm sorry for what happened…with Didi. When I heard…" She bit the bottom of her lip.

Matthew pressed a hand to her cheek. "Shh. Not your fault."

"But—" She fell silent for a moment, fighting some internal battle. Finally, she swallowed hard and spoke again. "It doesn't change how I feel about him. It should, but it doesn't. Do you hate me?"

He moved his lips to her wrist. "Never, my lady."

Rosaline was naïve and blindly ambitious, unable to see the monster that Malarath was, but that didn't make her one. She wasn't stupid. One day she would open her eyes, but she needed to get there on her own—pushing her to it would only drive her away.

"I misbehaved and was punished. Do you think he's still angry at me?"

"I don't know. He's been distant. But...he doesn't usually forgive. I was surprised he didn't kill Tarrick outright for bringing you in that night."

"It's not like he wasn't punished."

"True." She sat silent, the two of them gently touching each other, enjoying the feeling of closeness.

Matthew's eyes drifted to her neck, and he longed to sink his fangs into her.

"Hungry?" she asked.

"In more than one way."

"Prescott will give you blood later I think. Let's go feed."

A few minutes later, Matthew had dressed and they were riding down in the elevator. His hands wandered her back and came to rest on her round ass cheeks. "You know we didn't finish things last time we were in an elevator," Matthew said.

She laughed. "Maybe later. You're getting a feeder tonight. No diversions."

"Hm. Fine."

"You should start slow. Get to know whomever you pick. Let them pleasure you orally until you get more comfortable with them."

That was probably a good idea. Unsure of what to expect, he couldn't help but be a little nervous tonight.

When they arrived on the feeder level, Rosaline led Matthew past the pillowed waiting area, and paused in front of a curtain that opened into a room. Matthew could smell humans and incubi beyond it.

"I arranged it so that everyone you'll see is someone that wants to sleep with you. And, none of them can see you. The glass is one way. All you need to do is pick someone who interests you. There's no rush. If you don't like any you see, there are plenty of other options. The feeders are trained to handle rejection—you won't be hurting their feelings."

"Alright," was all Matthew could think to say. This all felt a little strange and part of him wished Holst had rejected Kyle.

Rosaline moved the curtain aside and they entered a large, circular room. Lining the walls were eight glass displays, almost like windows of a department store. Inside of each area sat an incubus or human, each as varied as their number.

The different displays were decorated to show off the interests of the occupant.

Rosaline walked over to the first one. Inside, a male incubus with the brightest blue eyes Matthew had ever seen, lounged in a chair with an eReader in his hand. He was wearing a short translucent robe similar to what the twins wore, only this male looked like an adult. Young, but still an adult.

His area looked comfortable. Chaste. Other than his body on display, there were no sexual objects in the room.

"He's been a feeder for almost a hundred and thirty years," Rosaline said. "He's skilled. Not the least bit demanding. He loves to read. I thought you might have that in common."

"Did you pick out everyone here?"

She smiled and walked to the next display, not answering him. "I know them all personally." Her smile dropped when she looked into the window of the next display.

Matthew came to see what had upset her.

He laughed when he saw Hiroto, sprawled out nearly naked on a cream lounger, wearing a big fat smile across his face.

Rosaline flicked a switch on the wall. *"Commander Hiroto."*

Hiroto teleported to the other side of the glass to stand before Matthew and Rosaline. "Yes?"

"What do you think you're doing?"

"Offering myself, of course. And really—" he turned to Matthew, then waved his hands at himself "—how can you resist me?"

"Where is Liao?" she demanded.

"Oh. He, uh, accidentally locked himself in one of the rooms.

It's tragic, really, that Matthew won't get to taste him, but with me around he won't need to."

"No. Matthew is picking a feeder tonight. You'll have to wait."

Hiroto whined. It was high-pitched and foxlike, and it broke Matthew's heart. He ran his hand through Hiroto's hair and up one of his ears. "Don't worry, we'll fuck eventually."

"Will we? I was starting to think you didn't want me. Or maybe that you still hated me for what happened last year...or because I'm tough during training...or—"

"Shhh." Matthew put his finger up to Hiroto's mouth to shoosh him. He grabbed the fox's hand and put it on his crotch, his leather pants strained tight with his stiff erection. Hiroto fingered Matthew's length through the leather. He had to bite back a moan. "We've just had terrible timing."

Hiroto's eyes half-closed as he continued to palm Matthew.

"Although," Matthew said, "if you want to go easier on me during training..."

"Not a chance," Hiroto said, pinching the tip just hard enough to cause Matthew to buck.

"You've fondled him enough. You're dismissed, Commander," Rosaline said.

Hiroto backed away from Matthew then bounded at Rosaline, planted a kiss on her cheek, and disappeared with a white flash. Rosaline looked half amused, half irate.

"He's hard to stay mad at, isn't he?" Matthew asked.

She sighed. "He's a pest sometimes."

"But a lovable one."

"Sure, when he's not murdering people."

"Have you ever slept with him?"

Rosaline moved her hands to her hips. "I don't kiss and tell."

"I thought all incubi kissed and told."

She shrugged slightly. "Only those who need to get ahead. I'm already at the top, who do I need to impress?"

Rosaline led Matthew through the rest of the displays. Most of the occupants were smaller, passive-types. Except one—a woman—built like a warrior; tall, thick muscles, hard face.

"She's an Amazon," Rosaline said.

"As in, 'island with only women' Amazon?"

"Yes. There are only a handful of them left, and they're all domi-nating in bed. I only included her because I know you like seeing crea-tures you never have before. But my gut tells me you won't be picking her. Besides, she doesn't really like men all that much."

Rosaline was right. Matthew found her appealing, but he wasn't in the mood to be ordered around. Or maybe it was just that he wanted Tarrick to be the one to order him around. Still, it was pretty damn cool to see an Amazon up close. He wondered if she ever fought. He'd love to spar with her sometime.

Matthew passed up a male with a collar on and bondage gear in his display and stopped in front of a young woman. She was human with light brown hair and brown eyes. She looked...normal. She wasn't walking femininity like Rosaline, or oozing mature sexual confidence like Carlotta, she was just...Matthew wasn't sure how to quantify her. Girl next door? A girl he'd want to eat a pizza with (figuratively, of course), then veg out on the couch while cuddling? A girl that didn't take anything too seriously and just enjoyed life? Any of those would fit her.

She wore jeans and a t-shirt and her hair pulled back into a po-nytail. She wasn't fat but she wasn't thin either. Her belly was soft, almost rounded, as were her hips. She was sitting with her legs draped over the arms of a recliner, eating string cheese. She wasn't too con-cerned with displaying herself like the others were. But it was the violin resting in the corner that caught Matthew's eye.

"Her."

"Are you sure?" Rosaline said.

"Yes."

Rosaline pressed her lips together as if she wanted to say some-thing but held back.

"Should I choose someone else, my lady?" Matthew asked, worried he had upset her somehow.

"No." She ran her hands over the front of her dress to straighten it a bit. "I just lost a bet is all."

Matthew blinked at her.

She sighed. "She's the only one Tarrick picked out. He was confi-dent you'd choose her. I thought for sure you'd pick Rya." She pointed to the first feeder they saw, the one reading the book. He would have picked him if this girl hadn't been here.

"I hope I didn't cost you too much."

"No. I just have to attend a party I was hoping to avoid. The King of Western Australia never shuts his cakehole."

Cakehole? Born somewhere in the 1900s, Rosaline sometimes slipped and let her era show. But not often.

"I don't think people say 'cakehole' anymore."

"Trap? Yap? Face? What is the slang now?"

Matthew shrugged, he didn't hang around normal humans too much these days. Hunters hardly counted since most of them were older than him.

She muttered something about asking Darius as she led Matthew into another room. This one was set up like a bedroom. Everything inside looked expensive and it was sexy without being cheesy. The bed itself was large with thick posts and silk sheets.

Matthew peeked into a cabinet to find it brimming with every type of dildo and sex toy he could imagine, and the armoire was full of kink gear. He wouldn't need that stuff right now. Hell, he didn't even know how to use half that stuff.

Rosaline left and a moment later returned with the human feeder. "Matthew, this is Felicia."

Matthew bowed to her.

Felicia's face lit up with amusement. "I'm not a lady, you don't have to bow to me."

"I disagree. You are a lady, and I might not have to bow, but I want to."

She smiled wider. "Smooth."

He returned the smile. "I try."

There was a short, almost awkward pause of silence where Matthew wasn't sure how to proceed. Felicia didn't let the moment linger long. She motioned to the bed.

She plopped down on it, and Matthew took a seat beside her. Rosaline came around the other side of the bed and took a spot there, giving them space but still staying close by. Matthew wondered if she'd be joining them.

Felicia looked him up and down. "I've never been with a vampire before. I have a few questions, if that's alright."

"Ask whatever you'd like. If I'm allowed to answer, I will."

"Are you going to bite me? Drink my blood?"

Matthew looked back at Rosaline.

"It's not common knowledge," she said.

"Ah. No, the High King removed my fangs, that's why the teeth are metal there." Matthew lifted the top of his lip to show her. "And even if he hadn't, I wouldn't bite you unless you permitted me to."

She studied them then asked, "Is sex with you any different than any other man?"

"My skin is colder, you won't hear a heartbeat right now, and I enjoy necking a little more than most. But other than that, I fuck and feed the same as any incubus male. How long have you been a feeder?"

Felicia reached out and ran her fingers up his arm. He liked that she avoided touching his shackles, the tangible evidence he was a slave. "You aren't that cold. And not long. Less than a decade. I'm told I taste fantastic, which is what earned me my place here. *Hamlet* or *Macbeth*?"

"Neither. The tragedies are too heartbreaking. *Twelfth Night* is my favorite. *Much Ado* is a close second."

Felicia leaned in and ran her fingers down Matthew's abs. "Strange. Warriors normally pick *Hamlet* or *Macbeth*."

"I'm not like other warriors."

"Hmm." She dipped her hand lower, her fingers brushing under his pants. Matthew's eyelids felt heavy as his body responded to her touch.

"You're like other warriors in some ways," she teased and moved so that she was standing between his legs. He spread his knees wider to give her room.

"I've never been with a feeder," he admitted. "I'm not sure if I should reciprocate or what's expected of me."

"How you eat is up to you. Usually you need to excite the feeder to generate sexual energy, but I'm highly trained and you're hot. You won't need to do that with me." She pressed closer into him, running her fingers through his hair. "Why don't you let me feed you for now, and next time you can eat me out?"

Before Matthew responded, she sank to her knees and unzipped his pants. He raised his hips to let her slip them down just enough to get his cock out.

"You're a good size. Beautiful cock." She licked her lips and glanced up at him, her eyes broadcasting her excitement. She gripped his length and ran her wet tongue up the fat vein that ran along the underside. Matthew leaned back on his hands and let out a shuddering breath.

Felicia took the head into her mouth, teasing it with her tongue, then pushed down to his piercing, working him with enthusiastic skill.

Matthew looked down and placed a hand on her soft, tied back hair. Her lips drew into a tight smile around his manhood. In ten years as a feeder, she had probably been with thousands of incubi, and yet she seemed genuinely thrilled to be sucking his cock.

Maybe it was because he was her first vampire, or maybe it was because it was her job, but right now he couldn't bring himself to care as she took more and more of him into her mouth, and he began to feed.

She wasn't kidding when she said she tasted fantastic; her energy was thick and filling.

From behind him, Rosaline crawled close, wrapped her arms around his torso, and slipped her soft hands under Matthew's shirt, caressing his skin. Her lips wandered his neck above his collar, heading towards his ear.

Matthew moaned as the two women pleasured him, their warm mouths driving his body crazy. He arched his back when Felicia increased her speed, bobbing up and down on his cock while gripping the base tight.

She worked him for several minutes, her tongue brushing against his piercing and applying pressure along the head.

"Oh god, yes. I'm close," he warned her. She kept her motion steady, and when Rosaline bit down hard on his earlobe, he came, exploding in Felicia's mouth.

She swallowed him expertly.

And as she licked the last drops off his tip, Rosaline snaked around to Matthew's lap and kissed him hard. Still floating from his orgasm, he returned the kiss, sloppy and wet.

When she pulled away from him, her eyes glowed bright green and her small red horns protruded from her forehead. Her wings unfurled as well, and her tail spiraled around his cock. He jerked when she squeezed his sensitive member.

"I need a few minutes to recover." He reached down to try and protect his cock from her aggressive squeezing and twisting, but she batted his hand away and hissed at him.

Felicia stood. "My lady?"

She growled at Felicia, then latched her claws into Matthew's shoulders and pressed in for a kiss again. This time, she began to rip energy out of him.

Matthew didn't mind, he'd feed her if she needed it, but it seemed kind of counterintuitive given that the whole point of coming here was to feed him.

Something had to be wrong. She wasn't acting like herself.

Matthew grabbed her hips and pulled her off him. She lunged at him, trying to lock lips again. Her tail still gripped tight to his dick.

"Shit," Felicia said and pulled her phone out of her pocket.

"What's going on with her?" Matthew asked.

"She just triggered her second transformation. Everyone's been expecting it, she's years overdue."

Rosaline struggled in his arms.

"Isn't that a good thing?" Matthew asked. "Aren't incubi more powerful the older they are when they go through it?"

Felicia shrugged. "Yeah, but it makes the transformation harder to go through. She shouldn't be here for it." Felicia looked down at her phone. "I've never had to call the Imperator before…"

There weren't any cameras in the room, and if there was a hunter hiding, they weren't showing themselves. It seemed like a strange oversight given that he wasn't supposed to be alone with Rosaline. Maybe she had arranged for his privacy somehow.

"Dial dispatch and give it to me," Matthew said. Rosaline moved onto Matthew's hips and began to grind against him, her normal posh behavior now reduced to incubi impulses.

Matthew remembered how *hungry* he was during his partial transformation. She had helped him through it. He wondered just how bad the physical changes hurt since he never had to experience that.

"Put me through to the Imperator, it's urgent," he said to the dispatcher.

"What is it, Matthew?" Prescott said, his voice sounding indifferent.

"It's Rosaline, sir. I'm on the feeder level, room 5810. Come quick," Matthew said and hung up. He didn't want to say anything over an unsecured line since incubi had big mouths, and he didn't know how transformations were normally handled.

Prescott teleported into the room. He was adjusting his gauntlet and continued to do so as he looked around.

"How long has she been like that?" he asked as he watched Rosaline continue to paw, kiss, and grab at Matthew. For his part, he was trying his hardest to keep her at bay without harming her.

"Like two minutes, sir. She won't let me go."

Prescott brought his comm up. "Delirium and Helldogs, clear everyone from level fifty-eight." He lowered his comm. "Felicia, right?" The human feeder nodded. "Rosaline would probably like to announce her transformation once it's finished—"

"I won't say anything, Imperator."

"Good. Thank you for your services, but you'll have to clear out as well."

She bowed and left the room. Matthew found himself looking forward to the next time he'd get to see her. She had made the entire encounter easy and fun; he wanted to repay her in some way if he could.

"Try not to let the little succubus overpower you. I'll be right back," Prescott said and teleported away.

Matthew rolled his eyes.

Outside, he could hear hunters clearing the level.

Rosaline started to make a sad mewling sound when he grabbed her wrists to keep her off him.

Matthew's body began to slow and his mind drifted as if he was submerged in water. He lay back on the bed, and Rosaline straddled his torso. She leaned in again and began to kiss him.

She was so hungry, and he could help her. He pushed his energy—from both his blood pouches and his soavik—into her. She fed greedily, pulling everything in, not even wanting to stop once his soavik had emptied.

Matthew managed to push on her shoulders, and she broke away.

"I need you in me. *Fill me*, Matthew. I'm so empty."

"Aw, Jesus," Matthew cussed. He felt his cock filling again as her tail worked it. She slid her hips downwards, hiked up her skirt, and pushed her underwear to the side, then sank her slick heat around him.

He clenched his teeth and tilted his hips to thrust into her. She matched him thrust for thrust, their bodies throbbing with pleasure. His hands gripped her hips tightly.

"Rosaline…maybe we should stop. I don't know if I should be doing this…" Matthew trailed off as she moved faster on him. His willpower had eroded and right now he'd do anything she asked. *Anything.*

"Bite me," she said, tilting her head to the side and brushing the tangled locks of her red hair away to expose her porcelain white neck.

Matthew released her hips and ran his hand over her dress, feeling the flat plane of her stomach, the fullness of her breasts, the smooth, delicate skin over her collarbone, and finally her neck. He could smell her enticing blood pumping under her skin, the warm life-giving liquid calling to him.

For so long, he had wanted to taste her, and she had never let him.

And now that she was offering it to him, how could he possibly resist that?

"I want to feel them in me," she said, as she leaned over, moving her neck close to his mouth.

What little restraint he had shattered. He pulled all four metal teeth painfully from his mouth, and tossed them onto the floor. It only took a moment for his fangs to reform, his body eager for their return, and they emerged for the first time in ages.

His world melted down to the sound of Rosaline's heartbeat, the feel of her velvet core wrapped tight around his steel, and the sight of her jugular pulsing.

Matthew moved his arms around her to hold her in place. His fangs were fat and long with desire, throbbing with achy need. It had been so long—so fucking long—since he had bit anyone.

He needed it.

God help him, he needed it bad.

And he couldn't wait any longer. He wanted to feel her hot blood filling his mouth and sliding down his throat. He moved to plunge his fangs into her neck and—

Rosaline was ripped away from him. Her warm body was gone and replaced with a feeling of desolation…then dread.

Matthew blinked hard and the real world came back to him.

He realized three things right away.

One. That Rosaline had wrapped a hold around him. A powerful hold.

Two. If he hadn't been thinking with his dick and fangs, he probably could have resisted Rosaline at least long enough for someone to intervene.

Three. That the room was far, far colder than it had been in the previous moments.

And it smelled of jasmine.

Fifty-Four

Matthew lay on the bed looking up at Malarath.

The High King towered above him, his eyes bright gold and his lips curled in a sneer. Rosaline stood pressed in his arms.

"Didi, I need you. Didi, *please*," she begged, her hands wandering the King's body, trying to undo his robes.

He folded one arm around her tighter and stroked her face, but his eyes never left Matthew, who was unable to move under the severe gaze.

Something akin to a growl came from Malarath. "Cage him."

He scooped Rosaline into his arms and left, carrying her from the room.

Able to move once the King was gone, Matthew buried his face in the crook of his arm and a sob escaped him. He hadn't meant to do any of that and now he was heading back to the cage.

"Matthew," Prescott said.

Matthew got a hold of himself. He swallowed hard, tucked his dick back into his pants, and sat up, facing the Imperator.

"I was gone for less than five minutes. How could you let this happen?"

Matthew looked at the metal teeth sown about the floor. He couldn't answer. Everything he could say would sound like a lame excuse, and it wasn't as if the Imperator actually knew what it meant to be a vampire. He couldn't understand the torture of drinking cold blood every day while the fresh stuff was just inches away.

The Imperator didn't repeat himself or press for an answer. "Come on," he said, and left the room.

Matthew followed him. Neither man said a word during the descent to the underground zoo nor when they got to his cage. Matthew froze in the door.

Prescott held the cage door open. "Am I going to have to force you in?"

Matthew squeezed his eyes closed. "No, sir," he whispered, the words sticking to the back of his throat.

He opened his eyes and forced himself to move. His feet felt like lead, and each step he took was agony. When he made it into the cage, he took a seat on the cot. Behind him, the sound of the cage door slamming shut was deafening.

Prescott sighed. "Every day since he learned about Apep—Devak—you've been a hair's breadth away from getting thrown back in here. I've been fighting him on it for a while now. Pulling your teeth out was bad, but taking advantage of Rosaline in her current state was worse. I know she had a hold on you and, personally, I would have forgiven the offense after punishing you, but he isn't forgiving. I wouldn't count on him letting you out of here anytime soon...if ever."

He turned to leave, pausing at the door to add, "For what it's worth, Matthew, I think you would have made a good Argonaut."

Matthew watched as all his work drained away to nothing.

The door shut with a heavy clang, and Matthew trembled as his worst fear came true. He was alone.

And he was alone for a long time.

At some point, someone had removed the daylight ring from his finger while he slept; they also removed his clothes, leaving him naked in the dark cage. There was still a nightly shower but no towel to dry off with after, which left him wet most of the night. After a while, he stopped bothering with the showers.

He spent most of his time in his vampire form, pacing the cage, looking for blood or sex and growling when he found none.

Matthew resolved to not fall to a blood rage or become a ghoul. He could resist it; he knew he could. Even with all hope gone, he would deny Malarath the satisfaction of seeing him completely lost.

A month in the cage—or at least he thought it was about a month—he still hadn't shown any signs of ghouling, and he still had his mind, even if his vampire and incubus sides were on the prowl.

The link he shared with Samantha helped him on the truly lonely nights. He'd tug at it gently, just to be sure she was still there, and he'd smile when she tugged back.

Every now and then, the tower would shudder, or he'd get that nauseous feeling that accompanied teleporting, but not much else happened.

Around the second month, he started hallucinating sweet wine and fragrant oil...or maybe the High King was just pumping the scent into the cage to fuck with him. It drove him mad. And it didn't help that his axe began to whisper to him:

Hungry. I know bud, me too. *Feed me.* Yeah, that ain't going to happen for a while. *Need.* You and me both, now hush, there's nothing to kill.

But it didn't hush. As time passed it grew louder, and while Hiroto's training helped him keep it under control, it didn't eliminate the urge he felt to satisfy it. In punishment, his tattoos itched.

In the third month, his loneliness grew so profound that he tried to escape into Hiroto's mind...just so he had someone other than an axe to speak to. It triggered the collar, causing him to fold over from the pain. He liked the pain. It reminded him that he wasn't permanently dead yet.

He started triggering it every night, and after a while it wasn't enough and he began throwing himself against the silver bars of his cage. And this time the pain wouldn't fade since he didn't have enough blood to heal the wounds.

His nights of doing that ended when he woke chained in the cell. Dangling helplessly, he hissed at the chains, flashing his fangs—which they hadn't yet removed.

Lost in a fit of growling, he stopped when a hand grazed his back. The tentative touch moved down his spine, taking the time to explore each vertebra. Matthew relaxed his body, his wrists sore from the strain against the shackles. "I still miss you," he whispered.

"I know, my prince," a honeyed voice said.

Matthew let his head fall forward and he closed his eyes, enjoying the touch. "Why'd you have to die? Everything was better when you were around. I was happy. Sam was happy. We were going to get a house together. Be a family."

"I'm sorry, my prince. I failed you. I hope you'll be able to forgive me one day." The hand moved off him, and Matthew's eyes welled in the absence.

"Please don't go," he begged. But it was useless...he was alone.

He stopped counting the days—tracking them was driving him crazy. Well, crazier anyways. He was pretty sure he was losing his mind.

He thought about Tarrick a lot. He wondered what the general was up to and if he missed Matthew at all. Probably not. The general was strong, with iron-like control over his emotions. Except…Matthew had seen the cracks when Tarrick had let him in just a little.

Not that it mattered now.

Somewhere in the fourth month, Matthew woke one night to a sharp temperature drop. The High King stood just outside the light, watching Matthew. He said nothing, and Matthew refused to beg, even though he was lonely, starving, and his arms hurt from hanging from the chains.

All night the High King watched him, saying nothing in his usual eerie fashion.

Matthew couldn't have been more thankful when the sun rose and shut his body down so that he didn't have to suffer through that shit for a while.

The next night, he was surprised to find himself lying on his cot and to feel a warm hand touching him. He thought maybe he was hallucinating again but it felt too real. His eyes snapped open, and a squeak of surprise escaped Felicia's throat. The human feeder reeled back, but Matthew caught her wrist.

"Don't run from me," he said, his throat sandpaper. "I'm too hungry and I'll chase." Adrenaline pumped through her, causing Matthew's vampire side to come forward. "What are you doing in here?"

"I was sent to feed you. I'm sorry I touched you, I just…your body…it was like…"

"A corpse?" Matthew chuckled. "Well, I'm dead sweetheart, and I haven't had blood in months."

Felicia looked down at her wrist, Matthew's claws still wrapped around it. He noticed the edges of her eyes were red and puffy. "What's wrong, dear?"

"They told me to tell you that I'm yours to do with what you want. You're allowed to come. And—" she swallowed hard, "—you won't be punished if you kill me."

"Jesus. Stay still, okay? Don't run."

She nodded, and Matthew released her. She pulled her wrist in and rubbed it but stayed where she was.

Matthew sat up. "I'm not going to kill you, but I'm pretty fucking hungry. Would it be okay if I had some of your blood and fucked you?"

She nodded. "Will it hurt when you bite me?"

"No," Matthew lied. It was a bite to her neck, of course it was going to hurt, but he didn't want to cause her more distress than she was already in. He was too famished to push pleasure or even compel her. "You never told me your favorite Shakespeare play."

She relaxed a little, and a slight smile curled at the edges of her lips. "Midsummer's Night—"

He was on her before she finished, tilting her head to the side with one hand and holding her body in place with the other. He struck lightning fast, his fangs sinking deep into her neck.

She cried out and tried to jerk away, but he was hardly going to let his prey go now that he had her.

The moment the blood filled his mouth, he moaned. God, her blood was like nectar. The warm liquid slid down his throat, filling him. His naked flesh began to color as life returned to his body, and he grew hard from the sheer joy of feeding. He subconsciously began to rub his erection against her pants.

Matthew drank fast and greedy, and as he neared the point where taking more would put her in danger, he whined. He needed more. His vampire wanted to take everything...but Matthew refused to let that happened.

It hurt when he forced himself to stop. He hadn't felt the pain of pulling himself off a victim in a long time. He licked at her wounds, healing them and kissing her neck with fervent hunger.

His hands slipped down to her ass and he lifted her closer while he moved to kissing her mouth. Her skin heated as she responded to him. Matthew yanked off her t-shirt and sliced apart her pants with his claws, splitting them down the center. He didn't bother to remove the shreds or her shoes.

He lay her down on the cot. Lining himself with her wet core, he paused and looked at her.

"Yes," she said.

With permission granted, Matthew grabbed her hips and took her hard. His hunger suppressed his normal regard for his partner.

She cried out with pleasure at each thrust and tried to move with him, but he kept her pinned as he fed. When her eyes began to drift, and her body slumped into the cot, he stopped feeding and finished inside of her with a few clumsy thrusts.

This wasn't his proudest moment—taking blood and sex from her and returning nothing—but he had been too hungry to care.

He lay down next to her, pulling her in close. "Would you like me to make you come?" he asked as his hands slid up her thighs.

"No, I'm too tired. Is it okay if I take a nap?"

"I don't mind, but can you tell me why you were put in here?" With the sharp edge of his hunger lessened, he was thinking a little clearer. It made little sense for her to be here. Normally, they'd just give him cold blood if they wanted to feed him.

"I...can't say. Please don't force me to say." Her eyelids fluttered as she struggled to stay awake.

Matthew wrapped his arms around her body and pulled her closer. "I won't, darling. You don't have to fear me. Get some rest."

"Your body is warm now," she said as she drifted off to sleep.

Matthew held her through the night. He studied her face and body, counted her heartbeats, listened to the rhythm of her breath. She was beautiful. And he was lonely. He let her sleep all night and didn't dare wake her even though he craved her company.

He was disappointed—but not surprised—when she was gone the following night.

A voice drew his attention. "Matthew."

He sat up.

The Imperator was standing there, wearing his full armor—helmet and all. He tossed some soap into the cage and the water turned on. "Shower."

Matthew snatched up the soap. Sore all over, he cleaned himself.

The water turned off, and he carefully set the soap down, wondering if he'd get to keep it. The door to the cage opened and Prescott held out a towel and Matthew's compression suit.

Matthew looked at it for a moment. When Prescott shoved it forward, he took the towel. Still mostly hairless, it didn't take long to dry. He put on the black suit; it was loose against his skin. He had lost a lot of weight, and one night of feeding wasn't enough to put it back on.

"Follow me."

Matthew kept his head down as they walked past the guards in the hallway and got on the elevator.

"What's going on, Imperator?"

Prescott said nothing for a while as they rode the elevator up. Then, suddenly, he slammed his fist against the runes, stopping the elevator's ascent.

He took his helmet off and faced Matthew. "The desire of the incubi to see you fight has been persistent over the months to the point where not even Mal can ignore it. He's giving the people what they want."

Matthew scoffed and looked at himself. He was in no condition to fight, even if his axe was urging him to kill. Right now, he could maybe take on a few vampires, lesser demons…maybe a werewolf, but a vampire lord or an alpha would kick his ass. "What will I be fighting, sir?"

Prescott swallowed, his Adam's apple bobbing up and down his neck. "A dragon."

Matthew rubbed his forehead. He didn't know a ton about dragons, only what Samantha had told him, but he knew their power rivaled that of a pit commander's. Besides being massive creatures, most had access to some magic, and then there was the whole breathing fire thing. Maybe with a year of training and at his fighting peak, Matthew might stand a chance against one…but right now? No. He didn't stand a chance in hell.

"I tried to stop this for Lily's sake. I wanted to spare her having to watch her father die but…at least you get to go out fighting. That's all us warriors can really hope for in the end."

And he would fight. He wouldn't just roll over and die but this was an execution, not a battle. As they stood in silence, a morbid realization came to Matthew: "Felicia…she was my last meal."

Prescott gripped his helmet and didn't answer. He didn't have to.

"Swear to me you'll take care of Lily."

"You have my word."

"And please be as kind as you can be to Samantha."

Prescott nodded once, then hit the rune to continue their journey.

Outside, the rest of the Argonauts were waiting and Matthew was ushered into a car. No one talked—not even Hiroto—as they drove.

Matthew wondered what had made the High King finally decide to kill him.

Twenty painfully silent minutes later, Matthew was in the locker room in King's Borough. This wasn't the same place Tarrick had brought him on their date. No. Above him was a *massive* structure; an arena. And he could sense thousands—maybe a hundred thousand—heartbeats.

He had to shut down his senses to avoid the overwhelming onslaught of sounds.

His armor was set out on a bench between rows of metal lockers.

"I've got this," Hiroto said to the Argonauts. They didn't move. "The King will want you guys up there for the spectacle."

Prescott paused.

Hiroto came to stand before him and pushed his mask and hood down. "Let me say goodbye. Please."

The Imperator nodded, and he, Lock, and Vik teleported away. Nellis stayed behind, his eyes darting between Matthew and Hiroto. "Don't fuck him."

Hiroto's fox ears twitched. "Why not?"

"Because you get too attached, and he aren't seeing the moonrise tomorrow." His Irish accent was thick.

"You're always so concerned with what I do with my dick...you want it or something?" Hiroto winked at him. "All you have to do is ask."

Nellis scrunched his crooked nose. "Fuckin' gaysian. Make it quick," he said and teleported away.

Matthew watched the smile drop from Hiroto, and he pulled his mask and hood back up. "There's blood in the locker behind you. Drink fast," he said, and teleported away.

Matthew opened the metal locker and, sure enough, there was a gallon of blood inside. Without ceremony, he popped the top off and knocked it back. He'd still be weak even with this blood, but it'd allow him to run faster and summon his axe easier.

Outside the various doors of the locker room were two teams of hunters standing guard. Distracted by the blood filling him, Matthew almost didn't notice them falling unconscious, their heartbeats slowing as they dropped to the ground one at a time.

When they were all unconscious, Hiroto teleported back in.

"What the hell is going on?" Matthew asked.

"Change of plans," a deep voice said. Tarrick came around a row of lockers. He was in his incubus form and armored, although he hadn't grown in size yet. In one hand, he held his kanabō and in the other, a large box. "Get his armor on," he ordered Hiroto.

Hiroto grabbed the armor and jumped onto the bench so that he was high enough to put it on Matthew.

"There's like a thousand hunters up there right now, I don't think I'm going to get very far if I try and run."

Tarrick shook his head. "There's ten times that number up there. Nearly a quarter of the corps is here tonight. We aren't running. We can't."

Matthew's armor expanded around him. "We?"

Tarrick set his kanabō against a locker and held out the box to Matthew. "We."

Matthew opened the box. Inside was a helmet designed to match his armor. It had a nose guard but the face was open and two large horns came out the top and swept backwards—just like Tarrick's horns. Matthew put it on.

He wished he had a mirror but the way Tarrick and Hiroto were eyeing him, he was confident that he looked formidable. Much like Prescott's helmet, the horns would give him the resemblance of an incubus.

"What's the plan?" Matthew asked.

Tarrick dismissed Hiroto with a, "Thank you, Commander."

Hiroto gave him a single nod of acknowledgement then launched himself into Matthew's chest, wrapping his arms around him. "Don't die, Demigod. You owe me sex and I plan to collect."

Matthew wrapped his arms around Hiroto and kissed the top of his head. Hiroto was gone with a glow of white.

"You going to tell me what's going on, General?"

Tarrick grabbed his kanabō and walked out the exit that led into the arena. "Come."

Matthew trailed behind as they passed through the door into a tall, poorly lit passageway. The bodies of two hunters slumped against the wall, their breathing steady, but they wouldn't be waking up anytime soon.

The ground turned to dirt, and the cheers became louder as they got closer to the arena. "Where did all this come from?" Matthew asked. He would have noticed something this large in King's Borough the last time he was here.

Tarrick stopped and looked at him. A smile crept across his face. "It is likely that you might die in the next few minutes and you're asking where the arena came from?"

"Okay, well, fine. Maybe you could give me a few tips how to fight a dragon..."

"You won't be fighting the dragon. What we are about to face is far more dangerous. Matthew, I have a plan, but it's a long shot, and it depends on variables that I am uncertain of. I can't guarantee both of us walk out alive. All I need you to do is stand in defiance of the High King. Don't kneel. And when it's time to fight, you fight."

A loud cheer rose from outside as an announcement came over the speakers.

"It's time, come on," Tarrick said and turned.

Matthew grabbed his arm to stop him from going anywhere. "Why are you doing this? Why are you risking your life?"

Tarrick tried to pull away, but Matthew clamped down harder on him. "We don't have time for this."

Matthew shrugged. He was not in that much of a rush to go to his death. "The show's not going to start without me."

Tarrick's face went hard. "I already told you my reasons. You were right—Malarath is not worthy to be king. Not anymore. I had hoped we could do this a different way but his decision to kill you has forced my hand."

Matthew tightened his grip. "You can't say it, can you?"

"Say what?"

Matthew let his arm go and ran his hand across Tarrick's jaw. "That you love me."

"I don't—"

"Stop." Matthew released Tarrick and took a step away as if putting distance between them might protect him. He knew it wouldn't. "I've had four months alone to think about it. From the moment you trapped me, I wanted you. I couldn't help it. Over the past few years

I thought maybe my feelings for you would fade but they haven't. There's a fire between us that refuses to extinguish. I want you, and I don't care if it's a fucking distraction. And you feel the same. I know you do."

Tarrick gripped his weapon tight. "Matthew—" he started.

"Please."

"Matthew—"

"*Please.*"

"I can't."

Matthew looked down at the dirt. The dim lights flickered, casting ominous shadows. "You could if you let yourself."

"Do you want me to lie to you? I will if you need it."

Matthew closed his eyes and put his hand over his heart, his fingers stroking his armor. He ached. God damn, Tarrick had a heart of stone. In a way, Matthew envied it. Things would be easier for him if he stopped letting himself get attached. Stopped falling in love. It was a weakness. One that wouldn't matter for much longer. Matthew turned away and headed down the passage towards the spectacle.

"Matthew, wait."

He ignored him, marching forward.

A clawed hand landed hard on his shoulder and whipped him around. Tarrick, in his full form now—fearsome and imposing—walked forward, forcing Matthew against the wall. He growled, then leaned in and conquered his mouth. He was rough; assertive. Owning him with his tongue.

Matthew tried to pull away but Tarrick wasn't letting him go anywhere. With no other choice, he surrendered to it.

Tarrick mapped Matthew's lips with his and passion ignited between them.

When Tarrick pulled away, he was breathing harder and Matthew had stopped breathing altogether. "You aren't mine. And—" A pained expression crossed his face as his hands gripped Matthew's hips and squeezed. "—you might never be mine. There is more going on than you realize, and everything is about to get far more complicated." More cheers came from the arena. Tarrick backed away from Matthew. "We need to go. Now." His command left no room for argument.

At some point, Tarrick had set his weapon down, he snatched it back up and approached the heavy doors that led to the arena.

Two hunter guards lay hog-tied and gagged. Silva stood above them.

She saluted and pulled out an egg shaped grey rock from a pouch on her belt. Grabbing Matthew's arm, she pressed it against his metal shackle. The rock glowed green, and the shackle began to heat. After a moment, it popped off and she began to repeat the process with the remaining cuffs.

Matthew's tattoos turned red. *Kill.*

Tarrick grabbed his wrist. "Don't bring it out until it's needed. The goal isn't to have you look intimidating, it's to have you look powerful."

Matthew stomped down the urge to let his weapon free, but his tattoos stayed red at the edges.

"The vamp trap and dragon barrier are down, General, but Necrus and Throne are still working on the barricade," Silva reported.

"Let them know that they have four minutes."

She finished with the last leg shackle, his armor reforming around the area when he was free of it. Matthew rubbed his wrist, then touched the armor on his neck. Underneath was the heavy collar. "Don't suppose that magic-rock-thing will work on this?"

"And summon the Judge right now? No thanks. Good luck out there." She put her hand on Matthew's arm. "I mean it."

Matthew placed his hand on hers. "Whatever's about to happen, you too."

She pulled away with a nod, saluted Tarrick, and teleported away.

The two bound hunters looked up at the general, confused. He offered no explanation as he stepped over them and pushed open the doors.

A deafening cheer rose and a spotlight beamed down upon Tarrick, who strode out into the arena.

Matthew drew in a breath out of habit and followed behind. He feigned confidence, holding his head high and keeping his shoulders squared. This was a show after all, and he had a part to play even if he wasn't quite sure what that was yet.

Tarrick's own confidence—which was genuine—reassured him. At least one of them knew what the hell they were doing.

The arena was like a football stadium, except there was dirt instead of grass below his feet. Large screens surrounded the upper areas, displaying the action below. He wondered if the fight would be broadcast to those who couldn't get a ticket.

The bleachers were overflowing with creatures. Humans, witches, shifters, incubi, dozens of races; many Matthew couldn't identify. No gargoyles though. Not surprising considering Matthew could command them.

Chained at one end of the arena was a woman. She was an ageless beauty—her skin brown and her eyes and hair dark. Matthew guessed that she might have been from somewhere in the Middle East. She wore a simple cloth dress but it was stunning on her.

Thick chains attached to the ground connected to shackles around her legs and wrists. She had a collar on, but it wasn't thick like Matthews, nor did it have any Night Stones in it.

Oh. And she radiated power that rivaled that of the High King.

A dragon.

Not quite what he was expecting, and Matthew had a hard time taking his eyes off her. He wondered what she looked like in her true form; how big she was, how powerful.

Kill, his axe whispered. His tattoos turned brighter at the edges as it begged to come out. Matthew ignored it. He wasn't about to run himself foolishly into a dragon no matter how epic that fight might be.

He forced himself to turn away from her to face the other side of the stadium.

To face the High King.

Who sat upon his golden throne in his incubus form, wearing a grey robe with a dark blue design down the left side and expanding along the bottom. His horns twisted back around him and his callous golden eyes stared down at Matthew.

Matthew supposed Rosaline—who was sitting to his left, looking more radiant than Matthew had ever seen her—couldn't get him into a suit tonight. But it didn't really matter because the High King looked fucking impressive.

So much so that it sent a chill down Matthew's spine.

The Argonauts stood guard around the platform with Prescott

standing just behind the High King. The twins kneeled on a pillow at his feet.

The incubus nobility sat near their king, including an extremely pregnant Queen Agleea and her ever-present consort Lord Ennius. Next were the highest-ranking Lords and Ladies. Matthew spotted Lily sitting next to Lord Teleclus, and near them were all six of Tarrick's children.

Despite the situation, Matthew was amused that they all in some way looked like their father—dusty blond hair, dark blue eyes, strong jaws. It seemed even Tarrick's genes were dominant.

Matthew spotted Vassu and Dennith near the Lords and Ladies but didn't see Samantha. He could feel her somewhere close by, but with his senses assaulted it was hard to pin down her location.

A familiar voice—Conor's, the man who owned the arena—came over the loudspeaker, introducing the demigod. The crowd surged with excitement—their fight, their spectacle, was finally going to happen.

Under normal circumstances, Matthew would have loved this. The energy, the battle, the show, the feeling of power. It fed him in a way he couldn't understand. He wanted to revel in the glory and fame. He wanted to be sated.

But this wasn't the time for it.

This wasn't his show.

This was the High King's…and the High Lord General was about to steal it.

Tarrick stood in the center of the arena, his wings stretched behind him, his weapon held fiercely at his side, the spotlights beamed down on him. Matthew stood just a few steps away. A single spotlight lit him as well, but it wasn't nearly as bright.

Tarrick said nothing, waiting until he had everyone's attention. And god damn, could he fucking command it. A hush fell over the audience as all eyes fell on him.

Fifty-Five

Tarrick lifted his comm to his mouth. "You've come here tonight to watch a demigod fight a dragon, but that is not what you'll be seeing." His masculine voice rumbling through the speakers. There was a pause for dramatic effect, then he continued. "For many millennia, we've been locked in a destructive battle. We bleed, we sacrifice, we endure great loss. And we continue to do so because we have been lied to."

The High King looked down at Tarrick, his eyes glowing bright. Cold air crept through the stadium. Not a person moved, not a sound was made.

Tarrick stood defiant against the King.

"We have been told this war is about power and wealth, territories and survival, but it is a lie. A terrible lie. This war is nothing more than petty revenge. Nebethah—the vampire queen—took Malarath's mate, and he wants her to suffer. I don't blame him. I've lost three mates to vampires, and I too want them to suffer, but not at the cost of watching my people die.

"War is all most of us have ever known. But it doesn't have to be. Early last year, the vampires offered their surrender. We could have forced their submission as we did with the shifters. We could have ruled them. But our king wants nothing less than complete eradication of vampires. It's not him or the vampire queen that suffers—it's us. We suffer. How much have you lost because of this war? How many loved ones have you watched die?

"The dragons have awoken—" Tarrick pointed behind him at the chained woman, "—and they will attack us. This war is about to turn against our favor when it could have been finished."

Malarath stood. The anger rolling off him made Matthew tremble. If not for Tarrick's presence by his side, he would have stumbled backwards.

"Kill him," Malarath said to Prescott.

Green outlined Prescott as he tried to teleport down into the arena, but he reappeared where he was standing. The other Argonauts tried to teleport and they were equally as unsuccessful.

"*Kill him*," the High King roared. Other hunter teams in the area pulled weapons but hesitated. Tarrick was their general. Matthew would bet good money most of the hunters here tonight had come up through Ashwood Academy and respected him for his leadership. Malarath, on the other hand, was just a distant ruler they rarely ever saw.

A hunter team tried to physically jump into the arena instead of teleporting but hit an invisible barrier. It was like a reverse vamp trap, one that kept everyone else out.

Tarrick continued as if he hadn't noticed the High King's orders.

"By my side is the demigod. Many of you have conflicting feelings about him because he is the sired son of Lysandros the Blood God—the god of vampires. But Matthew is more than that. He was born of Ilertha, the Goddess of Sex and Love—*our* goddess."

There was a breath of silence as Tarrick allowed them to absorb the information. A low murmur began to permeated through the crowd, growing louder as disbelief set in.

Matthew glanced back at the dragon. Her face was blank. But her eyes were locked on Malarath, and hatred poured from them. Matthew knew the look—it was the same one he had after being locked in a cage for a long time.

Had she also been held in the zoo?

A new spotlight turned on and beamed down onto a woman in the stands. Carlotta. Tonight, she looked the role of a high priestess, wearing white, long flowing robes and surrounded by other priest and priestess incubi dressed the same. She had a comm in her hand. "It is true. He is our goddess' son. And rather than honor him, Malarath took him prisoner. He made him a pet. One day, our goddess will punish the High King for his hubris."

She made it sound as if Malarath had known Matthew's lineage this entire time. Had he? Or was she lying as part of Tarrick's show? Matthew could believe either possibility.

He focused on the crowd around him and could see the threads that bound the incubi to Malarath weakening. It wasn't a lot, just a fray really—not anywhere close to what was needed if they were going to defeat him—but it was a start.

The spotlight on Carlotta turned off and she left the arena. No one stopped her.

"Malarath has not truly led us in centuries. He is hardly aware of the world passing around him." Tarrick narrowed his eyes at the High King to address him directly. "I reject you as my king, and those who wish to do the same may join me." Tarrick flicked off his comm.

Now Matthew understood why the arena wasn't filled with just incubi. Shifters, witches, hell, even trolls, would be useful to them. Most of these races existed in fear of incubi laws—and the hunters that enforced them—but maybe if someone gave them hope of winning, they might stand up to the High King.

Matthew watched as some of the strands leading to the High King snapped and began to work their way towards Tarrick. Tarrick didn't seem to notice.

Around them, some of the hunters were trying to break into the arena while others were trying to stop them. Small skirmishes were breaking out. Warrior incubi were shifting and seemed equally divided on what side they fell on.

"Matthew, your daughter," Tarrick said.

"Which one? And what about her?" Matthew asked.

Tarrick pointed down at the dirt between the two of them. "I borrowed the idea from you."

Matthew smiled and sank his hand into the ground. Samantha grabbed him, and he pulled her up.

"Father," she said as he pulled her into a hug.

"We have no time," Tarrick said.

"Yeah. 'Kay," she said, but didn't release Matthew.

Matthew kissed the top of her head. "What's going on? Why is she in here?"

"Samantha, it has to be now."

Samantha grumbled as she broke away, scooped up a small bag that had been in the ground with her, and ran over to the dragon. "So, here's the thing, I'm an oracle—"

"A vampire oracle?" the dragon asked.

"Yeah, long story. If I release you, who are you going to attack?"

"Are you the one who woke me?"

"Yep."

"And do you know who I am?"

Samantha nodded. "Zafirah. The one who tried to enslave the incubi. All the other dragons are a little pissed at you by the way."

A noise that sounded a little like 'humph' escaped the dragon.

"Listen, the dragon barrier is down, you aren't stuck in here anymore. You don't have to fight my father, but I need to know if you're going to try and murderface everyone or just the High King."

Zafirah tilted her head. "You are the oracle—you tell me."

Around them, whatever force was keeping everyone out was weakening. Witches loyal to Malarath were working on getting the shield down.

"Samantha," Tarrick said, raising his kanabō in a defensive position, ready to face hunters once they broke the magical barricade. "Release her. Now."

"But she might kill us all. I can't see it."

"*Now.*"

Samantha reached into the bag and pulled out a glass bottle full of oil. She poured it in a circle around Zafirah and began to chant. She pulled out a Zippo and lit the oil on fire. A cloud of thick white smoke rose, obscuring the dragon.

Matthew heard chains breaking, and a massive roar echoed through the entire stadium. Until now, the audience had been captive by the drama unfolding before them, but panic rose as people realized a dragon was about to be let loose.

From the smoke, a growing claw slammed down on the dirt. Emerging behind it was the dragon. Matthew watched as she grew and grew.

He had seen her before…in Devak's memory…she was the great black dragon Malarath was riding. Guess they had some sort of falling out between then and now. Or at least he hoped so.

He summoned his weapon just in case. Samantha came running over to him.

Around them, the barrier broke and hunters teleported in. Teams fought teams. Warrior incubi swooped down from the sky, joining the fray. It was pure chaos.

Matthew wasn't sure who to fight. Neither were others. No one wanted to harm anyone as lines were drawn.

A shadow fell over the stadium as the dragon continued to grow. She was fucking huge. She could easily snatch Matthew up and hold him in her hand like a doll. Yeaaaah…even if he wasn't weak as shit right now, there was no fucking way he could take her.

Her wings stretched out, her wingspan nearly covering the width of the field. She flapped them, testing her muscles. The downdraft she produced nearly sent Matthew toppling over and he grabbed Samantha to keep her upright. Others were faring worse.

Tarrick braced himself against the wind shear then swung his kanabō at a nearby hunter that was taking shots at him. The hunter ducked out of the way but Tarrick anticipated the move and kicked the hunter, his big hoof cracking against the hunter's stomach.

The general was dealing only non-lethal blows to his attackers. It was smart, he wanted these people to fight with him, killing them wouldn't help his cause.

Behind Tarrick, the Argonauts teleported in.

Matthew brought his weapon up, ready to fight them. But he never got the chance.

He watched as Hiroto appeared behind Vik and sank a dagger deep into her back. Shit. Matthew had been ready to fight her, but he wasn't prepared to see her die. Hiroto raised his other dagger for the killing blow when a bolt hit his weapon, sending it tumbling out of his hand.

Lock had his six-shooter crossbows raised. Without even taking a moment to question why Hiroto had stabbed Vik, the cowboy released bolts at the assassin.

Hiroto, weaponless, teleported in front of Lock. He held out his hands and both his daggers appeared back in them, forming out of black smoke.

Murder and Mirth flashed in the night, severing the muscles across Lock's wrists. Hands rendered useless, the cowboy's weapons dropped to the ground and he cried out in pain.

Nellis managed to get out a, "What are you doing?" before Hiroto stabbed him in his leg, piercing his femoral artery. The pugilist took a swing at Hiroto, but the fox was faster and teleported out of his reach.

Nellis grabbed at his wound and looked at Hiroto, betrayed. "You're my best friend, you cunt. Why?"

Hiroto's eyes were impassive. He was an assassin doing a job, not a teammate killing a friend. Matthew had never seen him look so dangerous. None of his team had been watching their backs for him and they paid the price for it. "I was a slave. And now I am free." Even his voice sounded different; lower, darker. All hint of his usual playfulness gone.

Nellis grabbed a vial of vamp blood from his belt and downed it, but it was too late. He toppled over, unconscious.

Prescott appeared behind Hiroto. "Traitor. I'll kill you."

Above them the dragon took to the air, its wings generating powerful drafts of wind, nearly knocking people over.

Hiroto tumbled out of the way of Prescott's swing, then pointed up behind him. "You can stay and fight me. Or you can save your lover."

Prescott looked back.

Above them, the dragon took in a deep breath.

The temperature around them dropped sharply.

Matthew watched as ice shards and cold mist exploded from the dragon's mouth, directed at the King's platform and royal area. Malarath stood motionless, unconcerned about the dragon.

Lily.

Lily was up there.

Matthew started to pour power into his speed when Samantha grabbed his arm and stopped him with a, "No."

He watched as the icy breath blasted the stands.

Fendrel—the hunter dragon slayer that wore plate armor and had a tower shield—teleported in front of the King and held his shield up. A force field expanded, blocking the icy breath as it hit an invisible wall.

The King didn't flinch as ice shards shattered against the shield just a few feet in front of him.

Hunters opened fire on the dragon. Fendrel teleported on top of its back and buried his sword into her. She roared and twisted, taking off into the air, disappearing from sight.

Off to the side, Prescott was wrapped around Lily, protecting her with his body.

"She'll be okay," Samantha said. "She won't come with us anyway, and you don't want to force her or you'll lose her forever. Let Prescott take her to safety."

Matthew's heart broke. "Won't the King kill her?"

"She wilts but not by his hand."

Matthew looked down at Sam. Was she saying that Lily was destined to die? "When does she wilt?"

Samantha frowned. "I'm sorry, Father. I don't know yet. But you'll see her again."

Gavyn teleported in beside them. He looked pretty damn pissed off. "You think you maybe should have told me we were betraying the King today?" he yelled at her.

Matthew snarled at him. His axe itched to sink into the hunter's chest. Or anyone's chest really.

"I couldn't ask you to turn your back on everything you've believed in," she said.

Three bolts came whizzing their direction. Matthew caught two of them and watched as one of Gavyn's tattoos—an image of a snake—rose like a shimmering ghost and knocked the third away. Gavyn looked at the battle raging around them.

"It's not safe here." He grabbed Samantha's wrist, and in response Matthew grabbed his neck, lifting him off the ground.

"Let him go, Father. He's going to get me to safety. You need to stay."

"I'm not leaving you, Sam."

Samantha's fangs came down and her eyes turned red. "Release him right now."

Matthew did. Her anger made her skin crawl, and he didn't enjoy the feeling. Gavyn fell into a coughing fit as he gasped for air.

"He's going to get me out of here, and you're staying. It's not an argument. That's what happens."

Matthew's fangs came out and his eyes went entirely red as he narrowed them at the hunter. "If you fail to protect her, I won't kill you right away—I'll keep you alive for years and destroy you bit by bit."

"Right. Got it. I die painfully. Let's go, Sam." Gavyn grabbed her and they took off together.

Matthew watched them exit the arena and fought the urge to go after her. He looked back up at Lily. She and Prescott were gone.

But the High King was still standing there.

The world was going to pieces around him; fire had broken out and raged in the stands; arrows and bolts filled the air; weapons clashed; brother was fighting brother. And all he did was stand there, watching Matthew.

"You will fail, pet," he said, his voice barely a whisper.

A woman screaming grabbed Matthew's attention. He glanced over and saw Queen Agleea holding the body of her consort. Lord Ennius was dead in her arms, his body riddled with icy shards. Hunters were trying to pull her away from him without success.

He looked back to the High King, who was unconcerned with what was happening to his granddaughter.

"*Lommi*," Malarath whispered. He glared down at Matthew one more time, then turned and left, his hunters and warrior guards flanking him.

The collar around Matthew's neck snapped open with a *hiss*. The collar stayed trapped in place under his armor, even if it was open now.

He wished there was time to remove his armor so he could be free of the collar for good.

"Matthew—" Tarrick yelled, taking down an incubus that had tried to attack him. Whatever Tarrick said next, Matthew couldn't hear over the sound of an explosion above their heads.

The sky cracked open and bright light flooded the area.

Tarrick was on his comm. "Dispatch, call for a retreat. Anyone still in the stadium needs to leave. *Now*."

Whatever madness was happening here didn't seem to affect the dispatchers who followed Tarrick's orders. On all the comms, the order for retreat went out.

Not that they needed it. All civilians had long since run. The hunters who hadn't joined the fray—unable to figure out whose orders they should be following—had busied themselves preventing a panicked stampede.

Thunder filled the air.

From high above, as if coming from the heavens, an armored figure descended.

The Judge.

She had no wings, but she levitated all the same. Her armor was white and steel, her face covered by an intimidating helmeted mask.

Scrolls floated around her, the paper twisting in the wind.

She was wielding a two-handed flail with a long chain. Incensed smoke rolled out of the round metal head like a priest's thurible.

When she landed in the center of the arena, all fighting ceased.

"Lariv Abernath," she said, her voice echoing with an angelic quality, "you have been judged and found guilty. Your sentence is death."

Matthew smiled. She didn't look so scary. "Really? My real name is Lariv? That's fucking lame," he said as he charged at her.

Fifty-Six

Matthew wondered just who had given him a name like Lariv Abernath as he sped at the Judge, who towered over him by several feet.

Before he reached her, she swung her weapon and smacked the ball of the flail on the ground. A great wave of force expanded from it and slammed into everyone still left in the arena.

Hunters went smashing into walls. Matthew watched Tarrick go tumbling across the dirt. Flying incubi plummeted to the ground.

Matthew slid to a stop, and rushed at her again, raising his weapon as he leaped into the air and came down on her.

She moved fast and held up her flail, the shaft deflecting the blow. Matthew sped around her, trying to use his speed to his advantage, but she moved as fast as he did, blocking another attack. And another.

She was faster than him.

Matthew ran to Vik's body and scooped out a handful of vials from inside her coat. He hurled them with great force at the Judge, who sidestepped about half of them. The rest met their mark, exploding with such force it knocked Matthew on his ass.

When he looked up, the Judge hadn't moved even an inch and her armor was unblemished.

Well, fuck.

He came at her again. Before his axe could make contact with her, the chain of her flail wrapped around his wrist. She hoisted him into the air. He clawed at her mask with his free hand but didn't pierce her armor.

She thrust her weapon up. The chain unwrapped from Matthew's wrist and he was airborne. Before he landed, she swung her weapon around and hit him square in the chest.

His armor—no longer drawing power from the Night Stones—might as well not have been there for all the good it did. His body shattered inside his skin. Bones broke and snapped, blood pouches and soavik burst, and his insides became way more mush than they should have been.

Nothing he had ever fought had hit him with such force—not even the pit commander.

He flew across the dirt field and crashed through a wall. Chairs and metal crumpled around him. He finally came to a stop in the lower bleachers. Everything was broken, and his body throbbed in pain.

Well, he might have underestimated her power just a smidgen.

He started the process of healing and watched as she strode at him. She didn't seem to be in any rush. She didn't need to be. He wasn't going anywhere, and he had no idea how to hurt her.

Tarrick had said they'd be facing something more dangerous than a dragon. Matthew had assumed he meant the High King...guess he meant the Judge.

What a shitty way to die, smacked around by something priests carry. Super lame.

Matthew tried to move as she approached. It didn't work.

She stood above him and raised her weapon.

"Wait," Matthew managed to get out, his lungs on fire.

She paused. Her features, hidden under the imposing mask, made her impossible to read.

"You never told me my crime."

"You were born of a god."

"Isn't that my parents' sin?"

"You are a demigod. You are guilty."

"You're an executioner, not a judge." Matthew tried to move again. Nothing. That hit had pretty much done him in. He struggled to keep his eyes open. If he was going to die, he'd face it.

She began her swing when Matthew heard a high-pitched whistling sound, like wind rushing through a cave, growing louder and louder. Before she could finish her attack, a streak of white and red light smacked into her, moving impossibly fast. The bright mass carried her down the field, through the bleachers, and out of sight.

Whatever the fuck that was, Matthew hoped it killed her, then he lost consciousness.

****

When Matthew came to, Tarrick had him in a fireman's carry. He was warm, and Matthew was extremely hungry.

He sunk his fangs into Tarrick's arm.

"Fucking asshole vampire," Tarrick said and tossed him hard to the ground.

Confused, Matthew looked up at him.

Oh.

It was Tane. Not Tarrick.

Fuck Tane.

"There's blood in the damned car. If you try to bite me again, I'm leaving you behind," Tarrick's youngest son said.

Matthew moaned in pain.

"I'm only doing this because my father ordered me to. If it were up to me, I'd let the Judge kill your pasty undead ass." Tane hauled Matthew off the ground and slung him over his shoulders again. "I have no idea what my father sees in you. And I don't care what my mother says either. I refuse to believe that you're Ilertha's son."

Mother? "Wait. Is your mother Carlotta?"

Tane said nothing and kept walking. They were in some sort of empty back alleyway in King's Borough.

"Seriously, Carlotta is your mom? But she's Tarrick's best friend's mom. And she practically raised him." That was a little weird. No. It was a lot weird. Incubi were super open about sex, but that just hit the 'nope' end of the scale.

"It was just an arrangement they made because the High King ordered everyone to produce a child. Don't look too deep into it."

Matthew started laughing.

"Stop it. You aren't exactly light," Tane growled.

"I've fucked your dad...*and* your mom."

Tane tossed Matthew to the ground again. "You can crawl to the car." He marched off, and Matthew laughed until he passed out.

✳✳✳✳

When he regained consciousness, he found a child standing over him. The boy's eyes were all black. Dark whispers surrounded him.

The demon body jumper.

"If you want to kill me, now's your chance," Matthew said.

It smiled. Oily saliva dripped from its mouth. "Tempting, but I'd be tortured for eons if I harmed you. You have been summoned by Saitenebris. It would be wise of you not to ignore the summon."

"Who the fuck is Sigh-ten-a-briss?"

The demon stared at him. It blinked its large black eyes slowly. Then it laughed. The wicked voice coming from the form of a child was unsettling.

"If you aren't going to tell me, then leave," Matthew said.

The demon bowed low. "As you wish…my prince."

Black smoke left the body of the child. The boy stood confused, then began to cry. "Run. Go find a hunter. They'll help you," Matthew said, compelling the child. He didn't trust himself not to try to eat him right now.

Matthew closed his eyes again. He couldn't stay awake, but his last thought was that he really, *really* hoped that his father wasn't the demon god.

****

Cold blood flooded his mouth, and he moaned. He suckled on the plastic tube that invaded him, and didn't bother opening his eyes. As he healed, he was happy to find one of his four blood pouches still intact. He wouldn't be completely useless while he healed the other three. He was, however, getting a little sick and tired of them always being fucked up.

The blood bag he was feeding from emptied with a slurp and someone removed the tube from his mouth. Another replaced it.

Slowly he opened his eyes.

He was in a stretch limo, driving along a bumpy forested road. Seats lined the interior of the limo, starting at a partition, continuing down one side, and ending at the back, like a giant C shape. The side that would normally have a bar was instead packed with weapons, gear, armor, and bags.

Matthew sat on the sideways facing section. Next to him, Silva held the bag of blood as he sucked it down.

Samantha and Gavyn were at the back of the limo. She had her hand on her lover, but Gavyn kept his hands to himself, eyeing Matthew.

Good.

He should be scared.

Matthew was far too grumpy, hungry, and aching right now to try to control himself if someone touched his child.

Opposite them, sitting with their backs to the partition, were Tarrick and Holst. Kyle sat on the floor, one arm wrapped around Holst's leg. Tarrick, in his human form but still armored, and Holst, in a suit, were making out.

Matthew's eyes went wide.

Silva coughed politely to get Tarrick's attention.

Tarrick pulled away from Holst.

"Ilertha's sake, you're a glutton," Holst said.

Tarrick shook his head and slid over to the spot next to Matthew's left. His cuts and scratches began to heal. "I was just in a battle. One which you sat out."

"Someone had to oversee the broadcast," Holst said with a shrug and pulled Kyle into his lap. The boy squeaked and smiled as Holst's hands traveled all over his feeder's body. Matthew wondered if those two were going to start fucking in front of everyone. They seemed to be heading that direction.

Matthew continued to drink the blood. But he had about a thousand questions.

Tarrick pointed out the back of the limo, and Matthew followed his motion, looking out the rear window. Behind them were dozens of other cars packed with hunters and incubi. "We're in Brazil," Tarrick said. "King's Borough has exits all over the world, including here. This is a caravan of only my most trusted. It's not much of an army, but it's a start. Others will join us."

Matthew continued to down more blood and noticed Tarrick's children were in the limo behind them. Only five of them though.

He looked back to Tarrick and shot him a questioning glance. Had one died tonight?

"My eldest...His loyalties lay more with the High King. He'll probably become High Lord General now." There was a terrible sadness in Tarrick's voice, one that he didn't—or couldn't—cover. If his son took his rank, they would be facing each other in battle eventually. Father against son. Matthew's chest ached for him, and his thoughts turned to Lily, hoping she would be safe.

"Holst can rapidly transfer sexual energy like you can," Tarrick said; a welcome change of subject.

Well, that answered why they were making out. Matthew wondered if the two of them had ever fucked. His eyes drifted back and forth while he sucked on his tube.

Tarrick chuckled.

"What?" Holst asked as he pulled away from Kyle's lips.

"He's trying to figure out if we've ever had sex."

Holst joined Tarrick in laugher. Matthew narrowed his eyes. He wished he wasn't so easy to read.

"Have you, Sir?" Kyle asked.

"A few times," Holst said. "We're both too dominant and end up physically fighting to top." Holst ran his hand up Kyle's back. "Although we've shared partners many times."

Kyle looked at Tarrick. "Who normally wins?"

Both Tarrick and Holst laughed, their mannerisms nearly identical. Holst pulled Kyle in and nibbled on his ear. "I'll tell you later. Maybe we'll even fuck again one day and you could watch. Would you like that?"

Kyle bit his bottom lip and nodded. Matthew wanted to watch too—that'd be hot as hell. But unlike Kyle, he wouldn't be content to just sit there. Maybe all three of them could fight their way onto the top...

There was a low whine between Matthew's legs, and a Rottweiler pressed its head into his lap.

Matthew finished the bag and raised his hand to prevent Silva from shoving another tube in his mouth. His insides were still mushy and he was hungry, but he could function just fine for now. He had questions he wanted answered.

"Jet, boy, I've missed you," he said, and rested his hand on Jet's head. The dog wagged its tail at an uncontrollable speed.

"How is the healing progressing?" Tarrick asked.

Silva moved over to the general and removed his armor. Underneath he was wearing only compression shorts that hugged his hips, leaving nothing to the imagination. Silva handed him a towel to clean off the mess of battle.

Matthew stretched his torso and rolled his shoulders, his armor feeling constrictive around him. "Slow, but I'm feeling better," he said, his voice scratchy. "Three pouches will be out of commission for a while. The remaining one is damaged. My soavik is too. I'm not sure how long that'll take to heal. A week maybe?" He pawed at his armor. He wanted to get the collar off for good. "Can you remove my armor?"

Forced to lean over a bit to avoid stepping on Jet, Silva had his armor off with a few words, setting it on the floor. She then sat by Gavyn. Both hunters were dirty.

Samantha had a little blood on her, but she seemed okay. Tired, judging by the way she was leaning her head on Gavyn's shoulder.

Matthew pulled the collar away and looked at it. He wanted to destroy it.

The scent of sweet wine and fragrant oil filled the air.

Matthew sighed. He really didn't need to be hallucinating now. Tonight, he had been pulled out of four months of solitary confinement and starvation, had his heart broken, and was nearly beaten to death by the Judge. It'd be nice if he could catch a break for once.

But no.

His dead lover was warming the seat beside him.

He ignored the illusion, refusing to even glance at it.

"Father?" Samantha said. Matthew looked at her, past the Devak mirage. She looked confused. "Are you okay?"

"Fine, darling. We should destroy this." He held up the collar.

"I agree, my prince, I died once wearing that collar." Devak's sweet honeyed voice wrapped around him like a blanket. Matthew pressed his eyes closed, if only to hide the tears that threatened to well in them.

There was a passing silence in the car for several moments. Then Tarrick broke it. "What happened with the Judge?"

Matthew opened his mouth to tell him what he had seen when Devak answered.

"I unsummoned her but it's temporary. A few days at most. Now that she knows he is on this planet, she'll be hunting him. I can mask him like I did before, but eventually she'll find him. And kill him."

"We'll have to figure something out," Tarrick said. "But my knowledge of the divine is limited. I'll need information from you."

Matthew opened his eyes and looked to Tarrick, turning his back on Devak. "You can see him?"

"Yes, of course I can, Matthew."

Matthew moved his hand to his chest and didn't take his eyes off Tarrick. "He's really here?"

Tarrick offered a reassuring smile and motioned at Devak with his chin. "See for yourself."

Matthew turned.

Devak sat beside him, his face serious as always. He was wearing his usual black outfit with a ridiculous amount of laces all over it. His coarse black hair was longer now but otherwise he looked the same: gorgeous, with bronze skin and amber eyes.

Matthew shook his head. This couldn't be real. "I don't understand."

Tarrick rested a hand on Matthew's shoulder. "I don't know the intricacies of the divine, but I do know the basics—"

"Thanks to my mother hounding them into us," Holst said, Kyle tucked into his arm.

"—guardians cannot be killed by a blade of their own god," Tarrick finished.

"What?" Matthew whispered, hearing the words but not understanding them.

"To be precise," Devak said, "I can only die permanently if killed by the weapon of an opposing god. The Imperator stabbed me with a blade of Ilertha because he thought I was a blood guardian. It didn't kill me, but it did desummon me. I'm not as powerful as someone like the Judge, and with our goddess missing, it took a long time for my body to reform."

"But—when I saw you, was that you or was I hallucinating?"

"It was me, my prince."

"But why...why didn't you save me?"

Jet moved out of the way as Devak slid to the limo floor, and kneeled before Matthew. "Forgive me, my prince. I wanted to, but I was only able to appear before you for a few moments. I needed more time."

As Matthew looked at him, every terrible thing that had happened to him the last few years came rushing through his brain: his captures, the torture, the rape, his failures…the collar slipped from his grip, forgotten.

Devak was alive? Here? There was no way that was possible. Life wasn't that kind to him.

Matthew looked at Samantha. A warm smile crossed her face. He looked back to Tarrick, who gave a single nod of support.

Devak was alive.

Matthew pressed his hands into his eyes.

Devak was alive.

He felt as if his heart might explode in his chest. And a feeling of exaltation overtook him, as if the universe had finally decided to give him a break for once.

Devak was alive.

Fifty-Seven

Matthew reached out and touched Devak's cheek just to be sure he was actually there. Devak sighed into his touch.

An overwhelming feeling of joy and relief welled within Matthew, and he fought to hold back tears. It was a fight he lost.

Devak met his eyes. "My pri—"

Matthew cut him off by running his fingers over Devak's lips and began to map his face. He couldn't believe this…he leaned in and their lips brushed together. It *was* Devak: his warmth, his skin, his taste, his scent. Matthew grabbed Devak, wrapped his arms possessively around him, and pulled his body into the space between his knees.

The need to be close to Devak overwhelmed him, and with one hand he began to unzip his compression suit to rid himself of it.

Samantha made a sound of displeasure.

"Hush," Holst said. "This is hot and I'm hungry. Let them go at it."

A low growl escaped Matthew, and he wanted to chase everyone else away. Devak was *his* and no one else's. He peeled the top of the suit then, unable to wait any longer, lost himself in Devak's mouth. Matthew's tongue explored every inch.

Devak's hands wandered over his chest and ribs as if they couldn't get enough.

Matthew wished he was in fighting shape, wished he was sexy for his guardian. His hands began to produce gel and he wiped it on Devak's neck.

"Uh, that's not good," someone said. Gavyn probably, but Matthew hadn't really paid attention.

"Father—" Samantha said. Matthew's fangs had come down at some point and he hissed at her, pulling Devak closer. "—you're doing that incubus thing where they go nuts. Stop it."

A low rumble escaped his throat…but a small voice in the back of his head told him that she was right.

Shit, his hands were all fucking messy now. And he had rubbed the viscous goo all over Devak's clothes and back.

Devak leaned against Matthew's upper body, not seeming to mind the mess. With Devak once more in his arms, the voice went away, and his need for his guardian surged. He wanted to mark him so that everyone knew who he belonged to.

"Tonight's critical. We can't afford this," Silva said.

Tarrick leaned over and grabbed the back of Matthew's neck, squeezing painfully hard as he shifted into his true incubus form.

Matthew tried to twist away from him, but he was weak right now and the general strong.

As he struggled, Tarrick pulled him down, forcing his face against his thick incubus thigh; forcing Matthew to submit.

Devak tried to shift out of the way as Matthew's knees moved together from the awkward position Tarrick held him in. But Matthew whined and refused to let Devak go completely, holding onto his arm in a death grip.

"Warrior—" Tarrick whispered in his ear, his upper body pressed on top of Matthew, "—it's been a hard year for you, and it would be easy to fall to your primitive instincts, but you need to control yourself."

Matthew pushed power into his strength and tried to get away from Tarrick, but the incubus' grip only grew tighter, his clawed fingers breaking the skin.

"It's not working," Holst said.

With his free arm, Devak stroked Matthew's head, his touch a tender contrast to Tarrick's painful grasp. "I am yours, my prince. There is no one here that is going to challenge you on that. You own me."

Desire surged once again in Matthew—he needed to be free and ripping Devak's clothes off. He wanted to take him and finish marking him, but Tarrick wouldn't let him move.

Devak leaned in, lips brushed skin as he whispered, "I love you, Matthew."

The words had a calming effect. What the fuck was he doing anyways? He didn't need to be rubbing his goo all over Devak...at least not in front of everyone.

His body went limp and his brain numbed. He loathed losing control but that was all his life had been lately. Everything—from losing Devak to his capture and rape, and even tonight—was out of his hands. And now he was losing control of himself?

Deep down, he felt tired and drained, and angry. And mostly, he was sick of it. His grip on Devak loosened.

"My prince?"

Matthew squeezed his eyes shut.

"Stay," Tarrick barked at someone. Probably Samantha. Tarrick returned to his human form and stroked Matthew as he broke apart. Curled up on the seat, loud sobs escaped him. He should be stronger than this but he couldn't hold back anymore.

A soft, reassuring humming came from Tarrick as he caressed Matthew's shoulders and back, while Devak's warm hand slipped into Matthew's, their fingers entwining.

Matthew tried to stop, but his body wouldn't listen to him. Bloody tears burned his eyes.

"Is he okay?" Kyle whispered to Holst. The human clearly had no idea how sensitive a vampire's hearing was.

"There's no need to worry, he'll be fine," Holst said, not bothering to whisper.

"You can come over now, Samantha," Tarrick said.

Samantha wiggled her way into Matthew's arms and lay against him. Still holding onto Devak, he wrapped his free arm around her, gripping his daughter tightly. His fangs came down and he bit her neck. Finally reunited with his daughter, he refused to let her go.

"No, hunter," Tarrick said to Gavyn, stopping him from doing whatever the hell he thought he was going to do.

"But—"

"He's not harming her. It's just something sires do sometimes."

"I've never seen one do that, sir," Gavyn grumbled.

Tarrick ran his hand down Matthew's arm. "And now you have."

Matthew wasn't sure how long he was there for but it was a while. His hand holding Devak's, his arms wrapped around Samantha, his head resting in Tarrick's lap, he came to a decision. One he had been running from for a long time. He could no longer afford to be the orphan trying to find a home he lost the night Lysandros turned him into a vampire.

He needed to be a warrior.

No longer would he allow anyone to collar him, make him kneel, or submit. He would fight.

And those who stood before him were going to fall.

The Judge, Malarath, dragons, gods, greater demons…all stronger than him and all a threat. And he would find a way to defeat them all.

"What is he?" Kyle whispered, breaking the silence. Matthew, eyes still closed, knew the kid was asking about Devak.

"He's—" Holst paused then chuckled, "—an angel."

"Are you serious?" Kyle said, his voice dropping a little lower.

Matthew opened his eyes in time to see Devak glare at Holst. Guardians hated being called angels, even if that's essentially what they were.

"My mother is going to love meeting you," Holst said with a slight nod of respect.

Devak nodded back. "I have heard her prayers many times and look forward to meeting the High Priestess as well."

"You look like an incubus," Kyle said.

Holst tilted Kyle's head up so their eyes met. "Is that your way of saying you think he's pretty?"

"I—" Kyle blushed.

Matthew chuckled against Samantha's neck, drawing everyone's attention to him. He removed his fangs from her, and they receded into his gums. She slid out of his arms as he sat up.

"You've made your choice, Father." Not a question or even a commentary. She simply knew he had.

"Yes," he said, sitting up straighter. "I'm going to kill Malarath and end this war. I'm going to unite my two people and keep the peace between them…by any means necessary." He turned to Tarrick, who was cleaning blood off his leg—blood from Matthew's tears. Even nearly naked, he looked every bit a leader. Smart, confident, an experienced general…Matthew needed to become that; Tarrick would teach him. Or so Matthew hoped.

Tarrick paused from his cleaning. "Good. Because if we don't kill the High King, he'll destroy all of us. It's too late to turn back."

Samantha bounced in Matthew's arms and, unable to wait any longer, pounced on Devak, kissing his cheek and hugging him. "You're so warm."

Devak looked amused. "I've missed you, Princess."

"If you leave again, I'm going to kick your ass," she said, not in any hurry to release him from her embrace. Jet excitedly licked Devak's arm and face.

Is this what Tarrick meant when he said that everything was about to get complicated?

Tarrick's expression had been impartial since Devak had shown up. Complicated was an understatement. Matthew's heart longed for both of them.

He doubted Tarrick was one to share. He wouldn't care if Matthew fucked a million creatures...but love? When Tarrick wanted something, he possessed it fully. And Devak didn't like Tarrick, most likely for what he had done to Matthew in the past. He had never said so directly, but the way his jaw clamped down every time he glanced at Tarrick spoke volumes.

Matthew had a million questions for Devak. But he wouldn't ask here. Instead, he turned to Tarrick. "I wish you had told me he was alive."

Tarrick shook his head. "I wasn't certain until he showed up in bed while we were sleeping."

Devak glanced over Samantha's shoulder. "It's not possible that you saw me."

The corner of Tarrick's mouth pulled up into a half-grin. "I didn't see you. Nor could I hear you, but Matthew was speaking to someone. It didn't take much to figure out who that was." Tarrick turned somber again. "What I didn't know—nor did Hiroto when I asked him—was if you'd be powerful enough to handle the Judge. I made a calculated risk. Matthew..." He paused for a moment, seemingly deciding to continue or not. "You should know that I knew Rosaline's second transformation was coming. I sent her to you."

Matthew rubbed his forehead. "You wanted me caged again?"

"'Wanted' isn't the word I'd use—"

"Four months alone and starved..."

"Five. I'm sorry, Matthew, but I needed more time to pull this off, and to ensure your guardian was strong enough to return. I couldn't risk having you interfere, or getting yourself killed early."

Matthew clenched his jaw and his hand fisted. "Say that again."

"I couldn't risk—"

"Not that part."

Tarrick looked Matthew up and down, then reached out. Fingers wandered across Matthew's ears, caressing them before moving across his jaw and finally tracing his lips. The surprisingly tender touch was made sweeter when the general said, "I'm sorry, Matthew."

The apology held the weight of years, and Matthew hadn't realized how much he needed to hear the words until they were spoken.

Matthew grabbed Tarrick's hand, gripping it hard as their eyes met. "Never again. No more cages. No more whippings. Or torture, or games, or lies."

Tarrick dipped his head in a motion that looked somewhere between a bow and nod. "Never again."

Matthew released Tarrick's hand and looked at Devak, his arms still around Samantha. Devak smiled at Matthew, and Matthew's chest began to warm. This was real. He was back.

And who else stood with him? Who exactly had joined this new faction of rebels? Matthew extended his senses to the three dozen or so cars following them in the caravan. "Where's Hiroto?"

Tarrick opened a cabinet and pulled out some clothes. "I don't know. I think betraying his team took a bigger toll on him than he thought it would. He'll show back up when he's ready."

"Cullip? Vassu? Dennith? None of them are here."

Tarrick frowned. "Cullip decided to stay at Ashwood to protect the recruits. And I was too uncertain who Vassu and Dennith would side with, both are extremely loyal to the incubi. I couldn't trust them enough to inform them of my plans." He handed folded jeans and a shirt to Matthew while he retrieved a suit for himself. "Teleclus got word to me that Lily is safe for now. Rosaline as well."

Devak swept a loose strand of hair away from Samantha's face and studied her silver eyes. "Your eyes are beautiful, Princess. My goddess' eyes are the same."

"They are?" Matthew asked. He had always assumed they'd be gold, like the High Kings. Like the color of sex when feeding.

Devak looked at Matthew. "Yes, my prince."

Samantha grabbed a towel and began to wipe off the gel that coated Devak. "I also have soavik nodes all over my blood pouch. I can nudge emotions a little, but I can't make this gross lube stuff from my hands."

Next to Matthew, Tarrick slipped off his compression shorts and stepped into boxer-briefs.

"Holy Mother of Fate," Samantha gasped and put her hand over her mouth.

Gavyn rolled his eyes, and Tarrick raised an eyebrow.

"Sorry," she said. She handed Devak the towel so he could finish cleaning himself. Devak, instead, started wiping down Matthew, cleaning blood and dirt from him. Samantha returned to her spot by Gavyn. "Sorry," she repeated. "It's just you have a *huge* penis."

Matthew groaned while Holst and Kyle laughed. Even Silva chuckled.

"Father, you let him fuck you with that?"

"Jesus Christ, Sam."

"How does it even fit?"

Tarrick slipped into his pants. "Your father is an incubus, it's not an issue."

"And, you know, with preparation it doesn't hurt…and if he, um, goes slow," Kyle said, his face beet red. Holst grinned at his feeder like a predator. Matthew had no doubt that Holst had dark plans for his human once they found a room.

Samantha giggled. And Gavyn shook his head and wrapped an arm around her.

Devak glared at Gavyn.

"This is Gavyn," Samantha said. "The guy I love, so don't be mean."

Devak regarded the tattooed man for a few moments. "I care about Sam. It would be wise of you not to harm her."

Gavyn leaned forward. "I care for her too. And if I hurt her, you'll have to get in line behind the big guy—" he motioned to Matthew, "—and the Lord General, who gave me a long speech, bullet-pointing all the dangers of dating her and exactly what would happen to me should I step out of line."

Heads turned to Tarrick, who was putting on a cufflink. He ignored the looks and adjusted his sleeve.

"I get it," Gavyn said. "You all care about her and you're all way more powerful than I am, but I'm an experienced hunter, a conduit no less, and not some fresh academy graduate. I earned my place in High

Tower, so give me a little credit."

Matthew held back his smile. He was sorta warming up to the guy. Although he did wonder what the fuck a conduit was.

"Oh. That reminds me." Matthew stripped out of his compression suit. Samantha put her hands over her eyes but no one else bothered. Almost everyone here had seen him naked at some point or another anyways.

Devak was brazenly staring at his cock. "You have a—" Before he could finish the thought, Matthew ripped the piercing out of his dick and tossed it away. He then pulled out the two from his tongue.

"Aw, man. You can unscrew those, you know. Or I could have removed them for you," Gavyn said.

"I don't want you anywhere near my dick again." Admittedly, the wounds didn't look pretty, but Matthew didn't give a shit. He wanted the piercings gone. He slipped on his jeans.

Devak's hand traced over the High King's brand. "I'm sorry, my prince," he whispered.

Matthew grabbed his wrist and pulled Devak into his lap. He didn't feel like talking anymore. His fangs slid back out from his gums and Devak tilted his head. Matthew licked him and opened his mouth wide.

"We're almost to our destination. Does his blood affect you the same as incubus blood?" Tarrick asked, putting on his tie. The limo slowed and pulled onto a back road. The branches and bushes whipped the limo as it made its way down the neglected dirt lane.

Matthew shook his head. "It's not the same, but it's powerful. Stuns me for a little bit."

"Then hold off. You're needed for this next part."

Matthew sighed. It was probably for the best, anyways. If he put his fangs into Devak, he'd want to fuck him and while most of the car wouldn't have minded watching, Samantha would have. Disappointed, he scooted Devak onto the seat next to him and finished getting dressed. "Where are we going anyways?"

Tarrick adjusted his tie. Clean and with his suit on, Matthew would have never guessed that the incubus had been in a battle not that long ago.

"I started a civil war tonight. As of right now, I only have the support of a small fraction of my people, and an even smaller fraction of warriors and hunters. We need an army."

The limo came to a stop.

Matthew could sense vampires—powerful ones—nearby.

Tarrick motioned to the door. "Let's go form an alliance."

Matthew stood by Tarrick's side in front of massive bunker doors hidden in a rock face.

It was just the two of them. Everyone else had been ordered to wait in the cars.

Matthew breathed in the night air, scented heavily of trees and dirt. Even at this late hour, the moon was still up, and what few stars he could see between branches shone bright above them.

Minutes passed and nothing happened. He could hear vampires moving around inside the bunker, fully aware that the incubi were outside.

"I don't think they're coming out. Can't we just call them?" Matthew asked.

"No. We tossed our phones. Holst owns a phone company, but Malarath could find a way to take control of it and I didn't want to risk being tracked. No phones, no comms, no computers. Problems I need to solve once this is taken care of."

"Holst is losing a lot by following you, isn't he?"

Tarrick nodded. "Most of his wealth. But he sees the bigger picture. And money can be made back."

They waited in silence for another few moments until Matthew couldn't stand it anymore. Wanting to get back to Devak, he was not in a patient mood. He walked up to one of the cameras. "Bryson, I know you saw the damn broadcast. We're not here to attack you. Either you come out here to talk to us or I'm coming in."

Nothing.

"Devak," Matthew said.

Devak was by his side almost before he finished saying his name. "My prince?"

Matthew's gaze drifted over his guardian's body, finding his lithe athletic build enticing. If they didn't have to talk to the vampires right now, he'd ravage Devak, pleasuring every inch of him. God, did he miss the feel of him.

The corner of Devak's mouth pulled tight in a knowing smirk. "Did you need something, my prince?"

"Yes."

There was a pause while Matthew studied him, his eyes tracing along his midsection; the tight laces there showcasing a trim waist and chest.

Devak cocked his head. "And how may I serve you, my prince?"

"He'd like you to break the doors down," Tarrick said, his arms clasped behind his back.

Matthew managed a nod. "Yeah. That."

Devak raised his hand to summon his weapon. Before he could utter the words, the bunker doors cracked open. In the dark, Matthew could make out a single figure. General Bryson.

He stepped out and joined them, the doors closing behind him. With his dark grey skin and black hunteresque outfit, he nearly blended into the night.

"Half my people wanted me to attack your convoy as it approached, the other half thought we should flee before you arrived. None want to speak with you. I have a near riot going on inside. Whatever you want, make it quick. And—" he looked at Devak, "—all the reports I had said you died. Even Sam confirmed it. It's good to see that they were wrong, guardian. And you look like shit, Matthew."

Matthew chuckled. "It's good to see you again, General."

"You saw the broadcast, General Bryson," Tarrick said. "You already know I've broken away from the High King. And you know why I'm here. For future reference, I do not like to be kept waiting."

Bryson regarded him for a moment. "It won't work."

"No?"

"Don't get me wrong. I want it too. But there's thousands of years of fighting between our people. There's no way they'll be able to overlook that. Fuck, even the peace treaties we had in the past dissolved."

"It will be different this time."

"Because of Matthew?"

"Yes. And other reasons we will discuss. But we should continue this inside, my people have been cooped up in cars for hours."

Bryson looked back at the door behind him then back to Tarrick. Matthew had to give it to the vampire general, he had to have a gigantic pair on him to not have fled when he had the chance. Their force of hunters and incubi was more than enough to wipe out every vampire in this bunker.

"I'm willing to entertain a discussion if you give me your word that you'll leave when I tell you to. And that your people will not kill any of mine. We have no daytime guards right now."

"I give you my word that none of my people will kill yours unless they are defending themselves. And as for leaving, it won't be necessary—you won't be kicking me out." Tarrick held out his hand.

Bryson looked at it for a moment then glanced at Matthew, considering the options. They were limited. But he and Tarrick had a mutual respect for each other. They could work together. He shook Tarrick's hand. "You're a presumptuous asshole. Don't let any of your social incubi walk around alone. I have a few sire-less, young vamps in there. The temptation to feed on their blood might be too strong."

"Sire-less and young like you?" a female asked. Silva was leaning against a tree, her arms crossed in front of her, stake in hand.

Bryson stopped breathing for a moment as he looked at her. Old lovers… "I can control my hunger just fine," he said, his voice deep and forceful as if trying to conceal the effect she had on him, and doing a terrible job at it. He ripped his gaze away from Silva and returned his focus to Tarrick. "How did you find me?"

"I've had someone tracking you for months. Can your bunker fit all these cars?"

Bryson gave a hand signal to the camera, and the doors opened. "Yeah, meet you down there. Come with me, Matthew."

He sped off, and Matthew and Devak followed.

At the end of a long ramp, they stopped in a massive cavern structure, already full of cars. It would easily hold the caravan. Bright lights flickered on for the sake of the incubi. Vampires had no need for them.

"I need to know," Bryson said. "Is this an incubus deception?"

"No. You saw what happened tonight—"

"I haven't verified the footage yet."

"It's not a trick. Tarrick wants peace, and Malarath won't let that happen. He's turning against his king so that he can end the war. Besides, you believe him or you wouldn't have ordered your people to stay in the bunker."

Vampires stood in the shadowy doorways and alcoves, watching them. Their eyes caught the light every so often. Bryson turned to the vampires. "The incubi are staying the day. If anyone attacks one, you forfeit your life. If you are unable to control yourself, or don't want to sleep with them here, I suggest leaving now and sleeping in the forest."

Matthew was hardly surprised when about half the vampires took off. They were the individuals banding together for survival, not the disciplined fighting force that the incubi were.

The limo pulled into the area, followed by the rest of the cars—a few other limos but mostly SUVs and heavy military vehicles.

Tarrick's people got out of the cars, stretching or looking around. The hunters kept their weapons sheathed, but most were jumpy.

"I'm listening," Bryson said as Tarrick came to stand by Matthew and Devak.

Tarrick eyed the vampires. With the exception of Bryson, all of them were keeping their distance, even the lords. "We're forming a new army. One that includes any creature that wishes to fight in it. The goal is to kill Malarath and any who stand with him. Once his remaining forces surrender, this ends for good."

Bryson put his hands on his hips and studied the incubi and hunters that had gathered behind Tarrick.

"Let's say by some miracle we pull this off. What happens after? You lead us? General, I doubt—"

"Warlord," Tarrick said, cutting him off.

"Warlord?"

"Yes. I'm now Warlord Tarrick, leader of the incubi faction. And you'll be Warlord Bryson, leader of the vampires. There will be four others as well, representing different species. And together, we'll form a council. One that will make new laws that all the supernatural community will follow. Laws that will be enforced by hunters who will no longer exclusively serve the incubi."

Matthew couldn't help but be a little envious; 'Warlord' was a pretty fucking cool title. Oh, and the council idea sounded kind of neat, too. It surprised Matthew that Tarrick hadn't simply insisted that he'd be in charge.

Bryson regarded Tarrick for a moment. "You've put a lot of thought into this."

"Of course I have."

"And Matthew? He'll be the seventh warlord?"

Tarrick shook his head. "Not a warlord, no, but he will be seventh. Our leader."

Bryson regarded Matthew for a moment. "No offense, Matthew, but being captured by the incubi, not once but twice, has made my people think you are weak. They aren't going to be lining up to rally behind you."

A low growl came from Devak, and Bryson took an uneasy step away from the guardian. Matthew appreciated the support, but Bryson wasn't wrong.

Tarrick laughed. "After tonight, no one will think he's weak."

Bryson raised his eyebrows. "Oh?"

"I didn't come here tonight to convince you to join me—I could have done that with a phone call or a messenger—I came so you could bear witness." Tarrick looked at the limo. "Samantha."

Samantha slipped out of the car, carrying a small duffle bag, Jet trailing behind her. Gavyn was already out of the car but he hung back, keeping an eye on her from a distance.

"Go ahead," Tarrick said to her.

She gripped her bag. "You knew?"

"You think you spent the last six months stealing from me, and I wouldn't notice what you were up to? Or that I wouldn't figure out what you were doing?"

"I, uh, yes?"

"Well, Oracle, you are mistaken. Go ahead."

"What's going on?" Matthew asked.

Samantha ignored him, walked over to Bryson, and clamped her arms around his torso. "Are you mad at me for running away?"

"No. I'm just glad you're safe." He patted her back, keeping an eye on Matthew to make sure it was okay. Yeah, totally cool to have everyone touching his child while he was still hungry...

Not that he could do shit to stop it—Samantha did whatever the fuck she wanted anyways.

She released Bryson and dug a wristwatch out of her bag.

A sharp gasp came from someone in the crowd. Darius, the social incubus who had been running Tarrick's household. Eyes widened as everyone turned to face him.

"Is that the Gen, *uh*, the Warlord's Eisher Marco watch?" he asked.

"Yep," Samantha said.

"But, that watch costs three hundred thousand dollars."

"It's alright, Darius," Tarrick said.

Darius clamped his mouth shut, but he looked like he was going to burst a blood vessel. And when Samantha dropped it on the ground and smashed her heel on it, he looked like he might faint.

She plopped down cross-legged on the ground, pulled out a mortar, and scooped the smashed watch into it. She poured some sort of blush colored liquid that smelled of strawberries over it, before adding more objects to the mixture: salt, splintered pieces of wood, a fang, and some sort of sparkly ground-up dust. Then she pulled out a golden dagger with gems on hilt—the same one she had used to open a portal in Chicago and to remove Devak's curse. How the hell did she find that again?

Samantha stood abruptly and marched over to Tarrick. "Blood. Yours and Devak's will do."

Tarrick brought out his claws and cut his own wrist, his red liquid dripping into the bowl.

A young vampire rushed out of the shadows, drawn by the overwhelming scent of the old incubus' blood.

She got two feet before a stake was in her heart. She tumbled over, unconscious, a hunter standing over the vampire's body.

Growls came from the dark.

"Enough," Bryson said, his voice boomed with command. "She's not going to be killed. We'll wake her tomorrow night."

That settled the vampires down.

When Tarrick had donated enough blood to the bowl, he took a handkerchief out of his pocket and pressed it to the wound. Matthew absently reached for Tarrick's wrist, intent on sealing it for him, but Tarrick pulled his wrist away.

"No. Not now. I'll be healed in a moment."

A small thread of disappointment worked its way through Matthew, but he stayed in control even if the incubus' blood—Tarrick's blood—called to him. Damn it, he was hungry.

Devak was next, giving his own blood. His wounds sealed quickly, also disappointing Matthew.

"Everyone ready?" Samantha asked.

Uh. Matthew looked around confused. "For what? What are you doing?"

Samantha smiled. "Oh. You know…" She began chanting, her eyes turned white, and the contents of the mortar burst into a bright flame.

"My prince," Devak said. "I once told you that one day you would become more powerful than I. Today is that day."

The mortar exploded and smoke billowed out. A dense haze settled in the cavern. Samantha dipped the tip of her dagger into the burning mixture.

"Father, I unbind you," Samantha said and stabbed him in the heart.

Pain, unlike any he had experienced before, rippled through his body. Every molecule of his being ripped apart. His flesh burned and muscles ached.

He looked down at his body and watched as it began to change. His skin grew darker, turning a smoky grey. His tattoos began to glow red.

Everyone around him backed away.

Pain erupted from his forehead, and he reached up to touch the source. Horns. Large fucking horns came out from the front of his skull, dipping forward then sweeping back above his head like two enormous boney crescents.

His body began to grow. He ripped his clothes off as they strangled his blazing skin, and yanked his boots off just in time to see his feet turn to hooves. His ears throbbed as they pinched together in points. Blood filled his mouth as he cut his tongue on new fangs—each and every one of his teeth had sharpened to long points.

As he continued to grow, his back split open. Leathery wings emerged and spread behind him. A long tail snaked out from his backside and, since he had no idea how it worked, it flopped uselessly to the ground.

He looked down at Samantha, she was tiny now. No. Fuck. It was *he* who was enormous. She only came up to his waist.

Everyone felt his aura and cowered from him. Even Tarrick took a step back.

The only two unaffected were Devak—who brushed shoulders with gods—and Samantha—who shielded her eyes so that she didn't have to look at Matthew's exposed sex.

Matthew's skin seared as it tore open across his chest and shoulders. Hard spikes emerged and the rest of his skin hardened.

Matthew sucked in a breath through the pain and arched back, releasing a furious bellow as power surged through him. The entire cavern trembled. He felt invincible.

Tarrick looked up at him. "You're beautiful, Blood Prince."

Matthew smiled and flexed his razor-sharp claws. He was unbound, and together they were going to destroy Malarath and end this war.

Epilogue

MALARATH

Malarath stood alone in his room, looking out across New York. The stars and city glittered in the night.

The air around him crackled; an announcement of the arrival of an expected visitor. Behind him, a black portal formed and a tall, thin figure emerged. His eyes were black, and death clung to him.

"Father?" Mazarus asked.

Malarath did not bother to answer his son.

The demon-corrupted incubus stepped forward and sucked in an angered breath. "The demigod and the oracle have slipped from your grasp. As well as your general."

"It will work in our favor." Malarath placed his hand on the window. By now the oracle would have unleashed the power that was locked deep within his pet. Power she would have never let loose if she had seen what he planned to do with it. Power Malarath would soon need.

"This is a mess. You're barely awake, and it's costing us."

Malarath began to tire of his son's disrespect, but he held his temper; the creature was fragile. Always had been. A failing on his part. "You worry much."

"I have reason to. They'll stop us, Father."

"They will try."

"And Apep? He's loyal to the Prince. He'll never follow you, even after you ascend."

"Devak—" Malarath paused, amused by Apep's new name. 'Trusted' it meant. "—is mine. We are inevitable."

"But—"

Malarath turned and faced his son, silencing him. "I will speak of it no more."

Mazarus averted his eyes; his limited control of his emotions rippled across his face. The High King grabbed his son's long, black hair and tugged, forcing him to expose his neck. His son stilled, submitting. "Father—"

"I will destroy the rebels, they are no threat. Are my armies ready?"

"Yes, of course. But, are you certain it will work? Once we start, we won't be able to stop, and the gods—"

"Are of no consequence."

His son sneered, pulling against the grip. Malarath clutched harder until the demon ceased his struggle. "Fine. But you will give me what I'm owed."

"Of course. When this is over, you will rule the Pit and Matthew's heir will be your queen." He released his son and turned back to the window. "Leave."

A pleased hiss came from Mazarus, and the air once again crackled as he departed.

Watching the city, a small smile crept up the corner of Malarath's lips.

Apep was alive.

Matthew returns in Blood Prince: Beautiful Monsters Vol. IV

Meet the hunters of Ashwood Red in late 2017

About the Author

Jex enjoys writing about hidden worlds full of vampire hunters, epic battles, steamy sex, and, of course, beautiful monsters. Find updates for new releases at:
www.JexLane.com

Made in the USA
Monee, IL
07 April 2024

56563894R00281